When They Made Us Leave

**A Novel
about Hitler's Mass Evacuation
Program for Children**

By award-winning author
ANNETTE OPPENLANDER

First published by Annette Oppenlander, 2019
Averesch 93, 48683 Ahaus
First Edition
annetteoppenlander.com
Text copyright: Annette Oppenlander 2019
ISBN: 978-3-948100-00-1 eBook
ISBN: 978-3-948100-09-4 Paperback
Library of Congress Control Number: 2019917020

Editing: Yellow Bird Editors
Design: http://www.fiverr.com/akira007

ALSO BY ANNETTE OPPENLANDER

A Different Truth *(Historical Mystery – Vietnam War Era)*
Escape from the Past: The Duke's Wrath I
(Time-travel Adventure Trilogy)
Escape from the Past: The Kid II
Escape from the Past: At Witches' End III
47 Days: How Two Teen Boys Defied the Third Reich
(Biographical Novelette)
Surviving the Fatherland: A True Coming-of-age Love Story Set in
WWII *(Historical Biographical Fiction)*
Vaterland, wo bist Du? Roman nach einer wahren Geschichte
(German translation of 'Surviving the Fatherland')
Everything We Lose: A Civil War Novel of Hope, Courage and
Redemption *(Historical Fiction)*
Where the Night Never Ends: A Prohibition Era Novel.
Boys No More *(WWII – Collection)*
A Lightness in My Soul *(Biographical Novella - WWII)*
The Scent of a Storm *(WWII and German Reunification)*
So Close to Heaven *(Biographical - Napoleon Wars)*
When the Skies Rained Freedom *(Berlin Airlift)*

GERMAN

Vaterland, wo bist Du?: Roman nach einer wahren Geschichte
47 Tage: Wie zwei Jungen Hitlers letztem Befehl trotzten
Erzwungene Wege: Historischer Roman
Immer der Fremdling: Die Rache des Grafen
Als Deutschlands Jungen ihre Jugend verloren *(2. Weltkrieg –
Sammlung)*
Bis uns nichts mehr bleibt *(amerikanischer Bürgerkrieg)*
Ewig währt der Sturm *(2. Weltkrieg – Flucht und Vertreibung)*
Leicht wie meine Seele *(2. Weltkrieg – Novelle)*
Endlos ist die Nacht *(amerikanische Prohibition)*
Das Kreuz des Himmels *(biografisch – Napoleon Kriege)*
Zwei Handvoll Freiheit *(Nachkriegszeit/ Berliner Luftbrücke)*

For the children who endure war
because their governments fail them

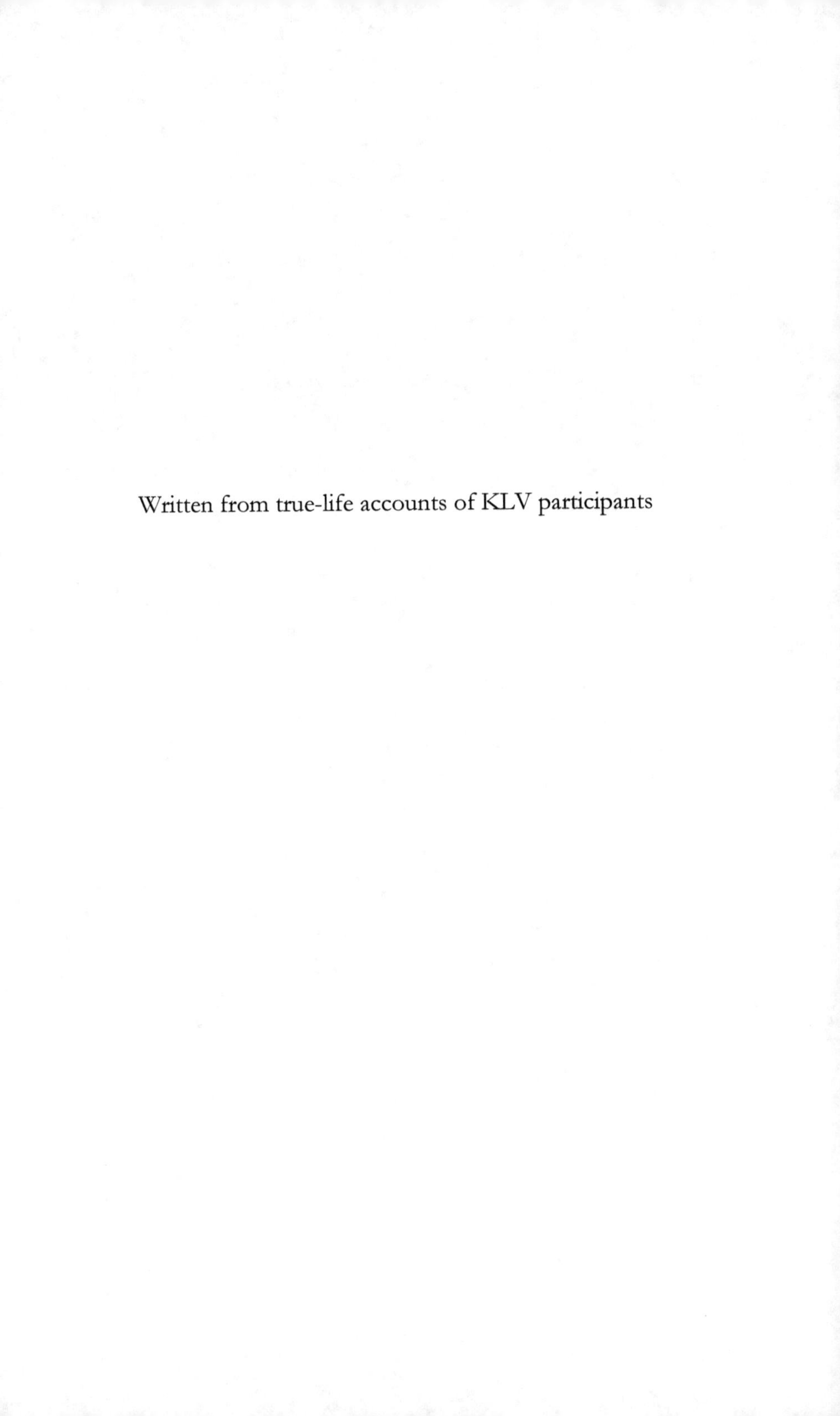

Written from true-life accounts of KLV participants

"He alone, who owns the youth, gains the future." –Adolf Hitler

"The more [Hitler Youth/young people] die for a movement, the more immortal it becomes." –Baldur von Schirach, Reichs Youth Leader in charge of the children's evacuation program KLV

"Collective fear creates collective silence." –Claus Günther, KLV participant

Book One: May 1943 – July 1944

CHAPTER ONE

Hilda

I wish I could tell you that what happened to me was an exception, that it was coincidence or just bad luck. The truth is that I was part of the greatest takeover of human minds, a clever plan concocted by Adolf Hitler and his henchmen.

The program I'm talking about was called extended *Kinderlandverschickung* or KLV, Hitler's mass evacuation program for children to the countryside. They called it a *happy* program, one to protect and nurture Germany's youth by providing them with beautiful surroundings in the mountains and alongside beaches, feeding them delicious food, cultivating their minds with excellent instruction, and strengthening their bodies with sports, games and dances.

All German kids were supposed to take part whether they were three months or fifteen years old. But undoubtedly, the focus of the KLV lay on its youth eleven and older, who attended camps overseen by the Hitler Youth.

The story I'm about to tell is not unique, not even close. In fact things that happened to me and to my best friends happened to millions of German kids, all trapped by Hitler's mad propaganda machine and his ingenious plan to separate Germany's children from the influence of their families, friends, neighbors, clubs and their churches to mold them into national socialist puppets.

Solingen, Germany, May 1943

Good, I've got half an hour before Mama returns from work, plenty of time to visit Peter next door. That's when the doorbell rings and Peter stands there all red-faced and out-of-breath. Since he lives exactly thirty-two feet from my house—believe me, I've measured it—I'm not sure what to make of his appearance.

"Can I come in?" he pants before rushing past me into the kitchen. Our place is small, just a three-bedroom flat with a modest living room. I've got the windows open to let in the glorious spring air and the chatter from a couple of house sparrows that nest under the eaves. In the middle of the kitchen sits a wooden four-person table, though it's been just Mama and me for the last few months.

Peter sinks onto a chair, his eyes dancing. Somehow he seems much taller even while sitting. He's been to the barber again, the hair above his ears shorn short. I like it longer, because he gets these funny curls on top, but the Hitler Youth requires all boys to keep their hair short as soldiers'. The best parts about Peter are his eyes: not quite brown, not quite hazel, some sort of curious mix of green mosses, bark and leaves like the earthy palette of a forest in fall.

We both love nature, especially the woods, not just the way they smell and look, the oak and beech trees, their roots covered under a carpet of acorns and beechnuts, hazel and wild rose bushes, or the mass of elderberries blooming in the spring, but the critters living there. Peter knows them all. He's even raised a baby squirrel. Right now he's taking care of a black bird that fell from its nest.

For years we've spent oodles of time in the forest. Maybe he'll suggest one of these weekend hikes that last all day. We'll carry a thermos and bread and jam. We might even swim in the creek.

"Tell me already," I say, noting how short his pants have gotten. I know something is up because I've known Peter as long as I remember, and I can read his expression like others read the paper.

Peter leans back in the chair, taking in the carefully set soup bowls, glasses and spoons for two.

"Something smells good," he says with a grin.

I huff. He knows how to push my buttons better than anyone. Not even my big brother, Paul, who joined the war four months ago, is that good at it.

"If you don't tell me this instant, I'll strangle you." I throw him a glance that is hopefully threatening, though I can't keep the corner of my mouth from lifting. Peter always makes me feel good, even when he teases.

"Your mom home yet?"

I shake my head. Does it show that I'm thinking about us being alone? We've been alone many times before, but somehow this feels different. As if he's hearing my thoughts Peter stretches out an arm. "Come here."

I take a step, then another. My knees tremble as I place my hand in his. His closeness is taking my breath. I can't speak right now and there is so much blood rushing through my head that my ears sound like a waterfall. I smell his body, fresh sweat mixed with chamomile soap, so familiar and—

"Here! For you." Peter waves the pheasant tale feather he'd found two weeks ago. It's a gorgeous brown and cream with a pattern of black stripes.

"But you love that feather," I cry.

"It makes a great bookmark. With you reading all the time…I mean…"

I take the feather from him and slide it along my cheek. He still holds my hand, his face so close, I see the tiny freckles on his nose. Is this the moment I've been imagining? Is he going to kiss me now?

"I'm going to *Pomerania* next week with the KLV." Peter's grin widens. "Our class is leaving together."

Silence descends as the word *Pomerania* echoes through my head. Say something, my mind urges. "How long?" I finally blurt. I stand there, so close, his fingers warm against mine.

"No idea. Maybe till the fall or Christmas."

Trying to hide my shock, I tear loose my hand and hurry to the sink. I wipe at some pretend water drop, search for something to say. Anything. I can't imagine staying here without him. The sink blurs. I force my shoulders to straighten and turn around. "Where in Pomerania?" All I know is it's way north, east of Mecklenburg along the Baltic Sea.

Peter shrugs. "They'll tell us all the details tomorrow."

"What about your mother?"

Peter looks at me funny. "What about her? It's not *her* decision." He jumps up and walks over to me. The waterfall returns to my ears. "Won't be long anyway, six months at the most. I thought you wanted to go too."

I shake my head. "I can't leave Mama. It's just…"

"What?"

"Nothing." I head to the stove to get away from his nearness. It's distracting right now, and I've got to keep my face from showing things. "You better go. I need to finish dinner," I lie. How can he be so happy to leave me?

"Fine then, I'll go. I don't know why you act like this," Peter mumbles and shoves past me.

I close the door as the tears start rolling for good.

Peter

I don't know what bites Hilda. She's always ready to go on adventures with me, climb up the steepest hills and dig through brambles and stinging nettles—she never complains. Here I thought she'd be happy. Sure, it'd be great if we went together, but who knows, she may end up in the same camp. After all, she's just a class below in eighth grade—

"Peter, why are you so late? I thought you were getting our bread today." Mother's voice is stern, so I hurry into the kitchen where she's ironing. Walter, my little brother, lounges on a chair doing homework. He's tall for nine and looks a lot like me with brown hair and square shoulders. But that's where our similarities end. A scar cuts his right eyebrow in half, and he annoys the heck out of me because he's terribly nosy—and loud.

Sure enough, he looks up from his math book and shouts dramatically, "We'll starve and croak." He rolls his eyes, grabs his own throat, and lets his head loll to the table.

Ignoring Walter, I sling an arm around mother's shoulders. "I forgot." I know she loves my hugs, especially since Father joined the war three years ago.

She carefully sets the hot iron on a stone and leans back, a huge frown on her forehead. It makes the wrinkle between her brows furrow deeper. "Why are you smiling? You should be sorry. We won't have anything for breakfast—"

"I'll go in the morning."

"But you have school."

"Not till nine o'clock."

"What about *my* breakfast?" Walter says, obviously back to

life.

"I'll go early, right at seven."

Mother sighs and pats my back. "Fine then. Better help me with dinner." She pushes me away, but then hesitates. "What is going on with you? Did we get mail? Did Father write?"

I note the hopefulness in her voice, her searching gaze at my hand as if I were carrying a letter from the mailbox. As guilt grips me, I begin to pace. "I'm going to camp in Pomerania." Like earlier with Hilda, Mother's eyes cloud over, so I hurry on. "You knew it was going to happen. The Führer wants us safe, and the Hitler Youth has it all set up for us. Lots of swimming this summer, hikes and campfires."

Mother rubs the red blotches on her throat. "What about school?"

I grin. "Herr Zimmermann, our math teacher, will come with us. He's going to make sure we have classes—most of the same subjects we have here. *Big Z* also loves literature."

But the frown doesn't lift from Mother's face. "What if I don't want you to go?" Her gaze wanders to the window. "We'll be completely alone."

"Come on! You've got…our neighbors…Hilda's mother. And Hilda can run errands for you."

"The girl is busy enough as it is." Mother's gaze wanders to the cardboard box on the sideboard. "What about your bird? I've fed him like you told me, but he's yours at night."

Damn, I forgot. I rush to Alex who squats on a sheet of newspaper, his shiny eyes on me. He hops and wiggles his shaggy feathers, his wings almost ready to support him.

"Hey Alex, you hungry?" I feed him an earthworm with tweezers. He swallows greedily, shakes himself and produces a tiny pile of poop that I pick up with a spoon. "Good boy."

Fighting down my disappointment for leaving Alex, I grab the metal container with the remaining worms. "I'll get a few more now. Alex will need another week, ten days at the most before he can be on his own."

Walter leaps from his chair and wiggles next to Mother. "I'll help."

She musses his hair. "Of course, *mein Schatz.*"

He grins his careless grin and sidles up to me. "What if you don't like it?"

A tiny jolt coils inside me, but then I smile back. "Impossible. I've seen the pictures. The beaches up there are incredible, white sand and huge dunes. And they say we'll get really good food— meat and gravy and pudding." I hold out the worm box. "Here, you said, you want to help. Why don't you dig up some worms for me?"

As Walter rushes outside, I notice a tear in Mother's right eye. It's shiny and hovers on her lower lashes. She angrily swipes her arm across. "I can manage the work. But you're my family and I worry… If anything happens to Father…you know there are more and more soldiers killed all the time. Walter needs you too— especially after that attack…" Her voice falters.

How could I forget? Walter got beaten by a couple of older boys and dragged into the alley behind our house. I shake off the memory and say, "That's why they want us kids to be in a safe place and away from the bombardments." When she doesn't answer, I go on. "You know there have been bombs in Köln. They may come here soon. We've got air raid alarms all the time." My gaze wanders to my brother's schoolbooks on the table. "Maybe Walter should leave too."

Except for a few bombs on factories, Solingen has been spared so far. They say our town hides under fog or the clouds and there are lots of hills and valleys that are harder to maneuver for British bombers.

"What if I say no?" Mother straightens a bit, her voice louder.

"You can't," I cry. "The entire class is going. They told us there won't be any more school around here soon. The teachers are going with us and…" Realizing that I'm shouting, I lower my voice. "Do you want me to be without school?"

"No, no…but there must be another way."

Dinner is muted and I'm the first to clear the table. From the corner of my eye, I see Walter remain on his chair. He's pretending to study, but his pencil just hovers. I hesitate because suddenly I feel the urge to put an arm around his shoulder. But then I remember my mission and grab the drying towel. Normally, that pleases Mother but tonight she silently pours water into the sink.

"You won't have to cook so much," I try again. "We'll play games, do sports competitions. Who knows? The war may be over soon. I'll be home by Christmas for sure."

"But—"

I rush up to Mother and capture her hands like the wings of a fluttering bird. "I'll write to you—a lot. I promise." Secretly, I wish Mother weren't so weak. German women are supposed to be fearless and strong.

A deep sigh rises from Mother's chest, and I know I have won.

CHAPTER TWO

Hilda

The soup tastes like sawdust, and I keep gulping water to chase it down. Mama's eyes don't leave my face, but she remains silent.

She's not one to pry nor open up herself, so we eat, our spoons scraping the bowls rhythmically. For once I'm not in the mood for seconds. Instead, I straighten and get busy with my dishes while Mama moves to her seat by the window with her cross-stitch to catch the last light.

I just don't get why Peter is so happy to leave. Isn't he the least bit sad to not see me anymore? My heart hammers against my ribs and I feel my cheeks warm. *You're a dumb cow, Hilda. He mustn't know…ever.* My mind wanders and I realize how tired my arms are. Even lifting the plates from the sudsy water is too much. I bite down on my molars and begin drying, wishing for once that my chore would take longer. I don't think I can handle sitting next to Mama tonight, talking about school or listening to the *Volksempfänger* radio, which Mama turns to every night as if she could summon my brother Paul's voice and whereabouts.

I'd much rather go to bed to read my new book, Erich Kästner's *Fabian*. My teacher, Fräulein Heinrich, gave it to me this morning under the pledge of secrecy. She knows I love to read and never forget a thing, but this book is forbidden. She also called it mature, whatever that means.

Not that I will use the things we study. Girls are supposed to have lots of children for the Fatherland. I'm not sure I agree. I'm not sure I want any children—at least not anytime soon. Unless…Peter's face swims into my vision: he grins as he urges me to jump into the pool… stretches out a hand to help me up a hill… shows me white nettles and a fox's burrow on a hike.

I resolutely put away the dried dishes and grab my school bag.

"I'm going to study," I announce. "Got a test tomorrow." Without waiting for an answer, I slip into my bedroom. It's the second lie today.

I'm still awake when Mama goes to bed, *Fabian* opened to page one next to me, Peter's feather nesting between the pages. Through the thin wall I hear her change, the swishing of fabric against skin, the suppressed sighs. I remember her laughs, her dry humor when we went on family excursions. That woman disappeared when my father left. And after my brother joined the war, her shoulders grew permanently hunched. She looks as if she shrank several inches.

My brother, Paul, is somewhere in France, we believe. He writes every few weeks, though his letters don't say much. I try reading between the lines, the way we used a secret language when I was little. What I see there isn't good. Paul turned nineteen yesterday, and I bet he didn't celebrate at all. Mama has tied the letters with a red ribbon and keeps the stack on the sideboard in the living room. Each time she walks past, she gives it a pat.

Now my best friend is leaving too, and though he won't be at some front, he'll be far from me and my bleeding heart.

Peter

The train station is flooded with people, mostly boys and their parents. Mother has come along to say good-bye, though I wish she hadn't. She wears a red and blue-flowered headscarf, and in her black winter coat that is too warm for today she looks drab. Her expression is worse, her cheeks reddened and her eyes glistening, but dry. Why can't she be happy for me?

At breakfast she kept watching me as if she wanted to implant my movements into her brain. She even organized an extra loaf of bread to pack a mountain of sandwiches.

Karl-Heinz is waving at me from the edge of the platform, pointing frantically at the numbers drawn on the wagon. Aside from Hilda, he's my best friend. We always share a bench in school, and he's the class clown.

Herr Zimmermann, who is tall and thin as a fencepost—thus his nickname Big Z—gesticulates toward the train. His voice isn't carrying in the mayhem of boys' chatter, screams and the chug-chug of the locomotive.

I bend low to give Mother a hug. When has she gotten so short? I feel her fingers clamp into my jacket as if she won't let go.

"I'll write soon," I say, suddenly breathless. I want to pat her cheek, but I catch myself. It isn't what men do. So I square my shoulders and march to the train door where Karl-Heinz is waiting for me.

"About time," he quips, throwing a glance at my mother, who waves again at the sight of us.

"Your mother didn't come?"

Karl-Heinz shrugs. "She was out late. Couldn't wake her this morning." I have the distinct feeling Karl-Heinz is glad about his mother not dissolving in tears in front of us.

The compartment is crowded with classmates. Everyone seems to talk at once as Karl-Heinz pulls me next to him onto a seat. Through the glass I see Mother standing outside. She's watching the boys hanging in the open window, and I can tell she's searching for me. But somehow I can't get up.

Karl-Heinz makes a comment about Big Z herding us like a flea circus, and I laugh as loud as I can. A shudder travels through the train car, drawing immediate hollers from us. As the boys find their seats, I spot Mother still waiting on the platform. Most people out there are waving or shouting, but she just stands planted like a black statue. For the briefest moment our eyes meet. Hers are filled with sadness too deep for tears.

I straighten and find the window, but by now the train is moving, and the image of my mother dissolves in a cloud of smoke. A lump chokes me with sudden ferocity. Sinking lower in my seat, I'm thankful that Karl-Heinz has decided to climb into the suitcase net above to give a welcome speech.

CHAPTER THREE

Hilda

I'm in the middle of making another soup when Mama comes rushing in. She's later than usual, but my cooking tonight is slow. I just got back from the weekly meeting of the *Bund Deutscher Mädel,* which everyone calls BDM, the German Young Women's Federation.

I'm tired of the endless hikes with heavy packs, and I can't stand the theatre and singing. Not only is my voice not meant to holler folk songs, but I loathe standing in front of others performing some pointless skit. Worst are the gymnastics we have to do with music. I love a good run, I can climb a tree, but don't ask me to dance like some monkey. According to our leaders, we're supposed to move *in harmony with each other* and skip gracefully across the lawn. Supposedly that prepares us to be mothers.

I'm in the middle of fixing vegetable soup with an onion, two potatoes, a can of green beans and a few pieces of macaroni I found sprinkled on the bottom of the food pantry.

Most of the time, one thing or another isn't available, and the lines are growing ever longer. We already ate our meat allowance on Sunday, a can of some sort of stringy roast without much flavor. Now that butter is no longer available, Mama fried it in a sliver of margarine, though even a stick of butter wouldn't have done it any good.

We have ration cards for everything—flour, sugar, salt, meat, fat, potatoes, fake coffee, coal, bread…even sauerkraut and shoe polish—but most coupons are worthless and our shelves ever more bare.

"Why didn't you tell me about Peter?" Out of breath, Mama hangs her purse on the hook in the hall. "I just met Frau Breuer, that's why I'm late. She said Peter left this morning?"

I give my ladle an extra push around the soup pot and keep my eyes on the few pieces swirling inside. "Nothing to say," I manage.

"But you two are friends. You see each other every day."

I shrug, afraid my throat will seize up if I say how much I miss him already.

But Mama keeps talking. "Frau Breuer is quite upset. She didn't want him to go, but Peter said they're moving his entire class and that there won't be any more school if he stays." She steps next to me to peek into the pot. "You think your class will go too?"

I detect uncertainty and worry in Mama's voice, which makes me feel a bit better. "I'm not going anywhere," I say. "I belong here with you." Mama puts a hand on my shoulder and I fight the urge to turn in for a full-blown hug. But Mama has already moved on to grab bowls.

"It smells good. I'm glad you're making our dinners. It saves me so much time." I don't tell her how easy it is for me. I rifled through all the soup recipes once, and now I can pretty much cook whatever we are able to get.

"But seriously," Mama continues as we sit down. "What if your school evacuates completely?"

"I don't care, I'm not going. They said the KLV is a *voluntary* program." I take a spoonful, vowing to look for herbs in the woods this summer. "Don't use that word…evacuation. They don't like it."

"What else is it?" Mama says. "They're taking you to God-knows-where, far out of our reach."

"To protect us from bombs."

"To fill your heads with propaganda." Mama's spoon sinks to the table. "Like they do at those meetings."

It's true. All boys have to attend the Hitler Youth and girls are part of the BDM. We march and we sing and do crafts. Maybe Mama is right, though I wish she wouldn't say these things out loud. It's dangerous when people speak their mind.

Just last week my best friend, Biene, told me about a neighbor who was taken away in a black car. Biene whispered to me that the woman was married to a Communist, and while he'd been arrested more than two years ago, the wife had been left alone. Until now. I'm glad Mama doesn't have friends in the *Partei*.

Peter

The trip takes forever. Our excitement shrivels with every passing kilometer. We've changed trains twice and are still not there. Once we stopped in the middle of nowhere because British bombers were near. Apparently, they love destroying tracks, preferably with trains full of people.

Our food has been eaten, water and tea thermoses drained. We take turns sleeping, the nearness of my classmates no longer fun, just annoying. Every time Karl-Heinz turns in his sleep, I wake up. Across from me, Dieter Maier snores up a storm. He has a crooked nose from a bike accident and can hardly breathe as it is.

I try to find a comfortable position, yearning for my bed with the feather comforter. Mother airs it every day in the open window under the eaves. Near the border to Pomerania, Big Z wakes us so we can change trains once again.

Sometime after midnight, I wake from a restless half-sleep to discover that my bones are filled with freezing lead. It's markedly colder up here, and a mean wind whips us on the bare platform. We huddle together, half sitting, half leaning on our packs. Sleep escapes me.

At dawn we arrive in Körlin. The train station is deserted, and after Zimmermann talks to the conductor, we march down some country road. The land is green and bare, bushes and trees short and leaning. Nobody has been working the fields. Off and on we see a modest farm in the distance. Zimmermann shakes his head and consults the map the conductor has drawn. We should've been there by now. The sun is crawling up in the sky and my stomach rumbles as if on schedule. We're missing breakfast. Some of us are muttering.

"I need two volunteers," Big Z says finally.

I immediately raise my arm and pull Karl-Heinz with me. Anything is better than wandering aimlessly.

"I need you to ask directions at the farm." He points down a narrow lane toward a red-bricked farmhouse with a reed roof. A thin ribbon of smoke snakes into the sky. "We're looking for the middle school they closed last year, a newly established KLV camp."

Karl-Heinz and I nod and march off.

The grass is long and wet, soaking my feet in seconds. It feels like a hundred years have passed since a person came along here. In the little yard in front of the house, a handful of chickens cluck.

"Hello? Anybody home?" we both yell.

The cow barn is dark and empty, and there's no manure. The door of the house opens slowly, revealing a mummy. At least that's what the woman looks like. Dressed in a layer of flowered skirts and a lumpy wool sweater, her face is so wrinkled, it looks like an old potato left over from last winter. Her hair is as gray as snow slush and pulled tightly into a bun.

"What do you want?" she says with a thin voice.

"We're looking for the former middle school. There's supposed to be a new camp for boys."

She mumbles something and I half expect her to send us away, but then she waves us closer with her forefinger. I'm reminded of the witch in *Hänsel and Gretel*. She even has whiskers and a huge mole on her chin.

"You from the west?" she asks, her dark eyes on us.

"Solingen…in the hilly land," Karl-Heinz offers. "Near Cologne."

"We walked from Körlin station," I add.

The woman nods, her expression neutral. "You went too far," she says. "Go back the way you came. Turn right at the old Linden tree. Go north about a kilometer until you reach the old Becker farm."

Next to me Karl-Heinz mumbles, "…back…Linden tree, Becker farm."

"Turn left…" the old woman taps a forefinger on her non-existing lips. It doesn't look like she's got teeth, her mouth and cheeks curved inward. "Better yet, go straight."

"Past the Becker farm?" Karl-Heinz asks.

The woman frowns. She's probably not talked to a human being in years.

"Maybe we should ask again at the Becker farm?" I say.

"The Beckers left last year," the old woman says.

I suppress a curse. I'm starving, my toes are freezing and I want to sleep. Badly. "You think you could draw us a map? We've got an entire class, thirty boys waiting—our teacher, too." Surely, by now, they must wonder why we're taking so long.

The woman hesitates, but then wiggles that forefinger again beckoning to us. We follow her inside.

At first, I'm blind, the room so dark I stumble along. As my eyes adjust, I make out a kitchen table, an old-fashioned tiled oven and a bunch of cabinets. Everything seems clean, but ancient.

The woman fumbles around in a drawer and emerges with a piece of thick paper. On one side are pencil marks and numbers. She begins to draw on the other side, but her hand shakes so badly, the lines are wiggling across as if possessed. She mutters to herself. I wonder if she can even see what she draws. The pencil lingers.

At last she shakes her head. "I cannot remember." Her gaze meets mine and there's pain and sadness. But then she smiles, an almost toothless grin that transforms her features.

"If you help me, I will show you."

Karl-Heinz rolls his eyes at me, but I pat his arm. "Of course, what do you need?"

The old woman shuffles to the door, then turns back and opens a box on the table. My nose picks up before my brain follows: bread.

The woman cuts two slices and holds them out to us. "I'm Augusta Weber." The toothless grin is back. We snatch the bread and start chewing. After we introduce ourselves in turn, we find out that Frau Weber has lived on the farm her entire life. She was even born here.

At the door, Frau Weber wiggles her finger again. We run after her. She creeps around the building to an ancient barn. Inside stands an equally ancient donkey. He's watching us with clouded eyes while chewing hay.

The old woman attaches a harness and leads the old animal past us outside. At last I understand. She's going to ride the thing and show us. But there's no saddle. Instead, she waddles to a roofed space with a collection of field tools, scythes, a wooden bench, and some kind of contraption on two wheels.

"Pull that out for me."

Karl-Heinz and I spring into action and drag out a cart no wider than four feet. Two wooden wheels hold up a tiny bench and an open flat surface in back.

Now I get it.

The return up the trail is slower than a sloth. I could run in circles around and still be faster. As we turn onto the main road, which is no more than a gravel path, whistles ring out, followed by shouts and laughter. Big Z only nods gravely and files in behind the cart. Catcalls and laughter die away.

The *race* to camp is on.

CHAPTER FOUR

Hilda

It's the first of June and we're having geography, one of my favorite subjects. I'm sleepy this morning because we had air raid alarms in the night again. Some nights there are three or four, cutting our sleep into ragged pieces. The only positive thing is that we get to start school an hour later.

Fräulein Heinrich's hair flames particularly red this morning. Every time she steps into the sun, it ignites like fire. I can't keep from staring.

"You all heard about Wuppertal?" Fräulein Heinrich asks, her gaze wandering around the room. She's good at that, keeping us on our toes. She nods gravely, the flames on her head flashing. "They say there were more than seven-hundred bombers and that there are thousands dead…many women and children."

Silence descends on our class. I haven't heard anything about a bombing, but that's no surprise. Most news about bombings reach us through word-of-mouth. Newspaper and radio only talk about us winning, about honor and glory.

I try to digest what I just heard, the numbers circling around my brain like a swarm of flies on a festering manure pile. I can't hold on to anything, can't focus, my palms sweaty.

Fräulein Heinrich's eyes shine with tears and I wonder how she found out and if she has family in Wuppertal. It's only ten kilometers away, and some parts of Solingen have seen smoke moving across the hills. Supposedly, the city has been burning for three days.

"That's why Principal Schmidt has decided to move all remaining fifth through eighth-grade classes with the help of the KLV, the children's evacuation program."

In an instant, arms fly up and the class erupts in shouts and questions. Fräulein Heinrich's green eyes move around the room to do their thing, but it's not working this morning. Everyone is talking, that is everyone except for me. The conversation with Mama replays in a loop through my head.

"Where are we going?" asks Susanne, the teacher's pet. She always wears perfect little dresses with white collars, and her father is some high up director at the city.

"And when?" Biene shouts next to me. I shove an elbow into her ribs because Fräulein Heinrich's brows slide beneath the fringe of her red hair, a sure sign she's irritated.

"If you give me a moment, I'll explain everything."

All afternoon, I'm pacing the kitchen. The class is leaving Friday—we've got lists of what to pack. That's in three days, but I'm determined to find a way out. It's almost summer holiday anyway, so I'm not missing much school. In my head I'm going over the arguments. I can study at home, read books. Most of the time it's boring in school anyway. Mama needs me. With Paul in the war, she's all alone. I can't go. Simply can't.

When the door lock turns, I run to meet my mother. She looks tired, the lines around her mouth deeper than I remember.

"Hallo *Kind*," she says innocently. Then she stops and looks at me with that penetrating stare that reminds me of Fräulein Heinrich. "What happened? Did you hear from…Paul?"

"No, no," I cry. "It's me. I'm supposed to leave and go to KLV camp with my class."

Strangely, Mama only nods. She slowly takes off her shoes, deposits her coat on a hanger, and places her purse on the hook. "Tell me," she finally says.

Unable to keep still, I begin to pace. "They say because Wuppertal got bombed, we have to go now. That it's dangerous and Solingen may be next. Principal Schmidt doesn't want to risk being blamed for killing the children."

Mama sits down heavily. "Oh, we blame the British bombers," she snaps. "And the men in Berlin."

"What are we going to do?"

"I'll talk to the mayor. Explain that you have to stay and help me." She smiles. "He doesn't know how smart you are."

I smile back, suddenly feeling relieved. Mama will fix it. We make sandwiches for dinner and share a fried egg, my mind preoccupied with the image of Mama telling the mayor about me.

Peter

When Frau Weber points down a narrow lane and turns her donkey around, we all take off in a run. After the slow walk I can hardly feel my feet. The bread was good, but my stomach rumbles again. Maybe they will put up a feast for us.

The building ahead is made of red brick, two stories with rows of windows. It sure looks like a school, but nobody is in the yard out front.

Suppressing our excitement, we fall in line, two in a row. The Hitler Youth runs all the KLV camps, so we don't want to make a bad impression.

Zimmermann takes the lead and into the building. It's unlocked, but as soon as we enter, I know something is wrong. There's nobody here. The reception and office are deserted, papers on the floor, drawers open as if the people hurried to get away.

Big Z sends four boys into the corridors and upstairs. I finally crumble against a wall as anger brews inside me. The lack of food and sleep are rearing their heads. The others aren't doing any better. A couple of boys are arguing with each other, Udo Lempski, the loudmouth, stomps outside, complaining. He's short and square, but makes up for it by commenting on everything and everyone.

"There's nobody here," says Dieter Meier, our snore master. He loudly breathes through his mouth, his cheeks red.

"We've got beds in some rooms," another boy reports.

Our teacher's serious expression turns grim.

"What about food?" Dieter asks. He's the only boy who's the slightest bit pudgy. His family owns a chicken farm, and he's used to eating well.

Zimmermann draws a paper from his bag and begins to make notes. I can tell that the pen is shaking almost as bad as the one the old woman held earlier.

We're all waiting as silence settles around us.

At last, Big Z turns to face us. "Boys, listen up." His gaze sweeps around the room as if we were in class. "I don't know what's going on or why they have send us here, but we're going to find out. In the meantime, I need all of you to pull together."

We nod and mumble, but Zimmermann raises his arm. "I want you to form five teams of six boys. Three teams will convert the classrooms upstairs to dorms. Collect the beds and sheets, furniture, etc. One team will prep a room on the first floor. We'll be having classes down here. One team will set up some sort of kitchen."

With what, I want to ask. We've got no more food and there's no grocery store in sight.

Herr Zimmermann waves at me. "You and Karl-Heinz will return to Frau Weber's farm and organize supplies." He hesitates before pulling out his wallet. "Here are fifty Reichsmark."

Karl-Heinz and I are retracing our steps. I'm beyond exhausted and hungry and can't wrap my head around the empty school building. Why didn't they know we were coming? Where is the Hitler Youth?

The farm looks just as tired and old, and the mummy stares. "I don't have anything to support thirty hungry boys," she says. I believe her. She waves us inside and we sit at her table—now almost familiar. "Here, eat." She pushes across a bowl of oat gruel with canned peaches on top and two spoons. She's giving us her food.

I want to shove it back, but my stomach is fighting mad at this point. When Karl-Heinz grabs his spoon, I take mine and we shovel in record speed.

"You will have to visit Lawinski's farm," Frau Weber says. "They may have enough stores…if you can pay."

Karl-Heinz produces the fifty. "I've got money."

The old woman shakes her head. "That will not feed thirty boys for long."

"Maybe we need to go home." It's out before I have time to think. In some corner of my heart, I wish it were true.

"And wait for the bombs?" Karl-Heinz scrapes the last bit of gruel from the bowl.

I shrug. "At least we had food and a decent bed."

"For how long?" Karl-Heinz is no longer funny. I've never seen him this way. Out of nowhere I feel the need to smack him—

hard.

"Boys!" Through the haze of anger, Frau Weber's voice reaches my ears. The lines around her eyes wiggle as she studies us. Kindness plays there, offset by a mouth that has seen great sadness. I wonder what her story is and why she is alone.

"Lawinski isn't far. I know he had a good potato crop…surely has some left." She rummages through another cabinet. "Here is a pot you can use for cooking." She sets a cooking vessel fit for a pumpkin on the table, also two ladles with long handles. "Now let me tell you how to find the farm."

Lawinski's farm sits in the middle of acres of fields and includes a two-story home, barns and assorted outbuildings built with red brick.

A woman Mother's age, a wash-water gray towel wrapped around her head, meets us at the front door. She must be the owner.

"We're looking to buy supplies for our class," Karl-Heinz blurts.

Frau Lawinski looks at us funny. "Not from around here, are you?"

I produce a smile. "We're here with the KLV, but they didn't know we were coming."

Frau Lawinski smirks, at least I think she does because the right corner of her mouth goes down and she folds her arms in front of her. "So we're supposed to come to the rescue?" she huffs. "All we do is hand out our hard-earned crops."

"We'll pay." Karl-Heinz digs out Zimmermann's fifty and waves it in front of the woman's face.

"We're just really hungry," I add, wondering whatever happened to the great holiday they promised us. Not only is there no beach and no swimming, there isn't even food and a decent bed. A headache brews behind my temples and my throat burns with thirst.

Frau Lawinski looks us up and down as if she wants to gauge the state of our bellies. Apparently, she's satisfied because she marches off to a side building.

We watch her go until she calls over her shoulder, "What are you waiting for?" As we walk across the yard, I notice a girl our age scoot around the corner and out of sight.

The storage barn is set up in compartments. "I've got potatoes from the last harvest, rutabagas, and onions. Some salad too."

"How much does the money buy us?"

"More than you can carry," Frau Lawinski says. Then with a sigh, "tell me where you are staying and I'll have it delivered."

CHAPTER FIVE

Hilda

When Mama returns home the next evening, I've already prepared dinner.

"The store had a delivery of white cabbage, so I've made cabbage with potatoes and onions," I tell her smiling. "There's no meat or sausage, but I think it tastes pretty good."

Mama hangs up her coat and purse and joins me in the kitchen. That's when I notice the blotchy spots on her cheeks. Instead of looking at me, she fusses with the soap to wash her hands.

"What is it?" I ask.

A shudder runs through her as she turns to face me. "I spoke with my boss and the youth welfare office. I even went to see the mayor." Her voice fades and I lean forward. "It's no good. They insist you go on Friday. I'm supposed to be an example because I work for the city. They said I was endangering your life, to think what kind of a mother I wanted to be…that I was irresponsible."

"Oh, Mama." I throw myself at her chest. "You're the best mother anyone could want."

"How dare they question me like that!" A quiver has entered her voice.

"What if we refuse?"

"They said you'd have to report to the unemployment office and work in the war effort."

I cross my arms in front of me. "I'm not going to make guns."

"My colleague said she heard they take away your ration cards, maybe mine too." Mama sinks onto a chair. "I don't know, but I can't afford to lose my job. Not now, with Papa and Paul…"

"But I can't go…I will hate it," I say, thinking how I despise Mama for calling my father *Papa* when he hasn't been near us in years. We don't even know if he's in the war. I don't want to care, resent the worry for him invading my thoughts.

A sigh rises from Mama's chest. "Maybe it won't be so bad and you'll get to come home soon. I heard they only plan for six months. That's not terribly long."

I note the resignation in her and know I've lost. She won't fight for me. "It's a lifetime," I cry. "I won't stand it."

"Your friend, Peter, likes it quite well. You might be surprised."

I stare at my mother. Is that the same woman who was talking mutiny yesterday? I hate how they scare her. Us.

I no longer care about dinner and slop it on our plates. We eat in silence as I go over the few possessions I have in my closet. Two dresses, one skirt, two sweaters—one of which is getting too small—a few sets of underwear. I doubt I can take my winter coat; it's already short in the arms and won't fit. Mama will have to come up with a replacement and send it. My stomach twinges, thinking about Mama being alone for Christmas. And Peter? A part of me was hoping to be here when he returns. I imagined this scene in detail, him walking in, the joy in his eyes, our embrace…and kiss.

"Maybe you'll be back after the summer." Mama's voice is hopeful. "Maybe this stupid war will be over."

But I can tell she doesn't believe it. And neither do I.

"I'll write as soon as I get paper and stamps," I say, rallying every bit of enthusiasm I can muster. "Then you'll know my address and can tell me about Paul." Paul's last letter arrived two weeks ago. It said pretty much nothing, except that they were moving into new positions and that he'd tried fried octopus for the first time.

I straighten abruptly and clear the table.

Mama sits and watches me. "Do you need me to help you pack?"

"I'll do it tomorrow. We don't have school anyway."

The train station is thick with kids, yet I feel completely alone.

There are screams and laughter, but also tears and unending hugs. That's why I told Mama to go to work. I don't want to cry in front of everyone.

I'm relieved to find Biene near the end of our platform. She's with her parents, a short and plump woman in her forties who looks like an older Biene and her father who works for a steel factory in some high-up position. He wears a dark suit and looks somber.

I detect wetness on Biene's eyelashes and am glad to be by myself. Just watching my friend clogs up my throat. It also feels a little bit better because I know I'm not alone.

A shrill whistle tears at my ears. The shouts increase and I see flaming hair near one of the train doors. Fräulein Heinrich is coming with us. Thank goodness for that.

I turn away from Biene, who's clinging to her mother like a lifebuoy. Next moment she joins me, wiping her eyes and pulling me along at the same time.

"Come on, let's hurry," she cries.

On the side of the train it says *Sonderzug*—chartered train— and a sign on our locomotive announces *Wheels must roll for victory.* As we squeeze in, the feeling of being lost returns. Some of my classmates are laughing and hanging out the windows. Are they truly feeling happy or are they putting on a show? I can't tell, so I concentrate on Fräulein Heinrich, who's walking up and down the aisle with a clipboard. She's usually pretty relaxed, but today her lips are pinched together.

A whistle blows, and the girls at the windows shriek and wave. The train rolls, then gathers speed. I used to like train rides, the chug-chug comforting. Now I see the familiar landscape disappear, replaced by roads clogged with Wehrmacht tanks and trucks. In the distance, ruins stain the sky.

Once we stop at a station where women in aprons and headbands offer hot tea and potato soup in paper cups. We eat and drink quietly, the warmth in my belly a welcome change to the wiggly sensation I've had ever since Peter left.

We're arriving in Bavaria after dark. We had to stop twice more in the middle of the tracks on open territory. Fräulein Heinrich says there are bombers about and that we're waiting for them to pass.

Biene and I take turns sleeping, almost as if one of us has to keep watch. Tilly, the youngest girl in my class is sitting next to me. Her hands and feet are tiny, like those of a child, and her eyes fill with tears off and on. I wish I could say something to make her feel better. Shreds of conversation reach my ears and I lift my head.

Across from me, Karin and Ilse are staring at Tilly whose sleeves are rumpled from all the tear wiping. "Sweetie is leaving the nest," Karin says. "Crybaby."

Ilse giggles. "Time to grow up."

They remind me of evil twins, always dressing alike. Both have dark brown hair and even wear their braids the same way: one long plait, draped once around their head. But while Karin has mean eyes, Ilse's mouth isn't aligned quite right and always looks as if she has a crooked smile.

"Do you want a piece of cake?" I ask Tilly. Mama has made the honey cake especially for my trip. It's sort of flaky, but it tastes pretty good.

Tilly nods and I stuff a pile of crumbles into her palm and smile. She's a small thing but has a sharp math mind, and her answers are always right.

"What about us, Hilda?" Karin's callous eyes try to look friendly, but they just can't.

"Yes, how about sharing?" Ilse chimes in.

"Sorry, she's already promised me the rest." Biene's hand lands on my wrist and I pass her the leftover cake with grim satisfaction.

When the train screeches to a halt, all of us jump up at once. Fräulein Heinrich's shouts are drowned out by our chatter. Of course, there isn't enough room in the aisles, so it's a wild shuffle until we're outside.

A man with a lantern talks to Fräulein Heinrich, and we're soon on our way—thirty girls and one teacher.

Thankfully, it isn't far to *Cloister Angel's Flight* where we're staying. The buildings appear tall and stark in the night sky. The wind nips at my legs and I wish I'd worn my thick hose instead of leaving in ankle socks.

A nun in a long dress and a sweeping head cover shows us to our rooms. Except for a bit of white fabric framing her forehead, she's dressed utterly in black. She doesn't smile and I'm glad when we close the door. We're six to a room, two triple high beds on each side of a narrow aisle. Across from the beds sits a wardrobe we have to share, and on a commode thrones a large white bowl and a pitcher.

Between the beds high on the wall hangs Jesus on a cross. His eyes are open and he mournfully stares at a spot on the floor between our bunks. Painted spikes hold him tightly, a bit of bloody red on his palms and the tops of his feet. I imagine him turning his head to look at us. He's probably never seen a bunch of girls in here.

Tilly takes the bottom bunk and Biene and I share the other two. Across from me, Karin and Ilse bicker about the thin blankets. They are right. My blanket is made from some kind of scratchy wool, it's flimsy, and the room feels like winter. The cloister was built in the Middle Ages and has thick walls and stone floors. I wish for my carpet and coal oven despite the fact that it's early June.

"I don't want to sleep on the bottom." Ursel Anton, the sixth girl in our room, stands, fists on her hips facing Ilse. "The air is bad down here and I'm claustrophobic." Ursel is as short as Tilly but solidly built. Even her hair is short, and a bit frayed like the hem of her dress. She looks as if she's ready for a fistfight.

"Says who?" Ilse squints, which makes her look even uglier.

"Says I."

"The top bunks are already spoken for," Karin says, draping an arm around her friend. "If you don't like it, complain to Fräulein Heinrich. I'm sure she has better things to do than listen to your whining."

As Ilse and Karin snigger, Ursel mumbles something and throws her bag beneath the lowest bunk.

I exchange a glance with Biene, wishing not for the last time to be on my way home.

We decide to skip brushing our teeth and turn off the single bulb dangling from the ceiling. As darkness descends on the little room, I curl up in a fetal position and massage my freezing toes. I could fold the blanket in two, but then I'd have to sleep in a ball. That's never going to work. I get back out of bed and rummage for my socks. Back in bed, I hear Tilly. She's sobbing into her pillow and trying to keep quiet. But the sounds seem to echo off the bare walls, and I know everyone is listening.

At last, even breathing comes from the other five beds. I'm still cold and envision white clouds steaming above our heads, icicles clinging to our noses in the morning. Then my mind wanders to Mama and Paul. I keep Peter for last, trying to think of the fun times we had and ignoring my irritation about his enthusiasm for camp. Mostly, I question my conviction that he's the boy I want…or who wants me. I know I've got an overactive imagination. He's probably sitting under some tree holding hands with a girl. The thought freezes my stomach until it feels like a ball of ice. I rub my middle, but the knot refuses to dissolve.

The door opens, and a shadow falls over our beds. Fräulein Heinrich, candle in one hand, is bending over us. I keep my eyes tightly shut and hope my lids aren't fluttering.

When she leaves, I let out a careful sigh. I don't remember when I fall asleep, but I awake to a blinding light. Biene has thrown open the shutters and leans out of the window as an early sun throws its rays on our beds.

"Time to wash," Tilly says. In her nightgown she looks even smaller, the seam of it dragging on the floor.

We all look at each other: six skinny girls in shabby nightclothes to share one bowl of cold water.

"Forget it," Karin says. She puts on her dress from yesterday, tears a brush through her hair and braids it to one side. Ilse follows suit. Ursel doesn't bother brushing her hair at all and instead examines the pitcher with the chipped handle.

"We've got to find water," I say to no one in particular. That's when a whistle sounds in the corridor. Moments later the door is thrown open and a young nun with huge blue eyes marches in.

"Good morning, girls," she says, a wide and genuine smile on her face. "I'm Sister Rose. Looks like you're up." She turns in a circle, her habit a black cloud around her. "Leave the water for now. Time to assemble and breakfast. We will give you a tour later, show you where you can wash." She hesitates. "There's a bathhouse, but the water is quite cold." She looks around the room and claps. "Now get dressed and follow me."

I self-consciously slip into my dress and shoes and refasten my ponytail, hoping my hair looks halfway straight. There's no mirror in the room—I guess the nuns consider it vain.

People are marching along the corridor. We turn right, then left…more marching. Most of us are quiet…expectant.

We assemble in a large room with oval windows, the smell of incense ticklish in my nose. A dozen nuns in black habits are upfront along with Fräulein Heinrich, her hair impossibly gaudy among the blackness.

"Now that we're all here, I'd like to welcome you to *Cloister Angel's Flight*. I'm the Abbess." A nun with a huge necklace of wooden beads and a cross dangling on her chest lifts her arms wide. "You may find the accommodations a bit Spartan." A tight smile plays around the sister's lips.

I can tell she's old, much older than Fräulein Heinrich, but there are no wrinkles. Not even around her eyes. Her face is round as a soccer ball with cheeks that reach from temple to chin. I return to her eyes, focus on the way they travel around the room. A shiver runs through me and I find myself wishing that they don't find me. "It is our way, so I'm afraid you'll have to get used to it." She continues to watch us, her eyes swooping this way and that like a hawk chasing its prey. "We will try to make your stay with us as comfortable as possible. In return, we expect you to honor our schedule, prayer and time of reflection. That means you walk quietly whenever in the halls and never speak in a loud voice—ever. You'll find it quite soothing, I'm sure."

She pauses and there isn't a sound in the place. "You will assume kitchen and garden duties, cleaning and cooking. And of course, you will study and do activities with your teacher." I know a nasty look when I see one, and that nun does not like Fräulein Heinrich. "You will eat and take classes in this room. Breakfast is at seven-fifteen—sharp. Class begins at eight. Now we pray."

I lower my head along with everyone else. The nuns mumble upfront but I can't make out any words. Just as well. I'm not interested in praying. My stomach demands attention, and I wonder what sort of food we'll be getting.

Too scared to talk, everyone sits down along skinny wooden tables that are as bare as the whitewashed walls. Four girls have been commanded to help. I see sweat on their foreheads as they push a cart with a huge pot along the aisle. The room fills with the aroma of hot milk. I loathe hot milk. I know that sounds picky, especially since we've got little to eat, but there is something in the odor that makes me gag. Sure enough, a bowl of boiled oats in milk appears in front of me. On top swim three cooked half plums and a smudge of purplish sauce.

While most girls scarf down their oats, I pick off the plums and sauce. The lumpy oats bring back an early memory, when

Mama wanted to feed me a similar dish. I couldn't have been older than three or four, but I can still recall the taste and her threatening looks. After a few bites, the whole mess returned onto the tablecloth. Mama yelled at me, but from then on I no longer had to try.

"Are you going to eat that?" Biene asks. She's eying my bowl—hers is scraped clean.

I push it across, worrying that I'll starve to death if this is a daily meal.

At eight on the dot, we sit to receive instruction. Fräulein Heinrich's cheeks glow, their red mismatched to her hair. Biene slides next to me at the last minute. She had to clean tables and wash dishes.

Her hand moves quickly to my lap and I immediately smell the delicious aroma of bread. Not just any bread, but a wholesome molasses and rye kind. I risk a side-glance to Biene, who wears the tiniest of smirks. Lowering my chin, I take a quick bite. When I raise my head I see Fräulein Heinrich's eyes on me. She knows.

To my surprise, our teacher begins, "You heard it, girls. Time to study. I've put up a schedule." Somehow the cloister has organized a blackboard, which now shows Fräulein Heinrich's orderly notes. "Copy it or commit it to memory," she instructs. I know that last bit is meant for me.

"We will study Monday through Friday mornings and, if the weather allows, take field trips on Saturdays. In the afternoons we'll do chores and, if time allows, exercises outside. Sundays we are supposed to do a flag ceremony, which I still must clear with the Abbess. Every Saturday and Tuesday, you will write letters to your families."

A mumble rises from the stark space as cavernous as a catacomb and likely as cold. A larger version of a somber Jesus on a wooden cross watches me from the wall. I imagine him winking at me and waving his red-painted hand.

In a way I feel like him. Watching from above helplessly, cold and sort of naked, and being far from what I know as home.

Fräulein Heinrich's voice drifts back. "You will write about your time here and I will have to read your letters before they are mailed." Her expression is guarded, her lips pressed flat as if it takes too much effort to form the words. "Those are the instructions of the *Reichsoffice*."

I'm lugging a galvanized metal bucket of water, soap and a brush to the latrine. As luck would have it, I'll be here all week. Every single girl received a job, and I was given the worst of the lot. My previous hunger has evaporated, the smell and taste of the watery barley soup now replaced by the stench of a group bathroom.

I stare in horror at the line of toilets along the back. There're no walls or partitions, just a row of ceramic seats next to each other. Strips of newspaper hang on a nail near the entrance. The only thing I can do now is think of something else—someone else.

As Peter's image rises in my mind, I get to work. I remember when he first found the black bird. It had to have fallen from the nest with barely any feathers, its yellow-rimmed beak open and its bulbous bluish eyes closed. "We may be able to save it," he'd said, picking it up carefully with his handkerchief. "It needs food and warmth."

At the time I thought that every other boy would've let it die.

Peter

After a week we've sort of organized sleeping quarters and classroom space. The problem is that none of us knows how to cook. Herr Zimmermann is a bachelor and seems to struggle turning on an oven. So we boil the potatoes and rutabagas we received, decorate them with shredded lettuce leaves and call it a meal.

The farmer has also delivered flour and a few eggs, so we attempt pancakes and bread. Neither tastes particularly good, the pancakes mushy and the bread crumbly. Still, it's better than starving. Big Z has written to the *Reichsoffice*, to our principal and to the mayor of Körlin to inquire about our quarters. Obviously, nobody knew we were coming.

This morning, a man in a suit showed up, some administrator from the *Reich* who walked around the school, mumbling and shaking his head. According to Zimmermann we are supposed to get help soon, but it has to be cleared through the proper channels first. The man in the suit explained that the Hitler Youth made a mistake, counting suitable buildings and listing them, but not assuring they were ready for kids to move into.

Big Z attempts to teach us math, history and literature in the morning. We found a world atlas as well as a few copies of Thomas Mann's *Die Buddenbrooks*. Big Z also likes to quote from Rilke and carries a collection of poems with him wherever he goes. Right now he is citing *Before Summer Rain,* something about scary childhood memories and creepy uncertainty. I don't get it and I don't care. I'd much rather explore the area and look for things to eat to add to our menu.

Karl-Heinz appears to be drowsy and he has this weird sheen on his forehead. He looks flushed, though it's not exactly warm in the classroom.

"Karl-Heinz, will you at least *pretend* to participate?" Big Z stuffs the dog-eared copy of Rilke back into his suit jacket.

Usually, Karl-Heinz offers some kind of dry comment. 'I've been listening with my eyes closed,' he'd say. Or 'I'd be happy to take over.' But this morning, he remains mute. That's when I get really worried.

It seems as if Big Z is equally concerned because he rushes up to us and puts a palm on Karl-Heinz's forehead. In its intimacy the gesture is at once comforting and alarming.

"You're burning up," Zimmermann says. In seconds we're putting Karl-Heinz between us and taking him to our bedroom. I feel the heat of his chest beneath my armpits as we half drag, half carry him. While we struggle upstairs, the steps blur and something sour rises from my stomach. Deep down I know that something terrible is going on with Karl-Heinz.

Eight straw sacks line up against the wall. Karl-Heinz sleeps on the last one in the corner.

As he slumps to his bed I lightly touch his forehead—positively ablaze. He wheezes, and when he listlessly tugs at his throat I notice that his neck is swollen. Now I'm truly worried. Karl-Heinz is never sick. In fact, whenever I had the flu or some other crud, he'd come and visit. "Bugs don't like me," he always said. They definitely like him now.

Christian appears in the doorway, his brows scrunched in a frown. "Big Z wants you to find a doctor," he says with a shaky voice. At least six inches taller than the rest of us, Christian's elbows and knees are bony and seemingly at odds with each other. When you see him walk, he looks like some marionette whose puppeteer is drunk. Right now his eyes are large and shiny as if he's about to cry. He lives next to Karl-Heinz, and they've been friends since first grade.

I take off in a run. In my confusion, I end up back at the old mummy woman's house.

"What's wrong?" she calls across the yard. I'm amazed how she can see me because her eyes are so clouded and rheumy looking.

"Karl-Heinz is really sick." Panic propels me to Frau Weber's door. "He needs a doctor."

"You'll have to go to Körlin," she says. I nod as I try to force air through my tight chest. I've got no idea how far the town is. The old woman points an arthritic forefinger. "Right up the path. Then left onto the main road until you see the city sign."

I nod numbly.

"Take Ingo," she says. "It is a ways." When I don't move, she hobbles toward the barn where the ancient donkey stands chewing hay. She can't be serious. That animal is about to fall over. When I hesitate, the old woman chuckles. It sounds a bit like a witch, but there's amusement in her eyes. "He's faster than he leads on—and he knows the way. We used to sell at the market."

And that's how I ride into Körlin on a donkey. Indeed, Ingo fell into a trot partway, though I likely could've run just as fast. My seat is damp with sweat and reeks of ass, but at that point I don't care. I've got to hurry.

After asking around I find the doctor, some old fellow with gray wispy hair who immediately snatches his black bag and asks me to join him on his buggy. I tie Ingo to the back and hope he'll survive. Because compared to Frau Weber's half-dead donkey, this black mare puts up a good clip.

Apparently, Big Z has given up on teaching this morning. Our class is lingering outside and in the halls. At the door to our dorm, the doctor puts up an arm.

"No further," he says. "Best you all go outside—and wash your hands. Now."

We reluctantly saunter off. Time ticks in slow motion as we wander around the school grounds. I can't concentrate because my mind rotates around the scene in the classroom, Karl-Heinz's hot face, the way his legs dragged up the stairs. He acted like an old man on life support.

I sink onto a rock and stare into space.

"You think he's all right?" Christian asks. I haven't noticed him approach.

Unsure my voice works right now I shrug. With a sigh Christian slumps next to me—the silence between us almost comforting.

So far, our retreat is not turning out the way I envisioned. This morning, Big Z asked us to raise the flag he received from the visitor, something we're supposed to do every morning. None of us is in the mood to sing the required songs…

Raise the flag! The ranks tightly closed!
The SA marches with calm, steady step.
Comrades shot by the Red Front and reactionaries
March in spirit within our ranks.

I tuned out the remaining two passages. *Our* flag hangs as limp as an old rag.

At some point, Zimmermann appears. His expression is even gloomier than when we first arrived.

"Karl-Heinz has diphtheria," he announces. "It's highly contagious, so nobody is allowed in the room. Körlin doesn't have a hospital, but the doctor has offered to organize a woman to care for Karl-Heinz." Zimmermann hesitates. "It is possible that some of you have been infected as well." He pulls out a scrap of paper. "Please raise your hand if you have *any* of the following symptoms: fatigue, problems swallowing, belly aches or pain in your limbs, nausea or vomiting."

I scan the crowd as I imagine various ailments. My bottom aches. Is that from riding the donkey or am I getting sick? My throat is thick as well, but that's likely from worrying and the effort not to cry. I've got questions. What is going to happen to Karl-Heinz? Will he die?

A couple of boys have raised their hands, one of them Christian. Big Z ushers them back inside where the doctor will examine them.

The rest of us file through the bathroom, washing our hands a second time.

Christian returns as we prepare another potato and salad meal. The leaves of the lettuce are getting soft and yellow, but we can't afford to throw anything away.

"I guess I'm fine," Christian tells me, taking a handful

potatoes to scrub in the sink. "What if he dies?" he whispers. Water drips, potatoes forgotten in his hand, his skinny arms by his sides—defeated.

I scoff. "Nonsense. Karl-Heinz is too stubborn to croak." I abruptly turn to search for the large pot. Must stay busy.

It's at least midnight, and the new dorm is quiet. I'm lying on a different straw sack because the doctor forbid us to retrieve anything from the room Karl-Heinz is in. Several times in the afternoon I suppressed the urge to run upstairs and peek inside to watch the caretaker, a motherly-looking woman from a nearby farm.

The wind rattles the windows and I wonder if Karl-Heinz is still breathing.

CHAPTER SIX

Hilda

I awake early this morning and immediately notice the smell. Pee. It's so strong I wonder if somebody has upset the night bucket we have sitting by the door. But the lid is in place.

I carefully climb down and realize it's Tilly. In the dimness that seeps through the shutters, her light blond curls glow like a halo around her cheeks. She's sleeping, and for once, she looks peaceful.

Any moment the bells will sound the alarm and everyone will know what Tilly did. So I touch her shoulder and gently squeeze. When Tilly's eyes open, I place a forefinger on my lips. That's when she notices her problem. Her eyes widen as she wiggles against the back wall and away from me.

I signal her to hurry out of bed. Before Karin and her mean twin, Ilse, find out. Or that nasty nun they call the Abbess.

I've got a plan.

Today we write our first letter home. Fräulein Heinrich has listed ideas on the board. 'Happy' and 'fun' are mentioned there along with 'peaceful' and 'safe.'

But Fräulein Heinrich doesn't look happy. She no longer wears lipstick and I suspect the nuns told her to quit painting her face. But there's more to it——

"As soon as you are done, we'll take a walk." Fräulein Heinrich's voice interrupts my thoughts, so I hurry to it.

Liebe Mama,

We have arrived at Cloister Angel's Flight, which is run by nuns. It is a peaceful place and we're quite safe here. Our teacher keeps us busy in the mornings and we have ~~to work~~ fun in the afternoon. I miss you very much. Please send me news soon. Especially if you hear from Paul. ~~Or Peter.~~ Please give Frau Breuer my address in case Peter wants to write.

Love and kisses,

Hilda

We spend the rest of the afternoon identifying herbs and edible plants in the cloister garden. It's my favorite spot so far. The beds are kept neat in little boxes with nametags. It smells of rosemary and lavender, lemon balm and mint. Next week I'll get to work here.

Saturday we'll be hiking the woods that surround the cloister in a thick green swath, so it's impossible to know how far it is to the next town. I plan on finding additional herbs to support the cloister's kitchen.

I got over the stinky milk issue. Had to because my stomach started aching so bad that I couldn't concentrate in class. The nuns are obviously poor—or maybe they just believe in living like they're on a hunger strike.

Dinners consist of soup and a little bread. Tonight it's pea soup. Not the thick pea soup I know from home, but a greenish water with a handful of mushy peas. Oh, how I miss cooking at home. But I'm afraid to write about it—just as I'm afraid to tell Mama about Tilly's bed-wetting, the strict nuns, and my homesickness.

The Führer says that fear is weakness. He wants us kids to be strong and brave like warriors. I don't know what the others think, but I feel like a fake. Not strong, not brave but yearning for the things—and the people at home—who I can't have.

After the meal we have a free hour to read, but I've got work to do. I pretend to go to the bathroom, but instead slip into the utility closet next to it. This is where the nuns keep the cleaning stuff. I've got a bucket sitting in the corner. Inside swim Tilly's sheets. I've got to rinse them one more time and then drape them some place warm. Ha! The cloister is dank and cold, and I don't want to even imagine how it'll be in winter. All I can hope is that we'll get to go home in November. That's when the six months are up.

I fill another bucket in the deep sink and move the sheets over. Thankfully, the smell is gone, but I had to use soap I was supposed to keep for cleaning. I wring out the fabric and decide to try the attic. A narrow staircase climbs up across from our dorm room. With luck I can get there unseen. Fortunately, Tilly has laundry duty and smuggled a set of fresh sheets under her dress. She's so skinny, nobody noticed.

"What are you doing up here?"

I'm so shocked, my bucket clatters to the wooden floor and spills over. A whoosh of black hurries to my side and I find myself face-to-face with Sister Rose, the young nun from the first morning. She's smiling, her teeth as white as the coif on her head.

"I'm so…so…sorry," I stutter.

The nun picks up my bucket and hands it to me. "Doing laundry so late?"

I nod. My cheeks are hot lava and my mouth dry. I'll be in deep trouble now. Probably have to pray on my knees for hours. Maybe go home—

The nun's young face is still close to mine. "Do not worry yourself. I'm not supposed to be up here either." She smiles conspiratorially.

Clearing my throat, I say, "Thank you. I just need to dry these."

"Let me help you." Sister Rose extends an arm and I hand her the end of a sheet. We drape it across two ceiling beams that are anchored in the floor. The second one goes across the handrail.

The nun turns toward the tiny window beneath the rafters. "Do you want to see?" she asks.

I creep closer, feeling self-conscious so near the black habit. Outside, beneath the roofline, clings a messy nest of mud and straw, and on top sits a swift. It looks like a tiny hawk with a white chest and long pointed wings, its brown feathers edged white. She has large black eyes that look a bit nervous.

"Oh," I say in wonder, "how pretty."

"She's got five eggs." Sister Rose giggles, a strange sound in this serious place. She holds out an immaculate hand.

I shake it and produce a grin.

She giggles again. "Your secret is safe with me. As long as you keep mine."

"Always."

Sister Rose's expression turns somber. "I better go before someone misses me. I'm supposed to be praying." She puts a forefinger on her lips and glides down the stairs. I look after her in awe.

I've got a nun as a friend.

Peter

While Big Z discusses Napoleon, my mind drifts. This morning, another woman arrived to take care of Karl-Heinz. I saw her whisper to our teacher, but nobody is talking. Equally worried and bored, I doodle on the precious paper Zimmermann handed out this morning.

That's when I notice movement outside. Before I've got time to tell Big Z, Udo Lempski, our class know-it-all shouts and points at something outside. "We've got visitors!"

In a split second we shove and push to the windows to watch three trucks pull into the yard and come to a stop in front of the main door. A bunch of boys in the beige and black Hitler Youth uniforms, red swastika armbands on their sleeves, are jumping out. The driver of the first truck wears the brown suit that people from the NSDAP party wear. We call them *brown shirts*.

As our teacher greets the guests, we hang out the windows. The group of Hitler Youths is unloading the first truck. They carry sacks and cardboard boxes inside. Two more march to the flagpole, raise the red swastika banner and salute. It's supposed to be part of the daily ceremony, but ever since Karl-Heinz got sick, it sort of fell by the wayside.

Voices rise in the corridor. Angry voices.

We rush to the door and peek outside. Big Z is talking to the man in uniform. Both are red in the face.

"I asked for supplies. Not to be ridiculed," Big Z says.

"Orders are clear. The camp leader will take over from here." The man waves at a boy who is maybe seventeen. He's blond and almost as tall as our teacher. He clicks his heels together and salutes.

"Sir, Werner Zeibler, it's all under control. We hear you have a sick boy."

My stomach pinches. Karl-Heinz.

"He'll be picked up shortly," Zeibler says as the man in brown marches off. "You may return to your classroom."

I stare in shock as Zimmermann, his expression frozen in anger, marches toward us.

"Inside," he huffs. "Close the door."

We scramble to sit and watch our teacher who doesn't seem to find any words.

"You heard it," he says at last. "Karl-Heinz will be picked up. That's safer for everyone." He bites his lip and picks up a piece of chalk. "Let's get back to Napoleon."

As Big Z continues, I watch the Hitler Youth finish unpacking the trucks outside. I hardly hear the knock on the door before Zeibler strides into the classroom, a folder in his hand.

"Sir, I realize it's still teaching hour, but the circumstances demand an exception."

"I'd appreciate—"

Zeibler raises an arm to cut him off. "I need six boys to take care of the kitchen, put away supplies and peel potatoes. I need six more to sort uniforms." He scans the room and makes a disgusted face. "I want everyone in uniform by lunch time. I need four boys to draw up rotating schedules. The others can clean." He hands Zimmermann a paper. "Here is the timetable. I expect everyone to follow it to the minute." He turns as if to leave, but then faces us again, his expression hard to read. "As of today, flag ceremony will be mandatory twice a day."

As Zeibler smacks shut the door behind him, Zimmermann just stands there. Then he sighs. "You heard it. Who wants to do kitchen work?"

None of us raise a hand. I hate peeling potatoes.

"Fine then, I will choose *for* you."

After lunch and a short break we assemble in the yard in our uniforms. Most of us brought what we had, but these are brand-new. Zeibler makes us stand in rows of six.

"Time to start your training," he announces. "We'll begin with marching. Left foot first. Forward march!"

We stumble thirty yards before the whistle blows. "Stop. STOP." Zeibler moves in front of us, his expression full of disgust as if he's stepped in a pile of dog shit. "Start again." He points at Christian whose dangling limbs don't even follow himself, not to mention some guy in uniform. "You there, pay attention. Your left foot first. Adjust your steps. Watch the person in front."

We march again, Christian's ears glowing right in front of me. This time we march five minutes. The whistle goes once more. I squint at Zeibler, want to throw a fist into his arrogant mug. What an asshole.

Zeibler points a bony forefinger at Christian. "You, what's your name?"

"Christian Koch."

"Can't you walk straight?" Zeibler spits. "It isn't rocket science."

Christian's ears glow while I imagine Zeibler bleeding from his nose. A light drizzle soaks our clothes, but the drill sergeant doesn't care. We run sprints, do pushups and sit-ups, run more sprints, and march again at the end.

"You're pathetic," Zeibler says, throwing a glance at his wristwatch. "Dismissed."

We drag ourselves inside in silence. My legs burn with fatigue and I'm ravenous. For the first time, I earnestly wish I'd stayed home.

CHAPTER SEVEN

Hilda

When I sneak back to my room after lunch the next day, a neatly folded set of bed sheets is lying on my pillow. *Sister Rose*, I think with gratitude. Unfortunately, Tilly has had another accident, despite the fact that she peed twice before bed and I told her to drink less during dinner.

I know what's bothering her has nothing to do with the amount of liquids she consumes. She's plain sad. And scared of the evil twins and the Abbess. I'm tempted to tell her about Sister Rose, but my promise to the nun must stand.

I quickly make Tilly's bed with the fresh sheets and hide the soiled ones under the bed before I reread Mama's letter.

> *Dearest Hilda,*
>
> *I hope this note finds you well. I miss you so. Frau Breuer says that Peter is doing well. He wrote that he's enjoying his new 'home,' a former school, and that they have lots of fun activities. He's sending greetings to you in the letter to his mother. Do you want me to give Frau Breuer your address? He could write to you directly...*

My mind spins off. Peter loves his life and I hate mine. What is wrong with me? I bet he isn't cold and starving half the time. I rub my neck because all of a sudden I'm all stiff and sore. What is wrong with him? How could he be excited—

"What are you doing in your room?" The Abbess fills out the

door like an oversized black tent.

I wince and stuff the letter under my pillow.

"What do you have there?"

"A…letter from my mother."

The Abbess extends a hand. "Give it to me."

Afraid my tongue may appear to show her what I think, I quickly bite my cheek. The words slip out anyway. "But it's mine."

"Give it to me this instant." Despite my fear, I note how the woman's eyes match her dark habit.

I hand her the paper and lower my gaze.

"You will report to your duty right this minute."

I rush past her without a word. I'm in the sock mending detail, but when I slip into my seat next to Biene, I can't even get the stupid thread through the eye of the needle.

"Let me do it," Biene whispers. We're not supposed to talk, and an older nun, who looks like she's chewing lemons, is reading a bible nearby. When she doesn't look up, Biene asks, "What happened? You look as red as a poppy."

"Shhh." The old nun's eyes are on Biene, so I shrug and try concentrating on the rubbed-through heel of the sock. My fingers refuse to cooperate as the scene with the old bat replays in my head. I feel sorry for the girl whose sock I'm supposed to fix.

At dinnertime we assemble as usual. Tonight we're having potatoes with watery gravy and bits of sinewy meat. I don't want to know what kind of animal died for it.

Instead of the usual prayer, the Abbess climbs the podium. "It seems that some of you have not yet learned the rules. This community can only function if we all work together and obey. We have schedules and we have made promises. I expect each and everyone of you to keep them." She nods at Fräulein Heinrich, whose cheeks glow like her hair. "Now let us pray."

I feel that every one of those words is meant for me and cower in my chair.

After dinner Fräulein Heinrich stops me in the hallway. "What happened?" she asks, her eyes hard to read.

I shrug. "I just wanted to read Mama's letter again."

Fräulein Heinrich puts a skinny hand on my forearm. "Hilda, listen. Be careful. We're guests here, and the administration has left guidelines. The Abbess is…strict."

"When will I get my letter back?"

"In time."

I know my teacher wants to say more, but she's afraid. My throat tightens as I realize we're both powerless. I want to tell her about Tilly, but I can't even risk that. So I hang my head and hurry to my room.

"…I can't believe it," Karin sneers as I enter.

"Like a baby," Ilse says. "The entire room stinks because of you."

I remember the dirty sheets under Tilly's bed. I meant to take them to the washroom earlier, but…Tilly cowers on a chair, sitting on her hands. She's pale, though her eyes are dry.

Karin and Ilse are towering above her, arms crossed. In the middle of floor lies a crumpled pile of sheets.

"She can't help it," I say, wishing Biene would be here. But Biene isn't in the room.

Karin swivels on her heels. "Who makes you the expert?"

Gosh, the girl is stupid. "Would anyone in their right mind pee in their bed on purpose?"

Ilse ignores me. "We better tell Fräulein Heinrich."

"And the Abbess," Karin says. "She has a right to know what pigs sleep under her roof."

"Please don't…" Tilly cries.

Ilse is already at the door. "You coming?" she addresses Karin.

"Why don't you shut your mouth?" I say, stepping in Karin's way. "It's none of their business."

Karin shoves me aside, her elbow digging into my ribs. That's when Biene enters, a towel over her shoulder.

"What is going on?" she asks, looking around the room.

"Tilly is a pig," Karin says, tugging at Ilse's arm. "Let's go."

I stand there in the middle of the room and don't know what to do. I want to run after the twins, and I want to hide Tilly. Take her away from here. Take both of us away from here.

"They found out that I wet the bed," Tilly says in a small voice.

Biene nods, but I think she already knew. "What now?"

"We brace for impact," I say. "Let's take your sheets to the laundry before they show up."

"I'll go," Tilly says and picks up her bedding. I look at Jesus, who appears even sadder than usual. I'm sure he never thought about the pain girls can inflict on each other.

At least tomorrow is washday. I wonder if Sister Rose is in the attic watching 'mother swift.' "You've been helping her," Biene says once Tilly has left. "I thought something smelled funny."

I nod.

"I hate that nun." Biene digs under her pillow for her nightgown. "She doesn't like Fräulein Heinrich either."

"How do you know?" I ask, as I change into my nightdress.

"I overheard the Abbess complain about us and that Fräulein Heinrich isn't teaching us manners, and that she is a bad teacher."

"She's a great teacher!" I cry.

"Sure, she is." Biene climbs into bed. "And she's young and pretty and the Abbess is a shriveled stinking onion."

I laugh.

Every time I wake, I hear little noises from Tilly's bed. Nobody showed up in the evening, but Karin and Ilse both looked smug when they returned. The waiting is worse than if somebody had yelled at Tilly. No wonder she can't sleep.

Tilly's bed is dry in the morning, but her eyes are bloodshot and her face pale. She looks like she hasn't slept a wink and will keel over any moment.

After breakfast, she's called aside by our teacher. Then she leaves and I can guess where she's going next. All morning she doesn't return while Fräulein Heinrich attempts to explain algebra.

During lunch, Tilly is back in her seat and I catch her on the way to quiet hour.

"What happened?"

Tilly shakes her head and avoids my gaze. She wordlessly climbs on her bed and turns her back to me.

Peter

A week has passed and there is still no word about Karl-Heinz. Big Z went to visit him at the hospital, but we're forbidden to leave the school grounds. I've considered sneaking away in the afternoon, but that new Hitler Youth guy, Zeibler, runs this place like a military barrack. Part of which is roll call and marching, fighting with sticks, and endless stories about becoming heroes.

We also have a new schedule, which means we get up at six forty-five, thirty minutes earlier, to allow for shoe shining, perfect bed making and room cleaning. At seven forty-five we assemble in the yard to raise the flag while Zeibler announces the flag quote of the day. One of his favorites is, *"You are nothing; your nation is everything."*

We've gotten much better at marching, but he still has it in for Christian, forcing him to do pushups and extra cleaning duty in the bathroom. Christian spends more time on his knees than his feet.

Food has gotten much better since the trucks arrived. But Big Z often hides his nose in Rilke's poems, a worry frown between his brows. He used to be patient. Now he blows up at us at the slightest provocation.

Right around noon, Zeibler walks into our classroom. He quit knocking three days ago and just takes over.

"Listen up, men." He puffs out his scrawny chest and looks around the room. "I know you'd planned soccer matches this afternoon, but I received a request from the Lawinski farm. They need help putting up fencing. I volunteered us for this afternoon and the weekend." Zeibler flashes his teeth. "After all, what could be better than working in nature and securing the food supply of our country?"

I stare at the ground, try to keep my fury under control. Something needs to be done about that man, just what, I don't know. Why can't he get sick like Karl-Heinz? Too bad they burned Karl-Heinz's bedding. It would've been great to sneak Zeibler diphtheria-infected sheets.

I smile grimly when Udo Lempski pipes up from the back. "We were going on a hike tomorrow." Big Z makes him sit back there, because he tends to annoy everyone he is close to.

Not a smart move as Zeibler zeroes in on Udo. "What was that?"

Udo's usual confidence falters. "I thought...we...Herr Zimmermann told us we're going on a hike tomorrow. To look for herbs and mushrooms."

"You need to work on your manners." Almost colorless anyway, Zeibler's eyes remind me of a frozen pond. "Report to my office in fifteen minutes." He throws a nasty glance at Zimmermann before yelling "Heil Hitler," clicking his heels together and marching off.

The door smacks shut and we all stare at our teacher. Big Z just stands there, clamping his jaws. He carefully lays down Rilke and looks at us. He's got brown eyes, but right now they appear more black, as if all the anger and frustration he's holding back is collecting there.

"Boys, you heard what he said." Zimmermann speaks very slowly. "We will postpone our hike until Monday morning." He sighs. "Our instructions are clear. We have to follow orders from the camp leader and that, *meine Herren*, is Herr Zeibler." He turns to Udo. "You better report to him now."

Cheeks glowing, Udo runs from the room. Part of me enjoys him getting punished; the other feels his dread.

By two o'clock we're heading toward Lawinski's farm near the old woman's place. Udo was seen marching in circles for an hour before being allowed to return to us. This time Herr Lawinski, a stocky fellow in a worn coverall with muck on his knees, is waiting and there at the entry door lounges the girl we saw the first time when we picked up potatoes. She's wearing coveralls and rubber boots, her blonde hair braided and snaked around her head. She's watching us with great interest, though her gaze nervously flicks to her father.

Sure enough, he shouts at her. "Bea, get in the house this instant."

I could swear there's regret in Bea's eyes, but she hurries off nonetheless.

Herr Lawinski doesn't smell too good, nor does he seem particularly friendly. Zeibler is gesturing and smiling, but we can't hear what he's saying.

We are sent to a field carrying wooden poles, shovels and wire. The wind blows fiercely out here, the country flat as a plate. Heavy clouds race above us.

Udo and two other boys work nearby with strips of cloth wrapped around their hands—none of us has gloves and the old wire fencing cuts into our palms. The rest of us are fighting the heavy soil, pulling out the old posts and replacing them with the new.

Zeibler doesn't move a finger himself. He just walks up and down the fencerows, shouting when one of us is too slow for his taste. Fury brews inside me and I envision knocking Zeibler to the ground, all of us taking turns giving him a good whipping.

The shirt I brought is too thin and already short in the arms. Swinging the shovel, I've torn the shoulder seam. At home I'd be spending time with Hilda, go exploring or just sitting some place talking. Oh, how we *could* talk about things. Anything really. All of a sudden I want to write to her. Tell her about our ordeal, about Karl-Heinz and Zeibler, the lousy school. She was right all along. A new ache joins the coldness in my bones. It surprises me.

"Ouch, damn," Udo cries, tearing me away from my thoughts. He's staring at his palm where blood pools and drips between his fingers. Zeibler appears, his expression full of disgust.

"Why don't you pay attention?" He grabs Udo by the elbow and half drags him across the field. Over his shoulder he shouts, "You better be done when I return or there'll be consequences."

"Asshole," Christian mutters under his breath. It's the first cussword I've ever heard from him. We join him inventing new expletives and repeat some not so new ones. But our banter soon fizzles and we return to work.

Zeibler never makes empty threats.

Karl-Heinz walks into our classroom, a shy grin on his face. It's the middle of July and he's as pale as the clouds outside. We holler and surround him, Big Z and *Aristotle* momentarily forgotten.

"How are you?" I say quietly as he settles next to me.

"Glad to be back." There are rings under his eyes and he looks much thinner than I remember, his wrists bony, and his voice a bit hoarse. Still, I'm elated to have my friend back. I notice Christian keeping his head low, hiding a huge grin.

We finally have a chance to talk during dinner. Thankfully, he didn't have to participate in yet another grueling afternoon of *war* exercises. I'm equally exhausted and famished. In fact, lately, that's all I feel. I want to eat and rest. It's getting harder and harder to write lie-infested letters. Mother is surely wondering about the lack of creativity. But Zimmermann told us to write good stuff and that he's forced to control our notes. In reality, it isn't our teacher. Zeibler is the one who noses round in our correspondence. He's looking for rebellion or negative comments, any sort of criticism.

So I write things Mother would want to hear. And maybe it's for the best because I don't want her to worry about me. She's got enough going on. I want to write to Hilda too, but every time I begin I don't know what to say. I've never lied to her and writing some bullshit is beneath her. Of course, if I did tell her the truth, she'd laugh and say 'I told you so.' Strange that she went away too. Mother mentioned that she was pretty much forced into it. I wonder how she is doing in Bavaria. Probably climbing mountains, eating bacon *Knödel*, and collecting blueberries.

Karl-Heinz is picking through his food: boiled potatoes, cabbage and greasy sausage. I'm waiting for him to start talking, but he's quiet, just staring at his plate most of the time. Where is my old friend, the joker, who could make the entire class crack up?

"So, what happened?" I ask finally. I've already finished my portion and am greedily eyeing his.

He shrugs. "I don't remember much of the first days. I couldn't swallow or breathe well. Everything hurt." He looks at me, his light blue eyes mournful. "I thought I'd be a goner."

"You lost weight."

"Couldn't eat."

I smack him on the shoulder. "You'll be back running around in no time."

He ignores me and watches Zeibler. "What is the matter with that fellow?"

"He thinks he's the Führer's first cousin."

Karl-Heinz smiles. It's the first real grin, which encourages me to go on. "He runs us around like we're already on the battle field. Big Z can't stand him, that much I'm sure of."

As if on cue, Zeibler gets up and whistles.

Karl-Heinz follows me outside where we assemble around the flagpole. As we salute with arms outstretched, Udo pulls down the flag. He hands it to Zeibler, who carries it like a precious carton of raw eggs.

After that we scramble to our sleeping rooms. Most nights Zeibler checks *organizational* skills by inspecting our lockers. Every piece has to be folded exactly.

"Room check," Udo yells. We all rush to the walls and stand at attention. Looking bewildered, Karl-Heinz follows suit.

Zeibler marches past us to the lockers, where he starts pulling out things at random.

"Whose is this?" He squints and points at the locker farthest to the right.

Christian straightens himself. "Mine."

"What a mess. Clean it up!" Zeibler quickly yanks everything from the compartment and throws it to the floor. As Christian bends low, more clothes and underwear tumble out.

Nobody says a thing. We all know what happens if we speak out. After Zeibler leaves I head to Zimmermann's room. He's settled in a former storage space, his cot squeezed between empty shelves.

Big Z hurriedly turns off the radio, he's keeping by his bed. "Peter, how can I help you?"

"Sir, Zeibler is crazy. We need to do something about him." When Zimmermann remains silent, I go on. "He treats us like dirt and is unfair."

If I were honest, I'd admit I want to go home. Stay with Mother and Walter even if there are bombs. But I can't make myself say it out loud.

"I'm going to tell you something that needs to remain a secret." Zimmermann's dark eyes bore into mine and I nod. "I've written to the National Socialist Teachers League and the KLV administration and requested a replacement." He takes a deep breath. "In the meantime Zeibler is in charge whether we like it or not."

"Can't we just transfer someplace else?"

Big Z shakes his head. "I heard from a couple colleagues. All of Germany is on the move. Children are even living in former hotels and inns. I doubt they'll give permission." He throws me a watery grin. "Maybe I'll try that next, if we can't get help. Now you better head for bed."

I take my leave, wondering how Big Z knows such things. It also makes me realize that we are being left in the dark—about everything.

"Where were you?" Karl-Heinz asks when I crawl under the blanket. It feels good to have my friend next to me again.

"Had to ask Big Z something."

"What?"

"Nothing."

"Why aren't you telling me?"

I turn my back to him. "Can't right now."

It occurs to me that this new life we lead is filled with harassment, cover-ups and lies. First I can't tell Hilda anything without being censored. Now I can't tell my best friend. Is this the new Germany the Führer talked about?

If so, I want no part of it.

CHAPTER EIGHT

Hilda

This afternoon I finally get to be outside. It's a glorious day, and for a moment I forget where I am. The cloister garden is a squarish area tucked between ten-foot walls. Beds are holding onions, potatoes, carrots and beans. Other beds have orderly rows of herbs. Parsley, chives, thyme and rosemary, but also strange ones I've never seen before. Small signs announce monk's pepper, nipplewort, feverfew, and lady's mantle. Along the west wall climb grapevines and purple clusters of lavender.

After the dankness inside, I take deep breaths. The sun stands high in the sky and I immediately begin to sweat—but oh glorious brightness. For a moment I close my eyes and soak in the warmth. I can feel the hairs rise on my forearms, feel my pores open.

Last summer Peter and I went swimming in *Schellberg*, an outdoor pool tucked into the hilly land of Solingen. I heard him laugh, the sensation of his newly lower voice, equally strange and familiar. We spent all day going back and forth between the pool, the soccer field, our blanket, and the kiosk, where Peter bought me an ice cream cone. I want to punch him for leaving us like that. Leaving me.

"What a magnificent day," a voice says behind me, and I snap to.

Sister Rose stands there, a smile on her face. "You are helping me in the garden today?"

I nod, taking in the woman's habit that concentrates

everything onto her face. Her eyes are the dark blue of a mountain lake. With that dazzling smile, the finely shaped nose and full lips, she could be on the cover of any magazine.

"Come on then, let's get our hands dirty."

I follow the nun, whose habit appears to float above the neatly kept walkways.

"How is the swift?" I say as we settle next to a bed with cucumber vines.

Sister Rose quickly looks around before saying in a low voice, "Mama Swift's babies will hatch soon."

"I want to see them again."

"Maybe tonight?"

I nod, taking a hand rake from the bucket Sister Rose brought with her.

The soil is fragrant and damp. Earthworms wiggle. Dirt creeps beneath my fingernails and up to my elbows as my knees grind into the gravel. I don't mind.

Sister Rose hums as she deftly pulls out a dandelion root. What could've possibly motivated her to join a convent?

"How long have you been here?" I ask.

"A while."

"Where did you grow up?"

"Berlin."

"That must've been quite a change."

Sister Rose's shovel hovers a moment before she digs in anew. "It was."

I wait for an explanation, some reason why she's chosen to hide away under the talons of the Abbess. But the nun continues her work in silence, her gaze downward and inward, where she's safe.

But there's one other subject I want to discuss.

"Where does Tilly go every morning?" Ever since the *incident*, Tilly disappears after breakfast and reappears at lunchtime. She's had more accidents, but now keeps a stack of sheets beneath her bed.

"The Abbess thinks that praying will heal her," Sister Rose says. Is there doubt in her voice?

"But Tilly is sad and upset. She misses her mother." *Like I miss mine.*

Sister Rose looks at me, her blue eyes grave. "I know."

"Why can't she just go home?"

The nun shrugs. "The program forbids it. She wouldn't have any school."

"I don't think she's learning much now." It's out before I have time to think. Sister Rose will be mad that I offended the bible.

To my relief the nun chuckles. "God works in mysterious ways."

I'm not sure I agree. The Abbess is supposed to work for God. And she's so awful, I doubt Jesus would approve. But I say nothing and return to cleaning away tentacles of clover and morning glories. The sun creeps around the building and bathes the garden in shadows.

The air cools immediately, and though I'm warm from the work, it's as if cold fingers creep up my spine from the soil. I can't explain the sudden unease I feel, just that the joy from earlier has left me.

Straightening my achy back, I rub off the worst of the dirt. Somewhere above us, a bell announces evening prayers. As Sister Rose rushes off to the chapel, I collect our tools. Time to clean up and get ready for dinner.

I catch Tilly in the washroom. She's bent over her legs so she doesn't hear me.

"Sister Rose says you're studying the bible with the Abbess," I say, filling a bucket with water and grabbing a brush.

That's when I notice Tilly's knees. They're bruised and swollen, and the skin is broken in places. "What happened?" I cry.

Tilly tries to cover her knees with her hands and turns away. But this time I won't let her avoid me. I lunge for her arm and bring her to a stop.

Tilly's eyes fill with tears, and the area beneath is gray from lack of sleep and likely fear. She shakes her head and tries to get away. I hold steady.

"What is wrong with your legs?" I ask.

That's when Tilly crumples against my shoulder and begins to cry in earnest. "I can't do it any longer. My knees hurt so badly, they hardly bend and the pain won't let me sleep. I want to go home. Please."

I hold her to me, feel the trembles against my chest. "Did the nun do this to you?"

Our eyes meet. Fury has joined Tilly's fear. "She makes me kneel for hours on the wooden floor in front of the Jesus statue. I'm supposed to read the bible and then tell her what I read." She hiccups. "I can't remember anything, though. All I know is that my knees burn and throb."

I pat her on the back. "I want you to go back to your room. I'll be there soon."

Filth and mud forgotten, I race down the corridors. So what we're not supposed to run. My breath comes in spurts. Not because I'm tired, but because I'm furious beyond anything I've ever felt.

I bang a fist against the door, and when it opens Fräulein Heinrich appears. "Hilda, I was just about to go to dinner." Then she stops and takes in my appearance. "What happened? Was there an accident?"

"Did you know what Tilly has to do every morning?" I shout. I don't care about the noise because all of a sudden, my head seems to float above my body.

"She's getting private lessons from the Abbess," Fräulein Heinrich says.

"She's being tortured. Have you seen her knees, all bloody and scraped?"

Fräulein Heinrich's eyes widen. "No, no, not that." She rushes past me and I slowly follow down the hall. My lungs are empty and I can hardly muster the energy to move. I'm still filthy, and dinner is about to start.

Mechanically, I walk to our room, half expecting to see Tilly. But the room is empty. With a knot in my stomach, I halfheartedly clean my hands and forearms with a rag, and change into my second dress, a flowery thing in white and yellow I used to like.

Everyone is sitting already, an elderly nun reading a bible verse. That's when I notice that Tilly isn't there. Nor are the Abbess or Fräulein Heinrich.

"Where were you?" Biene whispers as I slump onto the bench.

"The Abbess makes Tilly kneel until she bleeds." My vision blurs as I spoon two potatoes, green beans and a pale sausage onto my plate. I chew yet taste nothing as Biene peppers me with questions. I'm so tired right now. Maybe I'm coming down with something.

The last thing I remember is sliding off the bench.

Peter
July 28, 1943

Karl-Heinz has been ignoring me. It's as if he's an entirely different person. He no longer jokes or laughs, just slouches around like an old woman. He talks to Christian, but other than that, pretty much stays to himself. I know he's mad about me not telling him about the talk with Zimmermann. All I can hope is that Big Z will get help and Zeibler will be replaced soon.

After Zeibler inspects our fingernails, hair and beds, he lets us go to breakfast.

"Have you noticed that they don't tell us anything about the war?" Christian says. He sits across from Karl-Heinz and me, his black tie askew, his blond hair already messy.

"Or bombardments," Karl-Heinz adds.

I cringe, imagining Mother running from a burning house, Walter in the alley with a bloodied face. The image changes and Mother and Walter are buried beneath rubble, their faces translucent and still. I shake my head to make the pictures go away. "Big Z has a radio. Saw it in his room," I say, swallowing a piece of bread. It's hard and chewy, scraped with a bit of red jelly I can't identify. We haven't seen butter in two years.

"I'd love to hear *some* news," Karl-Heinz says. "Good or bad."

"Why don't we just *ask* Big Z?" Christian's eyes follow Zeibler, who is leaving the room. I know he's afraid of him. I guess we all are. "Maybe he'll let us listen in class."

"Doubt it," I say, draining the milk, a special delivery from Lawinski's farm. I've got table duty, so I get up and start collecting dishes. Though we only have four hours of class in the morning, I seem to have a ton more work. We're constantly rotating between cleaning, kitchen, and table duty, and afternoons are nothing but drudgery. I'm used to having free time, visiting friends, going swimming and spending time with Hilda.

I hesitate for a moment as Hilda's face swims into my vision when I saw her the last time. She scowled at me, her eyes shiny. How could she have possibly known about the camps? What made her the expert?

I smack the plates into the sink. Udo is already flooding the place, doing dishes.

Hard to believe it's summer. We still haven't gone to the beach. It's less than thirty kilometers to the East Sea and may as well be a thousand. We have no transportation and hiking there and back in a day can't be done. So we stay put as the summer fizzles away.

If you asked me now I would've definitely said no to leaving home—not that I would have had a choice.

As I hurry into the washroom I see Christian talking to Karl-Heinz. They're standing in an alcove by the sink and I catch a glimpse of Christian's expression. He's smiling, but that's not the strange thing. It's the way he looks at Karl-Heinz. There's something soft in the way he leans in. That's when it occurs to me that Christian isn't just Karl-Heinz's friend. He loves him.

I shake my head. Can't be. But in that instant it takes for them to realize that I'm there, I see that same yearning expression on Karl-Heinz's face.

Then several things happen at once. Footsteps clomp and Zeibler enters the bathroom behind me. Karl-Heinz and Christian scatter, their movement so abrupt, it draws even more attention.

"What are you boys doing?" Zeibler's voice is venomous. He pushes past me to keep Karl-Heinz and Christian from leaving.

"Nothing…" Karl-Heinz's voice shakes the tiniest bit.

Zeibler turns toward Christian, suspicion in his eyes. "Why aren't you in class?"

But Christian doesn't answer. All color has drained from his face, his cheeks as pale as the wall behind him.

I feel my body tense…have to swallow so hard—a gurgle escapes me. What are they thinking? Is Karl-Heinz queer like Christian? Zeibler will tear them to pieces. The Nazis hate homosexuals, call them degenerates and enemies of the state. Zeibler is going to have them arrested…put in some camp or worse.

"Sir, I asked them to meet me here," I hear myself say.

Zeibler swivels on his heels to face me, his lips downturned in a sneer. "What could you possibly want to do in the washroom?"

I stare at Zeibler. *What indeed?* I've got to have a good reason, a believable motive to take away suspicion from Karl-Heinz. Zeibler's colorless eyes are still on me, so are Christian's and Karl-Heinz's. What have I done? I need an excuse. Quick. In the past Karl-Heinz often came to my rescue, but I can tell he's shaken.

"Out with it," Zeibler shouts. Doubt has crept back into his voice as he turns back to Christian. "I've been watching you for a while. There's something rotten about you, a foul smell." He sniffs, though the only stink emanates from the toilets.

"Sir, I'm sorry," I cry. "It's just… I wanted to ask them to visit Lawinski's farm."

Zeibler faces me once more. "What in the heck for?"

"The girl," I say…*what was her name again?* "Bea, the blonde. I thought we'd see if she'd go out with us. Maybe she'd show us her…you know."

A slow grin forms on Zeibler's face. It's a strange sight since he hardly ever smiles. "You dogs. You were going to sneak off to visit Bea." Then he seems to remember his role as slave driver and the grin evaporates. He crosses his arms in front of his chest and stretches himself tall. "You leave me no choice but to punish you."

I drop my head. "Sorry, sir."

"I shall think about it. Now get to class before I lose my temper."

The three of us scramble off and Karl-Heinz slips past me onto his bench, not looking at me. I want to ask him about Christian, but then I feel my cheeks warm. What an embarrassing thing to talk about.

I just sit there, wondering what I've done, one half of me triumphant, the other half filled with dread.

When Zimmermann shows up, Christian immediately raises his arm.

"What is it, Christian?"

"We'd like to listen to the radio once in a while."

Big Z looks at him, then at me. He knows I told Christian about the radio. "I'm not sure I can allow it. I'll speak with Zeibler."

Why does he have to know, I want to ask. But I say nothing.

I used to enjoy math and literature. Now I can't concentrate. Zimmermann's voice drones in the background as I stare out the window or at the heads of Udo and Dieter in front of me. Udo's hair is a mess this morning, and I wonder when he last washed it. Shampoo has become scarce, so we use bars of air soap—soap filled with so many bubbles, it swims.

Sure enough, at lunchtime Big Z tells us that we're not supposed to listen to the radio unless the Führer or propaganda minister Goebbels gives a speech. Zeibler says it's distracting and that we're to concentrate on the important things. But then Zimmermann says something strange.

"I could use some help this evening, say around seven?" His gaze wanders around the room and comes to rest on Christian and me. "I want to rearrange my room, move some things."

Somehow I know I need to raise my hand. Christian and Karl-Heinz do as well.

As soon as we enter Big Z's room that evening—there are five of us with snore bear Dieter and his friend, Werner Niemann—Zimmermann motions us to close the door.

I'm still reeling from the meeting with Zeibler after lunch. This weekend, when Big Z takes the class on a hike, I'm going to march for two hours. Zeibler said we were lucky he didn't catch us in the act. *What act*, I'd wanted to say. *It was all a ruse.* But I know I can't, not now.

It's super crowded in Big Z's room. A desk cuts into my thigh, so I crawl on top. Karl-Heinz does the same, and Christian and the others climb on Big Z's bed.

"Boys, what we do in here must remain a secret," our teacher says. He looks old tonight, his chin a grayish shadow, the space under his eyes sunken. "I don't see any harm in you listening to the news. Keep in mind that what you're hearing is not always the entire truth." He swivels on his heels to watch us. "Do I have your word?"

Karl-Heinz rises solemnly and lifts an arm. "I swear to keep our meeting and what we hear secret."

"Me too," we chime in.

Zimmermann nods. "Then let's see what they say." He turns the little wheel on the radio that controls power and volume. We all lean in as the crackle turns into the voice of a reporter.

"Last night, the enemy struck into the heart of Germany, bombing Hamburg and setting in motion an unprecedented firestorm. Tens of thousands are presumed dead. Tens of thousands more have lost their homes. This is a direct attack on the German people that we must answer with equal ferocity." The radio speaker continues with troop advancements and victories of the German Wehrmacht as I try to wrap my head around the numbers.

I wonder if Solingen got hit yet and if Mother and Walter are safe. It's been two weeks since the last letter—an eternity.

When we leave Zimmermann's room, the shelves and desks are still inside. But something in our hearts has changed. If the Allies can bomb Hamburg and kill tens of thousands of civilians, what will stop them from bombing Solingen and doing the same?

CHAPTER NINE

Hilda

The room shifts and tilts—white on white, a sort of fog with shapes floating, shapes I can't make out. There are sounds too, voices near my head.

"Hilda, wake up!"

"She fainted…"

"What is wrong with her?"

I struggle to open my eyes and look into Sister Rose's blue ones. I can tell she's concerned because there are new lines around her mouth.

I find myself on the podium. Somebody has put a pillow under my head. My view clears enough to make out Biene's worried expression above me, and the evil twins, who both appear to gloat.

"What happened?" I ask.

"You passed out, probably got dehydrated this afternoon," Sister Rose answers, sounding guilty. "I should've made you rest and drink some water. I'm so sorry."

I try to grab her hand, fail and get tangled in her habit. "It's my fault."

Biene supports my back and puts a cup of something hot to my lips. "Drink up." I smell chocolate…hot cocoa. Oh, the last time I tasted something this good was Christmas. Tears flood as I remember Mama's proud expression, fixing us hot chocolate on Christmas Eve. "I traded it for some yarn," she'd said.

The warm sweetness gives me strength, so I wipe my eyes and sit up. "I feel much better already."

"Biene will help you go to bed." Sister Rose turns to face the class. "Hilda is fine. Finish your dinner."

"Where's Tilly?" I ask as Biene helps me slip into a nightgown.

"Haven't seen her," Biene says. All of a sudden she looks as worried as I feel. "I can't believe that old witch makes her kneel."

"Can't we write a letter to her mother or to principal Schmidt?"

"They read everything, remember." Biene tucks me into bed.

"What if we sneak one to the post office?"

"We need stamps and—"

"I'll ask Sister Rose."

Biene sits down on my bed. "We better write soon. Before they murder Tilly." She rubs her forehead in concentration. "I will organize paper. I think I know where."

At the door she turns and with thumb and forefinger draws a vertical line across her lips. I do the same.

"Tomorrow we write," she says before racing off.

Peter

The next day turns into a blur. I can't concentrate at all and the other four of us who went to listen to Zimmermann's radio are feeling the same. Karl-Heinz looks worse again and even Christian, who usually seems happy when he's near Karl-Heinz, walks around with his head low. They haven't looked at each other once since yesterday.

When I check my locker during lunch, Karl-Heinz appears by my side. He's pale again, his gaze on me almost hypnotic. He's trying for a smile, fails and then clears his throat.

"I'm…sorry, I…we wanted to thank you. It's not what you think…I."

I want to tell him not to lie to me, but maybe this is easier for everyone. "I much rather march with Zeibler on Saturday anyway," I quip.

Karl-Heinz's expression droops even more. "I'm so sorry."

Voices come from the hallway, so I say, "We better quit talking about it."

Karl-Heinz hangs his head, his eyes shiny. "I won't forget it."

"I want to tell the others about the radio news," Karl-Heinz says as we line up for afternoon inspection. It's raining buckets outside, so we're meeting in the gym. "They need to know what is really going on."

"We can't," I say. "We'll get Big Z in trouble. Zeibler will find out."

Zeibler enters just at the exact moment I mention his name. I want to kick myself for being so careless as Zeibler's eyes lock on mine, dark with malice. He may be the perfect German boy with blond hair and a spotless uniform, so convinced he's doing the right thing, so straight and perfect, I feel the urge to yank his shirt to make the buttons pop off or smear his shiny boots with fresh manure.

My smirk freezes when he shouts, "Breuer, you again! Do you care to repeat what you said about me?"

"Not really," I mumble. I can't afford another slipup, not now after the incident in the bathroom.

"What was that?" Zeibler is quick when he wants to be and now materializes in front of me. He's at eye level, but I can tell he's trying to stretch himself to appear taller.

"Nothing."

"Didn't sound like nothing." Zeibler's voice has gone quiet. I can tell he's enjoying himself, which makes my knees go soft. I rack my brain about what to say. He's going to punish me even more, probably make me clean the washrooms with a toothbrush.

"You going to tell me, or do I have to make an example out of you?"

Zeibler can't know, my brain cries. I think of the first time I saw him outside our classroom window, Hitler Youth boys jumping from the truck bed. That's when it hits me.

"Sir, I was talking about the delivery truck, the L 3000 that provided our supplies. How glad we were to receive support."

"What does that have to do with me?"

"The make of the truck…it's a *Daimler*." My jaw hurts with the effort to keep my expression neutral. "I know it sounds similar. You must've misunderstood."

Zeibler stands there. For once he is speechless, likely mulling over my explanation and what he remembered with his own ears. I remain still, keeping my gaze on the guy, holding my breath. At last he clears his throat. "All right, then. Let's begin drills."

I let out a sigh and Karl-Heinz boxes me in the ribs. I don't dare look at him for fear of breaking into a giggle.

"What if we get ourselves a newspaper?" Christian asks as we assemble around a bucket of potatoes with paring knives that some local has donated. On the menu are boiled potatoes, fried eggs and spinach. I've gotten better at peeling, wasting less, but it's still drudgery.

I quickly scan the room to make sure nobody is watching. Udo is washing spinach in the sink and Werner Niemann, the oldest boy in class, is counting eggs. Frau Landau, who took care of Karl-Heinz early on recently joined us to help fix our meals, is prepping several pots. She's lost her husband in Russia and doesn't say much, her eyes dim and sort of shuddered like closed blinds. But she brought spices, especially salt, and knows how to cook for a crowd.

"We can't leave," I say, picking up another potato.

"Maybe we can tomorrow." Christian keeps his gaze on the potato in his hand. "We'll be doing an excursion to Körlin. All we need is to find a store, buy and hide the paper. We'll just pretend we found one and have it lying around in the dorm. We just need to make sure, Zeibler doesn't see it."

"What about Big Z?"

"He won't care."

"That way we can listen to the radio again." I'm not so sure I want to, but I'm finding that not knowing is worse than getting bad news.

"If he lets us."

"Right."

"You boys about done?" Frau Landau adjusts the scarf around her dirty-blond hair and takes a peek into our pot where a few lone potatoes swim. "Better hurry it up. Dinner is at six thirty sharp. You don't want to upset *Herrn* Zeibler." She winks at me.

I grin back. She knows we suffer.

It takes less than an hour to reach Körlin and still, I'm drained as if we'd marched five hours straight. Zimmermann promised to give us time to explore, so we spread out. There aren't many stores, certainly nothing like downtown Solingen, but Karl-Heinz,

Christian and I enter the grocery store whose shelves are mostly empty. They offer a few farm crops…potatoes, beets, various salads and onions.

"Do you have any newspapers?" I ask the man behind the counter.

He shakes his head. "Sorry, boys, no papers. You may try the hardware shop or the pharmacy."

The hardware shop is closed. A sign in the window announces that the shop owner has been drafted. The pharmacy is a mix of a candy, school supply and drug store. They don't offer any newspapers.

"It's been months." The woman who wears a red and white striped apron eyes us suspiciously. "We used to get the paper from Danzig."

I nod but am temporarily distracted because there are three bars of *Sarotti* milk chocolate lying on a shelf behind the counter. I realize I haven't eaten chocolate in more than two years, and all of a sudden I'm hit with a craving so intense, I want to jump over the counter and tear open the wrapping. I see myself shove the woman aside and grab the bars before racing off.

In my mind the woman screams, just as Karl-Heinz tugs at my sleeve and breaks my reverie. He throws me a curious look as we exit and I swallow repeatedly.

"What is the matter with you?" Christian asks.

I shrug, all of a sudden stinking angry. Here we are in some forsaken corner of Pomerania, without news, without money. We're forced to stay in some run-down school, wondering what is going on at home, wondering if our mothers are still in one piece. Not to mention our fathers.

I march off in a hurry, Karl-Heinz and Christian scrambling after me. "Looks like we're out of luck," I finally say, taking deep breaths. I've got to do something…anything. That's when another idea hits me. "What if we find another radio?"

"None of us has any money," Karl-Heinz says. "Nor are there any stores here that carry radios." He doesn't even look that upset. If I envy him for one thing it's the way he takes things at face value. I know he wants to go home too, but he doesn't seem eaten up by it.

"What if we steal one?"

"You nuts?" Christian says. "That's a crime."

"What they do to us is a crime," I shoot back. "I want to go home." I'm surprised to hear myself say it. Zeibler always says we're tough and proud and brave. Whatever! Though I'm glad he didn't hear what I just said.

"We can't." Karl-Heinz chews his upper lip, thoughtfully watching us. Before his illness, he would've tried to make us laugh.

"How are you going to steal a radio?" Christian says. "We can't leave school, and the farmers have dogs and people who are watching. Imagine they catch us. Zeibler will make ground beef out of us. We may go to jail."

"I know!" I cry. A woman with a wicker basket dangling from her arm stares at me, so I continue quietly, "Maybe we could *organize* a radio—trade for one."

"With what?" Karl-Heinz asks.

"We'll keep our eyes open."

"That's not a bad idea," Christian says. "Frau Landau, that woman who helps in the kitchen, may know somebody."

At last Karl-Heinz nods. "All right. Let's ask her and if that doesn't work make a plan."

I box Karl-Heinz in the arm. It's almost as if I've got my friend back.

CHAPTER TEN

Hilda

It's taken until the quiet hour after lunch before we have time to write. I've slipped into Biene's bed, and we're hiding under the covers.

Tilly is resting below us, but I can tell she isn't sleeping. She showed up last night at dinnertime. Didn't talk or appear to even listen to anything we said. Overnight she had another accident, but this morning she was in class again anyway. Obviously, all the praying isn't working. I could've told the Abbess that before.

"What are we going to write?" I whisper, the task of finding a stamp heavy on my mind. Biene is better with words, so she begins:

> *Dear Principal Schmidt,*
> *Our friend, Tilly Lindner, has been having trouble. She's quite unhappy and sad and wants to go home. She has nightly accidents and the Abbess makes her kneel for hours and pray. Tilly's legs are bruised and sore, so she can hardly walk. The Abbess hates Fräulein Heinrich and treats her poorly. We all want to go home, but Tilly must leave soon or she may get seriously ill. Please contact her mother and tell her to fetch Tilly at once.*
> *Sincerely,*
> *Sabine Fuchs und Hilda Hagedorn*

We read the note a second time before folding it into the envelope that Biene traded with another girl.

I plan on finding Sister Rose after chores today. She wasn't in the attic last night, the swift sitting quietly on her nest. I didn't dare stay long for fear somebody would see me.

When the bell rings to signal the end of quiet period, we march to the common room for a singing lesson. I contemplate telling Tilly about the letter, but then I decide against it. She may tell somebody and we may get in big trouble.

I'm carrying twelve *Pfennig* in my pocket—Biene has donated ten, me the remainder. Mama was supposed to send money, but none has arrived yet. Not that we can buy stuff in a cloister.

While we practice *Alle Vögel sind schon da*—Fräulein Heinrich swings her ruler like a conductor and for once looks almost happy—I scan the room. There's no sign of Sister Rose. The Benedictine nuns pray a lot, sometimes their singsong drifts through the halls. They always meet at the Chapel—I've counted at least five or six times a day when they all march off.

The other problem I worry about is finding a letterbox. We've got one here inside, but I know they read what we write. Ten-foot walls surround the cloister and the wooden gate is always closed. When Fräulein Heinrich collects our letters every week, she hands them off to a nun, so I assume somebody leaves to drop them off.

In one of the sheds I've seen a ladder, but it's heavy and I wouldn't know how to get down the other side or back in. For all I know, the cloister is kilometers away from the nearest village with a letterbox. My only hope is to find the train station where we arrived two months ago. In her last letter Mama asked again how I was doing. I can't bring myself to tell her the truth. Besides, the Abbess would likely see it.

Since I don't have kitchen duty, I immediately slip out after dinner to visit the attic. No matter how I try, the stairs creak with every step. Isn't it laughable I feel like a thief in my simple effort to watch a mama swift raise her babies? Even with Paul gone, I'd always had a sense of freedom. Now everywhere I look I see guilt.

My insides twist painfully as I think about my father. Mama hasn't said a thing in years about Papa. Somehow I wish *he* were punished. The *Wochenschau*, the weekly show, I caught at the theatre a few times filmed horrific battles. Buildings evaporated in split seconds. Men shot at each other across seas of barbwire. I try to make the image go away, try not to think about Papa being stuck in a muddy hole—even if he left us.

In her last letter, Mama mentioned that Peter had written and said he and the other boys were staying at a former school in Körlin. They're busy with sports, marching, excursions and music.

I chew on my lower lip, the little voice in my head wondering why he hasn't written to me. Mama did say that they write their letters once a week and don't have much time for additional mail. "They even went to the beach and swam," she relayed. "The water was only fifteen degrees, but they all went in."

I wish I could see Peter's note for myself. I imagine him hiking through the dunes and jumping into the freezing waves, see his lips turn blue. Serves him right.

At least, Mama got word from Paul that he is still in France. What is happening to us? Everyone lives in some other place…alone. Is that how the Führer is winning the war? He talks about sacrifice and bravery. What if I don't want to make sacrifices? What if I want to live at home with my family? Like we did when I was little.

The swift sits on her nest. Her brown eyes are larger than most birds, and she has this cute white throat. I stare outside, beyond the walls. For the first time I notice a road leading away over a hill, forest-covered mountains looming in the distance. In this instant I feel trapped as if I were locked away in a prison. What else is it?

The door opens and I jolt out of my thoughts.

Sister Rose appears, concern in her beautiful eyes. "I'm so glad you're here. I've had to do extra work and couldn't come." She laughs, but I can tell she's miserable. "The Benedictine motto *ora et labora.*"

"What does it mean?"

"Pray and work."

"Is that all you do?"

"Pretty much."

I take in the young woman's expression. "Why would you do that?" The question breaks out before I have time to stop. "It seems so…so—"

"Boring?"

"Not just boring…you're so young and pretty." I search for the right words. "It seems a waste. You could lead a happy life."

"I'm not sure Germans will ever lead happy lives again." The nun seems to regret her words and hurries on, "I mean…that goes for me. I'm sure things will get better."

"How long have you been here?"

"Two years, two months and six days."

Why does she count days if this is her life for eternity? I want to ask her why she chose to hide herself away, but her upper lip trembles as if she's about to cry.

"I need your help," I say instead. "I've got a letter to send home."

"Oh?"

"I…it's private. Not for me, but for a friend." Better not name names. "I need a stamp and a way to send the letter without…"

"…it being read?"

I nod.

"I haven't written any letters," Sister Rose says. "But I can ask for a stamp." A wrinkle appears between her brows as she shakes her head. "Sending it without being seen is another matter. I must think on it."

She throws another glance at the swift, who still sits quietly. "They'll hatch soon."

I follow her gaze and nod, wishing I could sit outside this window and fly off whenever I please.

Peter

In my dream, Hilda takes my hand and leads me onto a meadow with wildflowers. Her eyes sparkle and she smiles, her lips so sweet that I bend down to kiss her. I wake up with a wonker of a hard on.

I've got no idea what she wanted or where we were, but the feeling of excitement and warmth is still with me. My hand wanders beneath the blanket, and after confirming that all is quiet, I soon forget everything else.

Still, I feel confused—I haven't thought about Hilda in weeks. At least not on purpose. She acted all strange last time we met, and I got angry and impatient with her. Hard to believe she's some place in Bavaria. Probably enjoying things way more than I am.

And if it were so, my mind argues. *Shouldn't you feel happy for her?* True, I'm an asshole. She's had it bad with her older brother being away and her father leaving them before the war. Hilda was only nine, and all us neighbors were shocked.

All of a sudden I want to talk to her, tell her all will be fine. That her father will walk into their kitchen one day and beg for forgiveness, and that Paul will be there as well. But I'm not home and chances are, Hilda will never see her father again.

My throat tightens with frustration. I can't even be there and comfort her because I'm stuck in this godforsaken place. Who knows how long we have to stay? Nobody talks about a quick end to the war any longer. It's all about enduring.

I remember Mother's sad expression at the train station, my sense of relief when the train started up. I'm ashamed I was nasty to her. Tomorrow, I'll write something nice and comforting. No need to worry her about this place. A new thought takes hold. What if she got bombed and injured? What if she and Walter are dead? Surely, I'd hear. Or would I?

It's dawn before I fall asleep.

The next afternoon, Karl-Heinz comes running into our workroom where we're building additional bedframes from former desks and chairs. "We're moving…I just heard from Big Z, it's official." His cheeks are flushed and I read relief in his eyes.

"When?" is all I manage.

"Soon, at the end of the week," Karl Heinz says. We all quit working and surround him.

"What happens to Zeibler?" Christian asks.

Karl-Heinz shrugs. "I heard a rumor he's being drafted. Either way he's *not* coming with us."

"Thank heavens." Udo Lempski sends his folded hands to the ceiling. These days, he's not nearly as loud and annoying. I just recently figured out that he's super religious and prays a lot, though always when Zeibler isn't near. Udo's family is Catholic and he used to be a choirboy.

"Where are we going?" I ask when the noise dies down. Udo is grinning and so is Christian. In fact we're all grinning.

Karl-Heinz sinks onto a chair. He's still pretty pale. "Big Z says that we'll talk about it during dinner. He wants us all present so he can explain what's going to happen."

Needless to say, we don't get much done after that, speculating where we'll move and hoping secretly to go home.

"Just as long as there isn't another Zeibler," Christian says. He sits next to Karl-Heinz, a little close, which makes me remember the washroom incident. I wonder if anybody else has noticed Christian's gazes at Karl-Heinz.

We used to talk about girls when we attended gymnasium. I seem to remember Karl-Heinz commenting about Hilda, my neighbor friend, who was in the class below us. But maybe I'm the one in the dark. Maybe Karl-Heinz likes boys better.

For a change we arrive early at dinner. It's mystery soup night. That's what we call the stews we get Wednesday nights. They throw in whatever they have and cook it a while.

Tonight it smells pretty good. Shredded cabbage leaves, potatoes, onions and some kind of stringy meat swim in the broth. Since Frau Landau arrived, we even have herbs and sometimes cake.

"You've probably all heard about the move," Zimmermann says as soon as we take our seats. There's a new light in his eyes, an energy in the way he paces before us. "We'll be leaving first thing on Friday morning to catch the train to Danzig. This is a large camp, I was told, so we should fit right in." Big Z's face remains neutral.

"Why can't we go home instead?" one of the boys asks.

"Visit our families for a while," Karl-Heinz says.

"I understand, but it isn't possible right now. Trains are scarce, many tracks destroyed and—"

"Man up." Zeibler's voice cuts through us. "You're supposed to get ready for war, not crawl on your mothers' laps. You've got no school there either."

Zimmermann's mouth opens and closes as he obviously searches for the right words. "Herr Zeibler is correct that we wouldn't be able to teach. And since we're heading into a new school year, you all should continue your studies."

We all begin to mumble, so our teacher raises an arm. "I want you to leave everything the way it is. Likely, another group will soon arrive to take over."

I already feel sorry for them, especially if Zeibler remains. I wonder if all German kids will move away from home. How the war is going. But the chance to organize a radio has come and gone. I must write to Mother and tell her my new address.

CHAPTER ELEVEN

Hilda

Fall has arrived at the cloister. I'd know even if it weren't for my visits to the attic—Mama Swift has taken her babies to freedom—where I catch glimpses of the colorful leaves beyond. The air inside the walls continues to cool with an added dampness as a bonus.

Today, Karin, one of the evil twins, was taken aside. Most of us received letters and I'm relieved to find that Mama is fine. She sent me a note from my brother, Paul, which makes me quite happy. She also mentioned that Peter has moved to a camp near Danzig and enclosed his address.

At last I can write. Only what, I don't know. Our letters are still censored and I'm not going to write some lies. Besides, why hasn't he written? The memory of our last meeting returns, his enthusiasm for camp, the fact he could hardly wait to get away…from me.

Tears press. Luckily, I'm on hall cleaning duty and the gloomy corridors are a good place to hide. I shall wait for him to write to me, no matter how long it takes.

The next time I see Karin, her eyes are swollen. My first reaction is that it serves her right to suffer when she usually enjoys hurting others. But then Biene whispers that Karin's father has died in the war, and all of a sudden, I feel dread.

"I'm very sorry," I tell her when we dress for bed.

She mumbles something I can't understand and climbs into bed. She doesn't even do her nightly ritual with Ilse, some kind of hugging and kissing thing.

Ilse makes a face and after the light is off, we all lie in the dark listening to Karin's muffled sobs. I'm frozen as I think about the horrible finality of death. It takes my breath as if somebody drags a black cloak across my face. The terrible uncertainty has become certain for Karin. She knows she'll never see her father again. *You won't either.* I press my hands against my stomach, feel the rise and fall of my breath. A sigh escapes me. Now they'll think I'm crying when in reality I'm what? Disgusted?

There were fights between Mama and Papa for a long time. I thought it was normal, even if I felt the need to shrink somehow. Surely, I had some fault in them being at each other's throats.

I wonder if it would it be easier to think of Papa shredded by a bomb. The finality of *his* exit, suitcase in hand, felt like death—even if I caught myself dreaming of his return. In the beginning I listened for the door all the time. I realize that nurturing this hope is much better than the certainty of death—like Karin's father. Though Papa could easily be dead like the millions of soldiers out there.

Silent tears run across my cheeks and drip into the pillow. I long for my mother and her embrace. Tonight our room feels like a graveyard, our beds like coffins and our souls ready to fly away.

The next morning, Karin's face is red and blotchy and her bed wet. She's whispering with Ilse before rushing from the room in search of clean sheets. My gaze wanders to Tilly who is silently bunching up her damp bedding. Karin and Tilly aren't the only ones with nightly problems. At least five other girls are wetting their beds.

Biene puts an arm around my shoulder and for a moment we stand together. Biene's father was recently drafted, and I know she worries about him because she chews her nails like rabbits chew carrots. She always had the most beautiful hands, but now she somehow looks injured as if a piece of her is missing.

How can humans force so much suffering on others? It seems all we do is worry, our anxieties disrupting our sleep and making us quiet. The Abbess likely approves because our initial noisy chatter has fizzled into halting whispers.

During breakfast, the entire room is silent. Fräulein Heinrich sits next to Karin, an arm around the girl's shoulder. Maybe Karin gets to go home now. Is that the condition, we must fulfill—that our loved ones die before we can leave? A gurgle breaks from my throat, a sort of sick laugh. I'm embarrassed, but I can't help it, not even when everyone starts looking my way.

Biene's pretty eyebrows scrunch into a frown. "What's going on with you?"

"Can't help it."

Biene shakes her head, but then she grins. Not the easy grin I remember, but a contemplative one. "I've got an idea about the letter. Let's ask Fräulein Heinrich to do a field trip to the village. To get us all to think about something different." Without waiting for my answer, she gets up and approaches our teacher.

Across from me Tilly nibbles on her bread. Her hair is messy and she has bluish shadows under her eyes. She looks like she has lost more weight. "What is Biene doing?"

"Asking Fräulein Heinrich for a field trip."

"I'd run away if I could," Tilly whispers. "I'm just too afraid."

I grip her skinny wrist. "Me too. We all want to go home, but it's too dangerous."

Biene returns, a smug expression on her face. "I think Fräulein Heinrich will agree. She said she'll speak with the Abbess."

"What does *she* have to do with anything?" Tilly says. Her eyes spit fire and I'm amazed at this small bundle of fury. Go Tilly!

"The Abbess likely has to give permission about anything concerning the cloister," I say dryly.

But an hour later we're passing through the cloister's gates for the first time since our arrival. As soon as the walls are behind us, we start talking. It's like a song of chatter. Our letter lies securely inside my pocket. The stamp is red and says *Grossdeutsches Reich*—Great German Empire. This morning after breakfast it was lying on my pillow.

Sister Rose works in mysterious ways.

We pass through meadows, along hedges and by fruit trees. Some of us rush off the path to pick pears. Juice runs down our chins and turns our hands sticky. Near the village we stop again to pick plums, adding purple stains.

It doesn't matter.

The air is warm for October and carries the scent of pine. The sun sends its rays to the ground, bright blades of light that illuminate my steps. I lift my face into the wind and close my eyes, listening to the rustling leaves beneath my feet. For that brief moment I'm back home, hiking the forest without a care. Any second Peter will say something funny or challenge me to a race.

My classmates' chatter brings me back. Ahead, Karin walks hand-in-hand with Fräulein Heinrich. I didn't think Karin liked our teacher much. But death changes things. Death offers no apology, no way out.

When we return, five military cars and a black Mercedes are parked inside the walls. A hush lies over the halls as we return to our rooms to wash and prepare for dinner.

A stony-faced Abbess waits at the door to the hall. Behind her stand two men in SS uniforms and a dozen soldiers. Nobody speaks, so we make our way to the tables. My stomach rumbles after the pears and berries, but there's no food, just empty white plates that mirror the emptiness in my middle.

I see the Abbess pull Fräulein Heinrich aside. The young woman nods and is introduced to the SS-men, who squint at her.

At last the Abbess climbs the podium.

"Children, *Oberst* Reidorf has joined us to inspect the cloister. Unfortunately, there was a misunderstanding and you left the safe walls this afternoon. That won't happen again. We must assure you are protected at all times and…" the chin of the Abbess disappears in the white collar above her chest, "exploring the countryside is not going to be advisable." She turns toward the man in uniform. "*SS-Standartenführer Oberst* Reidorf and *SS-Scharführer* Linker will inspect your rooms. There are some…adjustments to be made."

What adjustments, I want to ask. Once again the walls are closing in on me. No more fieldtrips, no more freedom to feel normal if just for a few hours.

"There's one more thing." The voice of the Abbess cuts through the rising mumbles. "I know you were planning to go home soon. That won't be possible…yet. I'm afraid," the expression of the Abbess moves toward a phony smile, "you'll be our guests for a while longer."

As the kitchen team brings in bowls of lentil soup—a thin version of my soup with hardly a shred of ham—my mind whirls. Tilly blinks rapidly as if she's about to cry, and Biene has gone pale. Karin buries into Ilse's arms while I sit there speechless. What does it mean…*won't be possible*? What is *a while*?

I want to ask our teacher, but at that moment the *Oberst* and Linker sit down next to Fräulein Heinrich. Everything on Linker is square and hard. His nose is curved like a fishhook and his shoulders turn into his arms in sharp angles. His jaw is angular too, the mouth straight. I feel sorry for Fräulein Heinrich, the man just towering and glaring at her.

Inside I'm all frozen, my rib cage tight. It's as if the air has been sucked from the room, a suffocating veil that snuffs out our breath and our hope.

Hope. Until this moment I've somehow managed to tell myself that it's a matter of time before we leave: just another day, another week, the certainty of an end. This new truth makes me want to stomp around and throw things at the Abbess. We've been nothing but obedient, playing along…quiet in the corridor, silent at dinner.

My fists curl beneath the table as anger grips me. "Bastards," I hiss.

"I want to be home by Christmas." Biene folds her arms in front of her. "They promised it wasn't going to be longer than six months."

"I'm going to ask Fräulein Heinrich." Tilly's voice is quiet but determined. It surprises me how calm she is when I've got a full-blown storm inside me.

The soup is cold, so I shove it down in record speed. There's hardly another spoonful in the terrines, and no extra bread. Either they didn't have time to bake or the Abbess wants to punish us. Fine then.

Eventually, Fräulein Heinrich gets up and leaves while Linker returns to the Abbess. While the Oberst shouts *"Heil Hitler,"* flings out a straight arm, thrusts together his heels and marches off, Linker, the second SS-man, who looks nearly as young as Peter, remains along with the soldiers.

Instead of listening to bible stories, we are ordered to return to our rooms. As we march down the gloomy hallway, Fräulein Heinrich materializes out of nowhere and calls for me. Biene throws me a curious look, as do Karin and Ilse.

I hurry after my teacher who slips into one of the alcoves. Red spots blaze on her cheeks. "Did you bring it?"

"What?" My mind is on our delayed trip home.

"The book I loaned you."

"I've got questions about going—"

Fräulein Heinrich grips my wrist and squeezes. "No time. I'll come and talk to you later." Her fingernails pinch my skin. "Did you bring the book?"

I nod numbly. Mailing books to us is forbidden, so I brought *Fabian* along. "You want it? I've read it…twice."

"No." Fräulein Heinrich's voice sounds like a cry. "Hide it! Hurry."

I stare at her, remembering the way she gave it to me after class a thousand years ago. As panic claws at me, I take off down the hall. Forget the *no running* rule.

My heart hammers in my throat when I reach our room. The door is closed. What if the men… I rip open the door.

Five pairs of eyes stare back at me, all of them equally curious and anxious.

"What is going on?" Biene asks. I shake my head, feel everyone's gaze following me. No time. I've got to get rid of the book, but where. I pull it from the dresser drawer where I kept it between my undershirts. Between its pages rests Peter's feather like a caress.

We all look at each other and Karin even pats Tilly on the back. They're no longer enemies, though Ilse seems to struggle with this new development, her expression rather sour.

Outside, muffled voices are audible, heels click. No time.

My gaze travels around the room, the bunk beds, the commode with its washbasin, our threadbare housecoats hanging on wooden pegs, Jesus watching me from his perch—he can't help me either. The window…but outside cars and men are waiting…watching. There's no good spot.

Karin asks something, her words bouncing off my ears unheard. Panic expands inside me, fills me. In the hall, hard steps echo. They're here. There's no telling what happens if I get caught. I mustn't.

My brain springs to life at the knock on the door. There is only one solution to my problem. In the moment it takes for the door to open, while my classmates watch open-mouthed, I stuff *Fabian* into my underpants. Then I freeze not to dislodge its new hiding place. Luckily, my dress is loose, even if it's too short.

Linker enters. Despite his squarish build he is short, his uniform with the sharp-edged SS on the collar perfect. He takes a sweeping look around the room before making us stand in a row.

"Arms forward, palms down." I carefully shuffle sideways and fall in line. The book under my dress digs into my hip. I'm afraid to move for fear it'll clatter to the floor. A wheeze escapes me and I imagine the SS-man singling me out. Biene nudges me gently in the side. She's got me.

The other two soldiers open our dresser and rifle through our clothes. Then they move to our beds and slip their hands beneath pillows as envelopes tumble from beneath, some from each of us, a bit of home while we're away.

That's when I see it: Peter's feather rests in front of my feet. It must've fallen out when I hid the book. I wiggle my fingers, my palms damp. I can't think.

The men trample across the letters, pick up our mattresses and after finding nothing return to Linker's side. The SS-man begins to walk past us, his eyes sweeping up and down as if he's searching for fleas. My knees threaten to knock. One more step and he's in front of me.

"Name?"

"Hilda…Hagedorn, sir."

"*Unterscharführer*," Linker hisses. "Why are you nervous?"

"I…am not nervous."

The man's eyes are the cold blue of a Norwegian fjord and they seem to freeze me in place. The book scrapes and any moment there'll be a sound coming from it.

Abruptly, he bends low and picks up the feather.

"Curious," he mumbles as he twirls my feather. "Whose is this?"

None of us speak, my throat so tight, I don't know how I continue breathing.

"Anybody?" The feather hovers in front of my nose.

Biene coughs loudly. "Excuse me, Unterscharführer," she shouts. "It's mine."

The cold stare moves on to my friend, followed by the click of his heels on the linoleum. I carefully let out a sigh. Not too loud. Linker has stopped in front of Biene. I admit her nails look gnawed and dirty, but that's because of her father.

He points the feather at her chest like the blade of a knife. "Then why don't you answer?" His mouth twists into a smile. "It's just a feather after all." He thrusts the feather at her and Biene takes it quickly.

"What's this?" the man asks, bending so low, I think he may kiss the backs of Biene's hand.

"My fingers," Biene says dryly. I love how strong she is.

"Being rude, too, *mein Fräulein*." Linker leans in, his nose four inches from Biene's forehead. "Name?"

"Bie…Sabine Fuchs."

"Age?"

"Sixteen."

It's true, Biene just turned sixteen last month.

The man pulls out a notebook and scribbles something. "We'll speak again," he says before nodding at the two soldiers.

The men move to the wall where they unfold a stepstool and climb on top. While one takes down the cross with the Jesus figure, the other hands him a framed picture. I imagine Jesus's eyes widen in shock to be so rudely removed from the wall where he's undoubtedly hung for decades.

The book scalds my skin. I've got to keep a straight face.

As the men leave—Jesus stuck under Linker's armpit—I collapse on the bed. Wordlessly, Biene hands me the feather. Sweat pearls on her temples, but her smile is warm.

From his high spot, the Führer solemnly watches us.

Peter

The camp near Danzig is huge, nearly two thousand youths stuffed into dozens of barracks lined up along a private road. I feel as if I'm in the military, our days organized by the minute, starting with washing and cleaning, flag salutes, singing, and marching.

The only good thing is that we have lots of sports events in the afternoon, running, jumping, and throwing balls. We also play soccer, do scavenger hunts and take excursions.

Bed wetters are numerous. That can't be normal, not among fifteen-year old boys. At first they were all ordered to sleep together. Now there are too many. The camp leader singles them out and makes them run extra rounds. They're yelled at and beaten with sticks by the older boys, their sheets taken away.

I don't sleep well most nights as a result.

When I return from the bathroom late one evening, I hear mumbles from the adjacent dorm. It's probably one o'clock and we're supposed to be sleeping, but I'm fighting a bout of diarrhea. Like us, the room next to us sleeps thirty in bunks of three high.

In the gloom of a candle I see four or five boys around a bunk, so I creep closer.

"Damn baby, why don't you go home? Crying for mama. I'll give you something to cry about." The boy I recognize as the room leader sinks a fist into a shape on the bunk. A muffled cry rings out.

A second boy follows suit, then another. Each time the recipient moans.

"Quit being a pussy. The Führer expects bravery, not whining," the leader hisses, starting a new round.

"Time to toughen up."

I stand there in the dark corridor wondering who is next. I've secretly cried on occasion. Many of us have. I cringe as another round of beatings begins.

My thoughts take me back two years to the alley where I watched two boys beat up my little brother, Walter. He was crying, holding his arms in front of his face as fists rained on him. I did nothing, just watched. Walter annoys me, his nosiness a constant barb in my side. He found my diary, eavesdropped on Hilda and me talking. And if I said something, Mother always took his side.

I remember smiling grimly as I headed off to school that day. Walter finally got his punishment…served him right. But after a hundred yards I turned back and found the alley empty. No Walter, no boys, just Walter's green and red-checkered handkerchief, engraved with his initials WB, soaked with bloody snot. I picked it up and contemplated going home to check on Walter. By now my heart was pounding and I had a strange tingle in my face as if it were on fire.

In my mind, the scene repeats as I see myself walk up to the bullies, yank them off my little brother.

But I didn't return home to check on Walter, I went to school and pretended that nothing had happened.

In the dorm, the boy is now crying outright.

"We better stop," one of attackers says.

"He needs to remember," the leader says with an ugly chuckle. "Let the others see it too. I'm tired of pussies."

Still I stand in the hallway, my toes frozen like me. In slow motion I turn toward the wall and switch on the hall light.

Instantly, I hear scrambling feet and voices, "Somebody is coming…hurry. Get to bed. Quick."

I hover a moment, listen to the quiet sobs of the poor soul in the bunk. Then I creep off to my own dorm where I lie awake until dawn, replaying my brother's attack in my head.

Book Two: August 1944 – April 1945

CHAPTER TWELVE

Hilda

The SS-men didn't stay long, but long enough to cast a permanent shadow over the cloister. The day after Biene mouthed off, she is called away in the afternoon.

When she returns she reminds me of Tilly the first time she wet the bed.

"What happened?" I ask. Biene is setting the tables with the usual white plates. She shakes her head and avoids my eyes. The plates rattle as she sets them down. I put a hand on her arm, but she tears loose and continues down the row.

I follow. "What can I do?" I whisper from behind. Biene continues as if she didn't hear me. "Did they hurt you?"

Biene abruptly turns and smacks the rest of the stack down. "They're gone, all right? I don't want to talk about it."

I shrink back, shocked about Biene's tears—she never cries— but I'm even more shocked at her tone so full of anguish. I want to hug her, but I know she won't let me. Not now.

So I nod and say quietly, "Thank you."

Biene resumes her duties as if I'm air and I stand there, arms hanging uselessly by my side. Something terrible must have happened.

Just like the day Papa left, I feel helpless. I see myself stand next to Mama, who has buried her nose in a handkerchief and seems to never want to return from that place deep inside her. I pat her arm, speak to her, yet she does not react, does not look at me. Even at the age of nine I understood that some hurts are too great to put into words. Mama's is one of them. Maybe Biene's is too.

That evening Biene embraces me from behind as she whispers, "I'm sorry."

We hug for a while and that is the last we talk about the SS-men. Biene keeps up a good front, but I know better. When she feels like nobody is watching, her shoulders just collapse. She looks as if she's carrying a hundred-kilo sack of potatoes, the kind Papa used to bring home when I was little.

Christmas passes with lots of singing and a few decent meals. But there is no joy in it, all of us longing for home, none of us able to voice our sorrow. Fräulein Heinrich spends extra time doling out hugs, but even she has lost more weight and embracing her feels like touching a skeleton with skin. Still, her warmth is welcoming and she's lost that tough look she used with us at the gymnasium.

We all welcome spring, then summer, fever for our turn at garden duty and a patch of blue sky. I didn't know time could pass so slowly. It feels as if we've been here five years and not one. The swift long left with her babies, and this year there wasn't a new nest. Sister Rose and I meet in the attic at least once a week to keep watch.

"Why do you think, she's not returning?" I ask.

"Probably doesn't like the Nazi stink around here." Sister Rose sounds like the sharp edges of an icy pond, so I turn to face her in a hurry. The Benedictine sisters still do their six daily prayers, clean, cook and garden, but they all appear subdued. The Abbess has been leaving Fräulein Heinrich alone. It's almost as if the women have banded together against the military men who broke in to torment us.

I'm so astonished about the nun's tone that I'm speechless.

Her usually calm eyes blaze. "I thought I'd be left alone here."

"What do you mean?"

She focuses on me. "My husband is…was in the communist party. They took him away." The nun's voice drops to a whisper. "I saw him once after that."

"Is he…?

"Dead?" Our eyes meet. "Yes. They said he tried to escape from some labor camp."

I forget my usual respect for the black robes and pat her arm. "I'm so sorry."

The nun's beautiful mouth is grim. "I went here to forget. Knew

Eddie since high school. He was studying to become a doctor, wanted to do good for all of us. He…"

Peter's image appears in my mind. He smiles as he offers a hand to help me onto a tree branch. Ahead in the meadow, a family of deer grazes. I massage my jaw to alleviate the tightness—resent myself for thinking about him when Sister Rose is the one suffering.

The nun's bitter laugh brings me back. "I wasn't even that religious, hardly went to church. Look at me now."

I think about the Abbess, the strict rules and the dank rooms. "Maybe you can leave again one day."

Sister Rose nods. "Maybe…once they're gone."

"The Führer?" I have a hard time imagining Germany with a different government.

"Him and all the rest."

"He could at least finish the war," I say.

"That monster will never finish. He'll kill all Germans first, destroy the country."

Once again, I'm speechless. Not only because Sister Rose calls the Führer a monster, but because she thinks we're all going to die. Unease grips me as I wonder if she's right. Paul is still in the war, Karin's father is dead. Many more men are dead, and we know from parent letters that cities are being bombed.

"I didn't mean to worry you." Sister Rose's expression is calm once again. She's squeezing the wooden cross between her folded hands. "I shall pray for you and your families."

"I've got something you may like," I say, pulling *Fabian* from under my skirt. I've been in the habit of carrying him with me, just in case.

"A book?" Sister Rose's voice is so full of wonder, I ask myself if she's seen anything other than a bible.

"A *forbidden* one."

"Where did you get it?"

I say nothing, but hand the book to the nun. "Promise me to hide it well."

Sister Rose's eyes light up as she rubs a palm across the cover.

That night I don't fall asleep until early morning, Sister Rose's hateful words about the Führer and losing the war. What if she is right and Germany is doomed? What will happen to us? To Mama and my brother, Paul…Peter?

I'm dragging at breakfast when there's a commotion in the hall. I can't see anybody, but hear the Abbess talking to one of the sisters. She sounds angry. Next thing I know, a nun appears and whispers in Fräulein Heinrich's ear.

The two of them leave, almost run outside as we all crank our necks. But the discipline of the cloister has long penetrated our bones and we remain seated like sheep, eating our gruel and scraping our bowls mechanically.

I watch Biene, who in earlier times would've shoved me in the side and tried to find out what was going on. The new Biene sits unmoving like everyone else. Out in the hall, more voices rise. There's a new one among them, a woman's voice that is soft and yet, strong.

From the corner of my eye, I see Tilly perk up and at the same moment, a woman in a coat and hat rushes into the hall.

Tilly jumps from her bench and cries something unintelligible before racing toward the woman. They embrace and that's when I see the resemblance. Tilly's mother has come to claim her. The huge grin on my face matches Biene's.

Our letter must have made it.

Peter

I'm about to nod off. *Herr Lustig*, our teacher, is reading from a dog-eared copy of Edwin Dwinger's *Die Letzten Reiter*, some war story with lots of blood and carnage that sounds like a field report, the man's voice sonorous and quiet, almost mumbling—so unlike Big Z, who always gave his best when he read to us.

Lustig is at least seventy-five, short and pretty much bald with brown and black age spots all over his skull. One of them looks like Italy, a boot-shaped area with the heel reaching toward his forehead. That's why we call him map head or boot because he certainly isn't funny like his name says.

A few boys are playing cards in the back row and some of us either read old letters or snooze. Ever since Big Z left, school has become a complete joke. I don't know why they bother. Every morning we sit squeezed into a room that used to be the overflow dining area of a restaurant. We're supposed to be on summer break right now, but they don't know what to do with us, so we continue having classes in the morning. A long time ago, I left home, thinking that we'd be going on a super long vacation. What a joke. All I ever dream of now is to go home and live with Mother and Walter.

Not a day goes by without me thinking about them. Walter has been staying with a family in Upper Palatinate who really likes him. Mother says he's doing well and growing.

And Hilda? Why doesn't she write? Why don't *you?*

Karl-Heinz is scanning a note he received from his mother yesterday. She was bombed out of their home, a nice villa with a huge garden, and now lives with her sister. Apparently, everything they owned is gone, including Karl-Heinz's collection of toy cars. He hasn't said much since he got the letter.

After Big Z left last winter, things got worse. We'd settled in pretty well, but they started using mail deliveries for punishment. Nobody was allowed to say anything bad in their letters and if they did, incoming letters were withheld. We also didn't receive mail when we misbehaved in any way. Some boys snuck out at night to run mail to neighboring villages.

Then supplies grew short and they forbid us to open the sandwiches we were served. Of course, we did anyway, finding the cheese in-between alive with maggots. Things went downhill from there and the camp leaders decided to split up the groups. Those who got there last, left first. Christian and a couple of other boys were picked up by their mothers. I don't know if Christian's departure had anything to do with the horrible food or if he was worried about being close to Karl-Heinz. Either way, I could swear that Karl-Heinz has been even sadder.

Our current place is a former country inn. Six of us are staying in rooms meant for two, but we've got a sink in our room to wash, a huge improvement to the shared washrooms in the prior camps.

Food is good. Our host, *Herr Sommer,* who lost one leg in France and limps around on a wooden stick, cooks like a first-class chef. He fixes delicious stews and dumplings with creamy sauces. We even get dessert on weekends.

Yet, I find myself drifting. I'm not sure what to think any longer. The Führer told us we'd all be part of this new great Germany. But there are lots of news of defeat, lost battles, dead soldiers and bombed cities—things they don't want us to know.

Except a few of us are listening to enemy radio.

Well, let me start from the beginning. In the last camp, I met this other boy, Bernd, who had a radio with him. We listened every night and made sure that our classmates heard what we heard. Soon, we all knew what was going on. At least what they wanted us to hear.

So, one evening, Bernd and I were sitting in a storage closet, listening to the radio, when he said, "I want to find out what the other countries are saying."

I got up without a word and opened the door to our room to listen outside. The corridor was empty so I nodded and after some crackling, an English voice came on. The reporter talked about the Red Army destroying the German front in the East and Hitler's refusal to pull back. The Führer was sacrificing half a million men. Then something amazing happened. The announcer mentions Thomas Mann, a German author living in the United States.

A knocking sound transmits through the radio as if somebody is trying to get in.

"German listeners!" says Thomas Mann. "The Nazis are the corrupters of the people. Everyone knows that Hitler has lost his war. Germany cannot win a war against the world." The Gestapo is mentioned, kicking humanity and its rights.

Bernd and I looked at each other. I don't think either of us knew what to say. Just listening to the reports was madness. We were mad too. Listening to enemy radio was punishable by death. What were we doing? What was Hitler doing? Was that why he always talked about sacrifice? Were we all going to sacrifice ourselves? Where would he stop?

According to Thomas Mann, Germany has committed horrible crimes. He says Nazis declared *total war* a normality, a German privilege.

I don't even hear all of it, I'm too confused and shaken.

"Don't tell anyone," Bernd whispered, turning off the radio with a click. That lasted a few days until he and I found ourselves back in the closet. It was like a drug we feared and craved. All day I was thinking about the words crackling through the airwaves.

The reports were similar, Germany being attacked by the Allies in the West, the Red Army in the East. The British RAF was taking care of Germany's homes and civilians. The writing was on the wall. We'd lose the war, lose big time. Thomas Mann was right.

Yet, the German news never talks about defeat or surrender, the camp leaders make no mention of bombs and war. They make us train and salute, raise the flag, lower the flag...Heil Hitler. All the while Thomas Mann's words echo through my mind: "Abomination and blasphemy of humanity wherever you look...to hell with them and their henchmen."

Be strong, be brave. Train your young and defend at all cost.

I feel like my brain is going to burst and yet, I can't say a thing. Not one word, not even to Karl-Heinz. Bernd and I have to keep this secret, or we may go to prison or be executed.

Leaving the huge camp meant leaving Bernd and the radio. In a way I'm glad. In a way I loathe the absence of news.

I haven't heard from Mother in three months. Mail is interrupted a lot, and I'm hoping it's nothing more than torn-apart train tracks and bombed post offices. Surely, they'd tell me if anything happened to Mother. Hilda hasn't written either. I've asked myself a few times why I didn't bring a photo of her. I'm not quite sure what her face looks like any longer.

"Peter, what do you think?" Boot's eyes, huge behind horn-rimmed glasses, seem to burn into my forehead.

"Sorry, I…" Nothing comes to mind.

"Can you summarize for us what I just read? Give us your thoughts, would you?"

From the corner of my eyes I see shocked faces. Karl-Heinz looks up from his letter, his cheeks bright red. I know he hasn't listened either. Boot usually leaves us alone.

Why is he picking on me now?

CHAPTER THIRTEEN

Hilda

This morning after breakfast, the Abbess shows up. That's highly unusual because ever since the SS-men removed all the crosses and references to religion and planted swastika flags and Hitler portraits in every room, she's made herself rare. Just as well. Though I miss Jesus watching over us, I won't ever forget the things the Abbess did to Tilly.

She marches to the podium and raises both arms. The noise dies down and we stare at the woman in the black habit. I'm thinking she may announce that we should celebrate our sixteen-month anniversary. Ha!

"I've gotten word that you'll be going home tomorrow. Pack your things and clean your rooms thoroughly. Tomorrow morning, a chartered train will be picking you up in Waldkirchen.

I don't hear the rest because hollers and screams rise as Biene presses me to her. "We're going home," she shouts. Tears run down Karin's cheeks; even Fräulein Heinrich is crying.

Home. I'm going back to Mama. Immediately, the anxiety of her long silence nags at me—barbed fingernails scratch my insides. Hardly any letters have arrived during the past months. But then the excitement returns and I'm patting Biene on the back. We smile at each other.

"I wonder how the war is going," I say aloud. It's true, I don't know. We don't hear anything, don't even get a newspaper to read or a radio to listen to. Once last month, I accompanied Fräulein Heinrich to the little village where we bought a few supplies. I told my teacher about the new owner of her book.

Fräulein Heinrich takes my hands. "Oh, Hilda, I'm so sorry. I should never have given it to you. I would've never forgiven myself if something had happened to you."

"Sister Rose doesn't know it was your book. I don't get why they forbade it—why they forbid any book."

Fräulein Heinrich quickly looks around as if she wants to make sure nobody listens. It's pretty unlikely because we're in the middle of a field.

"The main character, Dr. Fabian, believes that people should act from a moral point of view."

"They should do what is right," I say. "And they should be free to decide."

"Exactly." My teacher slings an arm around me, her nearness still strange even after receiving her hugs. "Our government," here my teacher's voice grows so quiet, I have to lean in further, "doesn't believe in such things. They tell us what to do and what to think."

"Some people like it."

"Lots of people like to be told things. It's easier so they don't have to consider if what they're doing is right...or moral."

I nod and the rest of the way we walk in silence. Fräulein Heinrich remains close and on the narrow path our shoulders touch sometimes. It's a comforting feeling, but it makes me miss Mama even more.

The village merchant, a shriveled woman with a navy wool scarf slung around her head, packed three bunches of green onions in a sheet of newspaper from the *Deutsche Allgemeine Zeitung*. It was from July 1944, but on the way back we take a break and I read every word.

Somebody tried to assassinate the Führer. Why hadn't I known? Hitler had escaped and now demanded unconditional loyalty. I wasn't really sure what that meant or why somebody wanted to kill him.

"Did you know about the assassination attempt?" I ask Fräulein Heinrich as we approach the cloister.

My teacher nods, her red curls bouncing off her shoulders. "I heard from the Abbess." She grips my arm. "Don't tell anybody, you hear? I don't want the girls to be upset."

On the last evening I climb to the attic. Sister Rose is already waiting and turns to embrace me. My respect for the habit is long gone as I press myself to the young nun's chest.

"I will miss you, Hilda." The sister's voice is muffled.

"I will miss *you*." I lean back and take in the beautiful face. "I hope you'll find a place to be happy."

She pats my cheek. "When the war ends…"

As we part ways, Sister Rose's cryptic words whirl through my mind. But then I remember that we're going home and bounce down the stairs.

Surely, it is safe again.

In the morning we hurry through our last breakfast and I marvel in the fact that I'll never eat oats and milk again, nor will I miss the Abbess. Everyone speaks quietly, a happy buzz of voices.

I grow aware of movement outside. Beyond the windows military trucks appear, but when I want to get up to take a closer look, Fräulein Heinrich calls us to finish and grab our luggage. I'm confused because I thought we would take the train.

The huge wooden gate at the cloister's exit is thrown open, and more trucks roll through. Already the courtyard is clogged with vehicles, medium-sized brownish trucks with red crosses on white background. As we march past, I see men lying on stretchers, their limbs, bodies and faces covered in bandages. Some lie still, some moan. A paramedic, wearing a steal helmet with a red cross, and two nurses carry a man on a stretcher past us. A white sheet covers the area where his legs used to be. He's awake and very pale, his eyes toward the sky, not noticing us haste past him. Several men lie on the ground, blankets beneath them stained brownish-red. The men's uniforms—or what is left of them—are as dirty as their skin.

A terrible stench cloaks the courtyard, one that makes me want to hold my breath and cover my nose. Here and there nuns linger while others direct the men inside. Sister Rose bends over a soldier with a wrapped head, her pretty eyes troubled, yet smiling at the suffering man. Now we know why we had to leave so suddenly.

We walk in silence to the train station, our happy thoughts of going home replaced by the images at the cloister. These men are our fathers and brothers. One of them could have been Paul. I shudder, throwing a glance at Biene, who's walking next to me. Her gaze is inward, her expression as serious as my own.

Oh how I wish we'd left earlier.

The train journey is taking forever. We pass by demolished buildings and torn apart streets. Much has happened in the year and four months since we left. Our train stops at a station and we wait. Last time there were women feeding us tea and sandwiches. This time there's nothing, just empty tracks and deserted stations.

My thoughts wander to Peter. Sometimes, at night I've run his feather along my cheeks, imagining Peter's touch. He was one who liked the activities of the Hitler Youth, the games they played, the fighting exercises, and the camaraderie. Does he still enjoy his time away? Does he ever think about me like I think of him? I imagine him on the beach or skiing and feel myself smile.

"What's so funny?" Biene asks. She's been super quiet ever since we began our journey.

My cheeks warm and I shake my head. "Nothing. Just looking forward to seeing Mama."

Biene's gaze is on me, her eyes a bit shiny. "You think they'll be all right?"

"Sure," I lie. "Why wouldn't they be?"

Biene turns her head toward Karin, who's staring out the window, away in her own world. I wish I could do that sometimes—just leave everything and dream away.

The train stops abruptly, wheels screech and we are tumbling off our seats. A few girls shriek and the formerly drowsy wagon erupts in chatter.

Fräulein Heinrich rushes past us out the door. That's when I hear it. A dull rat-tat-tat …thump, thump. The wagon vibrates as if the rails beneath have broken loose. Biene and Ilse are already at the window. Beyond the pasture lies a forest, and beyond that gray dots fill the sky. Planes.

My brain tries to warn me, but all I do is stare at the low flying specks. They're no longer small as pinpricks but shaped like flies with tiny wings and stumpy noses. That's when Fräulein Heinrich's voice pushes into my conscience.

"Off the train, this instant. Leave your things." Her voice is distorted, and its strangeness jerks me out of my stupor more than her words.

We push against each other and try to funnel through the door. Each second grows into a minute, stretching moments of agony. Ursel is in front of me, Biene in front of her. Somebody pushes against my back and steps on my heels. I'm through the door, blinded by daylight. I no longer see the planes—I hear them. Engines roar and bullets rain.

Outside girls are running in front of me, away from the train and the planes, through the fields toward the shelter of the forest. But oh, how slow we are. Ursel falls in front of me. I help her up and take her hand. We run as the rat-tat-tat of machine gun fire explodes around us. Dirt clods spray up from the ground in rows.

Don't you see we're kids, girls no older than fifteen, I want to scream. But no sound leaves my throat. If it had I wouldn't have heard my voice in the racket. The planes are ahead now and I'm still running. Ursel is dragging because of her short legs, her face pale as snow. I can't see Biene any longer. Cannot think about it, must run…faster. The forest is close now, no more than fifty yards.

Ahead, the bombers turn to make a second attempt to chase us down. Faster. The engine noise grows again as the shadows of the woods shield us in the moment the first planes appear above the tree line. Behind us curdles a scream. But I can't stop, not now. I drag Ursel with me between the trunks of the trees. Oaks and beech spread their wings over us.

It has to be enough.

We turn right, down a narrow path. Other girls join us. Some I don't know who boarded the train at some point. Ursel is next to me, still clinging to my hand. I'm glad Tilly got to go home. In the distance, an explosion rattles the air. The ground quakes and I make out bright lights between the trees. They've got the locomotive.

"Where's Biene?" Ursel asks. At last she's let go of my hand. We both swivel in circles, but I don't see Biene's black mane. The other girls around us, maybe eight or ten, are crying and whispering.

I turn on my heels and go back the way we came as the cries from earlier echo through my head—cries of people being hit with machine gun bullets. All of a sudden my legs turn to mush. I want to sink to the ground, my knees too weak to hold me up. But I can't…I must search…confirm. Ursel is next to me again, though I don't hear what she is saying. I keep walking toward the field.

It is quiet out there, so quiet, I can hear the crackling of fire. In the distance, the train sits aflame. I think of the gift I made for Mama, a couple of crochet potholders in pink and white. It took me four weeks because yarn and I don't get along. Add to that a crochet needle and there'll surely be a mess. What does it matter if a few potholders burn? So silly, so stupid.

My eyes search the brownish fields that were recently harvested—wheat or some other grain—short, hard stalks now brown and dead.

That's when I see it: a body lying forty meters from the train. It's still and sort of twisted. I keep walking toward it. I don't remember the last meters, only that I find myself kneeling and holding Fräulein Heinrich's hand. The skin is white and unblemished, nails clean. I know my teacher is dead without looking at her face.

Ursel falls to her knees next to me and cries out. I only stare, not crying, sort of empty as if I don't have tears. I'm all dried up like the stalks around me.

A reddish stain blooms across Fräulein Heinrich's middle. It is still spreading, seemingly alive. So much blood, so red…gaudy, like the lipstick our teacher used to love.

"What are we going to do?" Ursel cries.

I scan the remains of the train, black clouds billowing where the engine once was. The coal reserves are burning, the conductor likely dead. We have no supplies, no adults with us. I have no idea where we are.

That's when I remember Biene. She's not out here. My mind races over the events. She was in front of me. Or was she? I'm confused now… shake my head. Then my body begins to tremble and I bend over until my forehead meets the brown clotted earth.

A wail escapes me. Rises above the crackling flames of the train.

Hands pat my back, rub my head. A pair of feet comes into view. I know those shoes, the knee socks.

With a shriek I straighten and throw myself into Biene's arms. She just holds me as I sob.

"I thought…" I hiccup, "couldn't find you."

"I went the other way, left up the path," she says quietly. We look at each other. There're tears in her eyes as well. Everyone is surrounding us now. Nearly sixty girls have lost their teacher. Some of them cry, some just stare in shock.

"Where's Karin?" Ilse says behind me. "I can't find Karin."

We all look at each other as if one of us has her hidden in a pocket.

"Where did you last see her?" Biene says.

"Near the train." Ilse's eyes grow larger and she clamps a hand across her mouth. "She went back to get her father's watch, her mother had mailed it to her after he fell." Our eyes wander to the train, the blazing fire. Ilse takes a tentative step toward the train wreckage, stops, then takes another. "Karin!"

The only sounds are the flames hissing toward the sky and the sobs of my classmates.

Some place inside lies Karin. We'd all boarded that train thinking it was safe when nothing is safe.

I push down the new lump in my throat. Karin wasn't my friend, but she most certainly didn't deserve to die. "We've got to find a village," I say. "We'll need to ask for help."

"But we can't leave Fräulein Heinrich," a girl cries.

"We can't carry her," Biene says. Her upper lip quivers, but she's looking determined.

"We tell somebody once we find an adult," I say.

"Surely, they'll miss the train and pick us up," another girl says. Her right shoulder is bloody, a piece of fabric missing. She was lucky, the bullet just grazing her.

"We should stay and wait," another adds.

"I'm going," I say. "Who knows when they'll realize we're missing."

"We don't know the way." Ilse's face is wet with tears.

"I suggest we follow the train tracks. It's a matter of time until we come across a town."

"But it may be days," someone says.

"You can stay here," I say. "Germany isn't like Canada or America. There must be people nearby."

Biene puts an arm around my shoulder. "I'm going with Hilda."

"Me too," Ursel says.

Only then, as we're walking off, do I remember the feather that evaporated in the train. It's nothing, a trinket, and yet my heart breaks a little more as if a part of Peter has left me.

Peter

Boot's bottle-glass stare is on me and, for once, I don't know what to say. The entire class is silent.

"I…didn't listen," I finally say.

Boot's mouth pinches. It's tiny anyway and now disappears altogether. "I realize none of you considers my class important." He sounds offended. "I shall file a complaint—"

The door flies open and the inn's owner, Herr Sommer, stands there red-faced. "If I may have a word," he blurts at Boot.

Sommer is waving his arms, talking urgently... "overwhelming…need help…no room."

We look at each other, but I can't make out what they're talking about.

Abruptly, Sommer leaves and Boot snaps shut his book. "Something has come up. I need all of you to help. It's an emergency."

"Is something wrong with our mothers?" Dieter shouts.

"Did they bomb Solingen?" Karl-Heinz asks.

Boot is getting red in the face. "No, no, none of that." He opens his mouth and closes it. "It's best if you all come with me."

When we scramble outside, I'm about to fall on my behind. In front of us, beneath the old *Linden* tree, squat at least twenty people. Half of them are kids, some no older than one or two. A woman carries an infant in a blanket. There are old men in their seventies or eighties, six or eight women in headscarves and downtrodden shoes. They all have one thing in common. They look starved and scared, with tired eyes and hollow cheeks.

Sommer appears in front of us boys. "We've got to help these refugees. Put them up for the night, maybe two. Don't know yet." Sommer scratches his head while taking in the disheveled bunch. "Where to put them?" he mumbles. At last he resolutely stares at us.

"You six go to the barn and pack straw sacks. Bring them to the side room where you have class. We've got to put half of them in there.

"Two of you need to clear the room, take out the chairs and stack them in the attic. Ask my niece where the spare blankets and sheets are." He points at us. "You four come with me to the kitchen. We've got to feed them something now, so they don't fall over."

That's the moment I decide Herr Sommer is a decent man. All he wanted was to run a nice restaurant, host a few vacationers in the summers. First he gets all of us and now two-dozen refugees show up. But he doesn't say no. He's trying to help.

I follow our host, Karl-Heinz and two other boys to the kitchen where Herr Sommer's niece, Trine, a woman not much older than us, is peeling potatoes.

"Trine, show those boys where the glasses and pitchers are." Herr Sommer's forehead glistens. "Boys, give the people a drink of water. I'll see what milk I can spare to feed the little ones."

A moment later we're back outside, Karl-Heinz pouring water

from a carafe while I handing out cups to the refugees. They're a sorry bunch. I thought we had it tough when we landed in the old school a million years ago. But these people's clothes are shredded and dirty. They hardly have any luggage—a few cardboard suitcases, a couple of packs.

"Where are you from?" I ask.

"Near Königsberg." The woman's voice is deep and resigned. She's holding a little boy, no older than five, who focuses on me. Despite his obvious tiredness, there's a hint of curiosity in his brown eyes. "We've been running from the Red Army."

"How long have you been on the road?"

"Six or seven weeks." She offers the cup to the boy and then drinks greedily, absentmindedly patting the boy on the head as if she's some place else. "We're slow… had to hide and take detours. After they defeated the Germans, the Russians are gaining speed heading west."

Two things register. The Russians defeated the German Army and they're heading west…this way. While we waste time in camp, the Germans are losing. Thomas Mann has been right all along. I want to ask more questions, but there's no time. We've got to finish handing out drinks.

"I'll be back." I throw a smile at the little guy before following Karl-Heinz down the line. Herr Sommer has made sandwiches, which we hand out next.

Afterwards, the old men go inside to take possession of their straw beds in the barn. Our classroom is gone for now. Just as well, since Boot is no picnic. I'd much rather talk to the refugees about their experience and the news they may carry.

"You should be able to go inside soon. They're fixing beds for you," I say to the woman. She's resting on an old stonewall while her boy plays with a few sticks and two chestnuts. He rolls them around, before attempting to poke a hole into them.

I bend low. "Let me help you."

I take a pointy rock and force open the tough skin. The boy smiles and puts a stick into it.

"You making a person?" I ask. The boy quickly looks at me and then returns to his project.

"He doesn't speak," the woman says.

"Oh," is all I can say. I slump next to her and watch the boy with his stick figure.

"I'm Maria," she says, offering a surprisingly clean hand.

"I'm Peter." My gaze returns to the boy. "Is your son sick then?"

"Just in shock, I think. I'm not his mother." Maria's eyes glitter. "She was eight months pregnant and the strain, the fear…was too much." Maria wipes her face with her sleeve and shakes her head. "He hasn't spoken since. I'm his aunt."

"I'm sorry," I say, feeling inadequate and stupid. What can you say in the face of such misery and sadness? Nothing fits. "Will you tell me what you know about the battles? What did the Russians do? What is happening with the *Wehrmacht*?"

"All I know is there was this huge battle that started in late June and went through August. The Red Army pushed back the German front and have retaken Belarus and are moving into Poland." A sigh escapes. "Many men on both sides have died."

"Where will you go?"

Maria smiles weakly. "Berlin. I have a second cousin there and hope he'll take me in."

I nod while I imagine Maria and the mute boy sitting on a chintz sofa in a living room in Berlin.

"Your quarters are ready." Herr Sommer's niece stands in the door to the inn, waving both arms. "You'll wash at the pump behind the house. I'll make a schedule for the women and men."

Mumbling quietly, the hovel of humanity moves inside. I guess classes are canceled for now.

CHAPTER FOURTEEN

Hilda

My feet hurt, especially my toes. Mama didn't send new shoes, and the ones I'm wearing are too small and not suitable for long walks. My big toes scrape the inside. We left hours ago with most of my class.

Even Ilse came. None of us are talking as we hike along the rails. Sometimes, we have to detour because the tracks lead across bridges and through woods. I'm too afraid to walk on top of the rails. My throat is dry and scratchy. Sometimes tears roll on their own. The image of Fräulein Heinrich so still on the field makes me want to scream. But the idea that Karin burned alive inside the train is worse.

Hunger has joined my misery. None of us have anything—the carefully prepared sandwiches destroyed, the thermos bottles melted.

We pass by an old farm but when we excitedly knock, the door just comes open. The inside has been ransacked—broken glass and pieces of furniture litter the floor. There's no food, but in the front yard we find a well. We take turns pumping and drinking. We help one of the girls wash her bloody leg. Luckily, it's just a scratch.

After some discussion we agree to spend the night. Nobody has a watch, but it's late afternoon and none of us wants to be outside in the dark.

"I'm going to explore," Biene says.

"Going with you."

As the others clear the floor and look for suitable places to sleep, I follow Biene outside. The barn has a partially collapsed roof, but the door still works, and we peek inside. A few forgotten straw bales and a bit of hay are stacked against the back wall.

"I'll sleep on that," I say, taking a closer look. If we pull apart the straw, it's going to be much softer and warmer than a bare floor in the house.

Behind the barn are deserted fields, but when we go past the farmhouse, we come across a former garden and a few trees along the edges. In it grows a mess of weeds, and between them I find *gold.*

Carrots.

Glorious carrots, their tops a bit brown, but the roots in good shape. I yell at Biene who is eying a tree with purple fruit.

Biene has found plums. I race back to the farmhouse to tell the others, and together we harvest. There are so many plums, we could eat for days. We collect them in our shirts and dresses. Biene has found an old basket with broken handles. We fill them all and sit down in the dusk to eat.

Of course, all those plums have a way to upset our bowels. All night long, some of us visit the outhouse. It's horrible because we have no paper, and use hay and straw which sticks to everything. I don't have diarrhea, but my intestines churn and cramp.

In the morning we're heading out at first light. Chaffinches chirp around us without a care in the world. A jay calls a warning. I think about the swift and her babies, and how much pleasure I got from watching her raise her young.

We have to stop every half hour because some of the girls need to hide in the bushes.

By lunchtime we climb another hill. It's steep and we're out of breath and energy by the time we make it to the top. Below us, another valley opens. And there at the bottom lies a small village, its church tower clearly visible. With a cry, we scramble downward, across roots, bushes and rocks.

"You wait here," Biene says to the group. "Hilda, Ursel and I will look for help. If we all show up at the same time, they'll get scared."

Other than a few mumbles, nobody complains. They're all happy to wait and rest.

An old woman with her head wrapped in a flowery scarf watches us curiously before disappearing behind a door. We must be quite a sight, but I no longer care. We charge forward in search of a human being who will listen. Near the church we find the *Rathaus*, its doors closed. The church clock says eight thirty-five.

I march to the next best house and knock, Biene and Ursel at my sides.

Peter

The little boy, his name is Alexander, has been following me around all afternoon. He may not speak, but he doesn't miss much. I've asked him to help me sweep the floors. With that many extra people, the inn has turned into a pigsty. Afterwards, I promised him to organize games for the kids.

Every available surface is occupied, even during the day. Some of the older people are so exhausted, they're just lying or leaning.

In a way, I welcome the new tasks. At least they beat Boot's yawn-inducing lessons.

During dinner, Maria grabs my hand. "Thank you for taking care of him. He needs a bit normalcy, just somebody to be with who is not on the run."

I nod and grin at Alexander. Even though he's much smaller, he reminds me of Walter, my little brother. I have trouble remembering his voice. He's ten now, celebrated his birthday with strangers. Is that what Germany has become? All of us spread to the winds, torn apart, no longer families, nothing but nomads.

"We'll be leaving in the morning," Maria says.

I jerk out of my thoughts. "So soon? I thought…"

She shakes her head. "We all want to safely arrive in Berlin. The sooner we go, the sooner we'll get there."

How must it be to leave your home behind never to return? All this time I've been thinking about returning to the place where my family lives…where I have lived all my life. The thought alone brings me comfort. And yet, here is Maria, all these men and women who left everything.

Alexander doesn't listen. He's pushing his chestnut man across the table. I've added arms by attaching a stick with straw, and fuzzy moss shoes. I get the distinct feeling Maria isn't telling me everything…that she's afraid to stay longer.

The thought nags at me all night. The Red Army is obviously a lot stronger than the Germans thought. If they defeated the Wehrmacht, there is no telling how far they'll go. Why would they stop now? Why not go all the way to Berlin?

It's after midnight before I fall asleep, and I'm up with the first crow. Herr Sommer has a small flock of chickens guarded by a mean-spirited rooster. He's a skinny thing with green iridescent tail feathers and a shriveled comb tilting to one side. He's quick as a mouse and begins crowing at five o'clock.

Remembering Maria and the refugees, I ease out of bed and get dressed. The men are already in front of the inn, sitting and chatting.

"…another four weeks…if the kids hold up…if we hold up."

"At least the Russians aren't here yet."

"A matter of time…"

I turn away to quit listening when Maria exits the inn. Her eyes light up when she sees me, and Alexander runs over to grab my legs. He's still holding the chestnut man, who's lost a moss foot overnight.

"Thank you so much for your help," Maria says, taking my hands in hers. She's bound her dark hair into a scarf and carries a small bundle around her shoulders. "We'll leave after breakfast. If Herr Sommer feeds us again."

"I'm sure he will," I say. "He'd do it longer, if you stayed."

Maria squeezes my fingers. "I meant to say yesterday…" her eyes find mine, "you should leave. Solingen is far, and you should be with your mother. This…this whole thing isn't working out."

"The war?"

She nods. "Hitler is losing. I know it." She puts a palm to her heart. "The signs are there." She pushes a piece of paper into my hands. "Here's my address in Berlin. If you're ever near, visit us."

"I'll write," I say and know I mean it. My vision blurs and I'm not sure if it's the strange sadness of the woman, the mute little boy who lost his mother or the tattered refugees that renew the worry inside me. "I better go and help with food, so you can leave," I say finally.

My throat is dry and I almost want to hug Maria who could be my big sister. *Don't be a baby*, the voice in my head pesters. *What will the others think?* So I tear away and hurry into the kitchen. Herr Sommer's niece is already fixing bread and strawberry jam sandwiches. She's packed cold rutabagas, apples and a few bottles of milk.

Karl-Heinz is up and we carry everything outside. He looks like he didn't sleep too well himself, and I know he worries about his mother, but I've got to talk to him about what Maria said.

Our good-byes are short, but heartfelt. We're waving and yelling farewell wishes. "Be safe, travel well. *Alles Gute...*"

On the way to the barn—we're supposed to clean up after the men—I notice Karl-Heinz scratching his head.

"Maybe you should wash your hair," I comment.

Karl-Heinz makes a face. In the past, he would've made a snide comment, but ever since his illness, he's much more serious.

"The woman, Maria, said we should go home," I blurt as soon as we're inside the barn. "She said the Russians are coming this way."

"I'd love to go home," Karl-Heinz says. "I'm sick and tired of living this way."

"Then we should talk to Boot. Tell him we want to leave."

"He's spineless."

"So?" I cry. "He can't tell us what to do."

"How would we get home if he doesn't get us train tickets?"

I shrug. "We can at least ask."

That's what we do as soon as Boot shows his face outside. He's in a bad mood, his eyes squinty behind the thick glasses. He's shouting orders at a couple of boys who are doing ant races in the dust.

"Get busy, you lazy bones. We've got a classroom to fix." He huffs as the boys disappear inside.

"Herr Lustig, may we ask you a question?" I say as Karl-Heinz and I carefully approach.

Boot scowls at us "What is it? Make it quick."

"Sir, we're wondering when we'll be going home," Karl-Heinz says.

"The refugees are talking about the Russian Army coming this way," I add.

Boot stretches himself a bit, which is difficult because he only reaches to our collarbones. He's lost weight since he arrived, and his vest hangs loosely across his belly.

"Nonsense! Why would the Russians come this far? They've got no reason."

Thomas Mann's words ring in my ears. *Just defeating the Reich and everyone in it.*

"But they *could* come this way," Karl-Heinz tries again. "How would we know if we don't get any newspapers and hardly any letters?"

"You hear the radio broadcasts," Boot says. "Everything is going according to plan. Soon we'll have a unified great Germany and you can all go home to your families."

"But couldn't we at least ask—"

"No buts." Boot waves a stubby arm and turns toward the inn. "It's perfectly safe. Maybe you'll soon be called to serve the Führer."

"What do you mean?" I ask.

Boot looks us up and down. "I expect you'll become soldiers. Now be quick, it's time for you boys to resume class. In you go."

Karl-Heinz looks at me, his jaw muscles clenching in anger. He has a bit of fuzz on his chin now and looks older.

I shake my head. We'll need to talk about it again later.

CHAPTER FIFTEEN

Hilda

A man in suspenders and a grizzled beard opens the door. Everything on him is gray, even his skin tone. He stares at us suspiciously, so I blurt, "Excuse me, our train got bombed and we're trying to get home. Some girls are waiting by the train. Our teacher died and we don't know what to do—"

"Who's at the door?" A woman's voice yells from the darkness beyond.

"Girls," the man says. He squints and looks grumpy, the lines around his mouth drawing down to the chin.

That's when a woman in her forties pushes past him. She wears a blue apron and carries a washrag. Her eyes are alert and appraising as she takes in our appearance, the dust-covered scraped-up shoes, the stains on our dresses and likely our faces, our filthy hands.

"What happened?" she says.

I repeat my speech, hoping that things will get easier, because I'm about to fall over or cry when I get to explaining Fräulein Heinrich lying there with her eyes open.

To my surprise, Ursel pipes up. "Ma'am, we're lost and need to get home to our families. Our teacher died when the bombers came. There are more of us. We need help."

Something softens in the woman's face, her eyes a similar earth color as Peter's widen a bit.

"Likely story," the old man next to her says.

"Nonsense, Father, look at them."

"It's true," Biene says. "We've only eaten carrots and plums. Some of us aren't doing very well."

The woman steps back and waves us inside. In the back of the house is a large kitchen with a wooden table. Everything is very clean. The woman points at the bench and chairs. "Sit down and tell me everything."

She busies herself at the counter and puts mugs, bread and jam in front of us. "Drink, it's buttermilk. It'll be easier to digest than the plums."

When the woman opens the jar, I smell blackberries. She prepares three thick slices with jam and puts them on plates. "Eat, eat."

She nods and a tiny dimple appears on her right cheek. I want to hug her, but the smells are too delicious. I remember my classmates at the edge of town—I must tell the people about them. But oh, the aroma makes me salivate. So I dig in, trying to keep from gulping and chewing too fast. Obviously, Biene and Ursel are feeling the same, their glassy eyes focused on the food.

The woman watches while the old man stands leaning in the doorway, his arms crossed in front of him.

"You're too kind, Annie," he says. "If you feed every beggar who comes knocking, we won't have anything left to survive this insane war."

"Shush," she says and throws us a smile. Then she leans forward. "Now tell me. Then we figure out a plan."

While we devour a second slice of bread with jam, we take turns telling Annie about our ordeal. She nods and tsks, shakes her head and sighs. "There are thirty-five of us at the edge of town, twenty more by the train," I say. "We told them to wait until we got help. And there is Fräulein Heinrich…"

Somewhere in back, the old man clears his throat. When I look over my shoulder, he no longer crosses his arms, but listens intently.

"I'm going to see the Mayor," he says. "We'll need a lot more help."

"His heart is much softer than he admits," Annie says after he's gone. "He's lost his son, my brother, in the war and is angry most of the time."

I nod, thinking about Paul. I'm unprepared at the ferocity of my pain, realizing that I may never see him again. *What about Mama?* I straighten abruptly and ask for the bathroom.

Once inside, I wash my face and hands and stare in the mirror. The eyes looking back at me are larger than I remember, my cheeks more pronounced, almost angular. Hadn't they told us we'd gain weight with all the good food? All I know is that I'm taller and can't spend another minute waiting.

"We need to get home," I blurt into the kitchen.

Annie has cleared the table and pats my back. "I know. My father is—"

The door flies open and Annie's father and two more men enter. One is the Mayor, the other his son, who limps along with a cane.

We repeat our story and, once the Mayor produces a map, proceed to explain our route. The map shows villages and roads and is not too detailed. It's difficult, except that we know where the train tracks run.

"We've got an old bus we can use to pick up your classmates," the Mayor's son says. "I'll send my wife to pick up the girls nearby." He straightens his gimpy leg as pain tightens his jaws. "Just have to find somebody to drive it and gather a bit of gasoline." He limps off, obviously glad to have something to do.

"We need to find a way to get you home," the Mayor says. He's at least seventy and wears a heavy beard. If it weren't for the gray stripes, he'd almost look like Santa. Annie's father is no longer grumpy. He's sitting with us at the table, mumbling and making notes on a scrap of paper.

"Solingen, you say?"

Biene, Ursel and I nod in unison. "How far away are we?" I ask.

"Maybe two-hundred fifty kilometers," the Mayor says. "Too far to walk."

"How many people are you?" asks Annie.

"About fifty-five altogether," Ursel says. She may be short, but her voice carries and I'm proud of her. Ever since we've been heading for home, she's like a different person.

"You'll need an adult to accompany you, likely we'll have to find another train." The Mayor scratches his chin. The top link of his forefinger is missing and I can't pull away my eyes.

"I don't want to ride on a train," Biene says.

"You may not have a choice." Annie is placing mugs on the table as the kitchen fills with the aroma of some kind of chicory coffee. My mouth floods with saliva even though we just ate.

"It's going to take time," the Mayor says. "I've got to organize rooms for the other girls." He hesitates. "Annie, you willing to take those three girls?"

Annie looks at us, then her father. Serious at first, a smile crosses her face. "We've got the room. I'm sure they'll help me with the farming."

We all nod earnestly. I'll do whatever I can to help this kind woman. A giggle escapes me, at first it is soft, but then it grows louder and louder until I'm gasping for air. The others stare at me as if I've escaped an insane asylum—only Annie smiles. I do feel a little crazy right now.

Walking to the door, the Mayor shakes his head and mumbles to himself, "I've got to send notice. Thankfully, we've got farms to feed all those girls."

Peter

Indeed, we're back in class. The playing cards have disappeared, and everyone sits at attention. Somehow Boot has found his authority and is not afraid of using it. In fact, he enjoys pushing us around. He's not as bad as Zeibler, but Dieter had to go to bed without dinner yesterday because he wasn't able to recite Baldur von Schirach's poem about the Hitler Youth. Though I didn't sleep well again, the words echo through my head…

Firmly they march and different than the others.
Here goes power!
Of this kind there is much in far away Flanders.
A will grew and took proud form.

And their hearts, their hands
Fly above.
No, no power, not fire and not iron
Holds this life back from its course!

Von Schirach is the guy in charge of the KLV. It's his program. Early on I saw some photographs in the paper with him and a bunch of kids. I wonder what he's thinking now that we're spread all over the place.

I can't concentrate this morning because my body is itching as if a thousand feathers are tickling me. I've been scratching myself *down there* and wonder if I've got lice. It's sort of embarrassing as I scoot around on my chair, but the itch is making me crazy.

Karl-Heinz is scratching his belly a lot. He must have gotten them too.

By lunchtime, I'm going crazy. I've got to tell somebody, but it's so embarrassing, I feel myself flush just thinking about it. They'll believe I don't wash by privates. I do, but now all I want is to rip away my pants and scratch.

"Got to ask you something," I say when I see Karl-Heinz return from the outhouse.

He nods and follows me around the barn to the back of the inn. "I've got a terrible itch, you know, down there." I point a forefinger between my legs. "You think I've got lice?"

Karl-Heinz rubs his belly, then his crotch. "I've got a terrible itch on my stomach *and* below. It's all red and hot."

"Don't lice live in hair?"

"They can, maybe…" Karl-Heinz stares at my pants. "*That* hair."

I feel my cheeks warm again. Over the past year I've grown quite a jungle down there. "Possible." I look at Karl-Heinz who's scratching again. "You don't have hair on your belly though."

"Not really."

"Can I look?" This time Karl-Heinz blushes. Maybe he's embarrassed because he likes boys? "Come on, it's nothing that private. We go swimming together after all."

Karl-Heinz nods and pulls up his shirt, which has seen better days. The collar is frayed, and there is a tear in the elbow.

He didn't lie. From his sternum down to his waist, his belly glows an angry red. There are bloody spots where he's scratched too hard. I frown, wondering if my testicles look like that. "I don't see any lice, just little brown lines on the skin."

Karl-Heinz shoves his shirt back in his pants. "We've got to ask someone. I can't concentrate."

The only person we feel comfortable with is Herr Sommer. We find him in the garden, awkwardly balancing on one leg while pulling weeds and prepping the soil for winter.

"Herr Sommer," I call, my mouth dry as a sack of hay, "we need to ask you something."

The old man painfully straightens and holds his lower back. "I'm getting to old for this," he chuckles.

When we don't return his laugh, he gets serious in an instant. "I understand you've got a private matter to discuss."

How right he is. "You see," I start, looking at anything except for the old man's face, "I...we have a problem."

"An itch, to be exact," Karl-Heinz jumps in. He points at my crotch and his belly.

"It's nasty," I add.

Sommer looks at us. "Can you show me?"

"Eh," I say, "maybe Karl-Heinz can." I'm not going to drop my pants in the middle of the garden.

With a sigh, Karl-Heinz yanks up his shirt again. In the sunlight of the afternoon, the redness is much worse. Herr Sommer tries to appear calm, but I can tell he's worried. He huffs a bit and then clears his throat.

"We've got to fetch the doctor. This is likely scabies. Saw it in the Great War. Many soldiers had it, miserable buggers."

"What should we do, I mean, we wash..." I start.

"I bet the refugees brought them," Herr Sommer says pensively. "I shall send my niece." He sighs again. "If I'm right, we will have to clear the entire inn. Wash everything. Likely you aren't the only ones. Just a bit braver, maybe." There's the chuckle again. He pats me on the back. "I'm glad you told me. Waiting will make things worse...much worse."

By evening, the entire inn is on its feet. All of us are scheduled to see the doctor. Meanwhile, every bed sheet, comforter, blanket, pillow and towel has to be washed. So far, we've got nine boys with infections and there are still sixteen to go.

Karl-Heinz and I receive sulphur cream. We have to wash ourselves really well, apply the cream, and put on clean underwear. All our clothes have to be washed too because the tiny spiders infest everything. The doctor, an old man in his seventies, said they bury into the skin and lay eggs. Just the thought of some bug using my penis as a sleeping spot makes me queasy. The doctor said they can spread too. Karl-Heinz is really worried he'll have his balls infected and scrubs himself like crazy. For once, we're not mortified getting naked. The idea of the scabies taking over is way scarier.

CHAPTER SIXTEEN

Hilda

Four weeks have passed, four of the happiest weeks I've known since leaving Mama. Annie makes us work hard, but we don't mind. We all share in the cooking and cleaning. We eat breakfast together, a beautiful spread of bread, homemade quark, jam, cheese and on Sundays an egg.

The old man is no longer unfriendly. He asks us questions and often shakes his head when we tell him about the cloister and the Abbess.

Sometimes, I notice a shadow crossing Annie's face. It's as if her entire being becomes engulfed in some fog, something dreary and dark. She typically shakes it off quickly and I don't have the nerve to ask her.

The fall is glorious, but the news is more and more gloomy. We're listening to the radio every night—Annie and her father own a *Volksempfänger*—which sits on the kitchen cupboard. I know I should go home, demand a quick transport from the Mayor, but I can't bring myself to asking about that either. On the one hand, I want to go. Must go. See Mama and make sure she's safe. On the other hand, I dread the journey. And what if…

The Mayor has been working with the Hitler Youth and the regional KLV office to organize another transport. But it's difficult because they're concentrating on bringing back kids from the east. The Russians are taking back Romania, Tschechoslowakia and

Poland. They are heading west…toward Germany. Hardly any train tracks are intact, so the mayor is hesitant to be insistent with the KLV office. Privately, I think he sort of likes the girls here in the village even if feeding us must be a burden.

The worst part is that I haven't heard anything from Mama. As soon as we settled, I wrote a letter and mailed it with the help of Annie. I've heard nothing since, so I don't know if the letter arrived and if it did, if Mama can't write for some reason. During the day I'm doing all right, being busy and all, but at night, I lie awake and wonder. Worry is more like it. The uncertainty is terrible. Last night, Annie's father said the British came in the middle of the night and bombed *Darmstadt*. More than 10,000 civilians died, and the city burned for days. I've overhead him listen to enemy radio, likely the BBC. Neither of us talk about how he knows the latest developments when there's no newspaper available.

"I heard from the Mayor," Annie says, carrying a basket of potatoes into the kitchen. She's not exactly smiling, not really. Biene, Ursel and I are peeling and cutting apples for applesauce. It's amazing what I can do with a knife these days. "He's found a transport. We have to get you to Frankfurt. From there they'll have a chartered train all the way to Solingen. The mayor is borrowing three busses from neighboring communities."

"Really?" Biene carefully puts down the knife. "I thought we didn't have to go yet."

Annie piles the potatoes in the middle of the table and looks at us, one at a time.

"I'm sorry, girls, I sure have enjoyed having you. But we can't put any more burdens on the village. Food is getting scarcer, and we've got to think about winter."

"We're really grateful," Ursel cries, no longer the tough girl with attitude.

I'm not sure I can talk at all, thinking about setting foot on another train. At last I muster the energy, my voice strange in my ears. "When will we leave?"

"The day after tomorrow." Annie slumps down next to us and begins peeling potatoes. "Biene and Ursel, why don't you clear the table? Remember the compost? Hilda can help me finish the potatoes. We'll have green beans and a bit of bacon sauce." She throws me a glance that I can't read. "If we have time we'll make an apple pie, right Hilda?"

I nod numbly.

When the other two girls have left, Annie puts down her paring knife and leans forward. "I know you don't want to leave."

"It's just…"

"We've got to face what's coming," she says. "No matter how bad the news may be, it's better than the uncertainty. Uncertainty eats at us, hollows us out from the inside."

"I'm afraid of what I'll find," I cry. All of a sudden tears burst. "What if…"

Annie pats my hand. "I know. But isn't it better knowing than wondering? Isn't guessing much worse?"

I nod. "It's…I feel safe here."

"It's an illusion," Annie says. Now she has tears in her eyes. "It's all an illusion. We aren't safe here or anywhere. Not as long as this war continues."

"Maybe the Führer will win soon," I say.

"Nonsense," Annie shouts. All of a sudden she's red in the face, her eyes blazing. "That insane fool uses Germans for his sick war machine. He won't stop until all of us are gone." She grips my wrist and shakes it. "Wake up, Hilda, you've been living in a dream."

"Why do you say that?"

"Because it's true." Tears now drip from Annie's cheeks, but the fury in her voice is unmistaken. "My fiancée has been missing for more than two years." She angrily wipes her face. "I know he's dead even if they don't send me anything."

"My father is gone too." It's out before I can check myself. I haven't talked about my father in years.

"Oh no," Annie cries.

"It's not the war…he left us when I was nine." My voice has shriveled to a whisper. "I don't know where he is…if he's alive." Why do I care? He may as well be dead. The old helplessness rears its head as I remember the moment when I came upon my father in the bedroom packing his suitcase. I want to go there now and ask him why he is going. Why he sees no way to work things out with us.

Annie jumps up and hugs me to her. "I'm so sorry, I didn't mean…I"

I soak in the warmth from this woman who has been like a mother to me—in a way better because she is also my friend. So, we stand, two women whose lives have been changed beyond recognition.

At last she pats my head. "The war is lost, my dear. It's just a matter of time, never mind what Goebbels and Göring claim."

I sit back down as Annie gets busy at the stove. How can a woman know so much while we kids run around blindly? They kept us in the dark, locked away in some cloister while the country was being bombed to shreds.

All of a sudden, I want to go. I can't wait anymore. I must check on Mama, see if she has news about Paul…and Peter.

To make our last days special, Annie fixes one of her beloved geese. I'd never seen an animal being killed, but Annie just took an axe, grabbed the bird and chopped off its head. The kitchen turned into a stinking, feathery mess as we took turns plucking. But oh, the aroma that followed made it all worth it. The air smelled of roasted meat and we ate until the juice ran down our chins.

Peter

Karl-Heinz and I have snuck away. After the scabies incident— thankfully they have vacated the inn and us—we don't have much to do in the afternoons. We sit on a boulder next to a tiny creek we discovered last week, nothing large enough to hold fish, but pretty and peaceful. Sun dapples the forest floor sprinkled with colorful leaves, but there is sharpness in the air, a warning that winter is coming—the second winter away.

As if he can read my mind, Karl-Heinz asks, "You think we'll ever go home?"

I close my eyes against the brightness. "Hope so. They surely can't keep us away forever."

"And if the Führer loses the war? What will happen to us then?"

What will happen to our families stuck in the bomb zones? What about Mother and Walter?

Karl-Heinz continues. "You heard the refugees. We're much closer to Russia than we were in Solingen." He bangs his stick on the rock. Bits of bark fly around like harmless shrapnel. "I think these Russian soldiers are cruel. I overheard one of the men saying they rape girls and women."

"We could leave," I say. It sounds reasonable, a matter of planning and collecting supplies. I wonder if Maria was one of those women.

"Go home on foot?"

"Maybe we can catch a train or hitchhike on trucks."

"We should've joined the refugees." Karl-Heinz hurls his stick into the creek where it lands with a soft plop.

"Too slow. You heard them. They're going to Berlin, not the place we want to go."

"We'd get in big trouble."

Silence settles between us. It's a comfortable quiet only two old friends can enjoy.

"How is Christian?" I ask after a while.

"Don't know. There hasn't been mail."

Do I imagine it or is there pain in Karl-Heinz's voice. "Weren't you close?"

"He is my friend."

"Like me?"

"Like you."

"I thought you two had something else going on." It's out before I've got time to think.

Karl-Heinz shifts on his bottom as if he can't sit still any longer. "Something else?"

"I thought, you know…" My ears suddenly burn and I wish I could take back my words. "You never had a girlfriend and I thought…you—"

"*You* never had a girlfriend. Unless something happened with Hilda."

"What should've happened?"

Karl-Heinz makes a smooching sound. "You two seemed pretty close."

My cheeks are going up in flames as Hilda's earnest expression floats into my vision. Strangely, at this moment I see her clearly, the way she used to set me straight, arms crossed and eyes flashing, her lithe figure, the hips that were just beginning to round out, the small breasts.

My favorite part are her lips, sort of light pink, a bit curvy, and when she smiles with that odd lift on the left—kind of sweet and ironic at the same time. "An old friend," I lie.

"I think she really likes you."

"Two years ago maybe." My thoughts travel to our last meetings when I told her about going away. How excited I'd been to leave. What a fool I'd been. Last month, I celebrated my seventeenth birthday. She's sixteen now, wherever she is.

"I bet she still loves you."

Like you love Christian, I want to say, but the words don't leave my mouth. There're things that can't be mentioned. It's dangerous. Zeibler called men who loved other men degenerates. He said they'd go away for good…into labor camps, or maybe they'd be shot.

Karl-Heinz has retrieved his stick and sharpens the tip on the rock. "You think there's only one person meant for each of us?"

"Like a soul mate?"

"Yes."

"Hard to say. Maybe."

"What if that one person dies?" Karl-Heinz's voice is soft. "Then you'll have to settle for another or never know happiness?"

"With that many people on earth, you'd think there would be more than one."

"What if it's not?"

Hilda's face returns. Could she be the one for me? I've never known anybody like her. We used to talk about everything for hours. It was easy and fun. I smile.

Karl-Heinz abruptly straightens "You think it's funny?"

"Not that, I was just thinking…"

"About Hilda."

I look at him, the answer in my expression. Karl-Heinz nods quietly and holds out an arm. "We better head back before it gets dark. Boot will start the alarm."

I can't help but think how it would feel to trek hundreds of kilometers when we're not even comfortable staying out after dark.

And yet, the draw of home is so strong, it's like a rubber band tugging at my heart.

CHAPTER SEVENTEEN

Hilda

The train stops at the main station in Solingen. A strange feeling comes over me, sort of weepy and happy at the same time.

We've been on the road for an entire day, but in the end, all went quickly. I even have a bit of bread left that Annie sent along.

As Biene takes off down the street, I head toward our home near *Bülowplatz*. My steps speed up, then slow down as if my body can't decide whether to hurry or delay the inevitable. Annie's voice reverberates through my head. *Uncertainty is worse than knowing.*

I circle the roundabout toward *Schlicken*. My eyes are on the fall leaves, then slide past them. Heart hammering, my palms damp, I scan the street. It's all there, all the houses I know so well. When did they shrink? The streets too.

I run the last steps up to my house and ring the bell. Dusk is setting, but there are no streetlights. For years we've had to hide ourselves with obscuring blinds.

The door opens and there is Mama. Smaller and a bit withered, she searches the dark.

"Mama," is all I get out.

"Hilda? Oh, my god, you're here," Mama cries. Then we stand there in each other's arms. I'd forgotten Mama's scent, a mix of lavender she grows on the window ledge and something sweet, I could never define. In that instant it comes all back and her embrace, warm and familiar, dislodges those unshed tears I've kept inside me.

I am home.

After a while we lean back to look at each other. Mama touches my cheek. "You're so tall. I worried…oh, come in."

She takes me by the hand, the way she used to when I was a little girl. All the anger and frustration about her have vanished.

The kitchen is sparser than I remember. After Annie's messy assemblage of dishes, storage containers, flowers and bowls, it looks Spartan. A lone white porcelain bowl and a spoon sit in the drying rack. There are no food smells, no dinner pots.

Mama leads me to the table and rubs my shoulders. "You look tired."

I try a smile. If anyone looks tired, it's Mama. The lines on her temples and around her mouth have deepened, gray strands have joined her once honey blond hair. She looks old as if she's aged ten years since I left.

"Are you hungry?" she says. "You must be hungry…and thirsty." Without waiting for an answer, she runs to the cupboard and fusses through her supplies.

"I'm fine, Mama, I ate on the train."

I get up to fill a cup of water. "I can do it myself." All of a sudden I feel old, older than my mother who is so small, even frail.

"Why don't we sit?" I point at the couch, where a piece of knitting lies forgotten.

"Yes, yes, tell me what happened?"

As I tell her my story…our story, Tilly's and Biene's story, Karin's and Fräulein Heinrich's, I watch my mother. Her eyes are large and her lips form an o. Once in a while she claps a hand over her mouth or shakes her head.

"But what about you?" I say after a while. "What…" I want to ask about Paul and Peter, but the words won't come.

She pats my hand. "You didn't get my letters. It's just terrible what's been happening to our postal service. We used to always send things and now—"

"Mama, tell me." My mother looks at me, a bit disoriented and I wonder if she's all right.

"Yes, of course. Your brother…Paul is in a field hospital."

The old shakiness is back and I'm glad I'm sitting. "What happened? Is it bad? Tell me!"

"I don't know exactly. I received a letter from the war office that he's in France. I'm just hoping…" Tears trickle down Mama's cheeks.

"I'm just so glad you're safe. I couldn't bear the thought…"

The uncertainty…there it was again.

"What about…Peter?"

Our eyes meet, and I know there hasn't been any news. Mama just shakes her head. I slide onto the sofa and wrap an arm around my mother. We sit like that for a while. Somewhere in the corner, the mantle clock ticks. I'd forgotten about the sound, but it is part of home, part of my life. Above us, muffled voices argue.

After a while, Mama straightens. "I will go to bed." She turns at the door. "Your bed is made…I'm just so glad." She disappears into her room and closes the door.

I remain on the sofa. I can't move, am frozen in place. My palm rubs the thinning green velvet, fuzzy in some areas, shiny in others. I thought all I wanted was to go home and make sure that Mama was safe. Now I realize I'm right back where I started a year and a half ago—waiting. The moment of happiness was fleeting like a falling star, and one need has replaced the next.

Being far from home distracted me from many things, especially Paul and Peter. At last I get up to wash and climb into bed. My comforter is soft and familiar, but it takes a long time before I fall asleep.

Peter

Another refugee trek has come and gone. Boot still teaches, but none of us are paying attention. He scolds and he rants, but his insults roll down our backs. This isn't like school. We're not learning much of anything, just biding our time, waiting…

For what, is the question? Waiting for the Führer to win the war, waiting for the country to return to normal? How could it? We don't have a radio any longer, but one of the men from the last refuge group whispered of increased Allied attacks on German towns. Still, he was determined to head that direction. He was going to Dresden to find his sister.

There is also the matter of the draft, Boots ominous words that we may become soldiers. Karl-Heinz and I talked about it, neither of us interested in facing the front and shooting at people.

Food has steadily deteriorated. If it weren't for potatoes, we'd starve. We've been helping surrounding farmers with their crops, collecting the last hay, prepping fields for winter, planting cabbage, and, yes, you guessed it, harvesting potatoes. I'm still thin, but I've grown again—my ankles are showing—and my chest and shoulders are so wide, I had to find new shirts and sweaters. Luckily, the inn's owner, Herr Sommer, had a few leftover pieces. We've repurposed our Hitler Youth uniforms to rags. Buying things in the village is impossible. The stores are empty except for the crops grown in the area.

At least Boot lets us go in the afternoons. We roam the countryside, a mix of fields and forests, pretty and somewhat rugged. The air carries the salt of the East Sea, no more than ten kilometers north of here.

"We could look for mushrooms," Dieter says. His crooked nose seems sharper and larger in his bony face. All of us are bony and look like caricatures of ourselves.

"You know what the good ones look like?" Karl-Heinz asks.

Dieter shrugs. "How hard could it be?"

"I know a lot of edible ones," I say. "I'll get supplies." Happy to have something to do, I collect baskets from the kitchen. I try to remember what I read about gills, caps, rings and color combinations.

We hike up a dusty path through winterized fields. Some are wild now because nobody has worked them. A watery sun that doesn't warm shines above. In the flatness of the land the wind is fierce, bending the dried corn stalks along the edges sideways. It is a first glimpse at winter, and I realize I'm not prepared. My coat from last year is way too small and my shoes, the only ones that fit, have thin soles. The right heel is loose and I dread what's coming: a second winter away from home and cut off from news. The sense of isolation mirrors in the desolate landscape, and I'm all of a sudden in a stinking rotten mood.

Karl-Heinz and Dieter haven't noticed. They're talking about cars, an interest they share. I couldn't care less about stupid cars. All I want is my family.

Ahead, the path loses itself in a forest of oaks, pines and evergreens. Despite the gloomy appearance, it's a welcome sight because the incessant wind finally stops.

"That looks like a good spot," Karl-Heinz says.

Treetops sway and whisper above as we spread out.

"Call out, if you see some," Dieter says, turning off the path to the right. I head left toward a thick stand of beech trees. Their trunks are so big, it'd take three people to wrap their arms around. And there, right in the middle, the ground glows orange: mushrooms with wide tops and fluting stems—chanterelles.

"Found some," I yell. I pick and pick, and within minutes my basket is half full. Some mushrooms are as large as coffee saucers and quite meaty. I rush on, nose down like a blood hound.

Before the war, Father took me mushroom hunting. I hadn't been very interested and didn't pay attention, wanting to spend time with my friends. My insides contract as I suck in air. What a fool I'd been, thinking I could always spend time with my father later. He's been gone for such a long time, I can't remember his voice, not even his face. Only in my dreams, he appears lifelike and clear, but when I awake, everything fogs and his features dim.

I find more chanterelles and soon my basket is full. So full, in fact, that the top ones try to roll off. I bend down constantly to pick them back up.

When I straighten, I realize I don't know where I've come from. There is no path, just moss and roots and broken tree limbs.

"Hello," I yell. "Karl-Heinz?"

Nothing except rustling leaves and murmurs in the treetops. The air is rich with the aroma of earth and resin. It's beautiful, yet I feel the first tendrils of dread.

"Dieter?" I yell at the top of my lungs. "Where are you?"

Nothing. I swallow because my throat is dry. I'm thirsty, more like parched.

I scan the ground around me for signs of footsteps. But the moss is springy and the forest floor is littered with branches. I decide to walk in a circle by picking out one tree and rotating around it. Still, I see nothing except one spot where I've removed the chanterelles. Picking this new spot, I do circles again. Wider and wider I go. Still, I see no other signs of life, just endless trunks and roots and moss. How big is this damn forest? How long have I been walking?

Every time I stop I yell, but every time there is no answer. It's as if the trees swallow my voice.

In my head, I comb through scenarios. Spending the night, searching for water and something to eat, making a fire. Wait no fire—I don't have matches or a lighter. I see myself wandering for days, finally crawling and then lying still.

In my panic, I begin to walk faster. It's hard—the basket is wide and bulky, heavy with mushrooms. My thoughts are getting jumpy. What time is it? What will I do when it gets dark? What will Karl-Heinz and Dieter do? Are they lost too, or will they get help? I stumble across a huge root and smack to the ground, the basket tumbling from my hand. Dirt grinds into my palms and knees as I scramble upward, collect the mushrooms a second time, hurry onward.

When I turn right, I see movement ahead. No more than a shadow, likely imagined.

"Karl-Heinz?"

Nothing. I'm starting to hallucinate. The panic spreads to my bones like a wild animal. *Come on, pull yourself together.* I slow down a bit, pick my steps more carefully. No need to twist an ankle.

There, the shadow moves between the trunks. Ahead, the forest is darker, evergreens as tall as houses. I'm going mad. But then I see the movement again. Sliding in-between trees, trying to hide, yet moving slowly.

"Karl-Heinz?" I cry again. The shadow doesn't answer, just slips away to the right.

"Hey, can you help me?" I yell louder. "I'm lost. Please."

When there is no answer, I slow down further and pick my steps across decaying trunks that cross my path like oversized toothpicks. At last, I sink on a boulder and rest. I'm sweaty despite the cool air. Dusk is falling, the sun long gone. I wouldn't see it anyway down here.

I swallow and run my tongue through my mouth. Everything is dry, my throat a bit sore. I need water. Badly.

The panic I felt earlier returns full-blown. I'm truly lost and may have to spend the night. I have nothing to drink and no food. My friends don't know where I am—

"You have something to eat?"

The voice appears disembodied, almost dreamlike. *To your right,* my brain screams. I jump off the rock, twisting my head this way and that. Not five meters away stands a man, his face blackish gray, the color of his eyes washed-out in the gloom.

"I don't have anything," I manage, thinking about the man attacking. "I only have mushrooms." I lift the basket higher. The man's gaze is greedy as he scans the basket and me.

He nods, his shoulders slumping forward again. Even in the approaching darkness I notice how thin he is in his uniform. Wait a minute.

That's when it dawns on me that this man is a defecting German soldier. He's torn the insignia from his jacket, but the colors and style are unmistaken. "You're hiding." It's not a question.

The man nods and turns away. "Sorry to have bothered you."

My mind twists between taking off in the other direction and stopping the man. "Wait."

The soldier slowly turns. His uniform is filthy and hangs loosely from his shoulders. Even from here I can tell he's starving, his cheekbones sharp.

"Do you know the way to the path? I got lost and my friends…"

The man nods slowly, carefully. "You can't tell anyone if I help you."

"Promise."

He waves toward our left. "This way. I'll show you."

I follow in his footsteps and his stench. I could close my eyes and track him with my nose, it'd be just as clear.

"Where is your gun?" I ask.

"Traded it."

"Where did you come from?"

"Courland. Russians were closing in. I got out just in time."

"The Führer—"

The man abruptly turns. "The war is lost, lad. All of us are lost." Defeat swings in his voice, maybe shame as he turns down his gaze. "We had hardly enough to eat, barely any ammunition."

"But they told us the war would be over soon," I say. Somehow, my gut knows the man speaks the truth. It fits with everything else I've heard, the increasing bombs on Germany, the disruption of mail and transportation—Thomas Mann's soul crunching words on the BBC.

The man spits. "It'll be over soon enough. When we're all dead."

"Where are you going?"

"Bremen."

I cringe as I remember Herr Sommer telling us about the bombardment of Bremen in August.

"What?" The man has picked up on my reaction, his expression lurking like an animal watching his prey.

"N…nothing."

In a flash, the man is by my side, gripping my wrist. This close the stench is overwhelming. I notice that he wears a bandage around his left hand, the formerly white gauze black with filth. "You're lying."

I look into the man's eyes. They are brownish green like the moss beneath our feet—like my own. Fear shows in them, but also determination.

"So…sorry," I stutter. "You're hurting me." The man's grip loosens. "I heard they bombed Bremen in August."

"When?"

I rack my brain, trying to remember when I heard about it. "Around the 18th or 19th I believe."

The man lets go and shrinks in front of me. "I shouldn't be surprised." When he looks up there are tears in his eyes. "I'm sorry. I didn't mean to hurt you. It's just this damn war makes us all animals."

I nod. At least they haven't bombed Solingen. Immediately, I feel ashamed. The man may have lost his family. He fought for us, likely for years.

"It's getting dark," the soldier says. "We better hurry."

We continue our path much longer than I expect. In my mind I worry about the man leading me into a trap.

"There's the trail," he says after a while. It's just about dark now, but there is some light above from a half moon. "Remember what I said. Not a word."

"I'm sorry about…Bremen."

The man waves a dismissive arm, only the whites of his eyes visible beneath the trees.

I head onto the trail. "Karl-Heinz…Dieter?"

"*Mensch*, I thought you dissolved into thin air."

Hearing Karl-Heinz's voice makes me want to shout with happiness. I recognize two shadows fifty yards ahead. "We've been waiting for ages," Dieter says. I can hear the pout in his voice. "We're starving, will miss dinner for sure."

"Thanks to you, we'll get in trouble," Karl-Heinz scolds.

"Thanks for waiting," I manage. Remembering my basket, I ask, "Did you find any mushrooms?"

"Bunches," both say.

"Where were you anyway?" Karl-Heinz asks after a while. The path back to the inn seems to grow longer by the minute.

The dirty soldier's face appears in my vision. "Got lost." I wonder what he will do. By the looks of it, he's been living in the wild for months. Hard to imagine what he's going through. If anybody of importance finds him, he'll be shot.

"Next time…if there is a next time, we stay together," Dieter says.

Relief fills my heart when the lights of the inn appear in the distance.

CHAPTER EIGHTEEN

Hilda

I spend most days scrounging. We're supposed to get additional ration coupons for me now, but the administration is slow and so far, we're living from Mama's. It's not enough, not by a long shot, and having been gone a year, I see the difference and the shortages.

Mama receives five pounds of bread, a half-pound of meat and 218 grams of fat per month. How did the government determine that it had to be 218 grams and not 221 grams? If I weren't so hungry all the time, I'd laugh. But there is nothing to laugh about because we're heading into another winter with no coals or briketts.

Worrying about how we're going to heat the apartment, I head for the woods. It's less than a ten-minute walk, though I hardly recognize it. All the small trees have been cut. Beneath the rest, the ground is clean as if it were swept with a giant broom. There are no twigs or bark, no pinecones, acorns or beechnuts. Anything that can be burned or eaten has been picked clean. I continue hiking, and it looks the same everywhere I go. After three hours roaming the hills I turn back with an armful of sticks only suitable for fire starter. I will have to go much farther and most of all, I'll need tools…and luck.

In the afternoon I decide to explore the train station. Rumor has it that coal transports pass through and that people climb on top to fill their bags.

I go twice more and so far no transport has come through. I talk to a couple of boys about my age who had the same idea. They say it's hit or miss and that you've got to be patient and that it's dangerous. Thing is, I'm not patient and I'm past caring about danger. We need to prepare for the winter, and we're not ready.

The third evening I'm in luck. The boys are there as well as a dozen more women and older men. How did they know to show up today? A coal train is rolling past slowly. In the dusk everything appears black, the carriages impossibly high. The two boys climb on as soon as the wagons have cleared the station. I walk along the uneven embankment, trying not to twist my ankle while looking at the rust-colored sides and the vertical struts. The only place to climb on is in back or front where there is some kind of ladder. But that means I've got to jump in-between the rolling wagons with their iron wheels that are ready to cut me in half.

In the fading light, the boys are filling their bags. Some of the women have climbed onto a different carriage, all of them busy and intent on their task.

Somewhere, a whistle blows. The boys cry something from their lofty heights, but I shake my head. The wheels' screeching fills my ears. I just can't do it.

One of the boys climbs down part way and waves at me. "Quick, give me your bag."

I rush near and hand it to him. "Thanks."

But the boy is already on his way up. Behind me another whistle blows. The conductor or someone has noticed us stealing.

I keep walking along, hurrying now because the train is gathering speed. In the falling darkness it becomes almost impossible to see the ground. Above me the boys are gesturing. Then a bag smacks down next to me. I quickly pick it up. It's heavy now and smells like the coal cellar.

Moments later, the two boys are by my side as more whistles trill behind us. Cries ring out. They've got somebody.

"Come quick," one of the boys says. They turn on their heels and disappear into the bushes. I try my best to keep up, but they're much faster.

They wait for me in an empty lot near *Werwolf*. "You've got to hurry up," one of the boys says. In the blacked-out city, I can hardly make out his features. All I know is that he is tall and skinny as a fencepost.

"Thank you," I say, catching my breath. "It's my first time."

"We better go," one of them says. "See you around."

At home, I store the coal in the kitchen. It's too risky to put it in the cellar. Any neighbor could break the lock and steal them.

And so begins my weekly trek to the train station. The third time I finally get up my nerve and climb on top. There are briketts, large and bulky, and my bag fills quickly. The last time we could buy briketts was two years ago. Who knows where these wagons are heading.

During the day while Mama is at work, I roam around the woods behind *Eichenstraße* to collect sticks and cut down wood. It's slow, frustrating work, but late October the kitchen is well stocked. Needless to say there is no school. I met Biene a few times, but she is busy like me, organizing things for their home. She has a six-year old brother, Theo, who is kind of challenged and needs constant supervision, so Biene's mother stays home all the time.

The other problem is food. There isn't enough. I finally received my ration cards, but I crave fruits and vegetables, jam and cheese. Our apartment building doesn't have any garden and people who own houses with gardens keep them locked tightly. Everyone is wary.

That's what the need to survive will do to humans. They no longer think as a community or as neighbors, maybe not even as families. Real hunger makes you think about yourself and yourself only as your thoughts circle tighter and tighter around *one* thing: the next meal.

You can't blame them either. It is truly everyman for himself. I no longer have illusions about a great Germany. We are a doomed people who are paying for Hitler's ambition. Braunschweig and Bonn have burned. By now most men are somewhere on the front. There are so many, it is impossible to keep track. And not only men, but boys. Hitler has called them to join the *Volkssturm,* the people's storm. These *men* are only seventeen, barely older than Peter.

Peter. There isn't a day when I don't think about him—still. I went to visit Frau Breuer, who has aged like my mother, maybe worse. Peter and his younger brother, Walter, have gone into the KLV, and Frau Breuer's husband is some place in the Northeast.

Yes, we women and girls are left to fend for ourselves, keep the unraveled parts of our families together. Many women have to work in factories now because there aren't enough men to keep things going.

If I'm honest, I want to just lie down and sleep. And forget. But there is no such thing because every morning when I wake up, my stomach reminds me that I'm still around and that I will have to fight to keep going.

The other day I came across a field of potatoes. Of course, it was well protected, a man with a rifle walking around it. I will ask Biene to go with me. Together, it will work, one of us distracting the man, the other digging up potatoes.

I managed to trade a few carrots and three onions against a pile of firewood. Not sure that it's a good idea because collecting the wood takes at least as much if not more energy than eating carrots. It's hard to know what works and what doesn't. Every day feels like I have to climb a mountain with no gear, ready to free-fall off some cliff.

When the doorbell rings, I'm in the middle of devising a plan on how to distract the potato farmer. It's true, my breasts have come in, tiny ones compared to Biene's. But then her mother is really busty and Biene has likely inherited her figure.

Biene must be early, but then she often lives free of time. It's one thing I really love about her because I'm constantly checking and sorting and organizing. Biene sometimes teases me.

I rip open the door with the words, "You'll be the one to show your boobs."

"What?"

A man towers in the door and I quickly step back in shock.

"Sorry, I thought…"

A chuckle follows. It's deep and kind of happy, so I can't help myself but smile. That's when I recognize the figure in the door. "Paul!" I fly into his arms, something I wouldn't have done a year and a half ago.

"Ouch, easy, little girl." Paul's voice is so deep, I wouldn't have recognized it except for its tone. "Are you going to invite me in?"

"This is your home, you don't need an invitation," I jest. I always loved our back and forth squabbles and we fall back into the pattern without effort.

I step aside and let him pass. He smells of sweat and dust and…what? I'm not sure except that it's a smell I don't like— something alien and sick.

It's now that I notice the cane and the limp. He eases himself into the wooden chair, his seat at the kitchen table, a small smile on his lips. "It's good to be home."

I rush to his side and take in his face. He's looking pale, kind of washed-out like Annie's father, and there's something dead in his eyes. I've always loved his eyes, sort of blue or gray depending on the light. Lines run along his mouth, bitter creases I don't recognize.

"Can a man get a glass of water?" he says at last.

I clear my throat and get busy.

"I'm so happy you're home," I say, handing him the water. I take a glass too, but forget to drink. Instead, I watch my brother, who swallows greedily and wipes his mouth with a grungy sleeve. The skin of his hands is grayish black with filth. He reminds me of our father, the forehead equally square, the small ears too fine for a man's head. There's white on his temples like old man's hair.

He looks at me and nods. "I didn't think I'd ever see you again. Mama wrote that you went away south."

"A cloister near Nürnberg."

"You look thin." He shifts his weight and I see pain in his features.

"What is it? You're hurt. What happened to you? I was so worried. And when Mama told me you were in some field hospital I thought..."

"I was going to die?" Paul nods. "I almost did, but then I thought I needed to see my ornery sister again." He smiles, but when he moves again there's more pain. "I'm not healed, though, my leg is pretty much busted. Caught a piece of a grenade." He sighs.

"Do you want me to fix you a bath?" It's a luxury to use so much gas and water, but I don't care.

"A real bath? I would love one."

Already I think ahead to dinner and how we're going to feed everybody. I'll need to pick up ration coupons for Paul. It's almost the weekend and tomorrow...

Paul's voice reaches through the mist. "...Mama coming home?"

"Oh, soon. She'll be so happy." I refill Paul's glass. "Don't go anywhere. I'll be right back."

He chuckles and straightens his legs. There are reddish-brown stains on his left—the bad one.

"Can it get wet?" I ask when I return. The water is running. I've used a bit of air soap to make bubbles, laid out a great fluffy towel.

"I'll leave it out," he says.

"Well, then you better get in there before the water freezes over."

"Yes, mam," he says straightening. He limps off and closes the door. I take a deep breath, imagining him peeling out of those pants with a shredded leg.

Better get busy, I scold. I open the cupboard to search for ideas: a small package of noodles, two onions, three carrots, bread, almost the entire fat ration for November, two cans of mystery meat and cornmeal. I decide to make soup with cornbread, my thoughts wandering to the latest announcement in the paper that our monthly soap and detergent rations of 250 gram will have to last until December 11. They only say the allotment amount *can't be maintained*, never a why or that it'll return to normal. By now, even an idiot knows quotas only shrink, not grow. How will we wash Paul's clothes?

"Goodness, I'm glad it's the weekend." Mama is rushing in like she always does. She's already taken off her coat, hat and scarf and embraces me. Ever since I returned, we hug when she comes home from work. "What are we cooking? Weren't you going with Biene this evening?"

Biene! I've totally forgotten our excursion. "Mama, there's something—"

"What's that smell in here?" Mama's nose moves like a rabbit's. She'd be perfect as a hunting dog. I swear she can distinguish anything and anybody by their odors.

"Mama, listen." I grip her flying hands. "Paul is back. He's here…safe." Now that I say it, tears flood. All that waiting and worrying is finally over.

At first, Mama doesn't seem to hear me, but when she sees my tears, she puts a hand on her mouth, her eyes wide. "Paul," she whispers.

"He's in the bath."

"He's home, he's here with us." Wonder floats from Mama's chest. "Oh, Hilda, he's back." Then she laughs and I laugh and we cry.

By the time Paul returns from the bath, we're standing side-by-side at the stove, cutting things for the soup.

"Mama." Paul's voice is soft now and very tired. I can hear the tears in it. Mama runs to him and buries into his chest. He's wearing his old blue and white-striped pajamas that are four inches too short. I make a mental note that we'll need to find him clothes.

Then I turn away to give them space as joy fills my heart.

Peter

Herr Sommer fixes sauces and stews with the chanterelles and is full of praise. At last I did something useful and had it not been for me getting lost, I would've thought it fun, a welcome distraction from the boredom of camp—even if Boot was pissed and grounded us to our rooms the next day and do kitchen duty.

I don't mind being busy, and Herr Sommer is nice. He showed us how to clean the mushrooms—Karl-Heinz and Dieter found maroons, too, and some white mushrooms that were poisonous.

The boys tell me how happy they are to eat something different for a change. That's when I get the idea.

"You want to go back?" Karl-Heinz says. "You were lost for hours."

"But the mushrooms are too good. Chances are the small ones are large now. If we stay together and pay attention, we will be safe."

"Dieter won't join us again."

I produce a grin. "You and I can go. I bet, Herr Sommer will love it."

"We can't tell Boot."

"No way."

And so it happens that we head back to the forest two days later. What I haven't told Karl-Heinz is that I'm hoping to see the soldier again. I also haven't mentioned that I'm carrying a pail of boiled potatoes with mushroom sauce from last night's dinner in my pack. I siphoned it away because we had leftovers for once.

This time we both carry water.

The entire way I'm contemplating to tell Karl-Heinz about the soldier and that I want to help him. In the end I don't. I promised the man.

When we arrive in the woods, I again turn left off the path. This time Karl-Heinz follows. "Don't think for a minute that I'll let you go alone."

I scan the trees—back and forth I look, but the man is nowhere in sight. Karl-Heinz calls out, delight in his voice. He's found a bunch of chanterelles. I slowly continue on, keeping the path and Karl-Heinz in my sight.

At the same time I'm watching for movement, a shadow slipping in-between the trees. There isn't one. I almost step onto a patch of mushrooms, quickly bend low and pick. It's going to be another feast at the inn. The boys will be pleased.

I'm just thinking about how Herr Sommer will smile when I bring him the basket, when I hear Karl-Heinz shout. It's more of a gurgle, a kind of a guttural sound.

"What is it?" I yell back. "Where are you?"

"Over here."

I've known Karl-Heinz since first grade, and I know something is wrong. I hug the basket to my chest and begin to run.

He's leaning against the trunk of an ancient oak, his basket by his feet, arms hanging uselessly.

"What?" I cry.

That's when I see it. Rather him. The soldier from two days ago sits with his back against a fallen tree. He tilts a bit to the right, the bandaged left hand in his lap. His eyes are closed and his breathing is loud and raspy. In the brighter light, he looks even worse than last time.

"It's a soldier," Karl-Heinz whispers. "Not sure he can hear us."

"Let's try to wake him."

"No!" The fear is back in Karl-Heinz's voice.

"I met him last time," I say, keeping my eyes on the still figure. "He helped me find a way out."

"You *met* him?"

"I promised not to tell." I get closer and bend low. A horrible stink emanates from the bandage.

"What are you doing? You're too close."

I catch Karl-Heinz's eyes. "He needs our help."

"But…he is a deserter."

"On his way *home* to Bremen."

"We should tell somebody."

"No."

"You're crazy."

Once again I look at my friend. "Imagine if it were your dad. Wouldn't you want somebody to help him?"

Karl-Heinz's eyes widen. Like almost all our fathers, his is in the war. "You're right," he says quietly.

"Help me. Let's see if we can wake him. I brought food."

We get on each side of the man and carefully pat his cheek and shoulder. "Hello, sir? Wake up."

The man mumbles something, his eyelids flutter, but he doesn't wake. He is obviously a lot sicker than I realized.

"Sir, we've got food and drink," I yell. "Will you please wake up? We can help you."

At last the man's eyes fly open. He moans and says something unintelligible, his gaze crazy and unfocused. I lean into his face.

"It's me, Peter, the boy you helped back to the trail."

Movement goes through the soldier's back. His eyes focus. "It's you," he whispers.

"Are you hungry?"

"Thirsty."

Without hesitation, I get my thermos, the one I borrowed from Herrn Sommer and hold it to his lips. "Drink slowly."

The man swallows and coughs a bit, then wipes his mouth with the back of his hand. "Thank you."

I rummage for the container with the potato stew and open the lid. As the air fills with the aroma of fragrant mushrooms and sauce, the man's eyes zero in on the meal. Spittle appears on his lips as he swallows repeatedly. I hand him a spoon.

"Remember to eat slowly or you may barf." I read in some book that the stomach shrinks and people get cramps and throw up from eating too quickly.

I hold the bowl while the man spoons food into his mouth. There's a bit of light in his eyes now, a bit of life. He doesn't stop until the bowl is empty, not even then, because he keeps scraping until there is not a trace of stew to be seen.

I wordlessly take it from him and stuff it into my bag.

"Who is your friend?" the man asks.

"Karl-Heinz. You can trust him."

The soldier nods, his lids already droopy again. "I'm so tired, I just want to sleep."

"How is your arm?" I point at the filthy bandage.

The man moans. "I think it's gone gangrene. Will lose it for sure."

Visions of the soldier dying alone out here in the woods appear in my mind. "Maybe we can help you."

"Peter, we can't," Karl-Heinz says. "It's too dangerous."

"Your friend is right," the soldier says. "I'm afraid, I'll not see Bremen again."

"You can't give up now," I cry. "You can make it."

The man's eyes open fully as he looks at me. "Son, I'm afraid I can't."

"Nonsense," I shout even louder. Anger fills my stomach, climbs to my throat to choke me. A long time ago I'd refused to help. My little brother, Walter, could've been seriously hurt by those boys who beat him, the scar on his brow a constant reminder of my failure. Back then I failed him.

I won't fail again.

The man grips my forearm with his good hand. "Thank you for the food. It was an amazing last meal." A tiny grin appears on the man's face, hard to make out among the stubble and grime.

"I'm not going to let you," I say stubbornly. "Karl-Heinz, help me get him up."

"You heard him," Karl-Heinz says. But I can tell he's unsure too—unsure how he can let a man die in front of him and do nothing about it.

I ignore him and put a hand beneath the man's right armpit. I don't know what we'll do, but if he continues sitting here, he *will* die. Which means we'll have to take him with us. My fingers slip off the man as I imagine Boot seeing the deserter. Boot is a man who follows orders. Even now. He'll run as fast as he can to alert the authorities. Then—

"Will you tell us your name?" Karl Heinz squats in front of the soldier who appears to be asleep again.

"Arthur," the man says. "No last names. Now let me rest."

Karl-Heinz straightens and leads me a few feet to the side. It's getting dark, the ground hard to see. "You sure about this?"

"How can we leave him? I don't think he'll make it another night."

"We can't take him to the inn. Boot will have a fit."

"Herr Sommer would help."

Karl-Heinz's voice grows quieter. "How would we get him back? It's a long way. We're getting in trouble as it is."

"Let's at least try and see if he can walk."

"You're as stubborn as a donkey."

I think of Ingo, the old woman's obstinate ass I once rode like a cowboy. Grinning, I slap Karl-Heinz on the shoulder. "All right then."

We return to Arthur, who has not moved. "We'll take you to the inn where we're living," I say. "We'll get help there."

The man's eyes open in slow motion. "They'll call the authorities, the SS. I'll be shot."

"We'll hide you." It's out before I've got time to think. We do have a barn, and Boot never goes there.

The tiniest spark shows in Arthur's expression.

Hope has returned.

CHAPTER NINETEEN

Hilda

The next day I head out with Biene while Paul drags himself to the ration office to ask for cards. He's using a cane and walks like an old man, which makes my heart squeeze with joy and sadness. He's barely twenty and an invalid. So far he's refused to show us his leg. I'm not sure I want to see it—I may simply faint.

He insists he's very lucky, and judging by the many obituaries in the newspaper with crosses above them, I know he's right. But I do worry about his future. He wanted to become a policeman. There's no way now—he'd get laughed out of the building.

"His leg may heal," Biene says when I tell her my thoughts. "People overcome many diseases and injuries."

"You haven't seen him walk," I say. "Reminds me of a wounded animal."

"He is." Biene puts an arm around my shoulder. We're heading toward the potato field and she wears a dress that's a bit tight and shows off her curves. "He's hurt in here too." She places a palm across her heart.

I remember the way she looked when she returned from meeting the SS officer at the cloister. She carried that same wounded expression. There are things in Paul's heart that cloud his eyes. "I wish he'd talk about—"

"Shh," Biene whispers. "We better split." Bending low, she smears a bit of mud on her bare shin and across her cheek. She gestures for me to go right along a fencerow, bordered by hazelnut bushes. Beyond lies the field. I tiptoe off while trying to keep Biene in my sights.

Across the way I make out the man with the rifle. He sits on a stump, chewing a piece of straw and looking bored.

Abruptly he turns his head and there comes Biene, limping and crying, "help me, somebody please."

The man, who isn't a man at all, rather a boy of maybe sixteen or seventeen, jumps off his stump and rushes toward Biene. "What happened?"

"I don't know," Biene says, her voice clearly audible across the field, "somebody attacked me. I fought him off with a log, but I twisted my ankle and now…" She produces a sobbing fit that would make *Marlene Dietrich* proud.

"Where does it hurt?" The man leans low to investigate Biene's leg. She's standing facing the field, so the man has his back to me.

I climb through the brush and begin to dig. The earth is loose and rich, the potatoes fat and round. I dig frantically, shoving the tubers into my linen sack, hoping that the row along the edge is not so easily detected. I stick the plants back into the dirt, so they don't show what I did underneath. My sack fills quickly all the while I'm listening to Biene.

"I'm so glad I met you," she says. "You're my savior."

"You'll need to clean your leg," he says. "But I can't get away, got to watch the field. Thieves come at night and rob us."

"That's terrible," Biene exclaims. "I'll be all right. Maybe you could massage my ankle for me. I have to go home, so my mother doesn't get worried."

Out of the corner of my eye, I see Biene plop down on the ground, holding up her leg. Sure enough the boy kneels down to lift her foot to his lap. I grin, moving along the row. One burlap sack is full, so I begin filling the second.

"How strong your hands are," Biene says at that moment. "The pain is almost gone."

"I've got to return to the field," the boy says. "If the farmer sees—"

"Just a little longer. I have to walk back a ways."

"Where did you come from?" Is there a hint of suspicion in the boy's question? The second bag is nearly full. Just a few more minutes.

"*Widdert*," Biene lies.

"But I mean…why did you walk through the woods all by yourself…in a dress?"

"I needed to get away," Biene says. "My brother returned from the war as a cripple. I can hardly look at him and I'm so sad…I…I…"

"I'm sorry," the boy says, all earnest again.

"I lost my way a bit when this man appeared out of nowhere."

Leave it be, Biene. He'll get suspicious again about you fighting off a grown man. Sure enough, the boy asks, "you fought off a man all by yourself?"

"He wasn't really all grown, more like a young man…like sixteen or so."

"Like me?"

The sacks are full and I scoot backwards through the bushes.

"You are really nice, your eyes…are kind." Biene's voice is soft. "I think I can walk again. Mother is upset, so I better return home to help her with my brother." She abruptly pulls away her leg, straightens and limps quickly down the path. "Thanks again," she yells over her shoulder while the boy stands there staring after her.

As I turn and heft the bags over my shoulders, the boy returns to his stump, rifle at the ready.

"I'm sure glad it was you and not me talking to that boy," I say when Biene catches up with me a few hundred meters down the path. She laughs, but then grows serious. "I didn't like it. Lying to that boy. He'll be punished because of me. He was kind of excited too, saw him peek up my dress, his cheeks all red. I think he had a boner. Could feel it."

"I feel sorry for him too, but what are we going to do? We need to eat."

Biene takes one of the sacks. "I hope his mother will go easy on him."

We part with a quick hug, each of us equally happy and guilty.

It's after lunch, and I'm starving when I return. Paul lies on the sofa, his good leg on the floor, the other on a pillow on the armrest.

I slurp down a bit of leftover soup with cornbread, when the sirens begin. It's a sound I loathe, a shrill up-and-down whine that goes bone-deep. Paul is worse. His jaw goes slack as he scrambles to sit up. Panic shows in his eyes, something I have never seen before.

In the early years of the war, when Paul was still home and the sirens roared, he was pretty calm, almost flippant. He'd take his time climbing downstairs to the basement, our designated bomb shelter.

This Paul is somebody else entirely. He's fidgeting and almost falls as he straightens to stand. I rush to hand him his cane, and together we head toward the staircase. Mama appears from the bathroom, drying her hands. That's when another sound joins the sirens: plane engines droning…lots of them. Not just engine sounds either, but the bone chilling whistles of falling bombs, a kind of high-pitch howl that means only one thing: death and destruction, fire and burning buildings. I'm back on the field running from the machine guns, but now my legs are heavy and lethargic. They move in slow motion.

"Hilda!" Mama's voice jerks me back. "Help me with Paul."

Paul is leaning against the doorframe with his eyes closed while Mama tugs at his elbow. These whistling sounds are so close, they fill my ears and melt my brain. Then comes the inevitable: bombs detonating. The ground begins to vibrate, glass panes burst. One, then another, and another…

I see Mama's mouth move, but can't hear anything. I take my brother's hand and begin pulling. He opens his eyes and carefully, slowly, we coax him out the apartment door into the hallway. The floor bucks, the walls groan. The stairs are at the back of the house. It might as well be a hundred yards. The world has turned into a single explosion, the booms melting together. Plaster shoots from walls and ceiling into our faces, behind us the front door caves. *Get him down there*, my mind repeats over and over.

We reach the stairs and I line up Paul along the handrail. I tell him to hang on to it, but I can't hear my own voice. The stairs vibrate beneath us as if they're on rails. Somehow, Paul moves down into the gloom. There aren't any lights here, and I worry about Paul falling and breaking something. His knuckles are clamping around the handrail, his mouth pinched closed as he slides down one step at a time.

Above, there is a momentary pause, a breather. But they are not done. As we step onto the landing below, the second wave begins. If the house is hit, we won't survive anyway. These heavy bombs are constructed to slice through roofs and fall all the way to the basements. In a second wave, they throw burn bombs made from phosphor. They ignite everything and burn so hot, they suck the oxygen from the air—people don't burn to death, they suffocate.

The air raid shelter is filled with neighbors. In the light of a single candle, they hardly look up, their eyes filled with terror. We squeeze between them, my arm on Paul's shoulder, Mama's on the other side. The air smells of sweat—stinky, fear-filled sweat. I hold up my head in my hand because it's too heavy to carry.

How long do we sit? Is it a minute, five or thirty? I don't know. All I know is that I'm all soft inside with fear, but that I'm even more worried about my brother, who's acting like an injured fawn among wolves. My strong and confident brother, who used to tease me when I was afraid of going to the ghostly basement, sits next to me as if he's already dead. Even though his eyes are wide open with this sort of crazy stare, his mind is clearly some place else.

Is that what they call shell-shock?

I come to when my neighbors start moving and mumbling. I can hear them speak. Outside, it is quiet, the silence so complete it feels as if I have cotton in my ears.

"So glad to see that Paul is home," Frau Simon says. She lives above us, alone. She softly smiles at Paul who ignores her. He's still staring.

"Paul?" Mama pats him on the shoulder. "Frau Simon is happy to see you."

At last he comes to, his focus returns and he nods at the old woman. "*Guten Tag.*"

Frau Simon seems a bit surprised, but doesn't say anything and follows the other neighbors around the corner. Mama and I take Paul between us and guide him upstairs. The front door is lying in the hall, the spots where the hinges used to be torn away. More wood splinters cover the floor and I try to brace myself before we enter our apartment.

The cupboard doors stand open, its contents spread across the linoleum. All windowpanes are gone, the frames torn apart. I look in wonder at the sofa, which is now leaning against the half wall to the kitchen. In fact, all our furniture has moved.

"Why don't you sit?" I say to Paul, but then I notice broken glass and wood splinters covering the sofa.

While we put Paul on a chair, Mama and I get busy cleaning tables, beds, chairs, and floors. Broken china lies next to Mama's cast-iron cooking pot. Drawers have emptied cutlery and spread it around. There's no water in the line, and the electricity is out too. I fetch a blanket for Paul and put on my coat because the chilly November wind has moved in. The formerly blue sky is covered in gray clouds. Not any clouds, but smoke. Things are burning around us, the smell sharp in my nose.

"We'll need material to cover the windows," I say. "I doubt anybody has glass panes left to sell."

"Only for a fortune." Mama is lining up her spice containers and picking pieces of wood out of our meager sugar ration. She's put on her tough woman look, the one she carries when she goes to work. I'm grateful because if she'd be crying, I'd lose it too. And right now we have no time for that.

When we finish, the rooms are as cold as the outside. Paul has gone to bed, wrapped up in his comforter. Was it just this morning that Biene and I collected potatoes? Biene!

"I'm going to see Biene," I say quietly and pull on my knitted wool cap and gloves. Evening comes early as fiery clouds billow above the city. I rush along the streets, trying to avoid broken roof tiles, stucco and glass. Of course, it's impossible. To my left, a hole opens where a house used to be. The crater is several meters deep and littered with rocks and smoldering wood. Many of the roofs have lost their clay tiles, and I don't see a single unbroken window.

I breathe a sigh of relief when I see that Biene's home still stands. Its windows are missing like ours, and there are curtains swaying back and forth in the wind. Biene hugs me to her. We don't speak—don't need to. It's all there in our hug: the hurt, the fear, the curious wonder of our survival.

"I need material for our windows."

Biene nods and pulls me with her. Biene's mother is in the basement, sorting through a mountain of wood scraps, linoleum, planks, tarpaper and shingles. By the looks of it, Biene's father kept everything from the time they build the house. Biene's little brother, Theo, sits on the floor, playing with a ragged stuffed bear. He neither looks up nor acknowledges us.

"Hilda is here," Biene announces. "She needs some things."

Biene's mother nods. "How many windows?"

I go through it in my head…kitchen and living room share one, bath, and three bedrooms. "Five."

"All right, that should be fine. Take what you need."

Biene's mother straightens her back and points at a workbench. "Biene, help Hilda with nails and a hammer. Load everything on that wheelbarrow we have in the shed and take it over there. Then you come right back and help me." She nods at me. "Thank you for getting potatoes."

I nod back. Somehow, our smiles have vanished with the bombs.

Saturday evening and Sunday morning, Mama and I attach coverings for our windows, a mix of linoleum, tarpaper and wooden slats. It's not pretty, but it's keeping out most of the wind. The only problem is that it's now almost dark inside. There's still no electricity, and we have few candles.

We use way more wood than I'd like to heat the kitchen to a somewhat comfortable level. I can tell the entire building is cold, and the walls and leaky windows suck away the warmth. I don't know how we'll get through the winter, but I've got to remind myself only to think about today.

Around noon, Paul shuffles and limps into the kitchen. He's still wearing pajamas and his eyes appear only slightly more focused than yesterday.

Mama and I exchange a look. What will happen with Paul, we silently ask.

"You must be hungry," Mama says, but Paul limps wordlessly past her to the couch.

Seeing Mama's worried expression, I rush to his side. "Hey sleepy head, you ready for some food?"

At last his eyes focus on me. "I'm not really hungry."

"Just a little bread. You need to get your strength back."

As Paul sags on the sofa, I busy myself at the breadbox. The smell of the cornbread reaches my nose. I'm hungry again, but we don't really have enough to go around. I'll need to wait until dinner.

"We better fetch water," Mama says at my back. "Who knows when the lines will be repaired? At least enough to drink and cook with."

"I'll go."

Glad to get out of the house, I hurry to the well everyone calls *Pütt*. It's a ten-minute walk with empty pails and likely longer with full ones. At least the air is a bit better out here, but there are still black clouds above the city. Lots of things must be burning.

I wait in line before filling my buckets. On the way back, my arms grow tired. I put the pails down a few times before continuing.

Now I'm glad to return home, even if it is gloomy and Paul is unwell. At least he's here…with us.

Unlike Peter. *Stop it!*

"Put them in the kitchen. We'll reuse the dishwater," Mama says. "I'm going to lie down for a bit." She points her head toward Paul's still form on the sofa. It means I'm supposed to keep an eye on him.

Quiet settles as I sit across from my brother. He looks almost peaceful, though the hard lines around his mouth are still there. The eyeballs behind his lids are moving and I hope he's dreaming something nice. Something happy.

That's when I hear it. No, it cannot be. Not now. Again.

Engine sounds, a swarm of evil hornets grows louder, intent on destroying. Paul's eyes fly open the exact moment the first detonation hits. A vibration goes through the house. At least they can't break windows now, I think grimly.

The noise becomes deafening as bombs rain again. It's Sunday afternoon, no less. Mama appears next to us and like yesterday I can't hear what she says. She tugs at Paul, tries to get him to stand. But Paul curls himself into a ball, throws his arms around his head and begins to rock back and forth.

"Paul," I yell. "Let's go downstairs."

He doesn't hear me, can't hear me. I shake my head at Mama who slumps down next to me. Resigned, ready for what comes from above. I'm not leaving either. How could I if my brother is up here, living in agony?

I feel a dull pounding in my neck…I'm still alive, my heart still doing its job. The house continues to rock and vibrate. Paint chips drizzle from the ceiling like white rain. I pull a chair closer to Paul and lay my hand on his shoulder. He's shaking like the house. If we're supposed to get hit, we'll all go together. I quit listening to the pounding outside and watch Paul, infuse my strength into him. It's not working.

From the depth of the sofa rise whimpers. As the noise outside dies away, I listen to my brother's tortured cries, the bombers gone once more.

We're still here.

There is no joy in it, no relief—just a distant fact.

"Paul," I whisper. I rub his shoulder. "They're gone. You're all right."

What bullshit! What Paul lives through is way worse than bombs on the house. Somehow his mind is sick from all the war.

Paul's cries die away, but he continues to rock back and forth. I finally get up because I can't take it any longer. Mama follows me into the kitchen. "What are we going to do with him?" I ask, tears threatening.

Mama embraces me. "I don't know. I wish we could find a doctor to help."

We might as well look for the pope because the few remaining physicians are likely busy with the injured and dying. They don't have time for my brother, whose mind is sick with shellshock.

Peter

Arthur is hiding in the inn's barn. I still don't know how we made it back, only that it seemed to take half the night.

We bed him in the hay, cover him with blankets and sneak inside to find Herrn Sommer.

"You boys crazy?" he cries when he sees us. "Herr Lustig is very upset. We were all searching for you earlier."

"We need to show you something," I say. "It's a matter of life and death."

That's how Herr Sommer meets Arthur.

"He can't stay here," Herr Sommer whispers. "It's too dangerous."

"He can't leave," Karl-Heinz says. "He'll die. He needs our help now."

"What's wrong with him?"

I point at Arthur who crumples sideways against a straw bale, his bandaged hand cradled on his lap. "It may be gangrenous." Even from where I stand I smell the stench of putrefying flesh.

Herr Sommer lets out a bunch of air. "Oh, no." Then he starts to pace. We stand there and watch him. "It's a good thing my wife is gone. She'd have a heart attack." Herr Sommer told us that his wife died three years ago. He's never mentioned details, and judging by the pinched look on his face, we've never asked. "I know she'd want me to help this man."

A low moan comes from Arthur as he slowly tilts and slides to the ground. Apparently, that's all Herr Sommer needs. He abruptly turns to Karl-Heinz. "Fetch the doctor, but be quiet about it." As Karl-Heinz sprints into the darkness, Herr Sommer and I prepare a solid bed of straw and hay, wrap it in sheets, then add more blankets and a pillow on top. He sends me to fetch water and dinner.

The smells in the kitchen remind me that I haven't eaten, so while I collect supplies for Arthur, I stuff a few spoonfuls of fried potatoes in my mouth. I grab towels, washcloths and a bit of soap— we're running pretty low these days—and return to the barn. Except for an oil lamp by Arthur's new bed, it's pitch black. We've set it up in such a way that a person entering the barn only sees the straw bales and partitions where Herr Sommer used to keep a few cattle.

Herr Sommer takes the water pail and begins to wipe down Arthur. It's slow, painstaking work as Arthur is so filthy that his skin is near black. He's also weak and immediately begins to tremble with cold.

"Go back inside and grab a new set of clothes," Herr Sommer instructs. "You know where I live, just open the closet and pick something. When I return, Arthur has been stripped to his waist. His rips are showing and his sternum is sunken in. The bandage looks grotesque. The skin above the elbow is red and swollen to his bicep.

"We'll leave the bandage until the doctor arrives." Herr Sommer grips my arm. "Get the fire in the kitchen stove going. We need to burn these things."

While I rekindle the fire, Karl-Heinz shows up with Arthur's clothes. Immediately, the kitchen turns into a cesspool, so we stuff the things into the fire.

"Herr Sommer says we need to bury Arthur's shoes. I'm supposed to find a pair of boots in the store room."

"Speaking of boots, I wonder how Boot is doing," I say, keeping an eye on the stove. A bit of smoke is leaching out, but the heat continues to rise.

"He's likely stinking mad."

"Maybe we should tell him—"

"What should you tell me?" Boot shuffles into the kitchen wearing a threadbare housecoat. The few strands of gray hair are sticking from the sides of his head. Who knows how long he's been there. "You want to tell me what you're up to?" He sniffs. "What stink did you brew up this time? Herr Sommer will be angry."

Panic rises inside me like a creepy insect. What if Boot starts searching for our host and finds him with Arthur?

"Nothing, sir," Karl-Heinz says. "I'm sort of embarrassed, ashamed really," Karl-Heinz pulls a long sorry face, any actor could take a lesson from, "we got lost again."

"Mushrooms were wonderful," I add, pointing at the forgotten baskets on the counter. "So we kept collecting and soon—"

Karl-Heinz produces a huge sigh. "The woods are enormous. I was afraid we'd spend the night."

Boot stares at his watch. "It is night all right, way past your bedtime." Once more he squints. "What time did you boys return?"

"Not long ago."

"And you're doing what exactly?"

I look at Karl-Heinz, racking my brain what to say. Why are we making a stinking fire in the middle of the night—in the inn's kitchen of all places? I can tell he's equally confounded.

"Karl-Heinz shit himself," I say out of the blue. "We didn't want to tell anybody, so we burned his underpants."

"Eh, yes." Karl-Heinz lowers his head, feigning embarrassment. In reality, I know he's about to explode with laughter.

Boot looks back and forth between us, his expression somber...assessing. "Herr Sommer won't be pleased that you mess with his kitchen," he finally says. "I suggest you clean any traces and head for bed."

That second Herr Sommer enters the kitchen. I can tell he's flustered, his cheeks red and his eyes shiny with anxiety. "Better come—" He notices Boot and almost flinches.

"Ah, yes, Herr Sommer, I'm very sorry about the boys. They promised to clean up. There was a little accident, I understand." Boot stretches himself like he does when he tries to exude authority.

"What—"

"I told Herrn Lustig that I had an accident in the woods and had to burn my underpants. I am truly sorry for using your stove for such a task, I just didn't know what to do." As if to underscore his comment, the stove emits the last remnants of stink.

"Well, then we better air the room." Herr Sommer turns to the window. Just like Karl-Heinz he's obviously in a hurry to hide his face.

"Yes, yes," Boot says, "I shall think about adequate punishment tomorrow."

"Of course," Herr Sommer says. He's caught himself and returns to the counter. "If you like I shall take care of them for now. They can put away the mushrooms and sweep the floor, so we'll be ready to go in the morning."

"Excellent idea!" Boot smacks his heels together as if he's doing a salute, except he only wears old felt slippers. The thing looks so funny, I have trouble hiding my smirk. "Then I shall retire for the night." He turns to us. "Boys, you have heard the man. Do what you're told."

"Yes, sir," Karl-Heinz and I say together.

All three of us clamp our hands on our faces to snuff out our giggles. Even Herr Sommer laughs like I've never seen him.

But then he grows serious. "All right, Dr. Specht needs us. Arthur will have to have his arm amputated or he'll die."

The seriousness of the situation hits me like a bucket of ice water. Though I've hardly eaten, my stomach bucks in alarm and disgust. I don't want to watch. Not this.

But it was my idea to bring Arthur. And without us he'll die for sure. He still may.

I chomp down hard on my teeth until they grind, swallow the bitterness on my tongue. "All right, I'm ready."

CHAPTER TWENTY

Hilda

Mama dresses for work on Monday morning as I head for another water run to the well. But when I return with my buckets—Paul is still in bed—she is sitting at the kitchen table in coat and hat.

"What happened?" I ask.

Mama just sits and stares, and when she finally meets my gaze, she shakes her head. "It's all gone. Downtown is burning. I can't even get close to the *Rathaus*…if it still stands. The roads are buried too." She hesitates, her voice trembling, "There are hundreds of dead, wrapped in sheets…just lying there along the paths." She buries her face in her hands and I rub her back, trying to imagine the destruction of Solingen's downtown.

At last Mama straightens and takes off her coat. "Might as well see what we can do around here." She returns in her work clothes, a scarf wrapped around her hair. "I've got an idea."

She sits to face me. "We used to know this veterinarian. Maybe he could help Paul, at least visit and take a look."

"Wouldn't he be in the war?"

Mama chuckles. It sounds bitter. "Doctor Deichmann is at least seventy-five. Though they don't seem to mind sending geriatrics to war."

That afternoon my brother is being examined by an old vet. That's also how I get to see my brother's leg.

I wasn't going to be present, but then the old man calls from

Paul's bedroom. "Your brother needs help," he says as soon as I enter. "I want to take a look at the injury."

Paul sits on the bed, not really paying attention, so I lightly tap him on the shoulder. "The doctor wants to see your leg."

"Oh, all right." Paul tries to stand, but then falls back on the bed.

"I'll help you take off your pants." With the old man's support, we help Paul peel out of his pants. His good leg is stick thin. The other is swollen and appears to have been sent through a meat grinder. There are holes in the thigh muscle, the skin red and puckered, the knee some kind of blob of sinew and bone, the calf muscle half gone. It looks as if the surgeon quit half way through the operation and left half of Paul's leg on the operating table. I twist my head toward the wall to hide my tears as the doctor uses a looking glass to investigate further. He mumbles something I can't understand.

Then he waves at me and we put Paul's pants back on. Paul just sits there like a little boy, his eyes a bit glassy. Off and on he focuses on the old man.

"How about we talk for a while? Would that be all right?" the vet says, settling himself on the only chair.

Paul nods, so I tiptoe from the room. I run to the bucket and cool my burning cheeks. Tears and water mix together, and I'm glad Mama is upstairs, checking on Frau Simon. Mama will want to know what happened, and I don't think I can speak right now.

I busy myself with the wood and coal pile, trying to estimate how long it'll be before we run out. Maybe three weeks or four at the most, if we're careful and it doesn't get too cold. Maybe Biene will come with me to collect firewood. Or we could try the trains again, even if the rolling wagons turn my veins to ice. Boys like Biene, so maybe those boys I met earlier, will help again.

The old vet remains in Paul's room for a long time, so long that I'm wondering if they both fell asleep. But then the door opens and he waves Mama and me to him.

"Paul is a fine young man," he begins. But then his expression turns grave. "He has severe shellshock. Saw some of his best friends die in bombardments—the trenches—so the noise brings it all back. He really needs to be in a sanatorium, have peaceful surroundings." He sighs. "It isn't going to be easy. You may try the Wehrmacht, ask them for help." His hands flutter up, old hands full of bluish-corded veins. "He needs medication to help him sleep, maybe antidepressants." His eyes meet Mama's. "I don't have access to anything appropriate. But I do have valerian root."

Mama's fingers land on the old man's. "I've heard of it, an herb that helps you sleep."

"Yes, it is also calming and stress reducing." The vet chuckles, though there's a bitter undertone. "It tastes something awful, but it works even for my animal patients."

"But I don't know where I can find any. This time of year…"

"I've got reserves," the vet says. "If you send Hilda with me, I'll give her some. See that Paul takes it every day." He looks at the ceiling and shakes his head. "Who knows how often they'll bomb?"

Mama and I nod. I'll do anything to help Paul.

The same afternoon we start brewing tea with valerian root. It reeks just like the doctor said, but Paul doesn't seem to mind and is quickly asleep on the couch.

As soon as Paul nods off, I head outside. I need air so I can think straight. That's when I remember my previous task— planning for more fuel—and head to Biene's home.

"You want to go to the tracks look for coal?" I ask as soon as Biene opens the door. She's looking tired and irritated.

"Mother is visiting my aunt and I've got to watch Theo." A whine comes from the kitchen. "He's having dinner. If I don't help him, I'll scrape the food off the cabinets."

"Come and see me tomorrow," I say but Biene has already closed the door.

What is wrong with her? The same thing that is wrong with all of us. We're tired and hungry and afraid.

Wednesday morning Mama comes running into the kitchen with our daily newspaper, the *Solinger Tageblatt*. "I can't believe they're back to printing the paper," she cries. "The city is still burning, they must have some other print location."

We sit down side-by-side to study the news. The first pages— these days the paper only has four pages altogether—always talk about the war: how the German Wehrmacht makes all this progress, how brave they fight and how mean every other country is. Little space is reserved for city news and so we lean in to find out about the most severe bombardment in Solingen's history. I search the articles and small headlines. Down one column, then another. I'm quick because that's how my mind works, but there's nothing. I'm long done before Mama turns her gaze on me.

"There's nothing mentioned," she says. "Not a word." Her forefinger follows another line. "Oh, but they sure want us to black out our windows, even give us the exact times. And threaten with fines and cutting off power." She scoffs. "As if the bombers haven't found us already. They don't need to bomb at night."

My hometown has been burning for four days and wrapped corpses line the paths—likely, thousands are dead. And our local paper doesn't consider it newsworthy?

"I don't understand," I say.

"Oh, but I do." Mama's eyes blaze with irritation. "Don't you see? They aren't allowed to report. Everything is going so well for Germany." Mama's voice is full of sarcasm. "We're winning, always winning."

I stare at my mother as I try to grasp this new truth.

Peter

The night Dr. Specht takes Arthur's arm will forever haunt me. Going into the barn, I tell myself to be strong. Karl-Heinz is by my side and together we'll somehow work through it.

The space reeks so bad, I bury my nose beneath my arm. Dr. Specht waves us near, his forehead glistening and the wire-rimmed glasses at the tip of his nose.

"I need you to hold him," he says without preamble. "You boys take his legs, Herr Sommer, push down hard on his torso, I don't want him to move."

What I'd so dreaded now lies in front of me, a darkish, puffy hand so black it looks as if it were made from coal. Around the wrist, the color changes to gray and yellow, but Dr. Specht is obviously not taking any chances. He has fashioned a tourniquet near Arthur's armpit and is focusing on the area above the elbow.

Arthur's eyes are wide and crazy as an animal in a trap. He jerks his head back and forth between us.

"Now I want you to bite down." Dr. Specht stuffs a piece of wood between Arthur's teeth. "Herr Sommer, put your knees on his shoulders and squeeze his head between your thighs."

Herr Sommer adjusts his position. I now see that Arthur is lying flat in a heap of straw with the area immediately beneath his injured arm bare. Dr. Specht sorts through his tools one last time. He swallows repeatedly as sweat beads drip down his temples.

Karl-Heinz and I look at each other, neither of us wanting to watch, both of us staring at the unfolding surgery as if somebody has pulled our heads that way.

All that changes when Dr. Specht begins to work. As the saw blade bites into Arthur's arm, Arthur screams. Had it not been for the mouthpiece that turns the sounds into a gurgle, the entire neighborhood would be awake. At the same time, Karl-Heinz begins to sway and collapse to the side.

"Go outside," I shout into his ear. He seems to be far away, his eyes fogged over as if he were sleepwalking. I shove him sideways to get him away from the bloodbath unfolding. It isn't really that much blood, but the sound the saw makes when it hits bone pierces my brain like a hot poker. Thankfully, that moment Arthur passes out and Karl-Heinz staggers to the door.

Dr. Specht quickly saws through and gets busy sewing the open wound with a flap of skin. He carefully tucks and stitches as if it were no more than a piece of cloth. Herr Sommer's face shines pale in the lantern light, but he looks composed.

Since Arthur no longer needs to be held down, Herr Sommer straightens and wraps the severed limb into a burlap sack. "I'll take that if you don't mind," Dr. Specht says.

Without a word, Herr Sommer gets busy stuffing the soiled straw into another sack. I grab a clean cloth, dampen it and wipe Arthur's forehead.

At last Dr. Specht straightens and wipes his glasses. "I need to get sulfonamides. It may take a day. I hope I'm not too late, but the infection was strong." He washes his hands in a bucket of clean water and turns to me. "You did well, son. That was a tough one. You may have saved his life, but it's too early to tell." No sooner has the doctor uttered the words, tears burst from my eyes, followed by a terrible shaking.

Herr Sommer quietly takes me into his arms. "It's all right, Peter. The worst is done now." Leaning there in that barn against the man I only know as the inn's host, makes me realize that this is the first real hug I've gotten since leaving Mother. Which makes the entire thing worse because I can't stop crying.

Dr. Specht pats me on the back. "Let me give you something to sleep. And your friend. You both need it."

Apparently, Karl-Heinz has returned and lingers at the barn door, too afraid to come near. "It's safe now," Herr Sommer calls to him.

And that's how Karl-Heinz and I sleep until eleven the next morning.

Boot never utters a word about the previous night. In fact, from this moment forward he treats us like equals, never scolding or picking on us. I would give my right arm, well no, that was Arthur, but anyway, I'd give a lot to know what Herr Sommer said to him.

CHAPTER TWENTY-ONE

Hilda

The valerian root is helping some. Paul sleeps better and he's more relaxed. Luckily, there haven't been any more Allied bombardments, but right after the attack on Solingen, it began to rain and now, five weeks later, it's still raining.

Mama has tried to return to work, but she found the roads impassable. Last week, she made it all the way to the Rathaus, but the building had lost a part of its roof and all the windows were broken, without electricity and water. The mayor sent everybody home until they find an alternate location.

I've been out almost every day looking for opportunities, but the rain softens my brain along with my clothes. My feet are constantly wet because the shoes, my only pair, never dry. The forest is completely void of edibles, and there is not a twig on the ground. Everyone is looking for ways to heat their homes and cook some lousy meal.

The only thing to do is cut down trees, and that's a huge job, especially without a decent axe. A couple of times I stopped at a farm and begged. Each time the farmer's wife gave me a bit of bread or a couple of rutabagas, but the food was not even enough for me, not to mention for Mama and Paul. And the woman said not to return because with the winter coming, she can't feed any more people. That pretty much leaves stealing, which carries its own risks. The first problem is to find a location with something to steal. Any larger place is well guarded. They've even added sentries in the train station to protect the coal trains. There are fewer anyway and now each wagon has soldiers patrolling.

I'd hoped Biene would accompany me. Just having her with me lifts my heart. Lately, she barely ever comes to visit and if I go over there she's busy with Theo or has some other excuse.

I decide to ask her to help me cut down a small oak I've scouted out. Its trunk is maybe four inches across, so it shouldn't take too long.

"I can't go." Biene wears a skirt with black ruffles I haven't seen before. I figure she got it from her mother. She looks tired and doesn't meet my eyes.

"You going out?" I ask.

She sort of shakes her head and I all of a sudden know she's lying. She's never lied. Ever. Not to me. It's drizzling worse, and she's not even asking me to come inside. By the way she's dressed it has to be pretty warm in her home.

"I don't have time right now," Biene says. "I'll be by tomorrow."

I nod and turn on my heels. What is wrong with her?

The next day when I return from another trip to the forest, I ask if Biene visited. She hasn't. Nor does she show up the following day.

On the third day I stop by again. "Biene isn't here," her mother says to me.

"Isn't she going to be home soon? It's getting dark."

"I don't know." Biene's mother exhibits the same strange behavior as Biene.

"Will you tell her that I need to see her?"

All of a sudden I feel tears pressing. Biene has been my best friend for years. I wouldn't have made it through KLV without her and her rebellious head. Now she's avoiding me and going out secretly? I can't put my finger on it.

But the next day, Biene shows up. She embraces me in the doorframe and jabbers like the market vendor who used to sell us vegetables. "What do you want to do?" she asks. "It's almost Christmas. I've got no gifts for Theo and Mother. We need to find something."

She throws a glance at Paul who's on the couch reading a book. He has propped up his bad leg with a pillow and hardly acknowledges

Biene.

"Is he all right?" she asks. "I'm sorry, I've been preoccupied. I'm just so worried about Father. He's still imprisoned in that camp and now that it's Christmas soon, he'll have nothing…"

I blink, unsure what to feel. Relieved that I don't have to worry because my father has not talked to us since he left in 1938? I'm not even sure I know whether I wish him dead or not. Or should I be envious because Biene at least has a father?

Oh, there was a time when I did wish my father the worst. About a year or two after he left and it became clear he'd never return, I hoped he'd be run over by a truck or fall into a hole. I no longer remember how his voice sounds, nor do I know his face, unless I visit the portrait next to Mama's bed. I know she sometimes talks to him because I hear her whisper—the fool of a woman.

If I'm honest, I think he may be dead. But then there is that little voice of hope that insists I'd know. It's a small voice, no more than a whiff as if it isn't quite sure anymore.

I return to present and notice Biene's curious stare. "Are *you* all right?"

I nod but the smile I'm trying for doesn't work, so I clear my throat and say, "Paul is getting a little better every day." I look at the ceiling. "As long as it remains quiet."

Biene knows what I mean by the way she squeezes my shoulder. It's good to have my friend here. Still, I can't shake the feeling that something is wrong with her.

"So, what are we going to do?" she asks and it feels almost like the hundreds of times we took off on adventure when we were still in school.

"How about we scope out a farm or we could see if the grocery store has something to sell." After the bombing, many of our ration coupons are as worthless as the paper they're printed on.

Since Biene doesn't have any better ideas, we decide to visit the grocery store first and then head out of town to investigate. Against the rain, Biene has tied a shawl around her dark hair that is still shiny despite the lack of decent shampoo. I'm wearing one of Mama's scarves, but the rain is soaking through and soon our feet make sucking sounds.

The grocery store has a line in front of it, which is a good sign. It means there's been a delivery of something, so we join. The line moves slower than syrup, but we don't want to give up. The people leaving carry small wrapped packages, their faces a mix of relief and gratification. In this environment we've all become self-centered, each of us ready to fight for our share. Somebody says it's fat and meat.

All of a sudden Biene clamps a hand in front of her mouth. She's about to point at a young man when she half ducks behind the fellow in front of us. But the young man has noticed her too. And that's when I recognize him—the boy who was watching the potato field.

Within two seconds he's upon Biene. "I thought I knew you…you little thief," he hisses. His eyes spit fire. They're green and pretty as a forest of evergreens. He looks quite attractive, tall with a square chin and a straight nose.

"I'm sorry," Biene says. She appears genuinely guilty. "I…we were so hungry…and—"

"My brother needed food," I chime in. No need for her take the abuse, even if he never saw me.

"So, you were part of it," he says, his gaze now on me. His cheeks are flaming with anger, but his voice has calmed.

"I'm sorry too," I say.

"I got into a world of trouble," he says. "The farmer just about flogged me." His eyes are back on Biene and there's something else there now, something like curiosity…or interest. "Those weren't our potatoes. I hired on for a bit myself, but after that, the farmer let me go and mother never got her potatoes."

Biene's hand lands on the boy's sleeve. "I'm really sorry. It's not right what we did. We never stole before, but it's just so hard…"

"Maybe you should make it up to me," the young fellow says.

"What do you mean?" Biene asks.

"Maybe we should start with names. I'm Kurt."

"Biene."

"Hilda."

We shake hands and there is a tiny smile on Kurt's face now. On close inspection he's really handsome and I can tell Biene has noticed it too. She's smiling back and in that instant I feel like the fifth wheel.

"How about we meet some time?" Kurt says.

Biene looks up at him—he's at least ten inches taller—and says without the slightest hesitation, "I'm free tomorrow afternoon." She gives him her address and they shake hands again. The line has moved to the entry door, but none of us has really noticed. I'm plain speechless.

"I better take these home." Kurt pets the small package under his arm. "At least it'll please Mother." The grin on his face spreads. "I better not tell her who I met."

Biene laughs. It's the first real laugh I've heard from her in months. It's a strange sound, a bit otherworldly in the cold wetness of the December twilight. As Kurt marches off, Biene follows him with her eyes.

"I wonder why he wasn't in the KLV," Biene says as we move toward the counter.

"Maybe he's too old, or he returned early…like us." I want to say more, want to ask her how she can tell a perfect stranger her address and go out with him.

A bit of envy creeps into my heart as I imagine Biene and Kurt together. Peter's face appears in my vision. It's strange he hasn't come home yet. I've heard people say it's no longer safe in the east. How could it be, if we got attacked on the way home…in the middle of Germany? And right here…at home?

As the worry in my stomach expands, I vow to stop by Frau Breuer's home. For once, I'm glad Biene is quiet. When I look over, her eyes shine with excitement.

In the end, I say nothing. I know how I feel about Peter, but I sure wouldn't want to have to talk about it.

Peter

Arthur has slept for three days. Once again we've rearranged the straw bales so that it's impossible to see him, no matter where you stand in the barn. Thankfully, our classmates are preoccupied with the collection of food and staying on Boot's good side.

Off and on, those in the know sneak into the barn, usually under the guise of some excuse or other. On the fourth day, when Karl-Heinz and I climb behind the bales, Arthur is awake. Dr. Specht has been visiting twice a day, feeding him sulfonamides, some kind of antibiotic supposed to kill the infection.

"Good to see you, boys," Arthur says. His voice is low, yet there is some strength in it again. A bit of color has replaced the deathly pallor. He is clean, courtesy of Herrn Sommer, who fusses like a mother hen, bringing soup and cornbread. "Good thing, I'm right-handed," he quips, a weak grin on his face. I try not to look at the stump, but its white gauze draws me in.

"I'm sorry you lost your arm," Karl-Heinz says. Sometimes, it's good to have a friend with the right words.

"How do you feel?" I ask.

"Pretty well." Arthur nods at Herr Sommer who stands in the shadows watching. "Thanks to Siegmund here and Dr. Specht, I'm mending."

Siegmund? Herr Sommer and Arthur have become friends.

"He'll need a few weeks yet," Herr Sommer says.

"Herr Sommer, are you in here?" Dieter calls from somewhere beyond the straw wall.

We look at each other and I wonder if I should say anything. But Herr Sommer shakes his head and puts a forefinger on his lips.

"He isn't in here," Dieter says to somebody outside. "Look in the garden or in the hen house. Quick." There is urgency in Dieter's voice. Something has happened.

As soon as the barn door shuts, we scramble out from behind Arthur's hiding place.

That's when I hear voices argue, all tired and angry. We sneak to the barn door and Herr Sommer peeks outside. He waves us to come along and closes the door behind him. A new latch and padlock hang outside—he locks carefully and pockets the key.

Out here the noise is louder, and as soon as we round the corner, there is this throng of people: refugees once again with dirty faces and torn clothes, a few older men, mostly women and children, about fifteen.

"How can I help you?" Herr Sommer holds out both arms in greeting.

"We need food and place for the night," a man in his fifties speaks, his Polish accent heavy. He is the youngest of the men with the crooked nose and thick lips of a former boxer.

"Where are you coming from?" Herr Sommer asks, his tone a shade less friendly.

"Brest. Red Army come. We leave together." The man rubs his scraggly beard and I'm immediately reminded of the scabies we caught last time. It took weeks to clean and treat our skin. Karl-Heinz still has nightmares about his balls falling off.

"I can give you some food. We don't have much these days and I've got to feed thirty-nine boys."

"We sleep in barn."

"Sorry, no barn," Herr Sommer says quickly—too quickly because all of a sudden there is suspicion in the refugee's eyes. His brows lower themselves across his eyes. I'm sure he doesn't mind using violence to get his way.

"The last people coming from the east had diphtheria and slept in the barn," Karl-Heinz says loudly. "Some died. We haven't dared to go in there."

"Right," Herr Sommer says. "It's too dangerous. As I said, I'll get you food and you are welcome to sleep out here. There's a pump over there for water."

The man slowly nods as if he's trying to determine if our story is true. Then he turns and says something in Polish. The people mumble and settle beneath the old Lindentree in the front yard.

"You should leave," the man says when we distribute boiled potatoes and blankets. "Russians coming. German army finished." He cuts across his throat with the side of his hand, before taking a bite, potato skin and all. "Not safe here."

I nod numbly, trying not to show how much the man's words scare me. Dieter and Karl-Heinz have heard it too. I vow to ask Herr Sommer and Boot when the people leave.

For some reason, dinner is subdued. Outside the group has settled around a fire—with some of Herr Sommer's logs. But I can't get the words of the man out of my head.

"Maybe he's right," I whisper, watching absentmindedly how Karl-Heinz devours the last of his bean soup. There is no meat in it, but the leeks, onion and potatoes give it thickness. I long to return to the woods for more mushrooms, but we don't dare leave Herr Sommer to care for Arthur alone. Any day it's going to freeze and there won't be any more mushrooms until next spring. No way we'll still be here then. Or would we?

"Who is right?" Karl-Heinz wipes his mouth with the palm of his hand and picks a few crumbs off the table.

"The man outside. Maybe we *should* leave. The last group said the same. They've been close to the front, heard the artillery." I begin to whisper. "Remember the radio…Thomas Mann? It's exactly what he said, and that was a long time ago."

"I would love to go home." Karl-Heinz's voice is dreamy. "See my mother, make sure she is all right."

I see my own mother standing in her black coat at the train station, her sad expression as she searched for me behind the glass of the compartment. My cheeks heat with sudden shame as I remember my anger and embarrassment about her. I was a bastard, a stupid kid who knew nothing. How I long to embrace her now, tell her that I'm sorry, that I've missed her terribly.

She may be dead. Buried under rubble and shredded by bombs. No, I can't…I won't think about that. She must be alive. In that moment, my urge to leave is so strong, I want to jump up and race out the door.

My thoughts wander to Hilda, my friend. The way she looked when I told her about my plans for camp. How vulnerable and little she was. Even if she put up a brave face, she needed my help, my protection. And what did I do? Run off as quickly and happily as I could.

For what?

To hide in one camp or another and play capture the flag, get in fistfights with my classmates, far away from all I love and hold dear.

If I can't leave, I will at least write to her. Maybe Arthur can take my letter and mail it. I'm done telling lies.

The next morning the men, women and children are gone, along with the blankets and a few pots and pans, Herr Sommer had used to serve them food.

"Good riddance," Herr Sommer says as he places freshly shaped loaves of bread on a baking tray. "That fellow with the broken nose looked like trouble."

"He did say that we should leave, that the Russians are heading this way," I say, slicing carrots for soup.

"Entirely possible." Herr Sommer sticks the tray into the old brick oven, already producing a comfortable heat.

"Boot…I mean Herr Lustig believes it's safe to stay."

Herr Sommer chuckles, but then grows serious. "Arthur says the Wehrmacht is surrounded in Courland. It's a matter of time before they're finished."

"I've been thinking about going home."

Our eyes meet. "I doubt there are many trains or buses. It's a dangerous journey and you'll likely walk most of the way."

I shrug. "Better than being attacked by Russians."

Herr Sommer steps closer and in a rare display of affection, grips my shoulders. "I wish I could tell you what to do. Winter is coming, so it's dangerous. I told Arthur to wait, but he is determined to leave in a few days." He squeezes my arms. "Just promise me to take a friend or two and prepare."

I nod. "Why don't you go with us? We could all go together." I'm speaking faster. "You said yourself it's better in a group."

Herr Sommer let's go of my arms and starts wiping down the wooden counter. "This is my home, the place my wife…and I built together." He turns to me, his eyes moist. "I can't leave."

There is that word again—home. It's a small word but it entails our entire beings. How we define ourselves, where we come from and who we love. I want to argue and tell Herr Sommer to think about his safety, but I don't say a word because I understand him.

CHAPTER TWENTY-TWO

Hilda

The next afternoon Biene shows up at my house. She's red-faced and out of breath as if she's run the entire way.

"You've got to help me out," she yells.

I take her fluttering hands into mine. They're as cold as a frozen pond and I rub them and pull her to the kitchen stove.

"What happened?"

But Biene is not talking, she's crying. Biene never cries. Not even when the Abbess abused Tilly or we all half died from homesickness. Not when the evil SS-man called her to him.

But this Biene is a blubbering mess. I wrap an arm around her shoulders and pull her close. Thankfully, Paul is taking a little walk with Mama and we're alone.

"I can't...I." She puts a palm on my cheek, which immediately feels cold. "You need to go out with Kurt tonight."

"What...why—"

"I can't tell you, it's too..." She shakes her head and her arm falls uselessly to her side.

"Since when do we have secrets?"

Biene doesn't meet my eyes. So, my gut has been right. There's something going on with my best friend—something I don't know about. Worse, something she doesn't want to share. The hurt in my heart is immediate and twists into anger.

"Promise me to pick him up at my house," she says. "Six o'clock sharp."

"What do you want me to say?"

Biene shrugs. "Anything…that I'm sick, that I've got to take care of my brother." At last she meets my eyes. "Just make sure he knows I *wanted* to see him."

"Then why don't you? What could possibly be that important? Surely, your mother is home to watch Theo."

"It's not that."

"Then what is it?"

Biene turns on her heels and marches to the door. "Promise me?" There's fear and despair in her voice…and something else: guilt.

Kurt is surprised and upset to see me waiting at Biene's door.

"Biene had an emergency," I say before he can jump to conclusions. "She's really sorry to miss you."

"Oh." For a moment Kurt stands there, sort of undecided.

"It's fine, if you just want to leave."

"No, no." He produces a thin smile. "I'm surprised, is all." He looks at me, uncertainty in his eyes. "You want to take a walk?"

"Sure."

We wander a while, both of our attempts to talk awkward. I wish Biene were here to diffuse the situation. She used to be so bubbly, though ever since the abbey, with the war in its sixth year, she has been an entirely different person.

"…you go?"

"What?" I haven't heard a word Kurt said.

"I asked if you went away with the KLV?"

"Biene and I went to Bavaria, some cloister with the meanest Abbess." Fräulein Heinrich's pale face appears, her attempts to get along with the Abbess…her staring eyes in the field. "Did you go?" I hurry.

"Mother didn't want me to. I've been helping her at home. She's always been a housewife and…she has asthma."

When I don't say anything, Kurt continues. We're heading toward a little park on *Bismarckstraße*. It's pitch-black, the air icy and damp. "The smallest exertion makes Mama out-of-breath. Now they don't even have her medication anymore, so she's afraid to go outside. The cold makes it worse."

I hear the worry in Kurt's voice, recognize it from myself when I talk about Paul. "I'm so tired of this war. Things only get worse all the time."

"It can't go on much longer."

"How do you know?" I say.

"I don't know for sure, but how can it?" He lowers his voice. "I met a deserter in the woods. He said the Wehrmacht is finished. He said the Führer is crazy."

"I believe that."

In the darkness, he gropes for my hand. "So, will you tell me the truth about Biene? Is she…does she not like me anymore?"

"Nothing like that," I say, wishing I could see his face. "Honestly, I don't know what's wrong with her. She didn't tell me even though I'm her oldest friend. We never had secrets, but right now…I think she's ashamed of something."

I squeeze Kurt's icy fingers. "I think she really likes you. A lot."

Kurt squeezes back. "I'll wait for her, no matter what." There's conviction in his voice, something I'm suddenly envious about. How come Kurt just looks at Biene and falls in love? Peter never did anything to make me believe he liked me beyond casual friendship. He just left me like Papa…happily.

"I'll see her tomorrow and try to find out more."

Kurt gives me his address in *Unnersberg*. With no postal service I promise to drop off a note.

When I try to speak to Biene the next day, nobody opens the door. I can't tell if anyone is home, the windows covered in black and lifeless.

Tomorrow is Christmas Eve, and I've made Biene a wool cap from an old sweater. It's uneven because my knitting is as loopy as my attempts at crocheting and the light inside is terrible. The landlord has no glass or new windows. Nobody does, so every opening remains covered under wood and linoleum or whatever scraps people can find to keep out the frigid winter air.

Since I don't have any paper, I wrapped a piece of dried grass around my gift. I decide to wait a bit. At least it's not raining right now, so I find an old stone pillar up the street to sit on. The light is fading already, even though it can't be past three o'clock.

I've just decided to return home, when I see Biene hurry toward her home. She keeps her head low, her arms wrapped around a well-filled burlap sack. I'm about to rush up to her when I stop. Something is holding me back. Instead, I decide to wait five minutes and sneak around back. For some reason, Biene's villa has a couple of real glass panes in their kitchen window again.

Sure enough, the light comes on inside and I tiptoe closer to take a look. I've got to hurry before they lower the blinds. *Shame on you*, my mind complains. *Since when do you spy on your best friend?* Since she's been lying to me, I answer. My steps slow as I approach the window. It's fairly low, so I've got a good view of the inside.

Biene stands there in the middle of the kitchen, still in her coat while her mother is unpacking the burlap sack. I recognize cans with meat and fat, potatoes and onions. Despite the glorious spread— where did that come from?—Biene's expression is a mixture of anger and sadness. She's saying something, throws up her arms at her mother, but her voice is too low to hear.

I decide to do a frontal attack and knock on the window. Biene and her mother recoil at the same moment before Biene meets my gaze.

I wave and point toward the entrance. The door opens seconds after I get there.

"I wanted to drop off my Christmas gift," I say and stuff the wool cap into her hand. "Looks like you've been busy."

Biene's head droops as if it's too heavy to carry. "I…am sorry." She hesitates and looks over her shoulder. Likely weighing whether to let me in. Then she shrugs. "Come in, but only for a moment. My brother is ill."

Immediately, my internal fury turns to concern. "What's wrong with him?"

"We don't know. He's running a fever and mother has trouble getting it down."

"That dreaded cold rain." We've arrived in the kitchen and I notice how cozy warm it is. So warm, I'm hot in my coat.

"We've been heating the house, so Theo gets better."

"With what?" spills from my lips. I know Biene's mother is not looking for coal or cutting up trees. Nor is Biene—at least not that I know of.

My eyes narrow as I watch my friend, who's starring at her feet. "What are you not telling me?" I ask. I hear the anger in my voice, my throat almost too thick to force out the words.

"Nothing…I can't." Biene shakes her head and picks through the spread on the table. She hands me two cans of meat and a loaf of dark bread. I hadn't seen the bread because it was hidden behind the potato sack. "I'm sorry I didn't make anything for you."

My mind tells me to refuse the gifts, but my body has other ideas. I greedily snatch the food from Biene's fingers and tuck it under my coat. Then I turn to leave because tears press against my eyeballs and I don't want her to see how hurt I am.

"Hilda, wait."

But I don't wait, I go faster. Rip open the door, throw it shut and run. Why did I tell Kurt that Biene liked him? I don't know this person who I've considered my friend all these years.

Peter

Arthur left this morning. Herr Sommer tried to convince him to hang on until New Year, but Arthur was adamant. It's at least ten degrees below freezing, and a vicious wind howls across the open fields.

"Be careful," Arthur said before he left. We assembled in the barn, just Karl-Heinz, Herr Sommer and I, all of us sad and worried. Arthur's stump healed well beneath the knotted sleeve of the old coat that Herr Sommer had organized.

He turns from one to the other. "I owe you my life. I shall never forget it."

"Remember, this is a war injury," Herr Sommer says brightly. He has tears in his eyes though as the two men embrace. Arthur's injury happened *after* he deserted, but now nobody will know. Not as long as his commander, who is one of the thousands of soldiers stuck in Courland, doesn't show up anywhere. Which is unlikely.

"Be safe, boys, go home." Compared to the wreck we dragged in here, he looks like a new man. He turns back to face Herrn Sommer. "Remember, Siegmund, you are always welcome at my home. I will write as soon as I arrive."

Herr Sommer swallows and clears his throat. "Next year...I will visit."

The men look at each other one last time and then Arthur marches through the door and...is gone. In his pack he carries my letter to Hilda, an honest account of what's been going on. I ended the letter with "I miss you terribly." The time for hesitation is over.

The three of us look at each other in the shine of the lantern, our eyes wet, but our hearts light. We saved a human being, gave him hope. And by giving it to Arthur, we received all that hope back. A gurgle breaks from my lips as I begin to laugh. Karl-Heinz looks at me, then joins, and finally Herr Sommer. In the icy air of Christmas Eve morning, we stand and holler our heads off, if only for a moment.

I know that I'll leave too. Anything is better than waiting and wondering.

As we prepare for a second Christmas away from home, my heart is not in it. Around me, the boys are decorating the dining room with fresh cedar boughs and cones. Herr Sommer has dug into his supplies and produced a few red candles. There are straw stars and garlands crafted from chestnuts and acorns.

Karl-Heinz doesn't talk much either, and I notice Dieter's curious stare.

"Something happen?" he asks as we assemble in the afternoon. Herr Sommer has somehow baked cookies now piled high on plates in the dining room.

"Just missing my family," I say.

"Me too," Dieter says quietly. "I'm stinking tired of living like this."

Exactly!

We sing Christmas songs and give each other small gifts, mostly things we've scrounged or crafted, carved animals or knives, a candle inside a pinecone, leftover wax collected over months, a slingshot, the sling made from a piece of bicycle tire. Karl-Heinz gives me a small box, carved from a piece of oak root. He's done a fine job, hollowing the inside and it even has a tiny lid.

I quickly reach behind the bench where I've stashed Karl-Heinz's gift, a bow and three arrows. The bow is made from hazelnut and string I found on a field. The arrows are pretty short, but have feathered fletching and carved tips. I would've loved to strengthen the arrowheads with metal, but I've got no tools or supplies.

"We need to talk," I say to Karl-Heinz, watching the chatter in the room. The air is filled with the aroma of roast—Herr Sommer has managed to trade a wagon of straw bales against a small boar, a farmer shot on his field—and fried potatoes. Karl-Heinz keeps rubbing the little carving of K and B, his initials I added to the tip of the bow, so I bend low and whisper, "I want to go home."

Karl-Heinz quits what he is doing and looks at me. "Now?"

"Soon."

"All right, let's talk after dinner."

Only now do I realize that I want Karl-Heinz to go with me because if I'm honest, I'm afraid to be alone.

After the dining room is cleaned and things calm down, Karl-Heinz and I remain alone in the kitchen.

"Did you see the thermometer—it's at least minus twenty…the middle of winter," Karl-Heinz says. "Neither of us has decent clothes. We should at least wait until spring." He's leaning against the stove, warming his backside. Anymore, Herr Sommer let's the fire burn out to save wood. Over night, the most incredible ice flowers bloom on the windows.

"What if that's too late?"

Karl-Heinz's eyes widen. "You mean the Russians will be here already?"

"Maybe or maybe not. But do you want to risk being caught—a few dozen German boys hiding out from the war?"

The room turns quiet. Somewhere above, footsteps echo. Muffled voices filter through the walls. They're louder and deeper than they used to be.

"We may freeze to death instead." Karl-Heinz picks at a hangnail and finally chews it off.

"Herr Sommer will help us get ready."

"What about the others?"

I shrug. I don't really want a huge group to draw attention. It's easier to beg or steal and you don't need as many supplies to survive. "Most of them won't go unless they're told. And Boot insists we're safe."

"Right."

But I can tell Karl-Heinz is not convinced. Not the way I want him to be. If I'm honest, I can't blame him. Our shoes are too small and unsuitable for heavy snow. Just going outside for a few minutes turns our noses red. Our nostrils stick together so we wrap scraps of fabric around our heads to keep our faces from freezing. My toes often hurt and feel on the verge of frostbite.

Despite that, I've got to try. "Aren't you anxious to see your family, make sure they are all right?"

"Of course!" Out of Karl-Heinz's mouth it sounds like a cry and I immediately regret my question.

Karl-Heinz's home was bombed a long time ago. He doesn't even know where his mother lives right now. If she—

"Fine, I'll go."

"You are?" I rush to my friend and slap him on the back. "You'll see, we'll make it."

"You know how far it is?"

"Herr Sommer let me borrow his Germany map. I figure it's about a thousand kilometers."

Karl-Heinz's brows shoot up. "That'll take us forever."

I force myself to smile. "Six weeks at the most."

"If nothing unforeseen happens."

"Right."

Once again the room turns quiet. There is one more question that looms like a ghost above our heads. When will we leave? But neither Karl-Heinz nor I say anything, both of us relieved when Dieter comes running in with a broken cup.

"Damn, I didn't mean to..." He stops and looks at us. "What are you two doing here? We're playing games—"

"Coming," I hurry.

CHAPTER TWENTY-THREE

Hilda

On Christmas Eve morning I trek into the woods and cut down a three-foot fir tree. Its needles are soft and green, but even the piney aroma can't lift my spirits. At home Paul and I decorate with straw stars and pine cones. The few candles we own must be preserved for emergencies.

Mama has managed to bake a cake from cornmeal and a bit of sugar beet syrup she's traded with Frau Breuer. Together we fix a roast from the meat and potatoes that Biene gave us.

As we enjoy our dinner, Paul looks almost at peace. But I know he's had another valerian tea in the afternoon. We hold hands and sing *Stille Nacht* before opening our gifts.

Mama has knitted Paul wool socks. They're a bit large and almost reach to his knees, but he insists on wearing them immediately. I get a scarf from the same bluish gray wool and Paul presents me with a carved bunny. It's almost lifelike and I'm in tears, hugging it to my chest. I have no idea when he worked on it.

"Thank you," I whisper, carefully embracing him. We've found that he often flinches when we touch him, so we try to move slowly in his proximity.

He rubs my back. "Merry Christmas, little sister."

I present Mama with a couple of potholders I made from rags I found in the basement. They're ugly, the edges uneven, but Mama seems to adore them and hangs them near her stove. For Paul I made a pinecone gnome, complete with a tiny felted hat and matching feet.

"He's your guardian angel," I say quietly.

Paul pets the little figure on its pointy hat and smiles at me. "Then he better get busy." There's a bit of the old teasing Paul back in his expression, and I feel the tears rise again. I'm becoming a regular crybaby.

"What's going on with Biene?" Mama asks. "I haven't seen her at all."

I suck in air and try to keep a straight face. "Her brother, Theo, is sick with fever." *As if that explains anything.*

"Has he seen a doctor?" Mama asks.

"There aren't any, Mother," Paul says. "At least not for the likes of us."

I shake my head, try to think of something to say, but tears clog my throat and demand release.

"Oh, Hilda, don't take it so hard. I'm sure he'll get better." Mama pats my hand.

I nod and feel Paul's searching glance on me. He may be shell-shocked, but he's no dummy.

"Maybe you two can play a game," Mama says. "I'll see Frau Breuer for a minute." She packs a bowl of leftover stew and heads to the door. "Goebbels is speaking at nine o'clock if any of you want to listen."

Ignoring Mama's remark about the stupid speech, I call after her, "Ask Frau Breuer about Peter."

"Peter, eh?" Paul has a grin on his face—the first one I can remember since he returned.

"What's so funny?"

The grin widens. "You still love him." It's not a question, and all of a sudden I don't care.

I straighten my shoulders and meet my brother's eyes. "I think I always have."

Paul nods. "How lucky."

"What's lucky about that?" I hurry to the stove to heat water for dishes. "Haven't heard a word from him in a year and a half." Anxiety squirms through me like a disgusting worm. He never even wrote to me.

"You've got somebody to hold dear," Paul says. "I'm sure he'll be fine. He's quite capable."

Just not capable to write to me.

"Quit rustling around and play with me," Paul continues. He straightens painfully and limps to the shelf where we keep our chess set. "Let's see if you can still beat me."

"Ha." I join my brother at the table and we soon forget everything but the game pieces in front of us.

I win twice, the silence between us comfortable.

"Still the smart sister," Paul says afterwards. He looks at me curiously. "What's really going on with Biene?"

I sigh, sorting the chess pieces into the box. "I don't know—she's all weird. Doesn't talk to me or want to see me."

"You mentioned she gave you food?"

"Yes, she had all these things and it was really warm in her house." I swear I smelled real coffee when we don't even get a decent cup of grain beverage. In the newspaper they mentioned that the new fake coffee allotment is now smaller but better. Supposedly, one half teaspoon is enough to make three quarters of a liter of coffee. We boiled the mix for five minutes and Mama poured it into the sink afterwards.

Paul tips a forefinger on his chin. "I've got an idea, but..." He shakes his head.

"What?"

"No, let's not—"

"Tell me!" I cry.

He looks at me thoughtfully and I realize we're having the first real conversation since he returned eight weeks ago. "I could be wrong, but maybe Biene has a mentor. I mean somebody that helps them out."

"Why wouldn't she tell me then?"

"Don't know," Paul says and I can tell he's lying. He does know or at least have an idea.

"You're such a bad liar," I say just as Mama walks in the door.

"What is going on?" she asks.

"Nothing," Paul says. "A misunderstanding."

"Hilda?"

"Paul is right." I throw him a glance that says the opposite. I will ask him again tomorrow. And the day after. But that's unnecessary because the next day I figure it out myself.

Biene shows up around noon, her eyes wet with tears.

"You've got to help me," she says, hovering in the doorframe.

She's wearing my knitted cap and new brown leather shoes I don't recognize. "Theo is worse and we don't know what to do." She throws herself into my arms, the way she used to do, the rambunctious girl I know as my friend. "You had that doctor see Paul."

"The vet?"

"Maybe he could see Theo as well."

"We can certainly ask," I say, grabbing my coat. I like Dr. Deichmann. He's been by once a week, mainly to talk, and Paul always feels better afterwards.

On the way outside, I throw an arm around Biene. "I will take you to him, but you've got to tell me what is going on with you?"

Biene hiccups and wipes a palm across her eyes. "What do you mean?"

"Don't play dumb. I've been your friend for years and you've been acting all strange."

To my surprise, Biene begins to cry again. We keep walking because the wind is bone chilling. At last she begins to speak.

"I…mother knows this man, a coal merchant. Not long after we returned, she took me to meet him. That's when it all started."

"What started?"

Biene sucks in air as if she hasn't breathed in a month. "The visits…he asks me to stop by… And in exchange I…we get coal…and food."

"What kind of visits are you talking about?" Dark nasty things appear in my mind, but I'm still holding on to…what exactly? The goodness of humanity? Fair dealing?

"I…his wife died and he asks me to…undress."

"So you get naked in front of some fellow?" My voice has risen, and thankfully the street is deserted. After all it's Christmas and we are all *celebrating*.

"No different than the SS-man."

I stare at my friend. "That Linker…at the abbey?"

She nods, her gaze still on me, watching…my reaction.

"He made you get naked?" So that's how it started. Now she thinks she can throw herself away. My heart lurches. Oh, the shame she must have felt!

Biene scoffs. "At least he was young…"

My mouth opens and closes as I try to comprehend. I still see Biene walking off to report to the SS-man, head held high, shoulders straight despite the fact she must have been terrified. Tears threaten, so I cough hard. "How old is this coal merchant?"

"I don't know, in his fifties."

"In his fifties? Are you crazy?" A new thought crosses my mind. Her own mother did that to her? Sends her only daughter to see some old man to…

"At first he just looked, but then he moved on to other things." Biene's voice is so light, it seems to float in the frigid air, hot breath frozen in seconds. "He disgusts me."

"Oh Biene." I abruptly stop and pull her into my arms. "I'm so sorry."

Biene sobs against my shoulder as if she'll never stop again. "Mother says it's the only way we'll survive. With Theo needing help and her being stuck with him, Father in Russia…"

"But you aren't a prostitute," I say quietly. "You are a good person, kind and sweet, and my friend. Tell your mother that you won't do this any longer."

Biene pulls back and wipes her reddened eyes with her sleeve. "How will we keep the house warm? Get enough to eat?"

"We'll find a way. Somehow. It's worked this far, and we'll continue surviving."

"How do you know? What if the war keeps on going for two more years? Father may never return and there's hardly anything to eat in the stores now."

"I know, but it's got to stop soon. This stupid war has got to stop." I'm loud again, my voice an accusatory echo in the street. We've reached *Pfaffenberg* and I turn toward the doctor's house. As I grip Biene's hand and hold it in mine, I search for a way to escape…from this war and this life. Yet, I'm as firmly rooted as the burled oak in front of the vet's home.

"Right now, let's help your brother. Then we'll think about a solution to your problem."

Biene nods, her eyes filled with a mixture of relief and doubt.

That evening, I lie awake. Beyond the wall, Paul snores—with the valerian his sleep is extra heavy. I can't get the picture of Biene out of my head. The one where she takes off her clothes and sleeps with an old man.

She told me he grosses her out with his loose skin and hairy body. She often gets sick afterwards or right before, and only the thought of helping her family keeps her going. I ask myself why her mother isn't sleeping with the man. She's nearer his age and it was her idea. Instead she's selling her daughter for coal and supplies. I feel the anger brewing inside me like a caged animal. I want to smack Biene's mother, threaten her with the police. But who really cares at this time?

I also want to smack the idiots in Berlin. We didn't listen to propaganda minister Goebbels last night, but this morning the paper printed a long article. I only read the headline: *Germany to be called to a great future.*

What future? One where young women sell themselves for coal and young men return in pieces or not at all? Am I supposed to be thankful for a sixth Christmas spent at war? Or receiving a ration of 125 grams of artificial honey because I'm less than 18 years old?

It's almost morning before I fall asleep and I still don't have any idea how to help my best friend.

Peter

The day before New Year, it begins to snow. At first there are swirling flakes, tiny icicle-like bits that jab the skin like needle pricks. The sky is gray and laden, the wind fierce. It howls and pushes against the windowpanes, making them rattle. It creeps beneath the doors, turning our feet to clumps of ice. Just going outside for a minute is painful. The inn isn't exactly warm these days, our bedrooms unheated, but the dining area is doable as long as we wear our coats.

Every time I look at Karl-Heinz, I am reminded of our plan that now seems ludicrous. We wouldn't survive a single night without shelter. The other issue is Dieter. He's been with us for the entire time and more than once helped me out of a sticky situation. But involving more people makes everything riskier. What if Dieter tells somebody else and that person shares with another? Soon everybody knows. We may end up with ten or fifteen people.

I've drawn a crude map on a shred of newspaper, which I keep hidden between two boards in the barn. Paper has been non-existent for a while, so we now use cornhusks and straw in the bathroom. None of us are anxious to wash, not even inside where our breath rises in white clouds. I overheard Herr Sommer talk to Boot about hygiene and that he's worried we'll soon have lice or bedbugs.

The other day I watched Karl-Heinz stuff a cap into his locker. I don't know where he got it, but I see it as a good sign that he's preparing. Herr Sommer handed me an old canvas bag we can use to carry our things. He also gave me a lighter and a small box of matches. He told me we can take the wool blankets from our beds with us.

All of January, snow and wind bluster around the inn. The landscape outside is white and gray and frozen. Our mood has reached bottom, most of the boys are tired of Boot's dominant style and his attempts to make us study.

We don't care and mostly refuse. We trade the handful of books back and forth, whittle random pieces of wood, and argue and outright fight while our meals are getting increasingly smaller. Most of the time we have chores—cut wood, clean, assist in the kitchen, do dishes, wash laundry, air beds and clothes.

Herr Sommer looks exhausted, his wooden leg drags across the floor planks as if it's too heavy to lift. Off and on he loses his temper and yells, something I never heard him do in the past.

"I'm going crazy," I comment as Karl-Heinz walks past me in the hall. We haven't been saying much, none of us have. Worse is that Hilda hasn't written. Surely, by now she's gotten my letter.

"Have you seen the weather?" Karl-Heinz hisses. "We'll be dead in three days."

"I know, but we can't wait forever. We'll just have to find places to sleep. Like barns and garages and sheds."

"People will invite us to sleep in their featherbeds."

"No, but—"

"But what?"

"We've got to go soon. If you don't want to, fine. I'll go alone." I bluff, hoping that Karl-Heinz will come around. But he says nothing, just shrugs his shoulders and walks off. The worst-case scenario is happening. I'll have to go alone, likely get lost and die on the way.

From then on, Karl-Heinz doesn't even look at me. He simply turns his head or sees right through me as if I'm air.

"What should I do?" I ask when I catch Herrn Sommer alone in the kitchen. As usual he's prepping, his hands busy peeling the soft outer layer of a dozen onions. It's another soup day at the inn.

Herr Sommer frowns as he looks into the wintry landscape outside. "Not sure what to tell you, Peter. This could go on for another month or two, or it could be over tomorrow." He looks at me, his expression pensive. "Thing is, if you go out there right now, you're likely going to freeze. Between us and other towns are wide stretches of nothing, fields and woods and plain empty land. You'll lose your way."

"But the waiting drives me crazy."

"I know." He hesitates. "What about your friend, Karl-Heinz?"

My silence says it all. Tears press with sudden malice.

Herr Sommer shakes his head. "You going alone out there…it feels wrong."

I agree, but if I open my mouth this minute I'm going to ball. So, I turn abruptly and head for the door. Because I don't want to see anybody, I head to the barn. Behind the old straw bale wall I've hidden my pack and going through it calms my nerves. I'm doing something, getting ready somehow.

I almost jump out of my skin when a shadow stretches above me.

"Sorry, I didn't mean to scare you." Karl-Heinz slumps down next to me. He is carrying a bag. He throws it down next to me, a sly grin on his face. "I've got my knife, some soap and a towel. I guess Sommer will let us take our blankets."

I nod, the lump in my throat as large as a soccer ball. I cough and say, "I thought you weren't going."

"Can't let my best friend kill himself out there."

"We are a good team."

"I know."

And that's how on the last day of February 1945, Karl-Heinz and I leave the inn where we've spent more than a year for the last time. Herr Sommer has dug deep into his stores, our packs heavy with potatoes, bread, a bit of salt, an entire bund cake and a dozen apples from last fall.

The air is a bit milder this morning, not much below freezing, and the wind has died down. We plan on following the main road toward Koscierzyna and from there, southwest. It's going to be tricky to keep the direction, but I'm hoping the sun will help us.

CHAPTER TWENTY-FOUR

Hilda

At the end of February, I'm still no wiser. Winter has been brutal with snow and ice and long lines at the grocery store. I count every day, hoping for warmer temperatures. Biene still sees the man and she still receives coal and extra food. Sometimes, she sneaks some for me and I feel guilty for taking it. Yet, I do, even if Biene has shadows below her eyes and often cries when we're alone. I still take care of Paul, who had a relapse on New Year's Eve when the British bombers came once again. He curled into a ball beneath the table and kept his fists on his ears. Neither Mama nor I could get him to go to the basement, so we all stayed up there on the floor, rubbing his back and talking while bombs whistled and exploded over the town.

Biene has secretly gone out with Kurt, but there's no place for them to be alone. It's icy cold outside and she doesn't want her mother to know about him.

Meeting him seems the only happy thing in her life.

"She's always so sad," Kurt mentioned the other day when we met at the grocer. "I wish I knew how to cheer her up."

"Seeing *you* makes her happy," I say, forcing myself to appear upbeat.

"But she never has time."

"She's watching her little brother," I lie.

Kurt nods, his gaze far away.

"I saw Kurt today," I tell Biene when she stops by in the afternoon. She's wearing her dress again, so I know where she's headed. "He's worried about you…like I am."

"I'm fine," Biene says. "At least we eat."

A high price to pay. Out loud I say, "You'd think he'd run out of coal."

Biene's laugh is bitter. "He stockpiled and hid most of it in an old cellar, so his yard looks empty. The SS came by a few months ago and demanded that he give them his reserves."

That's when an idea forms in my head. "Is the cellar nearby?"

"On his property, beneath a half-collapsed storage building. There's a trap door in the yard we use when he refills my sack."

"Must be nice."

Biene shrugs. "I better go."

After Biene leaves I pace around the kitchen table, imagining what she's doing at this moment. What right do I have to mess with my friend's life and that of her family? But how can I watch her being destroyed by this man and the things he makes her do?

At last I sit down and write a note. After dark, pretending I'm visiting Frau Breuer, I head to the SS office. A thin light flickers behind the drawn shutters, so I sneak to the door and stick the piece of paper between the door and the frame. All I hear is my heart hammering in my temples. I don't want to be caught, not by these men who have the reputation of killing civilians at random or sending them away to labor camps.

As I hurry home, doubt creeps up in me like a toxic cloud that fills out my insides. What have I done? What if Biene is there when the SS come to investigate? My note mentions the man's name and address and that he keeps coal hidden from the government. I have mentioned the cellar door in back.

Lying awake half the night, I imagine Biene's happy face when she finds the coal trader gone, her burden lifted. At last she can concentrate on Kurt and forget the old man with his filthy fingers. I contemplate warning her not to go over there in case the SS is around.

In the morning I'm convinced I made a mistake. Who am I to turn somebody in? I've always hated people who spy and denounce. I'm no better. And Biene? I took their livelihood, the bit of comfort they have. Theo's as well.

Despite the near freezing temperatures in our apartment, I'm hot, the wool sweater scratchy on my neck. I leave right after breakfast and casually walk past the SS office. My note is no longer there.

The rest of the morning I spend in the woods, cutting down a small tree. I borrowed a saw from Frau Breuer and in exchange she's getting some of the wood. Oak and beech burn the longest, but they're also the hardest, and it takes hours to cut up pieces that fit into the stove.

Every few minutes, my thoughts wander to Biene and the coal merchant. Does she know? Did he say anything about her? What if the SS arrested Biene for profiteering? As soon as my hand wagon is full, I hurry home. But I never make it there, because I run into Kurt.

Even from a distance I can see something is wrong. He's red-faced, his movements jerky. My hearts sinks and I hardly have enough energy to pull the wagon farther—Biene must have been arrested.

"I've been drafted," he cries rushing up to me. "I've got to leave by tomorrow and I can't go without seeing Biene."

Relief takes my breath … not Biene. *You coldhearted beast, he's going to war.* "What happened?" I hurry.

"Had a second muster. We all have to go to Marburg and help with the *Volkssturm*…fight the Russians and Americans."

I stare at Kurt. He's so thin, just a boy. "But you have no training and you're really young!" I cry.

"Sixteen last month. They say the Hitler Youth will train us. And we'll receive weapons and uniforms." My thoughts wander to Peter, who I haven't seen in nearly two years. Hope is a curious thing. It shows up here and there, perks up its presence when you least expect it. Stupid me.

"Can you help me with Biene?"

I nod numbly. "Take the wagon and I'll go right over."

Kurt follows me to Biene's house. "I haven't told Mother. I don't know what she's going to do without me."

"Can't you hide?"

Kurt throws up his arms. "Where would I go—in your basement? I can't be seen by anybody or they'll shoot me for deserting." His voice falters.

I capture one of his arms and hold on tight. "Let's talk about it with Biene. Maybe she'll have an idea."

But the doorbell echoes and I can't help but wonder why Biene's mother never opens the door.

"Let's wait a bit," Kurt says. His eyes have that hopeful look that tells me he's head over heels.

"Do you have any family that could take you in…hide you?" I ask. Kurt is tall, but he's skinny, almost bony, and I can't imagine him wearing a uniform, shooting at Russians. In fact, you can tell from his expression how kind he is.

"Mother has a sister in Köln. She had to move after her apartment house was bombed. I don't even know where she is now."

"What about friends?"

Kurt shakes his head and I run out of things to say. We've been waiting for at least fifteen minutes, maybe twenty. If Biene got arrested I'll never forgive myself.

"…last?"

"What?" I focus on Kurt.

"You're so distracted. Did something happen?"

I shake my head, my throat too thick to speak.

"I asked you how long you think the war will continue."

How often do I ask myself that question? We all know that Germany is losing. Sister Rose's words return. "I don't think the Führer will ever give up?"

It's true. He's said as much in his speech at the end of January. We all listened squeezed around the radio. He talked about the people sacrificing and our will to fight and protect the Great German Reich. That we're strong…powerful.

Ha, I don't feel powerful. I feel weak and tired most of the time. And all the things I used to love and appreciate have either gone or are worse.

I meet Kurt's questioning eyes when I notice movement in the distance. Biene is walking toward us, but her pace is as slow as an old woman. She hasn't looked up yet, hasn't seen us.

Kurt, who notices my gaze, whips around and starts running toward Biene. I follow slowly. I only see Biene shake her head and keep walking.

"What happened?" Kurt's voice is exasperated and loud.

Biene keeps walking toward me. Only when she is two meters away, does she notice me.

"Are you all right?" I ask.

She shakes her head, but doesn't speak.

"Did you go…?"

She nods. She's about to speak when she remembers that Kurt is there too. So she says nothing and resumes her walk.

"Biene, wait," Kurt cries.

"Kurt has to leave," I say at her back. That's when she finally stops and faces us. "He's been drafted to the people's storm."

"When?" she says, her voice so quiet, it's no more than a breath.

"I have to leave by tomorrow." Tears have appeared in Kurt's eyes. He grips Biene's hand and holds it to his chest. "I don't know when I'll return."

If you return. Shut up, shut up, I tell my brain. I don't want to think about the men out there fighting and dying, those in prison camps or returning maimed like my brother.

Biene looks into Kurt's face as if she's seeing him for the first time. She caresses his right cheek with utmost gentleness. "I will miss you terribly."

"Where were you?" he whispers.

"Nowhere…"

"Maybe you should take a walk together," I say, feeling like the fifth wheel again.

"But something is wrong," Kurt says. "You're always upset and you hardly even noticed us."

Biene smiles, but I can tell it's false. "I was supposed to pick up rations from a friend." She opens her mouth, closes it.

"How about that walk?" I say into the silence, much too brightly. "Or maybe, you could come with me. Visit us…I mean you could…"

Biene shakes her head. It's one short shake as if she wants to cut me off. "I'm going inside now." She grips Kurt's hand. "I wish you well."

What? No! Surprise and pain show in Kurt's eyes, spread across his mouth, down to his shoulders. He literally sags forward.

"Biene, wait!" I cry. "Tell us what happened?" *As if I didn't know.*

That's when a terrible transformation happens on Biene's face. She sneers at me. "So you did know. I wonder why." She looks at Kurt with that same scorn. "Is he in on it? Did you turn him in together?"

Ignoring both us, she continues, "What am I going to do? How will I tell Mother? What are we going to eat?"

"I'll help you," I cry. "We'll find a way—"

"What are you talking about?" Kurt asks.

"So, you don't know?" Biene throws a fist at Kurt's chest. "I don't believe you."

"Please, Biene..." Kurt's voice is filled with more pain and...pleading.

"Please, Biene," my best friend mocks. I don't even recognize this person as she abruptly swivels on her heels and bears down on me.

"You did it! You turned him in." She grabs my collar and starts to shake me. "I asked myself who could've known and then I remembered." Biene's forefinger pokes at my face. "You asked me where he was hiding the coal. And stupid me, stupid trusting me, told my *best* friend."

"What happened?" I whisper because my throat is too dry for regular words.

"You know good and well what happened." Biene's voice is high and shrill. "They came and took him, took the coal. All of it." Her fingers slide off my coat. "What am I going to do now?"

"Live without that filthy man," I say.

"What man are you talking about? What coal?" Kurt looks back and forth between us.

"The one who gave us things," Biene says to Kurt.

I clamp my mouth shut. I will not tell Kurt what she did to *earn* the things.

"Why would he do that?" Kurt says just then. And that's when it dawns on him. "You slept with him for coal?"

Biene's gaze returns to Kurt, her eyes large and shiny. "So what if I did. We needed help. I can't go and steal like you do, I've got a sick brother. What am I supposed to do?"

"Hilda has a sick brother and she isn't doing it." Kurt's voice is almost calm as he watches the girl he loves.

"Hilda would do it too if she had the chance."

Would I? That's a question I haven't asked myself. I look at Biene, my friend, how she stands there all broken and ground to pieces from the guilt and the need to help her family. What are we turning into? What has the Führer done to us?

That's when Kurt turns to me. "Would you?"

I shake my head, unprepared for this question. Biene's eyes burn into my forehead. I feel them like a light, trying to illuminate my thoughts. "I don't know," I finally say.

I look at Kurt whose mouth is pinched flat from hurt and

now…anger.

"Will you please come to my house so we can talk?" I ask.

Kurt shakes his head very slowly. "That won't be necessary. I've heard all I need to hear. I'm going now."

Only when he walks off, Biene awakes from this…what exactly, a state of craziness? She finally understands that Kurt is leaving and may not return. "Kurt?"

He just throws up a dismissive arm and accelerates.

"Wait," cries Biene.

But Kurt doesn't wait. He begins to run and is soon out of sight.

Biene just stands there, arms hanging by her sides. "Now I've lost him too."

"He'll be back soon," I say, realizing how cold I am. I hardly feel my feet and my hands are stiff. But worse is the cold inside me, as if my bones have turned to ice.

Biene finally comes out of her stupor. "He'll die like the rest of them," she says before marching to the front door of her home and disappearing.

Peter

Karl-Heinz and I have been on the road for four days. Yesterday, we passed through *Koscierzyna*, a real town with little stores and stone homes. We hurried past, neither of us having any money or wanting to draw attention. An old man, his face darkish and wrinkly, watched us from the door of his reed-covered cabin. We nodded in greeting, then smiled at each other, because it sort of felt like a first victory. At last we are going home.

The weather has held, at least there haven't been any snow or super icy temperatures. Each afternoon we search for a barn or some other place, we can sleep. So far, it has worked. What worries me most is that we'll get lost. We're supposed to head southwest, but there aren't always roads, not even trails. We follow along fields and across patches of woods, then again wide-open expanses of land. There's so much land, why would the Red Army go through here in the first place?

The walking drains me, and though we have been limiting our meals, they're dwindling far too quickly. We haven't seen more than five people the entire time. The land in front of us is flat and bare, sort of dead. The few trees rear their bare limbs upward as if to pray for sun. The sky extends forever, a whitish dome of space that makes me feel insignificant, antlike.

In this cold and deserted vacuum we trudge, sometimes next to each other, sometimes one before the other. Neither of us says much, no more than a word or two. We stop to pee or to clear a rock from our shoes. Immediately, the air seeps into our clothes, slips beneath our skin to make us shiver, urges us to move on.

"You're limping," I say when Karl-Heinz moves in front of me.

"My heel hurts," Karl-Heinz says over his shoulder.

"What happened?"

"Nothing. My shoes are tight." Karl Heinz has huge feet, probably a size twelve. We used to be about even, now he is four inches taller than I am.

"Want to take a break?"

"No."

And so it goes. Karl-Heinz limps in front of me and I try to ignore the pain in his step.

When he abruptly stops, I almost bump into him.

"You hear that?"

I listen. Indeed, somewhere in front of us two women argue. One voice is young and high, the other gravelly and older. We're traversing a patch of evergreens, the air wonderfully thick with sap, so we can't see very far.

"You think we should wait?" Karl-Heinz says. Herr Sommer told us to trust nobody and to stay away from crowds.

"Maybe we should sneak up on whoever it is."

We leave the path and slowly work our way toward the commotion. The ground is soft and squishy with needles. Here and there icy patches remain.

Ahead, ten or so people sit and stand leaning against the trees, packs and carts beside them. Refugees. This group consists of women and children only. The two in question are facing each other, both red-faced, both spitting fire with their eyes.

"I shouldn't have listened to you," the younger one says. She's not much older than us, her hair cascading long and dark down her back. Her opposite is old like Mother and terribly ugly. Her nose, misshapen like a frozen potato, cuts her face into two, her eyes are small yet wide apart. Her fists are balled as if she wants to take a swing at the younger woman. The others in their company are watching wearily—none of them appears keen to take a side.

"You call me a liar?" Potato Nose asks.

"That's exactly what you are."

The ugly woman's eyes narrow. "If you don't like it, you're welcome to leave anytime."

"So you can take advantage of them?"

"You never liked me. Admit it."

"That doesn't mean you should steal our food or pretend you know the way."

"Enough!" Abruptly, Potato Nose smashes her fist into the young woman's face. The attack comes so quickly, the girl puts up no defense and simply sags to the ground. Blood gushes from a cut in her cheek, where the other woman has scratched her with her fingernails.

Without missing a beat, the ugly woman turns to the others and claps her hands. "Marta can continue on her own. Anyone against that?"

None of the tired figures makes a peep. At first it seems the young woman seems to want to argue, but then her arms drop to her side. Shaking her head, she crawls sideways and leans against a fallen tree trunk. Her right hand is bloody from where she wiped her cheek, but she doesn't seem to notice.

Movement creeps into the group of women and children, and ever so slowly they walk off, the ugly one shoeing them along. "Come on, let's go. Not much farther."

Karl-Heinz and I look at each other.

"We better go," Karl-Heinz whispers.

"We've got to help her," I say.

Karl-Heinz straightens and picks up his bag. "Why? She'll be a burden. We've got enough to worry about."

I get up too, facing my friend. I see irritation and questions in his eyes, questions I can't answer.

"I'm not leaving."

Annoyed, Karl-Heinz stomps toward the girl. "Fine then."

Running from our hiding spot, I cry, "Sorry, we saw what happened."

Marta about jumps out of her skin and shrieks. "I've got no money. Please spare me, please let me go." She straightens and in her haste trips and smacks on the forest floor. It's soft but the fall knocks the wind from her. Nonetheless, she scrambles to her knees and attempts to stand. I rush to her side and hold out a hand.

"We didn't mean to scare you," I hurry.

"We're not going to hurt you," Karl-Heinz adds.

The girl's gaze hops between us like a frightened bunny. It's clear she's trying to make up her mind about us.

"Look, we're going home…to Solingen," I say. "It's a long way and we're going to continue now, but you're welcome to join us."

By now the girl stands again. She sways a bit as she grabs her meager pack. That's when she notices her bloodstained hand and hesitates. "Rita…she and I—"

"We noticed. She didn't seem very nice." I offer my handkerchief, which has seen better days, but the girl takes it.

She even tries a smile. "Thank you."

"This is Karl-Heinz and I'm Peter."

"Marta Jawinski."

"You're fleeing?" Karl-Heinz asks.

"Going to Berlin," Marta says.

"You sure?" I say. "Berlin is going to be bad when the Russians get there."

"You think they'll go that far?" Apprehension darkens Marta's eyes. They're dark brown, but now they appear black. She hands me the even more soiled hankie and I stuff it into my pocket without paying attention.

"I don't see why not," Karl-Heinz says. "Germany lost the war."

I nod. Somehow hearing the words from Karl-Heinz makes it more real. A shiver creeps up my back that has nothing to do with the grayish cold of late winter.

Marta frowns. "Where did you say you're going?"

"Solingen." I watch the girl who somehow reminds me of Hilda.

"How far is that?"

"Maybe nine hundred kilometers."

The girl claps a palm against her mouth. "That will take you months."

"Another six weeks or so." Karl-Heinz sounds confident, but I'm not feeling it. We have no idea where we are, and it's entirely possible we're walking in a circle.

Today, at least while the sun was out, we headed somewhat west and south.

"I must think about it. For now I will go with you."

I produce a smile and Karl-Heinz says, "Great. Let's go then. We've got at least three hours of daylight left." I throw my friend a curious look—he hasn't been this talkative since we left the inn.

The first few kilometers we follow the footprints of Marta's former companions. But then we reach a lake that's so large, the opposite bank is at least a kilometer away. Ice crusts the edges in white ribbons. Somewhere in the reed a bird calls a warning. We have to decide on a direction and turn left. It feels like we're heading back east and frustration brews inside me.

"Maybe we should've gone the other way," I say after a while.

That's when the girl smacks a palm against her forehead. "Oh, I'm stupid." She rummages through her pack and produces a folded paper. "I've got a map."

I swallow a nasty comment and study the paper. It's only a piece that shows Prussia's northern coast. It doesn't reach all the way to Berlin nor does it show Germany, but there are roads and lakes and cities. Unfortunately, most of the area is uninhabited. There is no city nearby, not even a village, just lots of lakes and woods and emptiness.

"I think we're about here." Karl-Heinz points a grimy forefinger at a lake.

"Or maybe here," I say, aiming at a different lake.

We look at each other until Marta chimes in. "I'm pretty sure we crossed this forest earlier which would make Peter's location more likely."

I can't suppress a grin, which immediately disappears when I look at Karl-Heinz. The last thing we need right now is a fight over taking sides.

By the time we leave the lake's edge, dusk is settling. There is no barn or shed, no indication humanity has ever been here.

"We should sleep in the woods," Marta says, pointing toward a stand of evergreens. It is already almost dark beneath the trees, but the wind has quieted. A few trees have fallen and created horizontal roadblocks. Once again Marta takes over. "Here, this is good." She goes through her pack once more and produces a piece of canvas tarp.

If we make a fire in front and lower this across the tree trunk, it'll be warm enough. In the last light, Karl-Heinz and I rush around and collect wood while Marta sets up our camp.

Wrapped into our blankets we eat a freshly roasted potato—Marta gets one as well—and watch the fire. My back is cold, but thanks to the tarp it is tolerable.

When we fall asleep, Marta is lying between us, her long hair like a pillow beneath her. I imagine what she looks like beneath her cloths as Hilda scolds me with that special look.

When I awake in the morning, it is barely light, the spot next to me empty. Karl-Heinz lies on his back, snoring quietly. He looks peaceful. The fire is out and the dampness has made it up my spine. That's when I remember Marta. She's left us. She stole our things and disappeared in the night.

I sit up and smack my head against the tree trunk, trying to remember where I left my pack. Damn thief. Girls are just no good. Pain settles behind my forehead as I carefully inspect the growing goose egg. I straighten and am about to wake Karl-Heinz when something moves in the thicket behind me. I swivel on my heels and find myself face-to-face with Marta. She's carrying a bundle of sticks.

"Thought it'd be nice to have a little fire before we go," she says. Her smile is without guile and I feel my cheeks warm with shame. She's braided her hair, and though hers is dark and long, I'm reminded of Hilda again.

"Eh, yes, a good idea."

I busy myself with the blanket and find my pack underneath the tarp where I'd used it as a pillow. Even more embarrassed, I rush off into the woods with the words, "Got to pee."

When I return, Karl-Heinz and Marta are bending over the map.

"If we head left, we go south and should get to the road toward Schlochau," Marta says.

"Sounds good." Karl-Heinz nods toward me. "Let's make sure Peter agrees."

Studying the map, I frown, but can't find any fault with Marta's plan. So I mumble something like "all right" and pick up my blanket.

That's when I freeze.

The ground beneath vibrates and the trees appear to shake. This is how an earthquake must feel. We look at each other with wide eyes.

"Tanks...military," Marta cries and collects her tarp. Then she puts a forefinger on her lips and motions us to pick up our things. We scramble to pack, shove a bunch of dirt over the fire and follow Marta into the forest. Somewhere in the distance, tree limbs break and engines choke.

"Who is it?" I whisper.

Marta bends closer. "Russians or Germans."

That's when I see movement ahead. Men in brownish gray uniforms with round helmets are walking in-between slow-rolling trucks. *Not German* goes through my head. At the same time, Marta and Karl-Heinz yank me to the ground. We crawl behind a fallen tree and lie still.

The earth trembles worse—tanks. Over the noise of the engines I hear occasional shouts, nothing I understand. I don't care anyway; all I care about is staying out of sight. From the refugees, I know what soldiers do with girls. Bile rises to my throat. They may shoot Karl-Heinz and me or arrest and imprison us. Nobody would ever know what happened, just two guys lost in the woods, out of millions of people gone.

After a while, I've got no idea how much time has passed, the ground quiets. We peek across the tree and sit up. The forest is empty again.

"Let's wait a bit longer. Then we follow." Karl-Heinz stretches himself and holds out an arm to help up Marta.

"They're going west…like us," I say. It means one thing, and one thing only: the war is lost—Germany is lost—and all I heard before is true.

This time I swallow to hold back tears. I don't want the others to notice how seeing the Red Army is scaring me.

What will it be like at home? If we even make it?

Book Three: April 1945 – June 1945

CHAPTER TWENTY-FIVE

Hilda

I don't know how I made it through March. It was the worst month of my life. Biene refused to talk to me and I was eaten up by guilt. Still am. Why did I need to intervene? Why stick my nose into other people's business, try controlling them?

At least Biene's family would've been taken care of. Now they're starving like us and if anything happens to Theo, it'll be on me. Likely, I'd not even find out. Other than seeing Biene on the street once—at which she immediately turned around and ignored my calls—I have had no contact with her.

April brings some decent weather, so I've been able to build up a nice stash of firewood. The cutting and hauling helps me work through my emotions. At least during the day. At night is a different matter. I sleep terribly, wake up a lot.

Last night I dreamed that Peter returned. He stood in the door with his back to me though I knew it was him. When he talked I couldn't understand his mumbles, so I asked him to look at me. That's when he began to laugh and turn toward me. The right side of his skull was gone, showing the pinkish brain beneath.

I screamed and awoke, the sheets wrapped around my legs like chains, my face wet with sweat and tears. Had I not told the SS, Kurt and Biene would still be friends. He'd at least be having happy thoughts wherever he is.

The only bright spot is that I picked up a leaflet the Americans throw out of planes. It says we should surrender and hang white sheets out of our windows. It means the war will end soon. It must. Mama was quite upset when I came home with the paper. She's working part-time again in a different building. The city has moved their offices.

"They'll shoot us just for looking at the paper," she said, stuffing it into the kitchen stove.

"But we need to let the Americans know."

"The SS and Hitler Youth use martial law. They don't even need to ask or arrest you, they can just shoot."

"Mama is right," Paul says quietly. "As much as I want to see this end, we can't afford to…"

"So we choose between being shot by the Americans or the SS?"

Paul slowly nods. "We'll do the sheet when the time is right."

When is that, I want to yell. But I'm not supposed to speak angrily to Paul or raise my voice. It aggravates him. So I say nothing and get busy with another dinner of watery soup.

My first walk is to the tap. The service has been on and off again. A few days ago the water was all brown and silty. They say it's from the Rhine River. We can't drink or cook with it, only clean.

This morning the line hisses air, so I grab the buckets and head for the well. As I draw closer to the Pütt, I hear explosions toward *Widdert,* a neighborhood in the south of Solingen. Not from the air, not air mines or bombs, but likely artillery. There's a line at the well, and people are talking.

"The Americans are coming," one woman whose back is permanently bent forward says. "I hung out sheets."

"Me too," another, a black shawl wrapped around her hair, says. "I can't wait another minute for it to be over."

"You think they'll attack women and children, arrest us?" a third says.

We all look at each other. The Führer makes every other country sound like the devil.

"All I know is that the British kill women and children by the thousands. Who else are they bombing in the towns?" The bent-over woman purses her lips. "Dresden in February and now Würzburg."

"We're all paying the price," the woman with the shawl says.

"Shh," two others say.

That's when I hear the droning sort of noise, large engines make, heavy wheels rolling across stones, crunching everything beneath. It's coming from the main road, *Brühler Berg*. We all look at each other, at once curious and terrified.

"I'm going to look," the woman with the shawl says.

"I'm going home," the bent-over woman says. "They'll shoot us down."

"Why would they?" the question is out before I have time to think. "They want us to surrender."

"Young lady, you better hide. Never know what these soldiers are going to do."

I think about Biene, about the rumors of soldiers raping every woman and girl in sight. Still, I can't stop wondering about the noise.

"You think they're coming this way?" a small girl, no older than eight, asks.

"We can hide if they do."

From the well it's only a hundred yards to the main road. I quickly hide my buckets behind a bush and rush forward. I've got to see for myself. My ears are on high alert, so high, I hear the sparrows chirping under the eaves despite the increasing droning noise. Vibrations travel up my feet through my knees into my spine. Whatever is out there, is quite heavy—and huge.

Shortly before the little side road from *Unnersberg* opens onto *Brühler Berg*, I sneak behind the last building, past a little garden. Between bushes and trees I've got a decent view of the road.

From the direction of *Widdert* come a long line of tanks, grayish green monstrosities with turrets, long gun barrels and tiny wheels held by chained tracks. A single white star is painted on them. On top hover men in beige uniforms, black men with dark eyes. Across the street, sheets are being hung from windows. Women lean outside, one of them waving.

A couple of teen boys by the road hold white handkerchiefs, their eyes wide with awe and anxiety. That's when the tank nearest them stops. The entire line screeches to a halt just as my heart. The boys will be shot, I'm sure of it.

The American soldier on the tank yells something I can't understand. I know it's English and I know I should know, but my brain is completely empty. In my mind I'm urging on the boys to run—run fast and hide. But they just stand there and stare. Fools!

That's when the man in the opening of the tank, a soldier with smooth brown skin throws something to the boys. One of them catches, the other bends low to pick up the packet. They inspect their prize, the shiny white and red wrapper.

"Gum," the soldier shouts, nodding with a smile. "Enjoy."

My heart jumps a beat. The Führer lied to us. These men are not monsters here to kill us all. They're throwing chewing gum to kids. And then something else filters into my mind: *it's over*. The war, this terrible drawn-out, never-ending war, is over.

I half consider jumping from my hiding place to join the boys, but then the tanks resume their course. I turn on my heels, retrieve my buckets and race home as quickly as the sloshing pails let me.

"Hang out the sheets," I cry, entering the kitchen. Paul is on the sofa, reading a torn copy of Bertold Brecht's *Die Mutter*, he's borrowed from Peter's mother.

Paul deliberately slides a bookmark between the pages and sits up. He always moves slowly, but his eyes are showing the old spark I remember from years ago. "What happened?"

"The Americans are here." Now that I say it out loud, I'm all shaky. "It's over, the war is over."

Paul attempts to get off the sofa, but I'm faster. We hug, a long solid hug. Paul's eyes are wet when I let him go. "Better find something white," he says quietly. "Then you tell Frau Breuer."

As I drape a threadbare tablecloth from the living room window, Paul watches me. He's sort of like a wax figure, kind of lifelike but totally still. One thought repeats itself in my mind: At last, things will get better again.

I have no idea how wrong I am.

Peter

Every place we pass carries signs of war. Groups of refugees, sometimes hundreds, sit along roads. We overtake many, exchange greetings and bits of news. *Seen Ivan, yes, signs of him, yes, fires and torn-apart buildings yes, dead bodies in front of houses, shot dead, women raped and killed afterwards, children, even small ones, dead, farms ransacked, looking for food, hungry, yes.* We never stay long, the information always the same. *Where are you going? Be careful, keep your eyes open, travel safely.*

Roads and paths are mud holes, bridges destroyed, water soiled, rivers running murky. Our sleep becomes restless as one of us tries keeping watch. Whoever is on guard eventually falls asleep. It's been happening to all of us.

Marta's map no longer helps us. We're somewhere west, Berlin south of us. How far, we don't know.

The last days we have seen fewer signs of the military. It's as if they were all headed to Berlin. I'm thinking of the first refugees we met—Maria with her little boy, Alexander, who no longer speaks. Did they make it to Berlin? Are they being attacked by Russians in their new home?

But I can't spend much time on them or anyone else. We've got to concentrate every minute of every day on the task of survival. Food is hard to get, and the gnawing in my middle is like a nasty comrade who keeps picking at an old injury. Most days we steal, somehow managing to forge ahead in a state of exhaustion. Karl-Heinz sometimes stumbles, and my own legs are made of mushy bones that don't want to hold me up any longer.

Gray shadows circle Marta's eyes. We found out she is a year older than us, eighteen, but has only had seven years of school. After that she helped her parents on the farm—a farm that no longer exists, a father who left at the beginning of the war and a mother who died in childbirth shortly after.

The war tears at us all, makes us suffer. Nobody escapes. At least not people like us, normal working families. What families? There aren't any left, my own father gone for years, Mother and Walter somewhere alone…maybe dead. A gurgle escapes me as I imagine Mama lying in the rubble, dust-coated skin, still eyes. Like that day in the alley, Walter's face is covered in blood as he wanders past. And Hilda? Is she trying to walk home like us?

I suck in air to keep the thoughts from unraveling. Enough. I've got to concentrate. We've slept in a shed, but there's nothing edible inside. The hut is part of a *Schrebergarden*, a space where lots of people keep vegetable plots and little houses to spend the summers. Most sheds have no electricity or running water, certainly no toilets.

You've got to keep watchful because these communities have eyes everywhere…and they know each other. The owner of this one has prepared his plot for planting, but it's too early in the year. The winter bed is empty, the remnants of brown stalks indicate onions.

My stomach rumbles angrily as I move around the building, peek into the adjacent plots. Nothing.

"Hey, what are you doing there?" The voice belongs to an old man walking with a cane, which he now wields like a sword.

I roll my eyes, too tired to be afraid. But the man is surprisingly fast and soon arrives at the little gate. "You aren't Rufus's boy?" Humungous brows scrunch as he glares at me.

"No, just needed a place for the night."

"Then I suggest you get going before I…"

Before what, I want to say. The man is at least eighty and can hardly walk. Ignoring him, I call inside. "Marta, Karl-Heinz, time to go."

Both appear with hair sticking up, pulling on their coats and bags.

"I'm starving," Karl-Heinz says. "You didn't by chance—" His gaze lodges on the old geezer. "Never mind."

"We better go," I say, grabbing my own pack. It's light and only contains a change of dirty clothes, blanket and ragged towel, we haven't had a chance to wash.

"You better," the man huffs, shaking his cane once more.

Soon we're walking on a narrow path meandering through fields and forests. The air is filled with birdsong and the tangy smell of decomposing leaves from last winter. Smoky clouds hasten overhead and drizzle on us, just enough to soften our clothes and shoes.

We've been on the road much longer than I expected and even now, I don't know for sure where we are and if we're heading in the right direction. We're supposed to pass by Hannover, but haven't been on an actual street with road signs in a while.

"I can't go on," Marta says at last.

"Just a little longer," Karl-Heinz says. Marta and Karl-Heinz are close, much closer than I am. Sometimes, I wonder if I was wrong about Karl-Heinz liking Christian…liking boys.

Marta stops and drops her pack. She's grown thin as a stick figure, her cheekbones pronounced, her eyes almost hollow. "Maybe I should let you two go ahead. I just can't. You'll be faster without me."

"Nonsense," Karl-Heinz's voice rises in anger. "You're coming with us." He turns to me. "Right, Peter?"

I nod.

Marta sinks to the ground and closes her eyes. "Just let me sleep."

"No way." Karl-Heinz tugs at the girl's arm. "Come on, I'll help you up."

"Surely, this path has to lead somewhere," I add, stepping to Marta's side and squeezing her shoulder.

Marta mumbles something, but refuses to get up.

"If I have to I'll carry you," Karl-Heinz says. He *sounds* forceful, but there's doubt in his eyes. He looks like he'll buckle over any moment himself.

"Maybe we should try to find help," I say.

Karl-Heinz throws out his arms. "Where? How?"

"You both go," Marta says. "I'll be fine."

I pull Karl-Heinz aside who looks like he may burst into tears. "Neither of us can manage carrying her. It's the only way. There's got to be somebody. The longer we wait, the worse it'll get."

At last Karl-Heinz nods. I pat Marta on the head. "We'll hurry right back. Don't move, no matter what."

Karl-Heinz and I silently stumble off. The path continues to meander as I try to memorize the landscape. It all looks the same…trees and bushes, covered in fresh green, the path dotted with grasses and weeds. The only consolation I have is that the trail looks well used despite the quiet.

At some point the path leads to a narrow road. Nothing moves though in places wagon wheels have carved deep ruts.

We take a couple of fallen limbs and lean them against the trunk of a beech tree. It's not much, but we want to be able to find the path again.

We turn right. Walking is difficult because the ruts are muddy and filled with water. We hop left to right and back, trying to keep our feet half way dry. That's when I notice a thin ribbon of smoke to our left. At the same time, the smell of manure hits my nose. Through the trees we make out a couple of brick buildings—a farm. I poke Karl-Heinz and produce a grin. He nods and we rush forward.

Forgotten are caution and restraint. "Hello, anybody home?" I shout.

In an enclosure, a dozen brown-speckled hens cluck and scratch. The one rooster eyes us suspiciously, his comb swollen and unfriendly. Let's hope the farmer is in a better mood.

"Go away," a woman's voice says from a cracked window. Hard to tell who stands behind the glass.

"We need help," Karl-Heinz says toward it.

"Our friend is in bad shape," I add.

"I can't help you," the voice says. I detect fear in it.

"Please," Karl-Heinz says. "Marta has walked for hundreds of kilometers. She's very tired and weak. Will you not help us?"

Silence follows. The outline of the figure behind the window stands there frozen. Karl-Heinz and I look at each other. Somebody told me once that you should keep quiet when making a proposal to wait for the reaction of your opponent.

"It is a ruse, I'm sure," the voice finally says. "I've got a gun, so just leave now."

Sucking in air, I cross my arms. "Fine, then you have to shoot us. We can't go on and we need to get help for Marta. There's nobody else. We promise to be good, we just want to go home to our families."

"Where?" comes from the window.

"Solingen...near—"

"I know where Solingen is."

"We haven't seen our mothers in two years," Karl-Heinz says.

Again silence.

"We can work for you," I say finally.

As soon as I say that, the window smacks shut. Disappointment creeps across Karl-Heinz's expression, his shoulders slump. "I guess we'll steal a chicken and go back."

I nod.

But before we make it to the coop, the heavy oak door of the farmhouse opens. "Come closer."

We swivel on our heels and approach the entry. In the gloom stands a woman, though I can't tell how old she is. All I know is that she's in pain because she sort of hunches over, with one hand on her abdomen. There is no sign of a gun.

"I'm Peter and this is Karl-Heinz," I say, hope spreading through me like sunshine after a long winter.

"Where is your friend?"

"In the woods, about a kilometer up the path."

The woman points at the barn. "Take the handcart."

"Thank you," Karl-Heinz blurts.

By the time we return to the farm, dusk is setting. The chickens have gone some place inside. I smell wood smoke and something else...food.

My stomach seems to expand and grind inside me, an ache that crawls to my throat and takes over my mind. We return the cart to the barn and help Marta hobble toward the farm.

Before we can knock, the door opens. "Wash up at the pump and take off your shoes when you come in." I hardly hear what the woman says because the food aroma is so strong, I'm salivating and swallowing repeatedly.

Somewhat cleaner we creep inside. I'm embarrassed about the state of my socks, mostly holes with a few threads of yarn remaining. Karl-Heinz's and Marta's are no better.

The hallway opens into a spacious kitchen. Oil lamps spread warm yet low light. The table is set for four.

"Sit," the woman says, filling plates. The aroma is so strong now that I'm about to faint. I sink onto a chair when I see bread stacked in the middle of the table. It's real bread, not just corn mush. I swallow so loudly, the gurgle echoes through the room.

Marta's and Karl-Heinz's eyes swivel back and forth between the woman and the bread as she turns and sets steaming bowls in front of us. In the gloom I can't really tell what it is, but it smells heavenly. Again I swallow.

"I'm Frau Leitner," the woman says as she joins us at the table. Her eyes are tired as if she hasn't slept in weeks, the fine skin on her cheeks spidery wrinkles. She points a forefinger at the bread. "Better eat."

We all lunge for the bread, and when the first bite hits my throat, I close my eyes. The soup is creamy and thick with potatoes, carrots and onions.

"Better take your time," Frau Leitner says. "You'll get sick otherwise."

Quiet settles. I try to chew slowly, enjoy the glorious feeling of food sliding down and filling me. Shouldn't it be awkward to sit in a strange kitchen with a woman I've never seen before? But it doesn't matter. It's the reality of this new world that throws people together at random.

"This is Marta," I say into the silence.

Marta produces a smile. "Thank you so much. I just couldn't continue."

Frau Leitner pats Marta's hand. "I know, child, I know."

"Is your husband…in the war?" Karl-Heinz asks.

Frau Leitner blinks. "He left three years ago. I have not heard from him since January."

"Where was he?" I ask.

"Courland."

"Toward Russia?"

She nods.

I remember the refugees and their stories, Arthur's ordeal. The

Red Army had begun surrounding Courland in October 1944. They had attacked over and over, but the German Army Group North resisted. Frau Leitner's husband is either dead or a Russian prisoner by now.

I lower my gaze to hide the defeat that surely shows on my face.

CHAPTER TWENTY-SIX

Hilda

Two weeks after the Americans arrived, some things have changed, others haven't. Most houses show white signs of surrender hanging from their windows. Remainders of the Third Reich are disappearing. There are no more flags, swastikas or men in Wehrmacht or brown uniforms.

Mayor Brückmann has handed the keys to the city—rather the pile of rubble that's left of it—to the Americans.

Barb wired roadblocks have appeared at certain crossroads. American jeeps and trucks roam the streets. Major John O. Hall, an American commander, has taken over to establish the occupation. Chief commandant of the allied forces, General Dwight D. Eisenhower's *Proclamation No. 1* posters, which say that the military government is in charge, are plastered around town. Courts and schools are closed.

Mama returned home for a day, but is now back at work because the Americans don't want everything to break down. She speaks English pretty well, better than I do, and works for the Americans, helping them organize the city's administration.

After Papa left, we ran out of money. Until then Mama had never worked even though she attended school until tenth grade. During those months I thought we'd all somehow die…of hunger and heartbreak. I was nine then, and I still remember attempting to wake Mama, who'd been spending more and more time in her bed.

Our cupboards were empty and I'd gotten home from school famished.

I crawled into bed with Mama and crept into her arms. At first, she pushed me away, but in the end I wiggled through. As dusk settled in the room that reeked of unwashed clothes and sadness, Mama went into a crying fit. I didn't know what to do and finally called Paul who was studying in the kitchen. We both returned and snuck into bed with our mother, hugging her.

"Mama, will we die now?" I asked.

She didn't answer, just stroked my head for a while. We must have fallen asleep, but by the time we awoke the next morning, Mama was up. Not only that, she'd washed and dressed in her best outfit, somehow scraped together a few oats and nuts for breakfast. Before we could sit to eat, she was out the door.

A week later, Mama began her first job as an assistant at the city. She worked hard and often studied at night. Among other things, she did a refresher course in English. She's been working and supporting us ever since, even paying our school money so we could attend gymnasium high school. I love her for that.

Now she helps translate things and today, I decided to pick her up. Not just to help carry her bag, but because I'm curious about these men who are now running our city.

A sea of barbed wire surrounds the building and two GIs guard the entrance with machine guns. Behind the barricade several soldiers—so handsome in their crisp and clean uniforms—wash jeeps. They laugh and joke a lot, but I have trouble understanding their accents. Other than an occasional catcall, they ignore me. I envy them their white teeth and well-fed bodies.

Mama's new position helps her get a few extra supplies. She comes home with a packet most days, and we're eating a little better.

On April 21, the day after the Führer's birthday, Mama returns home in a tizzy, waving a shred from a poster.

"Paul, you have to report."

Paul calmly takes the paper and reads. When he looks up, he flops back in his chair, his expression hard to read. Do I see relief? "They want soldiers to report to police headquarters."

"But you're an invalid." I didn't mean to say it, hate the sound of that word.

Paul only nods. "They don't make a distinction between invalids and others, it only says *dismissed* soldiers."

"They'll arrest you," Mama cries.

"I don't have a choice." Paul straightens his aching leg. "I can hardly run with this."

"I'll come with you," I say.

Paul shakes his head. "You need to take care of things here. Stay with Mama."

Paul looks pathetic as he limps off down the street the next morning.

The things that haven't changed are less obvious—kind of shadowy and nagging in the background.

The stores remain nearly empty. Hardly any food or coal are available. The newspaper announces changes to our rations and it is always less than the month before. If there is a delivery, long lines form out of nowhere. The people in back usually go home empty-handed.

Lots of men are still missing. A few have shown up in dirty uniforms, their rank insignia torn away. They look tired and defeated, often sick, showing the same glassy-eyed expression as Paul. But the men *I* want to see are not coming. There's no word from Peter or Kurt. And now Paul is gone again too. Where is hope now when I need it urgently?

All I want to do is crawl into bed and cry. In the evening, Mama and I eat alone. The sofa is empty and cold. Living without Papa has been routine, the whole in my heart carefully covered. In fact, I'm happy I don't have to wait for him or wonder if he's alive, even if I study every obituary printed in the newspaper. There are many these days, usually decorated with a square black cross.

But having Paul gone cuts me like a blade," Mama says, her eyes damp.

"Tomorrow I'll ask to see the new mayor about Paul."

"New?"

"The Americans declared Herrn Rieß the new mayor."

Clinging to this new hope, I spend an almost sleepless night—only to find Paul sitting on his sofa in the morning. I rub my eyes because I think I'm dreaming, but then he grins and says, "good morning sleepy head."

"What happened?" I cry and throw myself into his arms.

"They didn't want this old invalid," Paul says. "Prisons are full and they don't have enough people to keep order. They're more interested in catching Nazis. So, they let me go."

"Where is he?" Frau Breuer cries, when I drop off a packet of flour and sugar a week later. It's pure luxury, but Mama insists on sharing. "You don't suppose Peter joined that *Volkssturm*?" She inspects the packages and hugs them to her chest. I remember her being pretty buxom, but now Frau Breuer looks like most Germans, reedy, almost a bit transparent around the edges. She's aged terribly, her hair gray and stringy, her complexion wrinkly. Yet, her mouth is set, her chin rigid as if she's decided to wait things out, no matter what.

"The roads are probably clogged."

Frau Breuer nods. "You're too kind. Walter and I are about to eat. Would you like to join us?"

"Eat with us," Walter cries from the kitchen. He returned before Christmas from a host family in Thuringia. Unlike me, he enjoyed it for the most part, his host parents old but kind, feeding him well. Even now he looks a bit rounder than the rest of us.

Silence settles between us as I try to decide whether to take food from my neighbors who must ration just like us. I want to say that it isn't necessary, that we're managing, but my stomach makes a happy jump. Somehow, I can't turn down food. Ever. Even if it is after nine.

"We are late, but who cares? Walter doesn't have school anyway," says Frau Breuer looking at her watch.

Dinner, a soup with various vegetables and a few potato slivers, goes slowly. We speculate about Peter's activities and Frau Breuer reads from his letters.

In the background the radio is playing depressing Wagner music, then stops and announces, "We fight with the Führer against Bolshevism, which threatens to swallow the world."

"I got the last one in the fall", says Frau Breuer after a pause when the music resumes. "Strange, they say there'll be an important announcement tonight."

"He's just too lazy," quips Walter. But in his eyes I read something else, something like dark anxiety.

"The mail has a lot of trouble," I suggest, while I greedily watch Peter's letters, his handwriting so familiar. But what good does it do? He never wrote to me. At some point I get up. "It's late, I better go."

In that moment the radio music breaks abruptly. Three drum rolls sound as Frau Breuer takes my arm.

"From Führer headquarters we report that our Führer, Adolf Hitler, fighting against bolshevism to this last breath, fell for Germany this afternoon in the *Reichs* Chancellery."

Frau Breuer leans back in her chair and puts a palm against her forehead. "He's gone. Finally, the monster is gone."

I'm speechless. Less about Hitler being dead, but about the hatred in Frau Breuer's voice. Her shoulders tremble and then from deep within her chest, a rumbling laugh erupts. "He's finally gone. I bet he killed himself—the coward. Killing half Germany, stealing our boys." She abruptly straightens and hugs me to her. Then she holds me at arm's length and smiles at me. "Now we've got a chance." She lets go of me and claps her hands together. "I shall bake a cake and send you all a piece."

I never thought much about Frau Breuer. I found her boring and sad, without will or opinion. How wrong I was. We have been living next to each other as long as I remember. And I knew nothing, assumed things because she wasn't loud or demanding, when she was likely afraid like so many of us.

Deep in thought, I return to our apartment. So, the Führer started a big war, killed millions of people in many countries, and then took the easy way out. Left all of us to fend for ourselves, be governed by foreigners. My thoughts travel to Peter, who nobody has heard from in months. I still see his flashing eyes, hear him carry on about the great KLV camps, all excited about the evacuation program.

My heart tugs painfully. By now I recognize it for what it is. Love—the same thing that goes on between Biene and Kurt. Silly me. Peter has been gone for two years. If he survived, he'll hardly know me.

Or would he look like Paul? Be injured with something dead in his eyes?

"Hilda? Everything all right?" Mama asks.

"The Führer is dead." Once I say it out loud, the finality of it hits me. I sink onto a chair across from Paul, who has propped his leg on the back of the sofa and now scrambles to sit.

"You sure?"

"We listened to the radio."

"When?" Mama asks.

I look up. "They didn't say. Frau Breuer thinks he killed himself."

"I believe it!" Paul shouts. It's the loudest thing I've heard him utter since his return. "Damn coward. Leaves us to clean up his mess."

Mama resolutely walks to us and hugs us one after the other. "Things will get better now," she says. "Things will get better."

How I want to ask.

The shrill buzz of the doorbell pulls us apart. "Isn't it a bit late for visitors?" Mama says. She hurries to the door and seconds later reappears.

"Hilda, it's for you. He didn't want to come inside."

I rush past her into the hall where I almost collide with Kurt. At least I think it's Kurt. He's thin as a pencil, his cheeks hollow.

"You're back," I cry, enfolding him into a hug. He's at least ten inches taller than I, but somehow I feel like a mother cradling her child. He clings to me, but then resolutely leans back.

"Got home yesterday," he says. There's no smile, not even a hint, his eyes large with stories written in them, stories I don't understand or comprehend.

"How are you?" I ask, immediately scolding myself. How can a person who has gone to war answer that? But Kurt doesn't seem to mind.

"Better now that I'm home."

"How is your mother?"

"She is happy I returned."

"Don't you want to come in?"

"It's late, I…want to see Biene." He runs a hand through his hair. "I was stupid. I know that now. We all *do* things to survive. It isn't always pretty."

"Have you been to her house?"

"She doesn't open the door." Kurt grabs my hand. His fingers are bony and rough, the nails bit down to nothing…like Biene's. Such nails were commonplace in the KLV camps. "I thought you could convince her to talk to me."

I want to shake my head. Ever since that night, Biene and I haven't been talking. I tried a few times, even wrote a letter, but she refuses to see me.

"I'll go with you, but Biene is mad at me for getting the coal trader in trouble."

"You did that?"

"It was stupid. I just wanted Biene to be rid of the man…you know, he wanted things, disgusting things." I grab my coat and yell something into the kitchen.

Kurt follows me outside. "The bastard. I would've done it too."

Peter

We are staying with Frau Leitner. Marta isn't in any condition to continue, and Frau Leitner can use the help. Her place is a mess: the farm equipment has been standing unused and her fields are grown over. She's managed to maintain a small garden, but it's too early for decent crops.

So Karl-Heinz and I clear weeds and plant potatoes. We sort the hay barn and clean the chicken coop. Karl-Heinz discovered a generator and takes it apart. Frau Leitner has a radio, but power has been out for months.

"It was all gunked up," he cries. "The cooling fan was stuck, the thing overheated."

I take a look at the mess of parts he's spread out on a blanket. "Can you fix it?"

"Maybe. I need oil or some other lubricant."

Scanning the rusty farm equipment, I realize I'm clueless. "Does the tractor have oil in it?"

Karl-Heinz follows my gaze. "Of course, yes. It's a *Deutz Bauernschlepper*." He grins. "That old fellow has got oil."

"Oh."

Karl-Heinz rushes past me and starts crawling around the engine. "My grandpa had one." He gets up and searches through the tools. "Need a wrench." And over this shoulder, "Find me a bucket or something."

When I return with a pail, he's wiping down the engine block. With the wrench he loosens a screw underneath and oil begins to drip. "All right, not too much."

"We've got a few gallons of gasoline. Why don't we work the fields?" I say.

Karl-Heinz emerges, his right cheek black with oil. "This fellow needs Diesel. But we can use it for the generator."

And that's how on the second of May we turn on the radio and learn about Hitler's death.

"I can't believe it." Karl-Heinz sits there staring at the now silent *Volksempfänger*.

"I can," Frau Leitner says. "He sent innocent people to their deaths. Told us all to be brave and strong and fight. Talked of honor and glory." She tsks so hard, it sounds like she's spitting.

"But he said we would win the war," I say. Only when it comes out I realize how stupid it sounds. Did I really believe that?

"I want to go home," Karl-Heinz says. "Surely, the war will be over now."

"But it's not safe," Marta says. "There are Russian soldiers about, you saw them…entire caravans. They'll shoot us or—"

"Shh." Frau Leitner pats Marta's hand. "You can stay here for now."

"Not me," Karl-Heinz says.

We look at each other and I nod. "Me neither, I need to see my mother."

The next morning Karl-Heinz and I leave the farm. Marta has our addresses. We agreed that it's too hard, and she's better off staying. Frau Leitner seems to be happy about it, the two of them helping each other.

At the end of the path, I turn one more time. The farmhouse stands as before. A thin line of smoke rises from the chimney and is torn apart by the wind. It's chilly today, but at least the sky is free of clouds. Inside of me spreads that same unease I felt when we left Herr Sommer's inn. It not just the uncertainty of what awaits us, but the worry of what will happen to the people we left, who took care of us, helped us through tight spots, didn't question our motives—our friends.

I smirk as I remember Herr Sommer's matter-of-fact expression when Karl-Heinz told him about his itchy balls. I mean, how did the man keep a straight face? But somehow he did. Not only that, he got help and made sure we healed. Only now do I realize what an exceptional man he was. I never really thanked him. I vow to write to him as soon as we're home.

"Frau Leitner said we should reach *Stadt des KdF Wagens* in a couple of days," Karl-Heinz says in the afternoon. It's the first thing he's uttered since we left. That city was created by Hitler to have *Volkswagen* make cars they call *KdF*—power through joy—some crazy motto. Just like we all could afford radios, Hitler thought every German should be able to buy a car. Frau Leitner mentioned the town was created overnight a few years ago.

We've been walking on some country road in search of a suitable place to sleep. Thanks to the farmwoman, we have enough to eat for a week if we're careful.

I pull out the makeshift drawing I've made from an old German map on Frau Leitner's shelf. It's pretty useless unless you can find a decent sized road or town. "Maybe we'll see a street sign or something."

We spend the night in a shed and head out at first light. Birds chirp, and the early sun feels warm on my skin. Even Karl-Heinz whistles a tune as we enter a wider road. The commotion to our right happens so fast, we're surrounded by a dozen men in dirty torn clothes much worse than our own in seconds.

"Where you going?" the leader asks, his cheeks darkened by a grizzled beard. His eyes are almost black but carry equal amounts of intelligence and cunning. The other men have surrounded us and stand so close, we can't move even a step. Hands tear at our packs, pull on our jackets like hungry wolves.

"Home," Karl-Heinz says.

"What do you want?" I ask, trying to hold on to the shoulder strap of my bag.

"Go home too," the man says. The other men are talking now, maybe it's Russian or some other Slavic language.

"Hey," Karl-Heinz cries, but it's too late. His pack disappears in the greedy hands of the gang. Something snaps and my bag is gone as well.

"Why are you stealing our things?" I ask.

Another man tears open the flap and brings out the food, Frau Leitner packed so carefully. Bread, cheese and potatoes roll on the ground where the men snatch them up and stuff them into their pockets.

A shudder takes over my limbs and I sway. That food was supposed to keep us going.

"Looks like you're not doing too shabby," the man says. His gaze slides over our disintegrating supplies, our towels and spare clothes. A shred of paper flies into the muck unnoticed—Maria's address in Berlin. A fight breaks out between the men as they tear at the new blankets, courtesy of Frau Leitner. They're dark blue and of heavy wool.

The man shouts something in his language and the fight ceases. Everybody looks at us.

"Where did you get the things?" he asks.

I swallow. Never in a million years will I give up the kind woman.

"Found it," Karl-Heinz says. "In an abandoned house."

"Where?" The man steps even closer, his nose three inches from

Karl-Heinz's head.

Karl-Heinz points to our left. "Near Berlin, after a bombing."

"Where you coming from?"

"We walked from near Danzig," I say.

"Going where?"

"Solingen."

"Where Solingen?"

"Near Düsseldorf."

The man looks at us suspiciously, then spits and extends a hand. "Give me your coat."

"But it's mine." That's the last thing I say because somebody yanks at my shoulders so hard, the tears that threatened earlier are spilling out on their own. The coat—Herr Leitner's spare coat— slides off my back, and the man tucks it under his arm. He's quite a bit taller than everybody else, and the stupid thing won't fit, but he doesn't seem to care.

"Your Hitler take everything from us," he says. "We work three years making cars."

"Forced laborers," Karl-Heinz mumbles.

The leader throws Karl-Heinz a nasty glance while a new fight breaks out among the rest of the men. They've distributed everything we carried, including our coats. One of them inspects the little box Karl-Heinz made for me and slides it into his pocket.

Apparently one of them didn't get anything and now tries to tear apart Karl-Heinz's jacket.

The leader shouts something at the man and turns back to us. "We live in *Stadt des KdF Wagens*, thousands, some prisoners no food, no good bed. Americans come and free us."

"The Americans are there?" I ask.

"All of us free now, but no food and no place to live."

I nod numbly. I'm stinking mad and yet, how can I blame the guy? He was taken from his home and forced to work in a German factory—a slave to do Hitler's bidding.

"Can we go?" Karl-Heinz asks. I can tell he's seething by the way he squints.

The leader says nothing, just watches us as if he needs to make up his mind. The men around him are saying things with their eyes, things I understand without words. They want us dead.

"Look," I say, trying to sound strong. "We were kids sent to a camp and now all we want is to go home to see our mothers."

"If they're still alive," Karl-Heinz adds.

For a moment we gaze at each other, try to comprehend the wrongs we have survived, try to measure how much blame we carry for the suffering of others. Two of the men say something to the leader, but he raises an arm to shut them up.

"How old you are?" he asks.

"Seventeen," we both say.

"You soldier, you fight?"

"We were too young," I say. "We went to school and then to camp near Danzig."

"What you do in camp?"

"Study and…" How can I explain the silly war games we played, the salutes to the flag, the songs of glory and valor?

"We had to leave," Karl-Heinz says. "The Red Army was coming."

"Russian Army," one of the men yells and pumps a fist. The others chime in and shout, some laugh. "Germany kaput." Glee mirrors on the dirty faces and again I want to be mad. But all I feel is emptiness, some big hole in my body that wants to swallow me.

The man who fought for a piece of my jacket now points at my feet and cries, "Shoes, I want."

A second man gesticulates at Karl-Heinz's shoes. "We take."

"Please," I cry. "We've got nothing left. We want to go home to our families."

"We not see our families in years," the leader says. "My wife dead from German soldiers."

"But we can't travel barefoot." Karl-Heinz's voice shakes with desperation.

"Maybe we kill you instead. Then you do not care."

"Yes, kill, kill," the others shout.

I feel like I'm looking at myself from the outside as I sit down to take off my shoes. Karl-Heinz drops down next to me, tears dripping down his chin.

"We didn't fight in the war," I say as my shoes are snatched away. The man who was empty-handed earlier puts on Herr Leitner's boots. "All we did is try to go to school."

I'm still sitting, don't really have the strength to stand right now, and risk a look at the leader.

Maybe he sees my despair, maybe he's tired of talking. "You go," he says. "Be careful. Next men will kill you." He grins. "Just for fun."

As Karl-Heinz and I stumble away, the men break out in song, something Russian that is loud and guttural and digs into me. We only walk a few hundred yards before I stop. My feet are sore already. Twigs and bits of leaves stick to the bottoms of my soles.

"Maybe we could stuff our socks with grasses or straw," Karl-Heinz says.

"And then what?" I begin to shake and sink to the ground, see and hear the Russian laborers again.

Karl-Heinz slumps next to me. "They almost killed us."

"The next ones will, we've got nothing left."

"Maybe we should go back to the farm."

"No." Even if our situation is grim, I cannot…must not turn back. It's like giving up, defeat. I won't allow it.

"But what will we do?"

I slide my hand into the pocket where Walter's old handkerchief rests like a hug. Then I set my teeth, my molars grinding in the back of my jaws—it hurts, I bite so hard.

"We will continue as long as we can walk."

CHAPTER TWENTY-SEVEN

Hilda

Kurt's and my visit to Biene was in vain. She didn't open the door, didn't even answer when we knocked repeatedly. Yet, I knew she was there, knew she was listening to our pleading.

Almost every evening, Kurt stops by to commiserate. He and I team up to organize supplies. Just having a man by my side is a great relief. He's capable and I can trust him. Paul likes him too. They sometimes sit together and talk, man talk that consists of fragments. It makes me happy to see them. Kurt hasn't said much about his time in the people's storm. I'm not pushing either, too afraid to rip open some hidden wound.

Ever since Hitler's suicide, we're waiting for the official end. Flags have disappeared, the red now gaudy, the Swastikas a repulsive stain on the history of anything German. There's talk of capitulation, Germany surrendering to the Allies. I hope so.

The Americans I've met since their arrival have been nice. They look so clean and well-fed, their skin shiny and healthy. Last time I picked up Mama, they gave me chocolate and a pair of nylons.

What in the world would I do with hosiery? But they may come in handy in trade. Kurt was mad that I went to watch the Americans. They've set up offices in some villas around town, have taken over the city's administration and are occupying an elementary school, the schoolyard clogged with trucks and tents.

Food has gotten even scarcer, so we spend many days

scrounging. At least the weather is better and firewood is mostly for cooking. Off and on we have gas to heat the boiler; off and on we have running water. I've gotten into the habit of checking the tap every so often.

The best part is that Paul is improving. The old vet still visits, but Paul is walking more, and I helped him outside the other day. We strolled…well, limped for a while down the street toward *Bismarckplatz* and sat in the park. Kurt fashioned a new walking stick from a hazelnut branch for Paul. The trees and wooden benches have disappeared, but there's still some green.

"What will I do?" Paul says. "Nobody wants an old cripple."

"You aren't a cripple and you aren't old."

"I feel old." Paul taps on his chest. "In here."

I rub his forearm. "I know." If his face weren't so young, my brother could easily be forty, Mama's age. "You think Papa will ever return?" *Why do I even ask?*

The day I came home from school to find Papa filling a suitcase is edged into my memory like a pattern into a knife handle. He was never home during the day because he worked as a mechanic at *Bremshey*. Mama was sitting in the kitchen and when I put my school bag on the table, I noticed her crying.

"What's the matter?" I asked.

She shook her head and buried her nose in her handkerchief. That's when I heard movement in the bedroom and found Papa packing. He was so intent on what he was doing, he didn't notice me until I stood next to him.

"Where are you traveling?"

To my surprise he dropped his shoulders and avoided my eyes. "Not traveling."

"Then why are you packing?"

"I'm leaving."

"Why?"

He hesitated then and finally took me by the arms. "I'm sorry, Hilda, I met somebody else and…"

Papa was a man of few words, and my parents married because Paul was on the way. It wasn't proper and nobody talked about Mama's seven-month baby, but in the end, everybody got busy. They were young and maybe not so well suited for each other.

But at that moment, I didn't understand that. I didn't understand love or social pressures. All I knew was that my father who until then had spent every day with me would leave. Well, I didn't get the *never* part. For years I expected him to return while Mama refused to talk about him.

By now I'm used to the hole inside me that won't heal, the ache of it buried.

Paul's expression darkens. "Not likely. Not now." He clears his throat. "We'll probably never find out what happened to him."

I wish Peter would come home. I don't dare say it out loud for fear I may cry again.

"But really, I planned on becoming a police officer." Paul moves his bum leg. "I couldn't chase after a mouse, let alone a criminal."

"Maybe you can do the police reports…or become an accountant."

Paul spits. "Hah, accountant. I'd rather dig myself a hole."

My mouth drops, but before I have time to digest Paul's comment, he cries, "I'm sorry, Hilda, I didn't mean that. I know how hard you work to keep us afloat. I just feel so useless."

"You aren't useless," I say quietly. "And you're getting better. We'll find a solution, you'll see."

"I just wish I could help support the family."

"You getting healthy is all the support Mama and I need." I mean it, too.

Paul squeezes my hand as silence settles between us. A lone black bird sings above us. I realize it's the first bird song I've heard in a while. Most birds have disappeared, people killing them or taking the eggs.

I'm thankful to have my brother back, though my heart is heavy wishing I knew how to help him.

In the evening, Kurt rushes in. "It's truly over. Germany has surrendered." His eyes dance as he embraces me. "The damn war is over."

"How do you know?"

"They said it on the radio and the Americans distributed flyers. They will be running things now, officially."

I pull him inside where Mama and Paul sit on the sofa playing checkers.

"The war is over," I say. All of a sudden my legs buckle and I sink on a chair.

Kurt embraces Paul. "Finally, things will get better."

With tears in her eyes, Mama goes to the cupboard. "We must celebrate." She pulls out a two-thirds empty bottle of brandy, she swiped from one of the American meetings she's attended.

The alcohol burns my tongue and edges a fiery trail down my throat. Heat spreads and warms my cheeks. We toast to each other, the clinking of glasses foreign in the austerity of the room. Nobody has celebrated here in years—birthdays with cake and coffee, holidays with roasts and chocolate pudding, always with family, friends and neighbors.

My heart fills with gladness as I imagine our lives returning to normal. Peter will come home—he must. Kurt tells Paul a dirty joke, both of them laughing as the brandy bottle empties.

Mama hugs me tightly and tucks a strand of loosened hair behind my ears. "Finally, we can heal."

Peter

Pace has come to a crawl. The only good thing is that winter is past and the ground, while cold, is not freezing. But our feet are not made to walk barefoot, and now that we have no shoes or jackets, I realize how I even took our basic clothes for granted.

Truth is I feel naked… vulnerable like that baby blackbird I once rescued a thousand years ago. The slightest mishap will be the end of us.

The slow walking has at least the advantage that we hear everything around us. And so it happens twice that afternoon and evening that we hear men talking. Each time we creep away from the path and hide.

Once, a group of men even larger than the last passes by. They look like the previous bunch of forced laborers, dirty and angry.

Karl-Heinz and I duck low into the weeds to wait. My skin itches from mosquito bites, scratches cover our arms and ankles, our faces and necks. I'm ravenous and terribly thirsty—so thirsty, my tongue feels thick and wants to stick to the roof of my mouth.

We've crossed a small river, but neither of us want to risk drinking the water. To be safe, we need a pump or a spigot at a house. But we are too afraid to come near the town with its hateful ex-prisoners and American soldiers, so we try to head south and west again.

After dark, we stop at a home at the outskirts of some village. We sneak to the back, where Karl-Heinz makes out a spigot. For several minutes we take turns drinking and washing hands, ears on high alert, nerves frayed.

As soon as my mouth and throat feel better, hunger sets in. It's roaring and furious like the anger that boils inside me. It pulsates and takes over my mind, empties my brain of thoughts until all I can think of is food…*any* food.

We lie down behind a shed, back to back to keep a bit of warmth between us. I wake up in the middle of the night, my middle an achy throb. I quietly straighten and peek around the corner. The house is modest, its roof in need of repair. No light shines nor is there movement from animals. Whoever lives here is likely struggling too. But the time to be nice is over. We've got to eat.

I take a few tentative steps to the back porch. When nothing stirs I try the backdoor. It creaks open and I tiptoe in. Two more steps and I'm at the door that leads into the house. The knob turns and I'm inside. By now my heart races, a loud knocking that reverberates in my ears. What am I doing here?

Still, my body continues forward. Beneath me, a floorboard creaks. I freeze and listen. Nothing. I take another step and another. It's so dark I only see shadows…the ghost of a cabinet to my right….

Ouch, something digs into my hip. At the same time I ram the table, glass splinters beneath me. At least I assume it's glass. In the stillness, the noise is deafening. I turn on my heels and smack my forehead against the doorframe. Above me footsteps clomp, a dragging, scraping sound.

Fighting the dizziness, I slip through and am back on the porch, when a light bursts on above me. For a moment I'm incapable of moving. My eyes ache and join the pounding in my skull as I recognize myself in the outer glass door, the mud stained pants, the bare feet. I've forgotten my hunger, forgotten why I came.

Why am I so slow?

"Hold it right there." The man's voice is deep and commanding…and kind of distorted.

I raise my arms. "I don't have a gun."

"Turn around."

I slowly swivel on my heels. A glass splinter must have dug into my right sole and I pull up my foot in pain. But that only momentarily distracts me from the man in the entry. He's tall, at least six feet, his shoulders wide and muscular. He holds an iron crowbar, but that's not what I'm looking at. It's his face, one that will stay with me for the rest of my life.

A part of his right cheek and jaw are missing and it its stead there is a gaping hole. Beyond gleam teeth, not front teeth like you see when somebody opens his mouth, but molars lined in a row. I want to look away, but I can't. It's like I'm a bear and the man offers honey. Except it's sick and revolting.

"Serves you right to see me like this," the man grovels. "Honest people meet me covered up."

"I…am sorry," I stumble, "so hungry. Russians took our things."

"*Our* things?"

"I mean *my* things."

"You're a lousy liar. Where is your friend?"

I shake my head, my gaze still on the man's disfiguring injury. "Don't know what you're talking about. I'm alone."

"Right." The man turns sideways to scrutinize the mess I made. From this angle he looks like any other man, actually quite handsome. "The least you could do is clean up."

I stare: at the crowbar, at the lit kitchen beyond and the splinters on the floor. I grip the doorframe to steady myself, because everything is moving and quivering.

"Broom is in the corner." The man turns his back and steps inside.

I throw a helpless look out into the night, send a silent warning to Karl-Heinz, and grab the broom. When I return inside, the man has wrapped a shawl around his neck in such a way that I only see his nose and ears. The terrible hole is hidden, but in my mind I see it just as clearly.

"Dustpan is over—" his gaze lodges on my feet that are leaving bloody footprints on the linoleum. "Never mind." He takes the broom from me and begins to sweep while I stand there like an idiot.

"You want to tell me what you were doing?" he asks. His voice is muffled behind the scarf.

"Looking for food."

The man hesitates and then resumes sweeping. The soft clink-clink of glass is loud in the silence. "Better sit then," he says at last. He stops sweeping again and takes in my appearance. "You're a mess."

I sink onto a chair and watch as the shards disappear in a pail.

"That was my mother's fruit bowl," he says. "Didn't care for it, but…" His gaze is back on me and I notice that his eyes are as deep blue as *gentian* flowers. "You suck at thieving."

"Sorry, I didn't mean to…break your dishes."

Saying nothing, the man moves to a cupboard and takes out a wrapped package.

"Just got it last night, so you're in luck."

"What—"

Ignoring me, the man rummages through a drawer and searches a shelf. "I don't usually eat this time of day, but why the heck not. Americans may arrest us tomorrow, Russians kill us."

As the man returns to the table, I try to comprehend what he's saying. Something else registers. Food. Glorious, delicious food. He's unpacking a loaf of bread—dark, firm bread that emits a delectable aroma of molasses and grain. Immediately, saliva pools in my mouth, threatens to spill. I swallow loudly, a gurgling sound in the quiet.

A piece of bread appears in front of me next to a jar of quince jelly.

"Mother's recipe," the man says. "I'm Wolfgang."

"Peter."

I spread the jelly and take a bite, chew like a maniac, then abruptly stop. My gaze meets Wolfgang's whose jaw is still wrapped in the scarf. Karl-Heinz is outside, maybe looking in at this very minute…seeing me eat. Guilt washes over me like a prickly blanket.

Wolfgang misunderstands. "Go ahead, I won't eat…it's a nasty mess."

I slowly nod as he focuses on my expression. "It's something else, isn't it?"

I nod once more.

"Tell me, tell me quick, what are you hiding?" Wolfgang growls. He's like a bear being disturbed after a long winter sleep.

"Not really hiding…my friend Karl-Heinz…is outside."

"I knew it." Triumph plays in the man's eyes. "All right then, where is he?"

"I couldn't sleep, he…we were behind the shed."

"To steal from me?"

"That was *my* idea. We were hiding from the forced laborer gangs."

"Is that why you look like the bottom of a scraped barrel?"

"They took everything," I say. Again I see the gang leader's cruel smile, the hunger and hate on the men's faces. I shudder and—

"War turns men into animals." Wolfgang adjusts the scarf. "Better get your friend or your food will not taste good."

I jump from my chair, nearly upsetting it, and rush outside. The backyard is quiet. I find Karl-Heinz rolled into a ball behind the shed.

Glad to have good news, I give him a shake.

We stay three days with Wolfgang, help him around the house in exchange for food and a sleeping spot on his living room floor. He's been home from the war for a year, found his mother gone.

"Mother went to visit her sister in Köln, where she died in an air raid." Wolfgang's voice is calm…accepting.

"What happened to you?" Karl-Heinz asks. Sometimes I'm glad he's with me because he'll not shy away from asking things I'm afraid to say. I told him about Wolfgang's injury when our host visited the bathroom.

Wolfgang tugs at his scarf. He's avoided eating with us and usually sends us to do a chore. "Got shot in the face…freak angle. I was lucky." The way he says it, I know he doesn't consider himself lucky. He would have wished for the bullet to hit his brain.

"What will you do?" I ask.

He shrugs and busies himself with the stove where he's preparing a soup. "Not much a cripple like me is good for. People don't like to look at me. I used to be a car mechanic. So far nobody is hiring. They don't want to scare their customers."

"You could work in the shop," Karl-Heinz says.

"It's an excuse." Wolfgang's eyes cloud over. "I can't blame them. I've turned into a monster…disgusting."

"Not a monster, that was Hitler," I cry.

Wolfgang's eyes show a glimpse of hope, then cloud over again.

We look at the young man who could be our older brother. He'll never find a girl and he may never work a decent job, all because of the war.

The war—I almost forgot. On the second day, Wolfgang returns from a trip into the village with the news that Germany has capitulated and signed papers. The war is officially over. Finally. As the Russian laborers attacked us, Germany was no longer fighting. Yet, it means nothing. Not to us. We've got weeks to go, and it's quite likely we'll meet more roaming bandits.

On the forth day, Karl-Heinz and I wear sweaters, hand-knitted ones from Wolfgang's mother. Karl-Heinz has sandals and I've got a pair of summer shoes—what heaven after walking barefoot. The cut under my sole aches a bit but no longer bleeds. I even washed Walter's hankie and carry it in the breast pocket of my new shirt.

A great sorrow settles in my chest as we wave good-bye. Wolfgang stands in front of his little house, a man whose life has been destroyed. He doesn't wave, his mouth and jaw hidden behind the scarf, a statue of a man who represents all that is wrong with war. Maybe he's right about wanting to die.

"I can't imagine how hard it has to be to walk around with half a face," I say.

Karl-Heinz remains quiet for a moment and I'm not even sure he heard me when he says, "we've got holes too, you know. You just don't see them."

I stare at my friend, the old joker, who has become a wise man.

CHAPTER TWENTY-EIGHT

Hilda

Encouraged by the good news, I head to the grocery store the next day. There's no line so I hurry forward in anticipation. I've got a sheaf of ration cards that entitle us to flour, sugar, meat and fat.

The door of the store is locked, and through a metal grated window I make out empty shelves. A shiver like a freezing wind creeps up my legs. But then I remember the Americans and decide to pay them another visit.

I'm not alone, wondering about supplies. A line of people in ragged clothes snakes around the building. Two hours later I am face to face with an American officer.

"Name?"

"Hilda Hagedorn."

"How can I help you?" The man says with a heavy German accent.

"I'm wondering when the stores will reopen." I pull out my ration coupons. "Now that the war is over and you are running things—"

The man lifts a hand to cut me off. "I cannot help you. We have no idea when there will be food available. The British military will take over from us shortly. You'll have to ask them."

"When will *they* come?" I ask trying to imagine what the British military will do differently.

"End of May at the latest," the American says.

So I leave the office empty-handed. There's still no food and nobody knows when there'll be any. Mama brings home a few things, but it's not enough to feed the three of us. I've got to ask Kurt for help. Once again we'll have to steal.

On a whim, I stop by Biene's house. It's been a week since I last tried and I really don't understand why I can't give up. When I turn into Biene's street I recognize her heading the other way. I reach her quickly because she ambles along as if she's asleep.

"Biene, wait," I say at her back.

She stiffens before resuming her walk. "I'm busy." She moves faster though the simple task of rushing off appears to be difficult.

I catch up to her side, am tempted to take her elbow. "Can't we talk?"

"I've got nothing to say."

"But the war is over."

Biene whips around to face me. I step back, almost clap a palm over my mouth. She looks horrible, her cheekbones pronounced, her eyes huge and dull—a hunger face.

"Thanks to you, *my* war is not over. And thanks to you, we've got almost nothing to eat."

My friend's words cut into me like a blade. "But the man used you."

Biene shrugs. "So what? At least we had food and coal."

"It was wrong."

"Who determines what's right and wrong, Miss High and Mighty? Who makes you the judge? War is wrong. My father being imprisoned is wrong. Theo having troubles is wrong. Us starving is wrong. You going to fix those too?"

"Aren't you glad the war is over? Maybe our families—"

"Just because they signed some paper, nothing changes. Germany is finished. We're finished."

She turns on her heels and walks away.

I just stand there with my mouth open. I thought I'd done the right thing, the moral thing. But what are morals during a war? They're the first to leave, starting with a government who sends their men and boys to be killed.

Tears burst as I stand there. Biene is right. I had no business interfering and now they suffer because of me. I hug myself as I wander home, wishing I could take it back.

If we owned a farm, I could supply Biene's family. But I've got nothing to give. All I can hope is that the British occupation will straighten things out and get us supplies.

And maybe find Peter.

Peter

We're somewhere near Hannover, but continue on. Wolfgang said downtown was completely bombed, that there isn't much left and many people lost their houses.

Every time I hear such news, my thoughts travel home, to the state our town may be in and whether Mother and my brother, Walter, are safe. And I think about Hilda, though my memory of her remains fuzzy. The glimpses my brain produces are fleeting like fog in sunshine.

Only in my dreams do her features become clear and defined. Last night she was a grown woman in a green and white-checkered dress and chin-length hair. She walked hand-in-hand with a stranger in a hat and coat, her lipstick glowing red as poppies. I knew it was her because she had that little mole by her right cheek. But she didn't smile at me, just sort of looked through me as if I were transparent. She talked to the man about renting an apartment and buying a leather sofa for the living room. I tried to get her attention, lifted my arm to wave, but my arm wouldn't move. It just hung there lifelessly. And then I noticed I had no feeling in the arm and when I looked down, I didn't have an arm at all, just an empty sleeve with a knot at the end. I woke up drenched in sweat.

Strangely, neither Karl-Heinz nor I talk about our homes or the worry about our loved-ones. It's a non-subject to be avoided at all costs. The only subjects we discuss are when and where we rest and where we may find food.

Our pace is slow. I can tell I've lost more weight because my pants are loose and hang on my hips. Wolfgang gave us a bit of bread, but he didn't have that much himself. So, we're back to organizing. Often we beg.

In the beginning I was embarrassed to knock on a door or enter a business. Now I don't care. So what, they say no. We just leave and try the next. Of course, that takes time. I thought that we'd be home by now. How naïve I was when we left Herr Sommer's inn.

Wolfgang said we could make it in ten days and that we should head for the city of Hameln next.

Today the sky opens to soak us. Gray clouds rush overhead, the wind cooling us further. All I can think of is a fire and drying my clothes, so when a sign announces Hameln, we hurry forward.

Around the next curve, we abruptly halt. The road is clogged with a tank, a boom stretches across, the eyes of four guards in uniforms on us—American soldiers.

"What are we going to do now?" Karl-Heinz says. He sounds as breathless as I feel.

I throw a glance over my shoulder, but there is no way we can outrun a bunch of men in excellent shape when my legs are filled with watery sludge.

"Come here," one of the men shouts from his guard booth. He carries a machine gun, his skin shiny black beneath a plastic-covered helmet. Fascinated I watch the water drip off his jaws.

We saunter near. The remaining three guards watch us from their posts on top of a tank.

"Where you going?" The black man's German accent is thick.

"Home," Karl-Heinz and I say.

"Here...Hameln?"

"No," Karl-Heinz hurries. "Solingen."

"Which is where?"

"Near Wuppertal," I add.

I used to be pretty good in English, but when the man calls something to his friends, I don't understand a word.

The second soldier rushes over to frisk us and checks the small canvass bag Wolfgang gave us. Out come the blanket we share, a towel, and a few crumbs of food. Everything slows down, the man's clean-shaven jaw so close, his fingers tearing at our things. Inside me fury mixes with helplessness. They're going to steal from us—again.

To my surprise the soldier hands the items back to us.

"Come," the second guard says. We're being herded through the barricade and marched down the street to a house. Next to it flies an American flag. Another tank and four jeeps are parked in front and on the side. Several GIs stand talking in the yard, but two men, machine guns at the ready, block the front door.

Once again my legs fill with liquid. Will the men arrest or shoot us? Karl-Heinz is pale next to me and when our arms accidentally touch, I feel him quake. Somehow this quiver transfers to me.

The soldier behind the desk is slightly older than the guards and motions us to sit while the guard explains in English... "stopped...Wuppertal...suspicious."

The man waves away the guard and focuses on us. His perfectly square jaw is cleanly shaven, his eyes piercing blue like a mountain lake. He emits authority without even speaking. I'm glad my left leg hides behind the desk because it's wiggling like crazy.

"Papers?"

"We have nothing left," I say.

"Names, ages, and addresses?"

We give our information, which the soldier notes on a form.

"What are you doing in Hameln?"

Karl-Heinz and I exchange a glance before he starts, "Two years ago we went to a camp near Danzig, in Körlin. It was bad, so we were moved to a different camp."

"They closed our school and sent us all away," I add.

"Then we moved again to an inn, a *Gasthof*," Karl-Heinz says.

"Why?"

"The large camp didn't have enough to eat."

The man leans back and folds his very clean hands. "Why didn't you go home?"

Good question, I want to say. Why in the heck didn't they send us all home instead of waiting for the Red Army to catch us?

"I guess, they thought we were safer there," Karl-Heinz says.

But that couldn't have been true. Anybody who knew anything, especially the German government with their spies and troops over there, must have known about the Russians advancing east.

The soldier looks at me. "What do you think?" he asks in impeccable German.

"Our teacher believed the Red Army wouldn't come this far."

Incredulity mirrors in the man's eyes, a slight twitch of the right corner of his mouth. But to his credit he lets it go and says, "Why are you here?"

"We are walking home…to Solingen," Karl-Heinz says.

Now the soldier unfolds his hands and straightens. "From Danzig?"

We nod.

"That must be…six- or seven hundred miles." He takes in our appearance. "How long have you been on the road?"

Karl-Heinz and I look at each other. "What day is it?" he asks.

The man scans his calendar. "May 12."

"Then it's been almost two and a half months."

"You *do* know Germany capitulated and that we're in charge?"

Karl-Heinz and I nod.

"You also know your…Hitler committed suicide?"

As the word *suicide* echoes in my head, I look at Karl-Heinz. He just stares straight ahead, but I recognize the shock on his face, his slackening jaw. So once he'd destroyed our country the man took the easy way out. Let the rest of us suffer. All of a sudden I can't breathe, the collar of my sweater too tight.

"You ever fight…wear a uniform?" The officer says, bringing me back. Do I imagine it or has his expression softened?

"No," I say. "We had classes and later we worked to get enough food."

This time the man's eyes remain impassive. Somewhere in the background a typewriter hammers. Outside foreign voices speak, followed by laughter, careless and light. It's a strange sound, somehow alien, something I haven't heard in a long time.

The man now writes something on his form. His hair is shorn to an inch, a bit of gray on his temples.

I smell myself. My armpits reek and the front of my pants is caked with grime. We must look like pigs to these clean, shaven, orderly men.

"All right," the man finally says. "You can go." He calls something to another man in the adjacent room who immediately hurries over and waves us along.

A last glimpse shows the man behind the desk sitting quietly, sort of contemplating. Then he shouts something at our guard who salutes and accompanies us outside.

"You come," he says.

I look at Karl-Heinz who shrugs, a new worry frown on his dirt-stained forehead. Did the soldier change his mind? Will we be arrested after all?

As we walk down the street, I'm having trouble keeping up. My legs are all soft again and I'm so hungry, my middle is one big ache.

After about a kilometer, we turn onto a side street, then turn again onto a path to a large building surrounded by barbwire. Two guards stand at the entrance. Two more are just inside.

Beyond lies a cavernous room with lines of tables, some of them occupied by soldiers. My eyes about pop out of my skull—they're eating.

"Sit there," our guard says. He's maybe a year older than us, but looks incredible in his spotless uniform and sturdy boots.

I slump onto a bench next to Karl-Heinz and take in our surroundings. A group of four soldiers sit at the next table, talking quietly…relaxed. They give us a curious look before resuming their conversation. I try to pick up words, but my ears are filled with cotton, my brain hollow.

The next moment a tray appears in front of us, the aroma of roasted meat and butter so heady, I want to sink my face into it. Instead, my hand finds a fork and I begin to eat. All I can do is look at the food in front of me. The meat is dark…beef…in a creamy sauce…mushrooms, oh… beans in butter and fluffy rice. I shovel and chew, shovel and chew. A platter of bread appears and I start dipping and wiping with the bread, stuff it into my mouth and repeat.

By the time I look up, my tray is as clean as if it had been washed. Across from me Karl-Heinz is polishing the last of the sauce with his bread. That's when I notice two bottles of cola sitting there, real American drinks. I take a sip, the fizziness tickling my nose— sweet and delicious. No wonder these men look so content and relaxed.

"They fed us," Karl-Heinz says with wonder in his eyes. "The Führer told us they were enemies and would kill us."

"True, maybe they took pity. I think—"

"But they didn't have to feed us."

"The Führer is dead, the war over." Deep inside me anger begins to brew as I wonder what is true about the things we were told in the Hitler Youth and in camp.

"You think it's true…that he killed himself?"

I bite my lip, hard, until I taste blood. "He killed our fathers…had our country destroyed." Pushing out the words takes effort. What was all that talk about honor and sacrifice? "Hitler was crazy…and in the end, a coward."

"You can go now." The young soldier is back and we abruptly straighten. "You take this." He hands us two green canvas bags and two pieces of paper. "Your passes. Show them when you are stopped."

"Thanks," I manage in English when we walk off. The soldier nods and hastens back up the street, probably reporting to his boss.

We walk about a quarter mile before my legs refuse to continue. My stomach is so full, I'm at the edge of nausea.

"They let us go," Karl-Heinz says next to me. As usual, he says the things I'm thinking like we're some old married couple who finishes each other's sentences.

I look over my shoulder. The street is deserted. Here and there, white sheets hang from windows.

"How much farther, you think?"

Karl-Heinz remains quiet, apparently calculating. "Ten days, maybe two weeks," he says after a while.

I shift the bag to my other shoulder, then set it down. I've got to see what the Americans gave us.

CHAPTER TWENTY-NINE

Hilda

Kurt and I have been banding together to look for food. He asked Biene too, but she still refuses to see him.

Every day we head out together into the surrounding countryside. Some places toward the *Wupper* valley are beautiful and pristine, the meadows full of flowers and fruit trees blooming. For moments at a time I pretend there hasn't been a war and that this is a spring like any other.

Many of the people here have gardens, but fences surround them, and there is always somebody watching. Kurt taught me about stinging nettles. They grow along paths and the river, are juicy and tall, sometimes six feet or more. And they taste like spinach. The trick is to use gloves when harvesting them to get past the hairs that break open and release formic acid, a liquid that burns the skin. Both of us carry old pillowcases and while Kurt cuts, I collect the nettles with a pair of old garden gloves that Kurt lifted from a shed.

It takes a lot of nettles to fill a pot because they shrink like spinach. We also collect dandelion leaves, chickweed, sorrel and burnet for salad. I particularly like to add wild garlic. Kurt had brought me a book he'd found on an unattended back porch with local plants, drawings and descriptions I memorized.

We've also climbed into bushes and trees to steal bird eggs. We especially like pigeon eggs because they're quite large—there are few these days.

On the way back we collect fresh leaves from red beech and the new growth from spruce trees. According to Kurt's book, they're all edible. Of course, Kurt no longer carries the book—he relies on my memory.

What we don't have are butter and oil. Fat is almost non-existent in any form even if our ration coupons claim that we're entitled to butter and margarine. The last fat ration during the war was 109 grams per month.

"You want to do something later?" Kurt asks as we turn into my neighborhood. It's early afternoon and our bags are filled with nettles and wild garlic. We have a few potatoes left, and I want to try making a soup.

"Like what?"

"Just walk around, maybe see if anything is open in town?"

I shrug. Not that I have any money, but wouldn't it be nice to window-shop and admire pretty dresses, shoes or even tools. Kurt wiggles from foot to foot, his cheeks glowing.

"All right. Pick me up at seven."

With the flavor of the soup still in my mouth, we wander into town. Footpaths lead past mountains of rubble. Here and there people walk past, their gaze downward to find some forgotten treasure, or perhaps not to stumble.

The stench of the fires and rotting bodies has dissipated a bit, but the scene is so alien, so ugly, I feel myself shrink. There are no shops open and certainly no displays of pretty things.

"Let's turn around. I'd rather take a walk in our neighborhood or down to the park."

Kurt doesn't answer, but then I feel his hand grab mine. "Sure. I'm sorry. This was a dumb idea."

I smile grimly. "You didn't know. It's just such a big job. I don't think they'll ever clean it up."

We return to the little park at *Bismarckplatz* and sink onto a couple of stumps. Somebody has managed to saw off several trees and carry away the wood. It sure beats transporting firewood from the forest, but the little park looks all hacked to pieces.

Again I hang my head.

Until Kurt drapes his arm around me. "You're sad," he says simply.

His nearness is comforting like our old sofa. Somehow I lean into it a bit and next thing I know, Kurt is kissing me.

His lips are soft on mine, but not too experienced. Who am I to judge? It's sort of fun, but strange at the same time.

"Didn't you like Biene?" I ask when he lets up. I push against his chest a bit and he immediately retreats.

"Biene won't even talk to me. I like you too."

"I see."

"No, I mean it." Kurt returns to stand in front of me, his eyes earnest. "You're a nice girl, Hilda. Good-looking too. We have fun together."

I'm not as beautiful as Biene and the way we dress these days, I don't even feel like a girl any longer. Only after my bath, when I study the mirror, I see the womanly things I was given, decent though tiny breasts and long legs. I've got no real hips, my stomach flat and lean. The pictures I have seen about movie stars like *Marlene Dietrich*, those women all look curvy and seductive. But what good does it do to look seductive when your cupboards are bare?

"Will you go with me?" Kurt asks. He reclaims my hands and squeezes them.

I look at the young man who is Peter's age, but somehow so different. My heart tells me that Kurt is a good man who will take care of me. He knows how to organize supplies and can help us a lot.

So I nod, and the next moment Kurt is kissing me again. This time he sticks his tongue into my mouth. I don't particularly like the feeling, but I keep steady and eventually we figure things out. Kurt seems to get all sweaty and breathes heavily.

"I better go home," I say quickly. It scares me a bit, the way Kurt acts.

Kurt pulls back and drapes his arm around me again. "Of course, I'll walk you home."

No need I want to say, but then I remember *we're going together now*, we're a couple.

At the door, Kurt kisses me again, but I cut it short, mumbling about neighbors spying on us.

As Kurt walks off, I rush into our bathroom. Except for the flushed cheeks, the image in the mirror looks no different. Relieved, I wash my hands and enter the kitchen.

Peter

Karl-Heinz and I made good time today. It's as if the American soldiers infused some of their confidence into us. Or maybe it's because we each have enough food to last us the rest of our journey.

When we finally open the bags, we each find thirty rectangular cardboard packages, a mess kit and canteen, and a fork.

"What do you think it is?" Karl-Heinz says, studying one of the cartons. I pick one of the stacked boxes and sniff it. Nothing. *Supper Ration Type K* is printed in green, a bunch of text below.

"Listen to this," I say as excitement floods me. "Coffee, biscuits, bouillon, confection, cigarettes, sugar and chewing gum." I turn over the packet. "What the heck is confection? You think all that is in here?"

"Pretty great if it were," Karl-Heinz says. "You think that's dinner?"

"Soldier ration, for sure."

"We better walk a while before we eat."

"Right."

By the afternoon we can't take it any longer. We come across an abandoned barn, its roof mostly caved, parts of the walls missing. Upon closer inspection we decide to stay. There's enough roof left to provide shelter if it rains—which it might at any minute—and the walls offer some protection from the wind.

The third reason always weighs on my mind. If another laborer or prisoner of war gang finds us, we'll lose it all again. And they may kill us. I've had nightmares already of the leader of those forced laborers wielding a knife and cutting Karl-Heinz's throat. I can't even tell my friend about it because it scares me so badly.

Karl-Heinz settles in the corner of the barn. "Let's see what we've got." His eyes flash as he studies the U.S. army packet, then rips it open. Out spill little packets, a can, and a stack of cellophane-wrapped biscuits. "Look at this," Karl-Heinz says, triumph in his voice. "This is chocolate." Indeed, the two packets say *Nestlé's sweet chocolate bar*. I stare in wonder before ripping open my own packet. There is sugar, real white sugar, bouillon, instant coffee, gum, matches, and even cigarettes.

Karl-Heinz giggles and I join him. We sniff each item, put it down, pick up another. I take a few kernels of sugar and let them dissolve on my tongue. Heaven. I will keep the chocolate for later.

"How will we cook the meat?" Karl-Heinz says.

I remember seeing some little contraption in my pack and rummage to find it. It's a foldable tri-stand with a spot for a heating element in the middle. Sure enough, there are paper-wrapped cubes.

We unroll the cans' metal tops with the little key and warm the meat in our pans. The odor of the cooking food makes me salivate so much, I have to swallow over and over. We take our time eating the meat with the biscuits.

"We need a cup or something to heat water in," I say after a while. "For the coffee and the bouillon."

"Maybe we can use the pan."

And that's how we first drink instant bouillon and then coffee, nibbling the chocolates. The taste is so foreign and so delicious I want to pinch myself.

Since neither of us smokes, we stash the cigarettes away for later. That night we sleep well, our stomachs calm and our minds at ease. As I relax on the ground, Karl-Heinz's even breathing calming in my ears, I think about a time when eating your fill and feeling safe was normal. When Father was home every night after work and Mother cooked roasts on weekends, and the worst I worried about was doing my homework. I long for that time, but as I lay there in Wolfgang's threadbare blanket, another conviction grows inside me like a terrible sore.

I realize I'm mourning instead because that time will never return.

CHAPTER THIRTY

Hilda

Today I went to Frau Breuer again. She and Walter are doing laundry in the sink, their living room and kitchen draped with a tangle of ragged clothes.

Not hearing from Peter is making me crazy. It's the middle of May and the war in Solingen has been over for a month. So what is keeping him? The possibility of Peter missing keeps me up at night. I imagine terrible things as nausea sweeps over me. In this moment I know he'll never return, and the ache is like a huge mouth that swallows me whole.

I lean backwards until my spine rests against the doorframe, hoping Peter's mother won't see my despair, hoping my legs won't buckle.

"I met Dieter Maier's mother," Frau Breuer says, wiping her hands on a towel. Her fingers are all shriveled and red from the cold water. "He's one of Peter's classmates."

Frau Breuer sags onto a chair across from me. "She received a letter two months ago. Dieter wrote that the boys are staying at an inn near Danzig."

"But that's…"

"…the territory of the Red Army, I know."

"You think Peter fought the Russians?" Walter says.

"Nonsense," Frau Breuer cries. "The letter was at least eight months old. They're likely long gone from there." Getting up, she ruffles Walter's hair and turns her gaze back on me. "Or they're just waiting for things to calm down."

"Right," I say, but inside I'm cold. Something isn't right. Why didn't he write like Dieter? What would the Russians do with a bunch of boys? Maybe Peter is in a Russian gulag like Biene's father. He may never come home.

My limbs grow so heavy, I can't move any longer. Nor can I see because my vision is all blurry.

"Mother, Hilda is crying," Walter says.

I want to wipe my face, but I can't even muster lifting a hand. The next instant Frau Breuer is upon me and I disappear in her arms.

"Poor girl, you miss him like we do." She rubs my back as I tremble and cry.

Walter awkwardly pats my hand. "I think he's just teasing us, knowing we're waiting for him."

I sob a laugh and lean back. "Peter was always good at that."

"There, there," Frau Breuer says. "He'll return in no time to make our lives miserable." Her eyes glisten as she smiles. In that moment I'm incredibly thankful for her encouraging words and her hopefulness.

Walter rushes off and appears a moment later with a navy blue scarf that has seen better days. "This is Peter's. You can hold on to it until he gets back."

New tears threaten as I wrap the scarf around my neck.

"Have you heard from your husband?" I ask.

Frau Breuer dabs her face and says, "Last he wrote he was near the Baltic Sea."

"He's probably having fun with Peter," Walter says. "I can just see them lie on some beach and forget all about us."

Again I grin.

Maybe having my father leave us before the war wasn't such a bad thing. At least I don't have to wait for him now. Taking a deep breath, I say good-bye. Strangely, I feel a bit better.

Peter

The following afternoon we approach Paderborn. At least that is the plan until we once again run into American soldiers. This time two jeeps park along the road.

"Where are you going?" one of them asks from his car.

"We want to go through to Solingen," I say, handing him our

papers.

"Not possible," the man says.

"Why?" Karl-Heinz says. "We won't stop, just try to cut across."

The two Americans look at each other, then both shake their heads. "Town is destroyed, roads impassable. You'll need to find a way around."

He returns our passes and points a thumb over his shoulder. "Back and around."

Without another word we march the way we came. It feels terrible to retrace our steps and extend our trip.

Karl-Heinz frowns. "How far around is he talking about?"

"What does he mean with impassable?"

At the next opportunity, we take a narrow side street. When we don't see any uniforms, we continue toward a row of homes. "Looks fine to me," Karl-Heinz says. He's perked up considerably since receiving all this food.

Strange is that we see nobody, the road deserted, the houses silent.

Around the next corner, a huge pile of rubble greets us. It's blackened stone, bent metal and reeks. Just during the last few yards, the air has taken on a sharp, acrid smell that burns my nose. Worse is the underlying odor of decomposition. Some place around here, dead people lie buried.

Karl-Heinz pinches his nose as we turn back and into an alley. Here the houses are still standing, that is until we come to the corner. The land ahead is flat and opens up to the west. All we see are ruins and piles of rubble—not a single house stands intact. It's like a huge wasteland after an apocalypse.

My lungs threaten to implode. I suck air, no gulp, because a noose squeezes tightly around my neck. Bile rises from the back of my throat. The American soldiers were right—Paderborn is dead.

I swivel on my heels and head back the way we came. Now I don't care how far we have to go, just get me out of this stinking graveyard. Karl-Heinz follows me, but right now I can't talk. I just can't say anything because I don't have the words to describe what I saw and how it makes me feel.

My thoughts gallop forward. What if Solingen looks like this?

We rush along, and because it's sunny today, we somehow manage to get back to the *Reichsstraße 1* toward Dortmund. The rest of the day we march with hardly a break. I can't stop and Karl-Heinz doesn't complain either. Nor do we talk. Not one word. Nothing.

In the evening when I think my legs will buckle, I turn off the road and sink to the ground. Karl-Heinz is next to me and I'm beyond thankful for his company. Silently, we unwrap another U.S. Army ration; silently, we open our cans and eat the cold meat.

Afterwards, I unpack the camels and light a cigarette. I've only smoked once in sixth grade when Karl-Heinz stole two cigarettes from his father and we hid in his basement. Karl-Heinz stares for a moment, then pulls out his own and lights up. We sit there in the waning light, puffing stinky smoke into the air, a black bird above us singing a happy tune. My tongue burns from the yucky flavor of the burning tobacco, but I don't care. I want to suffer, want to feel pain, want my mind to be numb and filled with senseless smoke.

We tear loose a few ferns and sleep on top, wrapped in our blanket. I fall asleep right away but then wake in the middle of the night. It's quiet, only Karl-Heinz's even breathing audible in the darkness.

I lie there listening, the smoke taste in my mouth bitter.

CHAPTER THIRTY-ONE

Hilda

Another week has passed, and though I'm plenty busy and distracted gathering food and keeping Kurt at bay, worry about Peter creeps into every part of my day. *This* worry is a constant companion, a revolting, black-hooded fellow who has long ousted hope and whispers into my ear whenever I take a break.

Paul and Mama often look at me funny because they wonder what is going on. Well, at least Mama does. I think Paul knows. Somehow he's figured out what ails me.

"I'm sorry, Hilda." Mama leans in the door. "I should've talked to you about your father a long time ago."

I drop the potato brush and turn to face her. Somehow she's mistaken my gloominess for missing my father. "Did he...die?" Somewhere in the recesses of my brain I envision Papa lying in some ditch with his helmet shot off, brain matter oozing into the mud.

Mama walks up to me and cups my face in her hands. She's three inches shorter than me now, her fingers soft against my skin. "He never contacted me again. I saw him a couple of times with a young woman, but I believe they moved. I don't know if he survived the war." I want to look away, but Mama holds me there, her gaze on mine. "You had nothing to do with his leaving. I think he was missing something."

I lean into my mother, thankful for her strength. I also realize how this new truth dissolves the worry that festered inside me.

Somehow I always thought I'd been partially responsible.

Is that why I tried to fix things all the time? Tilly's problem, Biene's arrangement, Paul's struggles. I realize that some things can't be fixed. People can't be fixed like leaky faucets. Love isn't perfect, nor is friendship.

Mama's gaze is still on me. "I also talked to Paul. He'd been so furious for so long."

"I guess we can never understand what motivates people," I say, thinking how Sister Rose ran away to hide in a cloister, or Biene's mother forced her daughter to sleep with an old man.

Mama rubs my back. "Sadly, that is true. No matter how well we think we know somebody, we never do completely. His leaving us made me grow, and I'm thankful for that." She leans back. "I forgave your father years ago. It's time you do as well."

I stare at Mama, swallow the lump in my throat. She's right. I did feel responsible, but I also blamed him for destroying our family. I think a part of me will always miss him and wonder what happened, but it is no longer painful, just a bit tender.

"Our family is perfect," I say out loud.

And it is.

I'm about to take off to the black market to trade a sack of nettles, when the doorbell rings.

And there, wrapped in an oversized raincoat stands Tilly. My mind immediately skips to the months we spent in the cloister, the dank walls and the cold eyes of the Abbess.

"I'm glad you're safe," Tilly says, a bit breathless. She has grown, her whitish blond hair longer than I remember. Before I can say anything, Tilly throws herself into my arms.

"Are you all right?" I ask, holding her at arm's length and studying her face.

Tilly nods enthusiastically. "I meant to come earlier. Our home got bombed and I had to move away for a while."

I pull her inside and we sit down on the sofa hand-in-hand. Paul and Mama have gone to ask about technical drawing classes. He wants to find an apprenticeship that doesn't require too much physical activity.

Tilly squeezes my fingers. "I found out about the letter you and Biene wrote. Turns out that Principal Schmidt contacted my mother and she about had a heart attack. It took a long time for her to find a way to travel to me."

"I'm glad it worked."

"I met Ilse and heard about your trip home. I'm so sorry. I will miss Fräulein Heinrich…and Karin. She and I sort of became friends after…"

Our eyes meet. I remember how mean Karin had been until she received the news of her father's death.

Tilly smiles. "I want to thank Biene too. I thought you and I could visit her together. It'd be fun after all this time."

I press my lips together, my mind heavy.

"What?" Tilly cries. "Did something happen to Biene?"

"Not like that," I hurry. How will I explain our spat, Biene's struggles, my misjudgment? When Tilly remains silent, I continue, "We had a fight and she's not speaking with me." I pat Tilly's pale hand. "I'm sure she'd be happy to see you."

"But you two were inseparable. I don't understand."

I say nothing because now that I think about it, I don't understand it either.

Peter

This morning we reach Wuppertal. The climb through my beloved hilly land has begun. In the *Wupper River* valley, the mountains are steep and woodsy or what you'd call ravines. Some slopes have been completely logged. People need firewood to cook and stay warm and they'll help themselves—even if it's against the law.

My heart seems to flutter as we climb the road to *Stöcken*. Once we arrive downtown, it's a matter of fifteen minutes until home. The road flattens toward the theater and town hall on the left. Not much further.

We halt abruptly because the town hall is gone…replaced by rubble, and as we look beyond, we see nothing but horrendous piles of rocks. Pieces of houses jut into the sky, singular walls still standing, their windows empty and hollow as dead eyes. Footpaths lead through this strange world of wreckage, up and down we climb through rocks, past doorsills with no doors, and past windows with no glass.

The old city to our left with its half-timber homes and cozy shops is gone. There is nothing but black rubble. At *Dreieck*, a central downtown location, the corner house where I used to get my school supplies stands alone. Everything around it is gone as well. The smell of destruction and decomposition hovers like a cloud above us. It's hard to breathe, and we both pull our sweaters over our noses. Women, their hair wrapped in scarves, work in long lines, stacking bricks.

Two older men are pushing wheelbarrows with iron beams.

As we pass them, my legs grow a mind of their own. They move faster and faster, jumping and stumbling across rocks and debris, weaving between people, always searching for sure footing in the rolling, smelly mess. My lungs are void of air and nausea curls around my throat like a poisonous snake. My town is dead like Hameln and still I hurry on like a madman.

Karl-Heinz follows, and the closer we get to home, the faster we walk. I don't remember how I get up the last hill, past the park so familiar and yet so strange. My eyes search ahead, along the street. The homes I passed so many times over the years are still here. At least the bombs spared this area.

At the roundabout we stop.

"Looks like you'll be all right." Karl-Heinz nods toward the row of apartment buildings circling the little park.

"If anything has happened, you come," I say. He's heading for his aunt's home where his mother took shelter. There is no telling if the house is still there. All of a sudden I feel pressure in my eyes. Here stands my oldest friend with whom I've walked for three months. Who helped me when I was down and spoke for me when I could not.

"Let's meet tomorrow for sure," Karl-Heinz says. "I better go." He hesitates, then slaps me on the back and grins. Not the old grin, the careless kind I remember, but a careful measured one. "We did it."

I squeeze his arm and grin back. "We sure did."

Moments later, I stand in front of my house as memories of Mother and Walter flood me. All this time I've avoided thinking about them because it was too dangerous.

I'm about to ring the bell when the entry door flies open and a kid rushes out and smacks into me.

"Oh, sorry," he cries. He's already past when he stops abruptly. As though pulled by a rubber band, he swivels around and returns. "Peter?" he cries.

"Walter." The boy in front of me has the same brown hair and has grown at least four inches—my little brother.

"You're back." He throws himself against my chest, a sob rising between us. I don't know if it's his or mine. This rambunctiousness used to get on my nerve. Now I can't get enough. I hug him to me, a lifeline to my family. "You're back," he says again, his face buried in my sweater.

"How is Mother?" I ask.

He leans back and shrugs. "She is holding her own…under the circumstances." He tears himself loose and grabs my hand. "Come on, let's go. She'll be so happy."

It hits me how familiar the smells in my hallway are: a bit of cedar—Mother's attempt to fight moths—a whiff of soap and leather and wool, I would recognize wherever I am. But Walter doesn't let me find my way slowly.

He's already yelling, "Mother, come here, quick."

I hear scrambling inside and then there is Mother in the door…and me in her arms in a flash. Just like Walter earlier, I bury my head. Except it's against her shoulder because I'm several inches taller. I'm unable to speak the lump in my throat large as an orange.

"Oh, Peter, my boy, you're home," Mother cries. Then we just stand there and hold each other. Some of the earlier guilt returns about the way I treated her at the train station, my urgent need to get away.

That's why the first thing I say is, "I'm sorry."

Mother holds me at arm's length and studies my face. There are new lines around her eyes and mouth, and her hair is nearly gray. She looks so old. "What happened?" And then she begins to fuss the way I remember, the way I used to loathe. Except now I love it and smile through the haze. "Oh, come in, you must be exhausted."

I follow her into the living room. Everything is still there—the sofa, the doilies and potted plants. I slump into the easy chair, but then straighten again. "I need to wash first."

"I'll make you something to eat." Mother pats my back and I'm tempted to go for another hug. But then I'm past and in the bathroom.

What I see in the mirror is a strange being with a dirt-and-tear-stained face, and longish hair that spreads in all directions. My cheekbones stand out, and I've got a jaw like that American soldier. Brownish hair sprouts from it. But the eyes draw my attention. They're the same earth color, but there are things written in there, things I don't want to revisit. So, I abruptly bend low and fill the sink with water.

"How are your classmates doing?" Mother asks as I sit down to a meal of cornbread scraped with jam and a bit of watery soup.

I swallow the bite of bread, its texture dry under the roof of my mouth. "Karl-Heinz came with me."

Mother slumps across from me. "What do you mean?"

"We left from near Danzig at the end of February and walked home." Now that I say it aloud, it seems ludicrous—outright crazy.

"I don't understand, why didn't the class travel home together?"

"Our teacher didn't want to. He said it was safe, that the Red Army wouldn't come that far."

"Ha," is all my mother says to that. She focuses on me. "You two went alone?"

I nod. What can I say, how can I explain the hunger and fear, the Russian laborers ready to kill us because we had food and shoes, the young man with half a face, the Americans?

"We were lucky," I finally say. "What happened here?"

"Americans came in April and the British Military just took over the town." Mother's fingers drum the table in little staccato movements. "We expected things to improve. Truth is, it's worse."

"How can it be worse?"

"There's nothing to eat. Stores are empty. We're supposed to get new ration coupons." Mother shakes her head. "I don't see how it will work any better. We have a new mayor, who has no power. Frau Hagedorn says the British occupation is inept or doesn't care. Meanwhile, people starve." Mother leans forward and pats my hand. "It's so good you're back." Fresh tears pool in her eyes.

My thoughts race to the girl next door. "How is Hilda?"

"She's working hard, helping her mother and brother."

"Paul is back?"

Mother nods. "He's an invalid, so young, and his leg…" She clears her throat and gets up. "I've got to plan dinner. Tomorrow, we need to get you registered for your ration coupons."

I abruptly jump up and mumble something before rushing out the door. I've got to see Hilda. Now.

I ring the doorbell. Again, I'm back in time…a hundred times I've heard that sound, never given it a second thought. My heart bangs against my ribs as I step back.

A man opens, fills out the frame. "Yes?"

I take a closer look, the eyes of the man familiar…Hilda's eyes.

"Eh, Paul?"

The man scans my face. "You are...?"

"Peter...from next door."

Recognition creeps into Paul's expression, followed by a smile. "Of course, come in. You are here for Hilda."

As I slip past Paul I realize how badly he limps. He pushes hard on a cane and wobbles back and forth. I immediately think about Wolfgang, who isn't much older than Paul—both men invalids.

"Hilda, visitor..."

CHAPTER THIRTY-TWO

Hilda

Why is Kurt early? He knows I've got to finish dinner before Mama gets home.

"I've got to prepare the soup," I say, not even trying to keep the irritation from my voice.

"Hallo Hilda."

The potato I've been cutting into slices slips from my fingers into the pot, the knife drops to the floor. I turn to face the boy I've missed for more than two years, who I thought was dead. Oh, what am I saying? The fellow standing in front of me is no boy. He is tall, with square shoulders and a shadow on his chin. Peter is a man.

I open my mouth but there is no sound. In fact Peter's face is all shaky and moves in and out of focus. The next moment he is there in front of me… holding me.

"I'm back," he says into my ear. What a useless thing to say. Don't I know it, don't I see…and feel? I lean into him, my cheek against his collarbone. The fabric of his shirt scrapes against my skin. I smell soap. He's bathed before seeing me.

"I missed you so," I finally say. It's not my voice, not even my body. I'm floating somehow.

Peter rubs my back "You're all shaky." There's wonder in his voice, so familiar and yet so strange, and definitely deeper than I remember.

Fury grips me and I step backward and out of his embrace. Why wouldn't I be shaky? Had I not thought him dead…or at a minimum injured and suffering like Paul? Yet, here he is all in one piece. As though he expects to just move right back into my life, the life he left in pieces.

"What happened?" I ask, almost afraid to test my voice.

"What do you mean?"

Anger grips me like a vise and I begin pacing back and forth. "I mean what happened to you? We hadn't heard anything in more than a year." I know I sound hysterical, definitely accusatory. "You didn't come home when the war ended. Most of the children's camps dissolved last winter. Kids returned home." I take a breath and continue. "You didn't even tell us or your mother. I worried terribly."

Peter's eyes go from wonder, surprise and something like tenderness—no, that has got to be my sick imagination—to clouds swirling, his brows scrunched.

"If you wouldn't just talk your head off, I could explain," he says.

When I remain silent, he continues. "Our teacher decided it was safe to stay. So Karl-Heinz and I decided to leave alone. We left late February and just got here. Today."

I grip the chair tighter because the shakiness is returning full force. Peter crossed the country in the middle of a war. No telling what he saw. How he must have suffered, likely starved. He looks so thin, even his hands are bony.

I remember our last meeting in this kitchen a thousand years ago when he was so excited to leave and go on adventures, and in the fraction of a second I'm angry again.

"You didn't even write," I say.

"I did."

"Not to me."

"Yes, to you." Confusion shows in Peter's expression.

But I'm on a roll now. "You wanted to go so bad," I shout. "If you had stayed…" *I could've stayed, and together—*

The doorbell rings. I hear Paul, who's left us alone, open.

Peter stares at me but I can't read his expression. It's been so long, there are new lines on his face, around his mouth.

Kurt rushes up to me. "I'm a bit early." He hasn't seen Peter who is hidden by the door and proceeds to kiss me. "Just didn't want to waste time at home. Wanted to see you quickly."

Across Kurt's shoulder, I see Peter flinch. He visibly shrinks before he turns on his heels. The door slams and he's gone.

And like stepping into an icy wind, I push Kurt away and hug myself. Peter was gone for two years and yet, his disappearance now feels worse, a void that keeps me frozen in place. I just stand there dazed and astonished to find Kurt touching my arm.

He looks surprised. "You had a visitor?"

"My old neighbor," I manage. Without looking at Kurt, I return to the pot on the stove. "Damn idiot."

I don't know if I'm talking about Peter or myself.

Peter

I don't remember when I returned home. It was dark and the cool drizzle had soaked me to the skin. I didn't feel it initially, just walked outside and marched off. Here I'd just returned after more than two years, had walked well over a thousand kilometers, had been shot at, threatened and robbed. I'd met with hatred and amazing kindness, had starved and been cold to the bone.

Had finally understood that I wanted nothing more than to be home. Not just for Mother or my brother Walter—but for Hilda. I'd missed her. At first like a friend, but later the image of Hilda had returned more and more. Until one day I understood that I loved her and that it had scared me. Is that why I'd been so keen on joining the evacuation program? No, I'd been thoughtless, lured by beach trips and games.

Now I was home, had fevered toward that moment when I saw Hilda again. Had imagined her jumping into my arms, holding on to me as I held on to her. I'd told her in my letter how much I missed her…and she never received it. Did Arthur lose the letter, did something happen to him or to the mail?

Either way, it is all over. None of what I'd imagined is true. Hilda is mad at me. She was when I left. She still is—likely more so.

After the suffering and the longing, she turns out to be false. Not at all what I remembered. She has a boyfriend and I've been chasing a dream, that's all it is. Stupid girls.

I drag myself to bed, curl together on the mattress. I don't even enjoy the clean sheets, the soft mattress and my beloved comforter. None of it matters. The longing I felt wanting to get home has been replaced by the longing for Hilda. Now that I know I can't have her, my heart is torn open. The joy I felt earlier today to find Mother and Walter unharmed in our home has evaporated. Of course, I'm glad they're all right. But this new thing dampens it all.

At breakfast I try to put on a happy face. Mother has set the table for three. Only Father is missing now. He may never return, or he may walk in like I did. Still, we have each other. I make a point of hugging Mother, remain in her embrace longer than I ever thought possible. Instead of feeling calmer tears press.

"What's wrong?" Mother asks.

I only shake my head and sit down silently. Breakfast consists of a few slices of cornbread and red currant jam. Mother has made instant coffee from a few of the packets from the American supplies I brought home. She is over the moon about all the cigarettes.

"Today, we'll visit the new black market," she says, taking a sip from the coffee.

"What black market?"

"At *Grünewald*," Walter chimes in. I can't believe how tall he's gotten.

"They started when the war ended," Mother says.

"Why don't we buy things in the stores?"

Mother looks at me with that knowing expression. "Thanks to the madman, Germany has nothing left, no food, no light bulbs, no coal, no nothing. And the Reichsmark is losing value as we speak." She chews on her lower lip. "I'm afraid, things won't improve for quite a while."

How do you know, I want to ask. *Who made you the expert?* But I don't because I realize that my mother is a lot smarter than I ever gave her credit for. When I left here in 1943, I only saw an aging woman in a frumpy black dress, one to be ashamed of.

Now I'm ashamed of myself.

When I look up, her gaze is on me. She's smiling. And behind that smile is unconditional love—for me.

I smile back and pat her hand, full of admiration for the grandiosity of her heart. "I'm so happy to be home."

"Those American cigarettes you brought will work wonders on the black market. On the way we pick up your ration coupons." She straightens and busies herself heating water. "I'm making another coffee…to celebrate my son's return."

To my amazement Walter hasn't said a thing, his gaze on me and for once quiet, even pensive.

The black market consists of men, women and youths milling about on an empty lot. Right next to it, sharp-edged ruins fill the sky. Some of the people have their wares on the ground…a hammer and rusty nails, hand-knitted socks, two-dozen brown eggs, bread.

A number of people show nothing, their goods hidden in bags or old cardboard suitcases.

We agree to make the rounds and find out what people are selling, then decide on what we can afford. Mother has brought two of the cigarette packs, four cigarettes each.

"I'm going to ask the people over there." Walter bounces off toward the back end where several men in hats stand talking with their hands in their pockets.

Mother and I go different ways. As I approach a couple of women, hair hidden beneath knotted scarves, they begin to mumble. "Cream, delicious fresh cream." The other says, "Rye bread, three loaves, rye bread, freshly baked."

"May I see the bread?" I ask.

The woman bends down and unpacks one loaf. "Can't touch."

I bow lower too. It's bread all right, but what kind or how old it is, I can't tell. It seems dry and doesn't smell like anything. Still, real bread would be incredible. "How much?"

"What do you have?"

"Cigarettes, genuine American camels."

The woman who is so wrinkled, she looks all scrunched up, focuses on me. I see interest in her eyes, maybe greed. "Four cigarettes for a loaf. Ten for all three."

"I'll be back."

I find mother talking to a youth about my age. He's selling rye and wheat grain in paper sacks. Mother is inspecting the contents closely, demands that the youth put two kernels on her palm. She looks at it, tastes it. "How much for two packages?"

"Six cigarettes," the youth says."

"Four." Mother's face is expressionless. Who is this woman?

"Five."

"I'll give you five for two bags if you throw in those shriveled potatoes." Next to the grain are the remains of last year's harvest—potatoes with roots sprouting.

The boy's gaze swivels back and forth between his goods and Mother who appears to be turning away.

"All right."

"They've got eggs over there," Walter shouts behind us.

Mother doles out the cigarettes and motions us to pick up the grain and potatoes.

"The woman over there has bread."

"Let's take a look at both." Mother tucks the remaining cigarettes into her pocket and leads the way.

The bread woman, emboldened by my reappearance, begins to murmur again. "Delicious rye bread, freshly baked."

Mother points at the wrapped packages and wiggles a finger. Apparently, the woman understands because she opens up the same loaf she showed me. Mother bends closer and sniffs. "Show me the entire loaf."

Reluctantly, the woman pulls away the paper. On the bottom edges sprouts green mold.

"Thought so," Mother says. She just turns away and pulls Walter along. "Show me the eggs."

Behind me the woman mumbles something like *old shrew*, but I can't be certain. Walter bounces to the egg vendor. Several dozen eggs pile high in enamel bowls.

"Can I pick one up?" Mother asks the man who leans heavily on a cane.

"Of course."

Mother carefully puts the egg on her palm, eyes it, sniffs it, and finally focuses on the man with the cane. "How old are they?"

"Fresh from the last two days."

She nods and looks at the egg in her hand as if it could whisper its truth to her. "How much?"

"Four cigarettes for six."

"I give you three cigarettes for seven."

The man eyes her, then his eggs, trying to gauge his chances. "Three for six then."

"Deal." Mother pulls a couple of dishtowels from her bag and carefully wraps the eggs and stores them in her basket. Then she looks at us, a glint of pride in her eyes. "Time to bake bread."

As we leave the market, triumphant about the prospect of fresh bread, Hilda and her boyfriend are coming up the street. From a distance she looks so skinny, a wind could blow her over. Worse is that I can't turn away because I'm helping carry the grain. Even if I wanted to, my eyes are drawn to the approaching figures. The fellow is talking though I have the feeling Hilda isn't listening. She's looking in our direction, in fact her eyes are on me.

I feel my cheeks warm and try to breathe normally. Walter is talking next to me, but I don't hear a word he's saying. Twenty meters…Hilda's hair is pulled into a ponytail. She looks vulnerable, kind of frail. My heart aches. *Breathe, you idiot.* Ten meters…Hilda says something, but her gaze remains on me. It's as if we've got magnets on each other.

"Look, there is Hilda," Mother says. I mumble something unintelligible. As we are about to pass each other, Mother calls out, "Hilda, why don't you visit us tonight? I'm going to bake. Isn't it wonderful that Peter is home?"

Hilda smiles, a pained smile, her eyes shiny. "Of course, Frau Breuer."

She hates to have to visit, but is too chicken to admit it to my mother. I bite down hard until my teeth grind. Fury and anger broil inside me, a toxic stew that will spill out any moment. I'm going to deck that dope she is with.

I feel my fingers curl and remember the grain. "I'm going ahead," I say, catching a last glimpse of Mother's surprised face. I fall into a run, slow at first, then faster and faster until my ribs ache with exhaustion. I've got no business running like this when I'm still worn out from the journey.

That's when I remember Karl-Heinz. I've got to talk to him. Now.

CHAPTER THIRTY-THREE

Hilda

I hardly notice what happens at the market. Seeing Peter walking toward me took over my brain. Frau Breuer didn't notice anything. She's her sweet self, even invited me for dinner. I don't think I can go, but I didn't have the strength to say no. Getting fresh bread is a mighty strong incentive. Leaving more for my own family helps as well.

"What's the matter with you?" Kurt asks as we exit the market, a kilo onions, leeks and a sack potatoes in our bags. The bread was either too expensive or didn't look fresh, so we opted for produce. In exchange, Kurt gave up his beloved pocketknife.

I didn't want him to, but he said we needed to eat and that his knife wasn't going to fill our stomachs. He's right, of course. Still, what are we going to use next time and the time after that? The new British occupation hasn't brought any relief, the stores still mostly empty. Every week posters announce what's going to be in the stores. Some days, it's hardly anything, even with the new ration coupons.

"I'm thinking about what to do with the food," I lie.

"Will you visit your neighbor for dinner then?"

"I suppose."

"Then I'll pick you up tomorrow night." Kurt has been aiming to get me into his room. His mother goes to bed early and he's told me, she won't know if we are there. So far, I have resisted. It's nice to be kissed, a bit wet maybe, but nice.

In front of Kurt's home, we divide the food. It's unfair because it was his knife. Kurt says it's his job to care for me. I don't argue.

All afternoon, I pace. I traded another book with one of the neighbors, but I can't concentrate. Dinner is made, a soup with today's black market finds and cornbread on the side. I can still go next door and cancel, tell Frau Breuer that I'm sick or that Paul needs my help. Any excuse is fine, yet I don't go. Instead I watch the clock move stubbornly slow. Mama returns around six o'clock.

She throws me a curious glance but doesn't say anything. Neither does Paul. He's been taking daily walks now and feeling stronger. His limp is bad, but he is no longer so pale. Sometimes, he visits the old vet and the two of them talk for hours. It does him good because he always returns with glowing cheeks and sometimes even a bit of a smile.

He's even gone with me a few times to scrounge.

"I hear you're going to dinner at the neighbors," Mother says innocently. "Isn't it wonderful that Peter is back? I heard he had a horrible time. Imagine him walking for months all alone…and those laborers even stole their shoes."

"He had Karl-Heinz," I say, wondering how she knows all this. It comes out totally wrong. Too late because Mama seizes on it.

"I must say I'm astonished you're giving him such a hard time." Mama's eyes are filled with anger. I can't remember the last time she was mad at me.

Tears threaten, so I jump up and go to the bathroom. I've got to get a grip. But no matter how I try, I begin to sob. Peter suffered, and I'm a nasty person. I'm cruel and…what? The image in the mirror has no answers, just red eyes and blotchy skin.

I take a cold washcloth and wipe my face. Time to eat bread.

Frau Breuer embraces me. "I'm happy you came." Then she holds me at arm's length. "Something wrong. Paul all right?"

I nod. "Everything is fine. I'm just tired from all the running."

Frau Breuer shakes her head and leads me into the kitchen filled with the most amazing baked smell. "Tsk, tsk, I know. What a time we all have just to eat."

Walter calls from his seat at the table. "Finally! I'm starving." The spotless tablecloth is buried under a large basket of sliced bread, some kind of red jam, and scrambled eggs with onions.

I force a grin. "Sorry, dear sir, for being late."

"You aren't late." Peter walks toward me, arms outstretched. He's smiling. "I'm glad to see you."

I blink. Twice. Is that the same man I saw earlier on the street, the same man who took off so he wouldn't have to look at me?

Peter

After seeing Hilda near the black market, I hurried to see Karl-Heinz. I smacked a fist on the doorbell, which loudly springs into action.

Karl-Heinz opens the door, his hair sticking up in all directions. Like me, he's not seen a hairdresser in months. "Better come in, looks like you're about to explode."

I follow him into a half-dark living room, heavy blood-red curtains covering the windows. "Mother and *Tante* are out," he says. "Just when I thought I'd have a moment to myself, you show up." He grins. "Just joking."

I stare at him. What's a joke? When has Karl-Heinz last said anything funny? Not that I feel like laughing. In fact, he's not funny at all. I slump on the couch, my head filled with thoughts I can't express.

Karl-Heinz sits down across from me. He's wearing a clean blue shirt with a collar and black pants I don't recognize. "Out with it. What happened?"

I sigh and stare at the somber looking men and women in picture frames. One of them is Karl-Heinz's father.

Abruptly, Karl-Heinz leans forward. "Something happen to your mother or Walter?"

I realize he doesn't ask about Father. None of us are ever asking about our fathers these days.

"Hilda has a boyfriend."

"What?"

"I went over there yesterday to see her and she…I…"

"You expected her to jump into your arms and cover you in kisses."

I look up. How did Karl-Heinz know?

Karl-Heinz shakes his head and says, "Come on, tell me."

"This fool comes in and acts like he owns her."

"The man is jealous." Laughter rings through the living room, a weird sound.

I frown as fresh anger brews. "What's so funny?"

Karl-Heinz slaps the pillow next to him. "You are. You're a fool,

Peter. Have you ever thought what Hilda's life was like while we were away? Did you ask her? She probably had to take care of things here, maybe she went to a terrible camp. Have you talked to her?"

I think about last night, the scene in the kitchen.

"Didn't think so." Karl-Heinz continues. Who makes him the expert? He doesn't even have a girlfriend…or boyfriend. "Maybe she needed him to help her?" He looks at me. "Weren't you the one running off to camp two years ago?"

I nod. Hard to believe now that I was so excited. A new feeling joins my anger: guilt. If I'd been home, Hilda would've had an easier time. We'd be together…lovers.

It's all my fault.

"I think you should talk to her, find out what happened while we were gone. Be the friend she missed for two years. Be the friend you were to me." Tears shimmer in Karl-Heinz's eyes.

My throat is closing up too, so all I do is croak "yes."

Karl-Heinz wipes his face with the back of his hand. "I hope you know I'd be dead without you."

We look at each other. Karl-Heinz's eyes are old as the world.

"It works both ways."

Karl-Heinz smiles. "Exactly. Now go and get your friend back."

All that afternoon, I worry Hilda won't show. I help mother grind the grain in the hand coffee mill. Help her mix dough, fix omelets, and set the table. I even get a bunch of daisies growing on a bombsite. Nature is funny that way. She just ignores us humans, or at least tries to.

Now Hilda sits across from me. She's serious and keeps her gaze on her plate most of the time. Still, I can tell she's enjoying the bread and omelet.

"It must've been terribly hard here during the bombing," I say. "Mother told me that they came over a weekend and you had no more glass in the windows."

A hint of surprise shows in Hilda's widening eyes. "It was very scary. We hid in the basement, but then Paul…"

"What happened to Paul?"

Hilda tells us about her brother's shellshock, the way his leg looked. "He's making a lot of progress now that the war is over."

"Glad to hear it," I say, trying to imagine my brother, Walter, with a horrible injury. "I want to help if I can. Just tell me."

Again there is that look of surprise on Hilda's face. When she nods, I take it as a good sign.

"What happened to *you*?" she asks.

In rapid succession, scenes play in my mind…the nasty Hitler Youth boy, Zeibler, the moment I thought the forced laborers would kill us, Karl-Heinz almost dying of diphtheria, the scabies and Karl-Heinz's fear for his balls. A grunt escapes me.

"It must have had some funny parts," Mother says dryly.

I burst into laughter as the others watch me. "Sorry, I can't…it was…Karl-Heinz would kill me if I told." I wipe my face. What the heck is wrong with me?

Silence settles, so I finally say, "I will tell you some time. Just not now. It's…hard."

They all nod, and I feel Hilda's gaze on me like a burning hand. "Paul doesn't want to talk about things either."

All of a sudden I feel it, that warmth and concern, Hilda always had for me. It's there, right between us, hovering above the table, moving to embrace me. I smile again. I know now that I love her and that I'll try to help no matter what she does in return. If she wants to marry that Kurt character, so be it. I'll be there, even if it kills me.

"That was nice," Hilda says at the door. She makes a point to thank Mother and insists it was the best bread she ever ate. Mother glows in return. Why can't I say nice things like that?

"I'm glad you came," I say, giving her right shoulder a light pat.

She nods and turns, almost shyly. "Good night."

It occurs to me that she didn't say anything about another meeting. But in former times we never needed to. Does that mean I can just visit her? Or is she done with me for a while?

Once again I'm confused, wishing I could ask Karl-Heinz.

I also think about Walter and the fact, he hardly said a word tonight. Something is definitely wrong with him.

CHAPTER THIRTY-FOUR

Hilda

Sleep refuses me tonight. I stayed way longer at Peter's house than I expected. I also didn't expect to enjoy it so much. It almost felt like old times when we shared dinners at each other's homes. Peter was so attentive—he really listened.

Apparently, Kurt stopped by around eight-thirty. He knew I was having dinner, so why is he showing up anyway? I feel a twinge of guilt and annoyance, but that's not what keeps me awake. It's Peter—

The doorbell rings. I about fall out of bed, turn on the light. It's fifteen past midnight. What could be so important to wake us all?

I climb out of bed and rush to the entry just as Paul and Mama appear in the hallway.

In the door stands Biene's mother. I haven't seen her in months and hardly recognize her. She was always very proper and a bit plump, her hair made up and her clothes expensive. No longer. The woman in front of us appears haggard, her hair stringy and not very clean, her clothes mismatched and ragged. To be fair, most of us look like this all the time, but it's shocking to see Frau Fuchs this way.

"It's Biene, I need your help," she cries.

"What happened?" Mama asks from behind me. "Won't you come in?"

"No time. She's gone...missing." Frau Fuchs's arms flutter like the wings of a moth.

"Maybe she went out late?" I say. After all, Biene is seventeen.

"She was in such a state. I tried…" The woman's breath comes in spurts.

Mama resolutely steps to the doorsill and guides Biene's mother into the living room. "Paul, get Frau Fuchs a glass of water. Hilda, help Frau Fuchs to the sofa."

I lead her by the elbow, help the woman sit when I'd much rather kick her in her behind.

As soon as we're all assembled, Mama asks, "Now, from the beginning, what happened?"

Frau Fuchs begins to talk about Biene, the way she acted lately. She leaves out the fact that she urged her daughter to have sex with an old coal trader.

"Why do you think she may harm herself?" Mama says.

Frau Fuchs looks up from her water glass. "I just know. She never leaves the house, unless she picks up rations, never at night. She was so sad lately, refused to talk, just sat there. Sometimes, she remained in bed all day, no matter what I said." Tears roll down the woman's cheeks. "I tried to cheer her up, Theo and I both. Theo isn't well, but he feels something is wrong with his sister."

Frau Fuchs takes a sip of water. "Then yesterday afternoon, she met Kurt, that young man she took a liking to, at the store. The only reason I know is that my neighbor saw them. Apparently, there was some kind of argument between Biene and Kurt. And when she came home, she went to her room…didn't want to eat dinner."

Mama turns to me. "Isn't that Kurt your friend?"

Heat rises in my cheeks. "He helps me organize supplies."

"I was sitting in the kitchen when she walked right past me. Didn't say anything, didn't answer, just walked right out of the house." Frau Fuchs puts the glass on the coffee table and hugs herself. "Naturally, I stayed up. Biene never came back. Wouldn't you know where she might have gone?"

I stare at the pleading eyes and say nothing. A long time ago, we used to visit the little park by the well—back then before the war reached us. Would Biene have gone there alone? Why? Most of all, I wonder what Biene and Kurt fought about.

"Why did you make her do those things?" I hardly recognize my own voice, sharp as Mama's best paring knife. The others are staring at me, but I keep focused on the woman in the coat, the rubbed-off lipstick, the slack skin around her jaw.

Biene's mother opens her mouth, closes it, the loose chin

trembles. "I don't know what you are talking about."

"The coal trader," I whisper.

"Hilda, what is the meaning of this?" Mama asks.

I ignore her. "You made Biene sleep with an old man."

Mama gasps, but I'm focused on the woman in front of me. She's blurring now as the fury and sadness I've carried for my friend demands release.

Biene's mother swallows before exclaiming, "Oh, my poor baby." She begins to sob theatrically, and Mama offers her a finely pressed handkerchief, her eyes darting between me and Paul as though searching for answers. "I must go home. Theo is alone and he scares easily."

"We should search for your daughter," Paul says. "It's just hard during the night. We'd walk right past her or fall into a bomb crater."

When the door closes behind Frau Fuchs, Mama and Paul hurry to my side.

"What was that all about?" The edge is gone from Mama's voice. "You all right?"

At that moment I'm dead tired, yet I can't move, can't even lift my arm. The pressure that's been building for months releases. I weep like I've never wept before, not even after I realized that Papa would never return.

"She made Biene sleep with the coal trader for food and heat. Biene was disgusted…I tried to help…" Little by little it all comes out. The SS-man…Biene's visits…my betrayal.

They say carrying a secret slowly poisons your insides. I can attest that the moment I let go I felt better—for a bit.

Until the thought of Biene jumping off the *Müngsten* bridge engulfs me like a toxic cloud.

Frau Fuchs and Theo are back at six in the morning, Mama decidedly cooler in welcoming them. Theo looks all sleepy, but perks up when Mama offers him a slice of bread with blackberry jam. He gobbles it down while the rest of us decide on routes and meeting points.

Though Frau Fuchs doesn't look like she's slept, she seems happy to get going. I decide to take the way past Kurt's house in *Unnersberg*. It isn't far to the park from there. Paul will head toward *Krahenhöhe*, Mama toward our old high school on Schützenstraße and Frau Fuchs wants to walk into town.

If we don't find her we will regroup at ten at our house. Frau

Fuchs mentioned going to the police and the British occupation.

Outwardly I'm calm, but my heart hammers as I rush downhill toward Kurt's place. It's early even for him, so I wonder what I'll find.

"Biene is missing," I say when he opens the door. "We're searching for her." He's only half dressed in a pair of high-water breeches and an undershirt peppered with holes. Even in the gloom of the entry I see his face turn ashen.

His lower lip trembles as he waves me inside. "I'm coming with you."

I wait for him to tell me about last night's meeting with Biene, but he says nothing. He gulps a glass of water and motions me back outside.

"I'm wondering if she went to the park," I say, trying to stay calm. "We used to go there before—"

"Maybe."

"I just don't get why she'd run off like this."

Kurt doesn't respond. He stares straight ahead, his arms fidgeting as he marches off in record speed.

We're at the park in minutes. Near the well house, the water gurgles in the trough. It is cool here, damp and shady under the trees. We quickly circle the area. No Biene.

"Damn. I would've thought she'd—"

"Let's go," Kurt says.

"Where?"

But again Kurt doesn't speak. He heads up the street into the *Schrebergärten*, the garden plots with their miniature cabins where people spend their weekends raising crops and relaxing. Kurt walks at such a pace I'm almost running.

To my surprise, he ignores the gardens until we arrive at one near the pond and the little restaurant. He opens the gate and marches toward the hut, which has seen better days, paint peeling on its only window, a few shingles missing from the roof.

He reaches above the entry door, no wider than two feet, and comes up empty. Ever so quietly, he twists the doorknob and peeks inside.

In the gloom I make out a cot, Biene lying on her side sleeping beneath a moth-eaten blanket. The skin of her bare arm shimmers pale, almost translucent. She's thinner than I remember.

My legs wobble as relief floods me. Until this very moment I didn't know if Biene was alive. Somehow, in my fuzzy brain, I notice Kurt get onto his knees and take Biene's hand.

"Hey," he whispers. The gesture is so tender, I feel like an intruder just standing here. The shack has a narrow stove and a few shelves on which sit banged up pots and a few garden tools, nothing worth stealing.

The cot creaks. Biene opens her eyes, and at first looks confused, but then focuses on Kurt and then me. "What are you doing here?" she asks.

I bend low to touch her shoulder. "Your mother thought…we did a search…we worried about you…"

Biene blinks, then looks at Kurt. "How did you know I was here?"

"I didn't, at least not for sure." Kurt's voice is hoarse and when I look sideways, I see tears. "After we spent time here." He squeezes her hand. "I'm so sorry about yesterday. It's just…I had promised Hilda—"

"What did you promise?" I say.

Kurt shrugs. "That we were…are a couple."

"You two have been here?" I say quietly. I'm eerily calm, though I had no idea that the two of them slept together.

"It was months ago," Biene says. "I have no right to be upset, but when I saw you yesterday, I just couldn't go on. Not with all the other struggles."

I stare at my best friend and my boyfriend. They're in love with each other, even a blind man…or woman can see that. Strangely, I'm not mad. A little disappointed maybe, but it's more my pride than anything.

"You're free to do what you want," I say. "I'll go home now and tell the others not to worry." My eyes meet Biene's. "Better tell your mother. She's quite upset."

Kurt hurries after me and catches me at the gate. "I'm sorry, Hilda. I didn't know, but then—"

"Wait," Biene cries. She rushes from the derelict hut as if a ghost were chasing her. She throws herself into my arms and begins to cry.

I feel my friend who I've done wrong, quiver against me and now the guilt I've carried pushes tears into my throat and then my eyes spill over. "I am sorry," I cry, clinging to her. "I was wrong to judge you. You wanted to help your family."

Biene wipes away my tears and smiles through hers. "You

wanted to protect me. I know that now. I never meant to take Kurt…it's just—I love him."

I place a forefinger over her lips. "I know…it's fine."

And strangely, it is.

Peter

I'm awake early. It's not only my stomach growling, but my thoughts about Hilda. Last night I lied—to myself and to her. I don't think I *can* be friends like Karl-Heinz suggested. Just thinking about that fellow Kurt touching Hilda turns my stomach. I'm going to keep my distance for a while, try to figure out a way to collect food, find out about school or at least find a job.

The few items I was able to get at the grocery store are laughable. A little bread, a few onions, a can of meat, and some sauerkraut. How are we supposed to survive an entire month with that? The storeowner said there'll be new posters every week announcing additional items we can collect. But the quantities are so small it won't matter. We'll all be dead in a year. If the war doesn't do it, the aftermath will—Hitler's legacy.

More and more news surfaces about concentration camps. Not camps like ours for German kids to study and play, but death camps dressed up as labor camps. Oh, how I wish I could go back to myself two years ago and talk some sense into me. How could we follow a monster like that? Not just him, but the likes of Goebbels and Himmler.

They destroyed the country, killed tens of millions, forced boys and men into the war. I'm lucky I didn't have to fight. Apparently, I missed the last Volkssturm in March when Hitler asked all the boys my age to fight one last time. Many of those boys are dead now. At least that's what people think because they haven't returned from the war. Father is still away. Some of the men are now in allied prison camps. Others are outright missing, likely dead.

A particularly loud growl emanates from my stomach and shoos me out of bed. Outside it's already light, birds chirping happily. I tiptoe into the kitchen and peruse the cabinets. We've got an egg left, some bread and plenty of grain. It was smart of Mother to trade grain instead of flour or other items that are eaten too quickly. Grain makes flour, and we can have pancakes.

Pancakes. My mouth instantly waters as I imagine a stack on a platter. But then I fill a glass with water and drink it down. And another. I can't make myself touch our food without asking permission.

"What are you doing?" Walter stands in the door, hair tussled, his pajama jacket inherited from me askew.

"Getting water?" Without a word he sidles up to me and grabs his own drink. "You're awfully quiet these days."

"What's it to you?" Walter's tone is outright hostile and when I put a hand on his shoulder, he yanks away and plunks himself on the sofa.

"You're quite a grump this morning," I say, trying a smile. "Did you get out of bed with the wrong foot?"

Walter shrugs and avoids my eyes.

"Oh, come on, what's eating you? Girl trouble, maybe?"

Walter's cheeks redden as he jumps up and leaves the room. A few seconds later he's back and shoves a red and green-checkered handkerchief into my face.

"You got an explanation for that?"

My mouth goes dry. I lean back, staring at the piece of fabric that accompanied me for two years. "It's a hankie, so what?"

"*My* hankie." Walter pokes a forefinger at the initials. "That's me." When I don't answer, he says, "Where did you get it?"

The words don't want to leave my mouth. They linger in the back of my throat as the scene in the alley returns. Walter being whipped, his flushed cheeks and muffled cries, dirt grinding into his shirt, his bruised face with the stitches in his eyebrow when I returned home. I'd feigned surprise, patted his head and helped make him comfortable on the sofa.

"The last I remember is that I left it in the alley behind our house." Walter's eyes are filled with tears. "I never wanted to see it again because it reminded me of Ralf and Otto who'd beat me up before school." He scoffs. "And then Mother comes in yesterday, handing it to me all clean, surprised where it may have been all this time."

"I must've found it," I finally lie.

Walter stomps his feet and shouts, "Bullshit," before running from the room. I begin to pace, around the table, twice…three times. I want to outrun the memory of Walter lying on the ground with a bloodied face…and my hesitation, even glee. I failed my brother. He'd been annoying, but he had been innocent and needed me. I'd done nothing.

And Walter knows it.

I feel my cheeks warm, then my body follows. Sweat pours from me. I've got to get outside…away.

When I leave the house, I'm tempted to go next door. I need a distraction from Walter's outburst, and Hilda's place is an invisible thread drawing me there—as if something were reeling me in like a fish. But then I remember Kurt in Hilda's kitchen and quickly march past. I've got to find a way to distract myself, so I decide to visit Karl-Heinz again. I sure could use another pep talk.

When nobody answers the bell, I bang on the door. "Karl-Heinz? It's me." *Why do I sound so urgent, downright pitiful?*

Karl-Heinz opens, his cheeks a bit flushed. "What happened?"

"Can I talk to you?" I say, pushing past him into the hallway. "I don't think I can go through with it."

Karl-Heinz closes the door behind me, but isn't moving.

"Who was it?" Someone calls from the living room—Christian's voice.

"It's Peter." Karl-Heinz motions me to follow him before I have time to comment.

"Good to see you in one piece." Christian sits on the couch, his arms and legs as lanky as ever.

I step into the room, having the distinct feeling I'm disrupting something. Indeed, Christian's throat flames as red as Karl-Heinz's face.

"I can return later," I say.

"Nonsense." Karl-Heinz slumps onto the couch next to Christian and points at the chair. "What happened? I'm sure Christian won't tell."

Christian taps a forefinger across his closed lips and shakes his head. Now I'm feeling silly.

I look at the two friends—Karl-Heinz, my oldest friend and Christian, our classmate. All of a sudden I know exactly what's going on. I was right all along. "I don't want to disturb you," I say and head to the door.

"Peter, wait. I've got to tell you something." The tremble in Karl-Heinz's voice makes me turn. "Sit, would you?"

Karl-Heinz swallows loudly as if he has a huge ball in his throat. He looks at Christian and then at me. "I've lied to you. I was afraid you'd not understand…but when you told me about Hilda, I…" He looks helplessly to his friend who pats his hand and then links his fingers with Karl-Heinz's.

"I love Christian. I thought…*we* thought… that it'd go away somehow. That we'd find a way to like girls." Again the helpless look. I stare back and forth between the boys. "You're my oldest friend. I'm going to burst if I don't tell somebody. And when you asked me about Hilda, I thought…"

"You said I could be her friend, just be a shoulder to cry on," I yell. "Here you sit all happy like a couple."

"I'm sorry," Karl-Heinz says. "Maybe it was wrong, but I still think…"

I jump up, shouting, "What do *you* know about girls?"

Karl-Heinz shrugs. He squeezes Christian's hand. "It isn't that different."

"Oh, it isn't?"

I don't hear the rest of Karl-Heinz's words, only that he and Christian both call after me. The door slams shut and I rush up the street. Idiot.

He was afraid, the voice in my head says. *Like you were afraid to talk about Hilda until you were about to blow a gasket. For Karl-Heinz it was infinitely worse because the Nazis considered homosexuality deviant. And I doubt the law has changed.*

But you knew anyway. Your gut told you years ago. Karl-Heinz never showed interest in girls, he never talked about them. If you weren't so distracted and self-centered you could've discussed it. Been there to support your friend.

I'm about to unlock the door to my apartment, when I hesitate. It took a lot of guts for Karl-Heinz to tell the truth. Way more than me admitting about Hilda. All of a sudden I regret running off. It's just…I feel abandoned somehow…even jealous.

My chest tightens with embarrassment. Or is it envy? First Hilda has a lover and now Karl-Heinz does too. Where does that leave me?

I'm floating without purpose—in a vacuum. No school, no work, no belonging anywhere. Just a few days ago, all I wanted was to survive and see my family again. That's no longer enough.

I find Walter in the kitchen reading. He ignores me as I slump next to him. My brother's shoulders have broadened, and the pants he wears show bony ankles. He's growing up. A lump forms in my throat then, so I push against it and blurt, "I'm sorry."

When he doesn't answer, I continue, "I saw what happened…the boys beating you up. I returned a few minutes later, but you were gone. I picked up your hankie and…" The lump bursts into my eyes, but I don't care. "I felt terrible seeing you like that…afterwards."

Walter turns to me, his eyes wet like mine. Still he says nothing.

"You've got to believe me," I cry. "I regretted it ever since."

"You took my handkerchief with you?" Walter's voice is so low I hardly make it out.

I nod, thinking about the times I kept touching it in my pocket, the relief I'd felt when the forced laborers didn't steal it. "It was a little part of you." I grab my brother's hand that is almost as large as mine. "I should've protected you. Will you please forgive me?"

Somewhere in the quiet that follows, wood settles in the stove. Outside, a neighbor calls a greeting.

With a sudden movement, Walter throws himself at my chest and we hug like we've never hugged. We don't say a thing, just sit there as the burden I've carried lifts.

I've got my brother back.

In the afternoon I walk next door. I've got one more thing to do and won't wait another minute. Hilda opens, her eyes that beautiful gray of an early winter evening when you sit near a cozy fire with a cup of cocoa. Even in the shadow of the hallway I notice they're curious…appraising.

"I've got to talk to you," I whisper.

Hilda opens the door wider. "Everyone is still gone."

Before she can slip back in, I grab her arm. "I've got to tell you something. I've been an idiot, I…love you. I just came here to tell you that I'll wait and I'll do whatever. Even if you like Kurt, I want to help." *So much for my earlier thoughts*, my mind quips.

To my surprise, Hilda throws her arms around me. "Oh, Peter, *I'm* the idiot. I didn't really mean to be with Kurt, it was just easier than spending every day wondering what had happened to you and whether you'd return. What I mean is…I love you too."

I lean back to see her better. "What about Kurt?"

"He's in love with Biene, always was." Hilda smiles at me, tears shimmering. "He and I were sort of lost, we just didn't understand it."

Silence descends as we sink into each other. I no longer think, only feel: Hilda's chest against mine, that slight pressure of her breasts, the scent of soap on her skin, her quickened breath and the

shine in her eyes. I lean closer and we kiss.
    I've arrived.

The End

EPILOGUE

July 1948
Hilda

If it weren't for Kurt, Karl-Heinz and Peter, we wouldn't have survived the last three years. Peter's father, who returned in July 1945 on foot from the Baltic Sea, has been a huge help as well. Not only by organizing farm trips to trade food, but by mending Peter's family.

Food continued to be sparse and in the hunger winter of 1946/1947, we thought we'd all perish. But we didn't and finally, last month, the government introduced the new currency, the *Deutsche Mark*. Overnight, we no longer starved or waited for food to arrive at the stores. Overnight, store shelves overflowed with everything from chocolate, honey, pasta, and licorice to light bulbs, camera equipment, umbrellas and women's dresses.

Black markets ceased to exist, and we no longer use ration coupons.

When the doorbell rings, I rush to open it. Peter embraces me in a whirl. He wears his hair longer now so that curls form around his ears. "Ready? I've got sandwiches with real cheese and beer." He kisses me fiercely and I melt against his body. It shouldn't be allowed to feel this happy.

"Karl-Heinz and Biene will be here soon. We'll pick up Christian on the way."

"Does this mean we have a few minutes?"

I smile and we slip into the kitchen.

Peter's hands move beneath my shirt to my bra, loosen the straps. His fingertips are soft against my skin, the feeling exquisite. As I pull him toward the sofa, I strip away my underpants. His hands find me as we sink into the pillows. Bodies and breaths melt into one—nothing else matters. If somebody enters now, we won't stop.

When the doorbell rings again, we're sitting at the kitchen table sipping peppermint tea, our secret safe between our glowing cheeks.

"You ready?" Biene stands there arm-in-arm with Kurt.

Peter and I exchange glances before bursting into laughter.

"Did we miss something?" Kurt says.

"Just happy," Peter says, grabbing his pack. "Let's go."

As we're hiking through the forest toward the public pool, I watch my friends. Biene and Kurt are holding hands. They are quiet—as quiet as Karl-Heinz and Christian. We all know they're a couple, but we don't talk about it. It's not safe for them—a crime called sodomy. And there is Peter next to me. I feel his gaze on me like a warm embrace, making my steps light.

Peter's return made me realize I could let my father go. In a sense, Peter freed me. I no longer have the need to fix and control everything.

The future is finally looking up, even if we tend to party too hard and drink too much. I think what we want is a sense of normalcy. Nothing fancy, nothing extraordinary, just a decent life with a bit of fun doing things normal youths do. Is it so strange that we're looking harder for it than people who didn't experience war? Or do we want to distract ourselves, at least pretend we are like typical people? Is there such a thing in Germany, where most everybody had a lousy childhood?

Each of us carries a burden, a package of experiences and memories. They're invisible and yet they are as real as the clothes on our backs. If you look carefully, you see Biene's solemn expression, the wariness in her movements. It's still there four years later. There's Kurt, who has still not told us what he saw in those last two months of the war. Karl-Heinz's face is peaceful, but I know from Peter that he almost died in camp, far from anything he knew, and again on that long march home.

We later heard that most of the boys who stayed behind with the old Nazi teacher, Boot, were drafted in early March to help stop the onslaught of Russian soldiers by digging trenches. Most of those boys didn't return at all; they vanished as cannon fodder for Hitler. I only know because Peter, my love, told me bits and pieces after one of his classmates, a Dieter Maier showed up. He only escaped because he'd been running an errand for Zeibler, the old Hitler Youth leader, when the Red Army rolled past with their tanks and he managed to hide and flee. According to Dieter, Zeibler had been even worse than the first time he'd been running the KLV camp near Körlin. Now he was gone...along with Peter's former classmates.

At night, we revisit the memories in our dreams, the cruel Abbess, the SS-men...Fräulein Heinrich with her staring eyes. We are forever scarred, and yet, I know we're the lucky ones—the ones who survived the madman. I can still not comprehend the evil he spread, the millions of Jews he killed, the country he was supposed to protect treated with such disdain and destroyed, all those families forever marred.

I know one thing: for me, the KLV was a failure. Yes, we were away for some of the bombings, yes, we learned to live without our families and become more independent. But the emotional scars we carried back home may never heal. The fears and cruelties we experienced would've been more easily alleviated if we'd stayed with our mothers.

In the end, we served a purpose for Hitler and his twisted ideals. Even if some children had a good time—that was never the intent of the Third Reich. They always meant to separate us from our families and mold us into Nazis.

I'm glad that didn't work out. I'm glad we persevered.

Thomas Mann said in his last radio address on May 1945 that he felt joy about the allied victory as well as grief. But he also said that this was a great hour: The return of Germany to humanity.

I know all of us will work hard to make it so.

AUTHOR NOTE

While the stories of this novel are fictitious, I pulled together experiences from many eyewitness reports and sort of melded them into something that allows insight into the state of Germany in the later war years. Once again I write from the perspective of children/youths who are faced with circumstances that are formidable even for adults and must have seemed overwhelming. What struck me when reading more than a hundred eyewitness accounts, was the lack of emotion in the retelling of cruelties and seeing friends and parents die in front of them. I do believe that some hurts are too deep to put into words. Nonetheless, these war children overcame all that is connected with war, including Hitler's propagandistic mass evacuation program.

Can these children and youths who were taught to believe in Hitler and the National Socialist doctrine be exonerated? Or should they share responsibility for the atrocities committed by the National Socialist regime (NS)? It's clear that many of their parents followed what they were told—some with enthusiasm, others because they were afraid, and many because they simply accepted the status quo. It's also clear those KLV participants who do speak out only share select memories, some because they're traumatized, others because they may not want to remember their own convictions in the teachings of the NS or may not have recognized them as such.

To me it is important to approach Germany's problematic and guilt-ridden history with honesty. No matter how much time passes, we can never truly walk away from it. Instead we must continue examining every aspect of its truth in the hopes that such horror will never be repeated—not in Germany or anywhere else.

I welcome you to share your thoughts or questions. Please contact me anytime at hello@annetteoppenlander.com.

The Children's Evacuation Program (KLV)

In September 1940 Hitler ordered Baldur von Schirach to head the new 'extended children's evacuation program' or *erweiterte Kinderlandverschickung* (KLV). Divided into three categories, the KLV was supposed to include all German children.

Children up to five years of age were supposed to be accompanied by their mothers, school age children six to ten went to host families, and kids aged eleven to fourteen attended camps. Older youths, who by then attended the Hitler Youth (HJ) or League of German Girls (BDM), were then deployed to help run such camps. Initially, children went for several weeks, in some cases three to six months. As the war expanded and lengthened, schools were closed and entire classes went on extended stays with their teachers. Some kids spent the last two years in camps, in come cases beyond the end of the war.

The word evacuation or *Evakuierung* was not to be used because it carried the wrong connotation not suitable for the propaganda of the Third Reich. Instead, the KLV was sold to parents as a vacation during which children could study, exercise and play in healthy environments, eat well and enjoy themselves tremendously. Posters showed happy children going on adventure, newspapers ran beautiful stories of summer trips and joyous parents sending off their kids.

Despite the propaganda the majority of parents was leery about shipping off their children for extended periods. They fought back and either refused to send their kids or retrieved them from camps without permission, arguing that the KLV was a voluntary program.

With the increased bomb threats in the later war years, the KLV turned into something entirely different. Employers, schools, and communities pressured parents to enroll their kids in the KLV. There was talk about 'endangering' the lives of their children. German children received compulsory education, but could, due to the school closings, no longer attend. Thus, entire classes and schools were evacuated together and parents forced to go along.

Since teachers accompanied children into camps and younger

kids attended the schools near their host families, this became a new argument of the Third Reich to make children join the KLV. In many cases parents were threatened with losing their ration cards, making them unable to care for their children.

Nobody knows how many children participated in the KLV. At the end of the war, documents were either destroyed by German administrators or by the ravages of allied bombardments. Participation estimates reach from 800,000 to more than five million children. Many researchers think that a participation rate of two million is likely. Considering the large numbers who traveled away, relatively few witness reports are available. Studying those it becomes clear that the KLV was as varied as the children who partook in it, making them unsuitable for statistical analysis.

Some children were gone for six months, others for years. Some stayed in one camp, others in five, even seven. Some enjoyed themselves—most of the time—others experienced nightmares, including cruel classmates and abusive camp leaders, life-threatening illness and vermin. Some had plenty to eat, others received meager meals because kitchen personnel misappropriated supplies or there simply wasn't enough to go around.

Undoubtedly the KLV saved lives. With the increased British RAF bombings on German cities, and later the sophisticated combination of air mines, impact-bombs and phosphor bombs to incinerate buildings by the thousands, targeting civilians, women and children often succumbed in firestorms. On the other hand, children who went to camp in the east/west, in German-occupied territories like Poland, Hungary and France, encountered life-threatening situations when the Red Army and Allied troops advanced through these regions.

Whether the KLV administration was inept, uninformed or plain didn't care is unknown. Fact is that children and camp leaders were told to 'stay put' or that the enemy wasn't going to reach them.

From the research it is clear that many teachers rose far above their duties, teaching, protecting, safeguarding and comforting their often-substantial student groups. Without their commitment, the damage would have been much larger. Not to say that some teachers weren't inept or fervent NSDAP party affiliates who indoctrinated their students and took off when allied troops arrived.

That children experienced serious trauma becomes clear from the many incidences of bedwetting, nail chewing and serious illness, reaching from diphtheria to hunger typhoid. Infestations of bedbugs, lice and scabies were common and difficult to combat. Weaker children, bed wetters and those exhibiting sensitivity were beaten and abused by their classmates and/or camp leaders.

Children were homesick and worried about their loved ones. It is hard to imagine what they felt and thought when news about ever-increasing bombings, fallen fathers and perished family members reached them—often months later. The constant anxiety and uncertainty must have been horrific.

But that was never of any concern for Hitler and the Third Reich's leadership. They had intended to separate children from their families, friends and churches to influence them and raise them in the image of national socialist philosophy. Boys were supposed to be tough and heroic and become soldiers. Girls were supposed to be strong and brave, but also beautiful and healthy to grow into mothers to produce more children to become more soldiers and mothers…

The KLV presented one more program to control the population, but because it affected children and youths, it added to the long-term effects of already existing war trauma. Such trauma not only influences a person for life, research shows it also manifests genetically and is carried on by future generations.

When you realize how Hitler wanted to *ab-use* Germany's children and add this to the genocide of Jews and other minorities, the wars he began with more than thirty countries, the way he trampled over the lives of so many millions, you understand what dictatorship truly means—a complete contempt for the dictator's own people. That Hitler is likely the worst and most wide reaching dictator in known history doesn't mean we should close our eyes to dictatorial movements, including autocracies and plutocracies—the government powered by a few wealthy.

They all have one thing in common: to use their nation's people for their own gain.

Additional Information about the KLV Program

Since nearly every resource about the children's evacuation program is in German, I put together a brief overview called *Hitler's Mass Evacuation Program for Children: an Introduction,* you can order quite reasonably as an eBook or small paperback. This is my first non-fiction work which may be useful to those who are interested in this time period.

Solingen

First mentioned in 1067, Solingen is an industrial town in the hilly land near Wuppertal and Köln, a city of 155,000 people famous for producing cutlery and all things with a blade.

While Solingen is the main location for this novel, this story could've easily been told in any other German town. The same is true for the characters who, while fictitious, represent some of the experiences of German youths during the KLV.

Indeed, on November 8, 1944, Solingen's daily newspaper did not report the biggest news in the history of the city, the devastating bombardments on November 4 and 5, 1944, when at least 1,700 private citizens lost their lives, thousands of homes, including historic downtown were destroyed in a weeklong fire. Propaganda minister (yes, that was his official title) Joseph Goebbels had prohibited the media from reporting about and describing the extent of the destruction of allied bombings. Not only that, photographing or filming bombsites was strictly forbidden and severely punished. That's why hardly any German image material about the destruction exists.

But that is to be expected from a man and this regime when he said this to the men and women working in his own ministry on April 21, 1945 (nine days before Hitler's suicide and two and a half weeks before Germany's total capitulation):

"Everything is lost…a nation of cowards! It lets its women be raped. It lets its earth be soiled. In the east it flees. In the west it surrenders. It wasn't worthy of National Socialism. But its cowardice, its defeat, its humiliation will be more costly than a victory, whose price was too high for this nation."

Thomas Mann

Thomas Mann, who takes on an important role in this novel, was a German author who won the Nobel Prize in Literature for his family saga, *The Buddenbrooks*.

Criticizing the right-wing shift in Germany early and calling National Socialism "a huge wave of eccentric barbarism and primitive mass democratic carnival truculence," he went into exile in 1933, at first in Switzerland and then 1938 in the U.S.A. He left behind his assets in Germany, lost memberships and honors before WWII started. Between 1940 and 1945 and broadcast by the BBC, he made fifty-five radio speeches he always began with "German listeners."

Thomas Mann is not without critics and by some considered uncreative as he used real-life people and scenarios for his stories. However, he is one who recognized early the dangers of National Socialism and lived with the consequences of exile. He was criticized by some for leaving and speaking to Germany from a safe distance. At the same time he took on the important role of addressing Germany's conscience, even if by then few people heard him—listening to 'enemy' radio was punishable by death—and the German people were unable to rise up against Hitler's dictatorial leadership.

TIMELINE

September 1940
Hitler gives the order to evacuate all German children through various programs of the KLV. He selects Baldur von Schirach to oversee the program.

October 1940
The first KLV participants leave on chartered trains.

1942/1943
The winter of Stalingrad turns the tide, ultimately leading to Germany's doom and the loss of WWII. More than 700,000 people, Russians and Germans die during the battle.

Feb 2, 1943
The German army surrenders in Stalingrad. Large-scale air attacks bomb and devastate German cities. The civilian population, mostly women and children, without food or heat, seek refuge in bunkers and cellars.

Feb 18, 1943
National Socialist propaganda minister Goebbels declares "total war" – the Third Reich's reaction to the defeat at Stalingrad

April 19, 1943
The Warsaw ghetto's remaining Jews start to fight the German SS and resist until May 16.

1943
To scare the German civilian population, British and American Air Forces execute large scale bombing attacks, carpet bombs cover large areas. The German flak anti aircraft fire, in charge of protecting the homeland, is unable to reach the high flying planes.

June 6, 1944
The Allied Forces land in France

June 22, 1944
Dissention erupts within Germany's military leadership to end Hitler's regime

July 20, 1944
Oberst Klaus von Stauffenberg's attempt to assassinate Hitler fails

Sept. 11, 1944
The Allied Forces enter Germany.

Oct. 16, 1944
The Red Army enters Germany.

Nov. 4/5, 1944
Solingen is leveled and burns for a week. The bombing on November 5 lasts 18 minutes and leaves 100 large, 300 middle sized and 500 small fires. 921 tons of bombs and air mines, followed by 138 tons of phosphor bombs fall. Thousands die and more than 20,000 people lose their homes. On November 5, 1944, the British radio announces: "Solingen, the heart of the German steel industry, a destroyed, dead city!"

Jan. 1945
As the German Army lacks ammunition and food and soldiers retreat on all fronts, families are asked to sacrifice yet again. In what has been called the "final war", boys and grandfathers are drafted. The Allies move across Germany to finish the job, no longer expecting

much opposition. Air attacks blanket the country. The Red Army liberates the Concentration camp (KZ) Auschwitz—most of the prisoners have died in SS-organized gas chambers and during death marches.

Feb 13, 1945
RAF and USAAF bomb Dresden, burning it to the ground, killing 18,000-25,000 civilians.

March 1945
In the desperate last wave of the *Volkssturm*, Hitler orders all boys, born 1928 and 1929 as well as old men to defend the 'fatherland.' With Russians and Americans already on German ground, the German government threatens to execute anyone who displays white sheets or flags as a sign of surrender.

April 16/17, 1945
American troops arrive in Solingen. Its citizens surrender without a fight.

April 21, 1945
Battle of Berlin, 2.5 million Red Army soldiers surround the city, fighting one million German soldiers. The last fanatics, SS, Hitler Youth create stand-up desertion tribunals, shooting surrendering German citizens on the spot.

April 30, 1945
Hitler commits suicide by shooting himself.

May 1, 1945
Magda Goebbels, the wife of propaganda minister Joseph Goebbels, poisons their six children with cyanide. Both parents commit suicide.

May 2-8, 1945
The German government surrenders.

June 5, 1945
Baldur von Schirach, initially hiding from authorities, surrenders and stands trial in Nürnberg in 1946.

Summer 1945
British and American military release German prisoners while the USSR continues filling its camps.

1945-1948
With its infrastructure and production facilities destroyed, the German population starves. Families go on barter trips, trading and stealing to survive as run-away inflation and black markets emerge throughout the country.

1946
US, British and French occupation governments pass "Denazification" laws, trying to stop former affiliates of the Third Reich to reenter leadership positions. Most adult Germans are required to complete a 130-question survey about their involvement with the Nazis.

June 1948
The new currency, the Deutsche Mark (DM) is introduced. Every German receives forty DM. Stores that have hoarded for months fill with merchandise overnight. Black markets and the ration system disappear.

1966
Baldur von Schirach is released from prison and spends the rest of his days in a small B&B in Kröv on the Mosel River. He dies in 1974, apparently still convinced about Hitler's cause.

ABOUT THE AUTHOR

Annette Oppenlander is an award-winning writer, literary coach and educator. As a bestselling historical novelist, Oppenlander is known for her authentic characters and stories based on true events, coming alive in well-researched settings. Having lived in Germany the first half of her life and the second half in various parts in the U.S., Oppenlander inspires readers by illuminating story questions as relevant today as they were in the past.

Oppenlander's bestselling true WWII story, Surviving the Fatherland, received eight nominations/awards. Uniquely, Oppenlander weaves actual historical figures and events into her plots, giving readers a flavor of true history while enjoying a good story.

Oppenlander shares her knowledge through writing workshops at colleges, libraries, festivals and schools. She also offers vivid presentations and author visits. The mother of fraternal twins and a son, she now lives with her husband and mutt Zelda in Germany.

FROM THE AUTHOR

Thank you for reading When They Made Us Leave. My sincere hope is that you derived as much entertainment from reading this story as I enjoyed in creating it. If you have a few moments, please feel free to add your review of the book at your favorite online site for feedback (Amazon, Apple iTunes Store, Goodreads, etc.). Also, if you would like to connect with previous or upcoming books, please visit my website for information and to sign up for e-news: http://www.annetteoppenlander.com.
Sincerely, Annette

CONTACT ME

- ➤ Website: annetteoppenlander.com
- ➤ Facebook: facebook.com/annetteoppenlanderauthor
- ➤ Twitter: twitter.com/aoppenlander
- ➤ Pinterest: annoppenlander
- ➤ Instagram: @annette.oppenlander
- ➤ Blog: annetteoppenlander.com/blog/
- ➤ Amazon: amazon.com/Annette-Oppenlander/e/B00W8QRTJ4/
- ➤ Email: hello@annetteoppenlander.com

9 783948 100094